W9-CCP-284

YELLOW EARTH

YELLOW EARTH

John Sayles

Haymarket Books
Chicago, Illinois

Published in 2020 by
Haymarket Books
P.O. Box 180165
Chicago, IL 60618
773-583-7884
www.haymarketbooks.org
info@haymarketbooks.org

ISBN: 978-1-64259-021-0

Distributed to the trade in the US through Consortium Book Sales and Distribution
(www.cbsd.com) and internationally through Ingram Publisher Services International
(www.ingramcontent.com).

This book was published with the generous support of Lannan Foundation and Wallace
Action Fund.

Special discounts are available for bulk purchases by organizations and institutions.
Please call 773-583-7884 or email info@haymarketbooks.org for more information.

Cover design by Abby Weintraub.

Printed in Canada by union labor.

Library of Congress Cataloging-in-Publication data is available.

10 9 8 7 6 5 4 3 2 1

For Maggie

STAGE ONE

EXPLORATION

FORGET THE WOOLY MAMMOTH. Let the big ice creep back where it belongs. Start with tribal people, some nomadic, some content to stick around a while if the eating is good, moving up and down what will later be known as the Missouri River and the Yellowstone that meets it. They chase elk and bison, they fish and farm, they have their enemies and alliances. The smallpox reaches them before the white men do. Then come trappers and traders from the north, men of the Hudson's Bay Company who live with the people in their earth lodges whenever welcome. In 1804 the Lewis and Clark Corps of Discovery arrives, probing into what the Americans are still calling Louisiana all the way up to the Canadian border. Here, well north of where the tall-grass prairie gives way to stubbly, nearly treeless plains, they build a fort to take shelter from a brutally cold winter. They have relatively peaceful relations with the neighboring Mandan and Hidatsa people and impose English names on peaks and tributaries and other places of note, adding these to the names or simple descriptions the various local tribes know them by. It is on their return trip from the Pacific that moody, self-important Meriwether Lewis, mistaken for an elk by the near-sighted, fiddle-playing *voyageur* who serves the expedition as river guide and translator, is shot in the buttocks. Lewis is carried most of the way back to St. Louis, and a journal kept by one of his men reveals the name given to the scene of this accident.

Yellow Earth.

THERE IS CHAOS IN the colony. They are all popping up, males, females, even some of the bolder juveniles, and Odysseus is using the opportunity to pull a young virgin from Ajax. Blacktails, en masse and on alert, twitch their heads north, south, east, and west, not knowing which of their fifteen, or is it seventeen? distinct alarm cries to join chorus in. Leia stands by her lease car and pans the field glasses. She's never seen them all out at once like this, a thousand-headed indignation of prairie dogs stretching back toward the scrub-and-dust horizon. She looks to the sky– not a hawk soaring. The lot of the p-dogs are so accustomed to her by now– the same Wildlife drone in the same uniform driving the same Toyota– that even the pups barely glance at her when she walks close among them from the highway.

Leia finds her coterie in the glasses, little wooden stakes from Ace Hardware, labeled A1 to A83, driven into the ground by each of the dome or rim craters. She's been able to dye-mark twenty-two of the group with the Nyanzol-D, the animals such junkies for a handful of oats that they'll stroll into a live trap suddenly parked right outside their burrow, metal two-doors from Tomahawk Co. in Wisconsin apparently not on their instinctual checklist of things to avoid. Odysseus is hip-checking the young female toward his favorite hole while the multitude remain upright in vigilance. Ajax has been in his face several times this week, the Big Heat likely to kick in any day, and the boys (though Ajax is likely the father of Odysseus they look nearly identical) strutting their p-dog machismo, stretching their pear-shaped bodies long then hunching them low, staring at each other nose to nose for a long minute, then both spring-shooting into the air before landing already on the shuffle in opposite directions, each somehow knowing if it was win, loss, or draw. Altitude? Attitude? Hang time? The females aren't watching, aren't even interested yet, but every now and then something is decided, and the coterie realigns.

Odysseus has the big **O** sprayed on his left side, and the young female– Leia has to check her laminated chart– is Niobe, due to come into estrus with the rest in a few days. Leia is pretty sure Niobe's mother killed her own sister's last litter, the lactating sister suddenly pup-less and available for nursemaid duty. Intrigue and high drama in the coterie. Odysseus is not yet as husky as Ajax, still something short of three pounds, but sneaky and ambitious.

Or Leia is so benumbed watching this passel of busy grass-munching clones that she is making it all up.

The population suddenly joins in on a strange, high-pitched chattering cry, and Leia points her phone toward them in video mode to capture the moment, then turns her head as the residents of the smaller, incest-ridden town on the other side of the highway, a scrawny couple dozen she has christened the Outcasts of Poker Flats, join in the chattering. And then she thinks she feels it.

Not a tremble, exactly, more like a sudden energizing of the ground beneath her feet. Something is moving down there, and it isn't a prairie dog.

Will passes the Wildlife Girl, binoculars and cell phone in hand as usual, parked at the side of the highway. Poking along at sixty, he considers for a moment stopping to ask if she's seen the Kosters' half-wolf moping around, but figures if it was anywhere close the critters would all be in their holes instead of out taking the sun and sticking their noses in the air. Wolfie– the Kosters didn't rupture themselves thinking up a name for the animal– has been taken with canine Alzheimer's and can't seem to find his way home lately. Five concerned-citizen calls so far, two in fear, one in outrage, and two worried about the mangy old thing. Problem is, it will amble up to anybody with two legs, including Busby Curtis, who has already accused Wolfie of serial chicken murder and would like nothing better than to unload his shotgun on him and then stretch the pellet-riddled half-wolf pelt on his tractor-shed door as a trophy. And then you got another Koster-Curtis revenge deal going like back in the '30s. When what is really called for is to put the animal down or find some sort of assisted-living arrangement involving a collar and a chain.

Whatever, it's good to get clear of the office and out in the county for a spell. It's still March, pretty much all yellows and browns on the seemingly endless northern plain, nothing tall enough to block Will's view of something looming up ahead that he ought to have been told about.

Six white trucks like none he's ever seen before, the power plants on their tail ends whining steadily, the vehicles spaced evenly and rolling slowly in single file maybe fifty yards in from the edge of the highway. Not too far off is a little square truck with antennas sticking out from it and a couple white-collar-looking fellas watching the progress of the conga line. The bareheaded one turns when he notices the patrol car has stopped and shuffles over without pulling his fingers from his ears till he is close enough to offer a hand to shake.

"Sheriff! Or is it Deputy?"– bowing slightly to read the badge– "No, Sheriff, glad to see you! I'm Sig Rushmore, Case and Crosby."

"Law firm?" Will ignores the proffered hand and steps out of the car.

"Oh, we've got a whole remuda of lawyers, but I'm mostly Energy and Development." Rushmore has a round face and a sunburned nose. He nods toward the lineup. "Geology boys throw the right charts back at us and things might start to develop real quick."

"You get a permit for this?"

"Sure did."

"How come I didn't hear about it?"

Will sees Harleigh Killdeer's pickup coming and knows the answer before the company man says it.

"We were assured this is reservation land."

Will looks around to get his bearings as Harleigh skids to a stop in his usual cloud of dust. "You're cutting it awful damn close."

"If we find what we hope to, Sheriff," Rushmore beams, "they be plenty for everybody in the deal."

Harleigh steps out, wearing ostrich-leather boots and a couple pounds of Navajo turquoise. He adjusts his Stetson and strides up to the patrol car like he's going to kick the tires.

"Will."

"Harleigh."

"What brings you out to the Nation?"

Harleigh likes to call it that, singular, even though three different tribes, each with its own unpronounceable language, are involved in the government. Will makes a show of turning a full circle, and Harleigh narrows his eyes.

"I can walk you to the nearest boundary marker if you'd like."

Will shakes his head. "You know A. J.'s gonna have the surveyors out once he sees this." A. J. Niles owns a big chunk of the land to the east of the rez and has chosen to carry the white man's burden. Another one that will shoot Wolfie on sight.

"We contacted Mr. Niles," says the company man. "He was rather abrupt."

"Abrupt is what the A in A. J. stands for. What's the story here, Harleigh?"

"That remains to be seen," says Sig Rushmore. "Right now we're just giving the earth a friendly little hump or two, see what she's made of."

There's a cab at the front of each of the machines, with an open power plant, transmission, and pumps mounted on the rear, but the middle is nothing but a big piston-looking thing, a square base plate that's raised and lowered on four shiny steel hydraulic stilts. Another white collar fella, this one wearing a baseball cap, steps over from the front of the data collection truck. Give him a Stetson like Harleigh's and he'd be the Marlboro Man.

"This is our PG, Randy Hardacre," says Rushmore. "He'll be doing the work-up on all this back at the lab. This is Sheriff– ?"

"Crowder."

"Sheriff Crowder. And you already met Mr. Killdeer."

"Seismic vibrology," says Harleigh.

Will has never seen it before, but the trucks are pretty much what he imag-ined. "How far you mapping?"

The geologist shrugs. "Right now, everything on the reservation."

"Got some tight oil underfoot, is what we're hoping," says Harleigh.

"Shale rock."

"There's an oil field?"

Rushmore barks out a professional laugh, then touches a finger to his lips. "Shh-hhh. Don't want to start a feeding frenzy, Sheriff. We've got to sound out the rest of the area, maybe punch a few test holes, see the extent of it. And then there's inter-national price fluctuations– they can change your attitude toward a play real fast."

"It's all just dollars and cents, Will," says Harleigh, quoting something he's been told no more than a day ago. "The value of the deposit has to greatly super-sede the expense of retrieval."

"Here we go again," says the geologist, nodding toward the line of trucks.

One by one, starting from the front, the trucks roll to a halt, shaker assem-blies sliding down their metal shafts till the base plate pushes onto the ground, then keeps pushing, the bodies of the massive trucks seeming to stiffen as they're jacked up, huge tires almost lifting off the ground. There is a brief shudder at the base of the shaft, a spurt of dust, and then the vibrator plate pulls back up, the trucks' great mass deflating back to earth with a visible sigh. They roll slowly forward again, the entire procession no more than a half a football field long.

"Not much foreplay, is there?" winks Sig Rushmore. "We got sensors and ca-bles laid out in a grid all around here– hired some of Mr. Killdeer's folks to help us put and fetch. The sensors read the vibrations, give us a snapshot of the layers underneath and what they might be made of."

The trucks stop rolling and the huge pistons slide down again.

"And all this is just to see *if* we're interested," the company man continues. "People don't grasp the scale of the outlay that's required."

Will looks around at the flat, almost featureless land. When the weather permits it will be put up in feed barley or alfalfa hay, with the profit margin pretty damn slim for the work that's required. Hell, vibrate your little hearts out. He turns to Harleigh.

"The council ordered this?"

Harleigh gives him the great stone face. Harleigh could model for whoever carved the Indian on the nickel. "It will come up for a vote," he says, "next time I call a meeting."

Will holds the council chairman's eyes for a knowing moment, then turns to the geologist.

"So what's next? Drill rigs? Or you just dig a giant pit and blast it out in chunks?"

Sig Rushmore jumps in first. "There's any number of methods for retrieval," he says, his smile slapped onto his face with a nail gun.

"You have to consider the economic feasibility, Will," quotes Harleigh, not smiling at all.

"And, of course," Rushmore adds, another wink skipping on the paper-thin surface of his words, "the ecological impact."

Will pulls the patrol car up next to Wolfie near where the Canada road cuts off from the highway, the animal standing with a dead prairie dog in his mouth and no idea what to do with it. Will gets out and opens the rear door on the far side.

"Come on, Wolfie," he calls gently. "Leave your friend behind and I'll take you home."

RANDY HARDACRE CAN TURN the numbers into rocks, and the rocks into dollars. He has the readouts spread before him, Houston on his headset, and a cold Shiner from the case he drove up here with in his hand.

"We got to get down to the late Mississippi, early Devonian before it gets interesting," he tells Houston, "and it's kind of bowl-shaped– deepest point right under Yellow Earth. Layer of shale, four layers of Three Forks dolomite, then more shale, all of it loaded."

He sees the layers, like he's in a glass-walled elevator heading to the Earth's core, senses how tight or loosely the molecules are packed, feels the tension of restless atoms straining for a way up and out.

"I'm guessing three, four billion barrels easy out of the shale at our present recovery rate, but hey, we frack that much, the technology is bound to improve. And the first layer of the Three Forks stuff is definitely worth taking a crack at."

In his dreams Randy has witnessed the molten, spinning ball flung free and then roped into orbit, has seen it cool and crust over, seen gasses condense into liquids and the crust crack into plates, seen thousands of centuries worth of bio-mass build up and then be yanked under and pressed thin beneath miles-thick strata of heavy rock, volcanoes and earthquakes the tiniest of adjustments to the geologic maturation of the planet. It is a tale with innumerable twists and turns, rarely predictable, and in the great Energy Treasure Hunt he is the man who draws the map.

"We might want to consider tightening our well spacing," he says, "and it'll merit a pipeline or two."

If they've sent their landmen here already, his opinion is mostly confirmation, but a different sonic picture could bring the whole deal to a halt. Back in '03 he blew the whistle on an offshore play and the Company was able to stop short and watch a couple of their competitors sink a fortune into a sucker hole. Took nearly three years for that to prove out and let him unpucker his asshole, but it cemented his reputation as their favorite oilhound. And it is so, so much more satisfying to say yes to a new deposit, or bring an old one like the Bakken back into the game. Randy saw the white whale movie on TV when he was a kid, and when he imagined himself into the story, as he always did, it was as the lookout in the crow's nest, spotting the great harpoon-scarred back as it broke water, the spout of foul breath and blood-tinged seawater arcing in the air. But unlike that exultant sailor he's learned over the years not to shout, to keep his excitement out of his reportage and adopt the controlled monotone of a friendly-skies pilot cruising into Bush International for the five-hundredth time.

"Price per barrel holds up, this'll be the gift that keeps on giving," he drawls, twenty years in Texas having permeated his affect. "All my numbers say we go for it."

Houston is pleased. Houston, without popping any champagne corks, says to sit tight till the production folks get there and he can ramrod the first wave of penetration. Houston thanks him for his information and signs off the call.

There is another dream Randy has, a couple times a month, that probably comes from his diving trips in the Gulf. He's standing out on a plank suspended over a huge, circular shark tank, with way more sharks than you'd think could fit in it circling under him, all in the same direction, bumping each other for position and rolling on their sides to point their soulless eyes up at him as they slide below, a relentless slow-motion whirlwind of sharks, hungry and primed to boil over into carnage. He is not at all nervous. In his hand he holds a heavy, bloody chunk of meat, still warm from the body of whatever it's been torn from. He has an idea what comes next, and it will be something to behold.

Time to toss that puppy in the water.

ICED TEA, UNLESS YOU put a heart-stopping amount of sugar in it, will go right through you. Rest rooms being few and far between out in these hinterlands, you want to just sip a little politely, maybe pour some out in the sink if you get a minute alone. Because it's almost always the kitchen they choose for the sitdown, nice big table to spread the contracts out on.

"Oh dear," says Mrs. Sanderson when she sees them. "Ernest always took care of the paperwork."

"I'm sorry for your loss," Sig tells her. She uses the powdered mix tea, which has a stronger smell. "It was what– two years ago?"

Two years and two months, according to the record at the county courthouse, where the lady at the desk wore headphones and listened to books on tape– she told him she had *Mill on the Floss* running– while she worked her keyboard.

"I get my son to come do the taxes."

Please, no sons. Sons get all possessive and show-offy and, yes, you have to invoke the G-word. Sons are Greedy.

"Well, Mrs. Sanderson, in this case, the land– the *stew*ardship of the land– is your responsibility. The way I'm sure Mr. Sanderson intended."

She is early eighties maybe, starting to dim and forget to wipe her glasses clean, frowning with constant concern as he explains.

"You farmed this land I assume?"

"Fifty-seven years. One of the Buford boys has been leasing some acres the last little while, trying to make a crop– "

"Not an easy life."

"But a good one."

He smiles, leans back. A V-formation of ceramic ducks on the wall, calendar flipped to last February, snaps of the grandchildren under whimsically shaped magnets on the refrigerator door– Sig has spent half his working life in this kitch-en. "I think of the labor you put in, the time spent to keep a place like this up, raise the little ones. There should be a reward."

"We did well enough, Ernest and me."

"That's obvious. But I was thinking about the land. This part of the country you need a lot of acres, whether its crops or cattle, to pull a living out of the ground. You have some children, *they* have children, and pretty soon when it comes to passing those acres on– "

"That is a worry. How to be fair."

"But with *cash*, it's so much easier to portion things out."

"You want to buy our place?"

He chuckles. "Oh no. I'm here to discuss a *lease*– something like what this young Buford has with you– but this is to lease the right to harvest the oil and gas that might be sitting thousands of feet beneath your land."

She nods solemnly. "I remember back in the '80s, there was some oil."

"A smallish play, relatively close to the surface. But my good news to you, Ma'am, is that the techniques used to bring these riches to the top have shot ahead in the last thirty years, and it's now possible for us to access deposits much older and much deeper than could have been considered in those days. The Company is betting that you and your heirs might be sitting on a very valuable layer of shale rock."

"And you want me to let you drill into it."

"I think, Mrs. Sanderson, from now on it would be best to think of this as a 'we' rather than a 'you' situation. I'm proposing a joint venture– your mineral rights, our technological expertise and years of extraction experience."

She looks at him blankly for a long moment, then gets to her feet. "Excuse me," she says.

When she is gone Sig quickly jumps up to riffle through the mail piled up on top of the microwave. He hears Mrs. Sanderson turn down the volume of the TV in the next room, Dr. Phil dealing out some tough love. Three different outfits soliciting to meet and talk leasing– he slips the envelopes into his briefcase and rearranges the pile, back in his seat before she returns.

"I want to do the right thing," she says, as she sits across from him again. "With Ernest gone– "

"I asked around in town," he says, leaning forward, lowering his voice as if someone might be there to hear what comes next, "trying to get an idea of who the key people are– the folks who've been in this county the longest, earned everybody's respect– in order to set the right kind of precedent. If I'm going to invite somebody onto the ground floor of this deal it should be people with real roots, real history."

"Ernest's great grandfather founded the county."

"Exactly what I'm talking about. Somebody who can set an example."

"Nobody pays attention to me."

"You'd be surprised. Getting started in an area, it's important to choose the right people to get the ball rolling."

"So it's not just *our* land that's got this shale under it."

He sighs then, his storm-clouds-on-the-horizon sigh, and spreads the papers out a bit, pretending to ponder.

"The decision you're going to make today, Mrs. Sanderson, is an important one. It affects not just you but your friends and neighbors in the community, and that's why it's important to understand the– the pitfalls and ramifications, and also why, besides that my time in this area is very limited, it behooves you to move quickly."

She clearly doesn't like the pressure, but without pressure the oil will sit down there for another couple millennia. Psycho fracking, Dick Whittaker used to call it when they worked as a team.

"In the oil industry as it stands," he continues, adding the ominous note where it will do the most good, "we have to acknowledge the concept of *pooling*."

"The oil is sitting in– ?"

"The oil may be sitting under your land, as well as that of your neighbors on each side, et cetera, and since these modern wells are drilled horizontally, meaning sideways– "

"How can they do that?"

"A wonder of modern technology, which I am unqualified to explain. But what is important to grasp is that oil, no matter the characteristics of the rock it is trapped in, *flows*."

"You mean somebody next door could pump out all my oil?"

Two minutes ago he was explaining Geology 101 and now it's *her* oil.

"The pooling statutes, Mrs. Sanderson, are formulated to insure both efficiency and fairness in the drilling operations." He pretends to read the next bit from one of the documents laid out on the kitchen table. *"In the absence of voluntary pooling, the Commission, upon the application of any interested person, shall enter an order pooling all interests in the spacing unit for the development and operations thereof."*

With men this is when the anticommunist diatribe usually starts, and Sig has to invoke the evils of Foreign Oil and call on the rights holder's sense of patriotism. Mrs. Sanderson just looks horrified. "There's a commission that can make you do that?"

Sig nods. "Duly appointed."

If he has to, he can explain that the statute is from Oklahoma, and that even the owners who choose not to lease but are pooled get an averaged royalty from whatever is retrieved from under their land, but that's all in the literature.

"In fact, a penalty as high as two hundred percent can be assessed for cost and risk of the completion. Of course this is America, and you'd have your day in court."

Mrs. Sanderson seems to flinch at the word 'court.'

"So what is your company offering?"

Sig smiles. "This is my favorite part. All this"– he indicates the lease forms and literature heaped between them– "boils down to three important items. Term of lease, signing bonus, and royalty. Now, I like to offer my mineral owners– that's you– a five-year lease. That gives the exploration and completion people more time to look for and pump up the good stuff that's gonna make you and them a good deal of money."

"They'll be drilling for five years?"

"Drilling any individual well, Ma'am, is only a matter of weeks. Well stimulation, a different process, adds a few days onto that. For most of the life of the well it will be a set of pipes sticking out of the ground, not much bigger than a Christmas tree, and maybe a holding tank or two. Quite honestly, we have to make a map on a big property like yours to *find* them after they're operating, they're that low profile. Now, the bonus is just that– you've heard of professional athletes getting a bonus when they sign with a team right out of college, and like them this is a bonus not for services already rendered but a kind of good-faith payment to seal the deal. That ballplayer could have an injury in practice and never suit up for his professional team, but still he gets to *keep* his bonus. If for some unforeseeable reason the Company either fails to drill on your property or the formation beneath proves not to contain profitable resources– what we used to call a 'duster' back in the Texas wildcat days– you still got your bonus, safe in your pocket. The Company, at this rather speculative juncture, with an unproven field in consideration, has authorized me to offer you fifty dollars."

"Oh."

Once you've got them on the hook, once their imaginations are running away with *$$$$$$$$$$$???!!!*, you can play them a bit. Otherwise there's no fun in the fishing.

"That's per *acre*, of course."

"Ah." Face brightening, then the worried look again as she tries to add it up. Sig already has his phone on Calculate.

"That was what– four hundred twenty-seven acres? That times fifty is– "

He punches it out and holds the tally under her nose. Mrs. Sanderson squints behind her lenses and rewards him with another 'Oh,' trying not to seem too impressed. A month from now it'll take another zero on that sucker to get their attention.

"But that's just the good-faith money," he continues. "Your *royalty*, which is your partnership with the Company, is where the real potential lies. It's what assures you that you're not selling your rights short– for every dollar of profit the Company makes, you make something too, only you don't have to put out for equipment and wages like they do– all profit, no risk. And once the shouting's over– and there will be some bit of noise and inconvenience for a couple weeks, I promise you– you just sit back and let the cash roll in. The royalty percentage is fixed, so the amount of money you receive over the years depends on the productivity, the *richness*, if you will, of the mineral deposit itself. We're in this together, Mrs. Sanderson, and there's nothing that makes me feel better than hearing that one of my lessors has struck it big."

She considers this for a moment. Sometimes the ones who have worked themselves to the bone on unyielding land for their whole lives don't trust it, don't approve of it. "So it's just luck then, isn't it?" she says.

"I would call it Providence, Mrs. Sanderson. There ought to be a book– *When Good Things Happen to Good People.*" He slides the master form over to her. "These early leases, while we're still exploring, I'm able to offer you a twelve-

and-a-half-percent royalty. That is one-*eighth* of the profits from any well drilled on your property."

Sig remembers one old Cajun, set of teeth that'd make you cringe, who'd allowed as how one-sixteenth of the gross sounded a whole lot better than one-eighth.

And what am I, a math teacher?

"One thing I can tell you with total confidence about the Company," he says as she picks up the pen he left lying casually to the side of the main form, "is that we *drill*. You may be contacted by other landmen in the next few months, but many of them will be merely speculating– trying to buy your rights on the cheap and then resell them to a legitimate E and P company like ours– that's the main signature box right there, Mrs. Sanderson, but there are some side documents we'll have to go over. Rules and regulations, making sure nobody can just storm in and do whatever they want on your surface land."

He loves it when they sign at the first sitting. Her hand is a little wobbly, some of the fingers bent with rheumatism, but she looks pretty pleased with herself.

"Now, you understand, Mrs. Sanderson, that this is a *private* contract. You have my assurance that I'm not going to wander all over the county blabbering about your sudden good fortune. Don't want to set good neighbors to envying each other."

Again the frown. "We're not supposed to compare offers?"

"Let's just say that that sort of– col*lu*sion– leads to bad feelings. We have in this country what is known as the free-market system," he smiles, nudging the rest of the forms in her direction. "Golly, in most other countries the *government* owns all the mineral rights."

HARLEIGH IS HALFWAY BACK to the tribal center when Danny Two Strike gets him on the radio. It's Fawn again, this time out on the Reservoir Road by the boat ramp. As if I need more brushfires to stomp out.

He's at least on the right side of the water and doesn't have to drive all the way around. They'd named the lake after the Shoshone girl who went along with her trapper husband to guide Lewis and Clark to the ocean. Most of the pictures and statues have her pointing over the horizon, looking noble, though a few show her with infant child in arms. There is something creepy about the look of the reservoir, something unnatural about its low, nearly treeless banks. 'Sterile,' Teresa Crow's Ghost always calls it. The old fellas talk about what it was like before the government forced the dam on them– everybody grew table crops and fodder for their livestock, people got by pretty good. But the Missouri was cranky and would go over its banks pretty regular, flooding the white towns downriver, so General Pick and the Army Corps of Engineers got busy in Washington, and pretty soon it was either take what we give you for the most of your land, the best of your land, or we'll eminent-domain it and you get nothing. Harleigh has a big reprint of the signing photo behind his desk at the council office, bunch of white bureaucrats in suits standing around looking official, and then the tribal chairman from those days, over to one side with his glasses off, weeping into his hand.

And not only do we take it, they said, you Indians don't get to use the new shoreline for hunting or grazing. And no cutting down trees for firewood before you go. Harleigh's grandfather on his father's side, not Granpaw Pete, got a job with the dam construction and for years people called him a traitor.

There were still stone walls and foundations under the water when Harleigh swam in it as a kid– him and some of the others would go out on the float with a big rock, then dive down holding it to get deeper. Spooky. The old folks talked about the fasting areas and sacred places that went under with their houses, and didn't seem so thrilled by the record-sized walleyes and Chinook salmon folks started catching, maybe because they'd seen the Wildlife people out shooting the fingerlings into the lake with a hose. What are salmon from California doing in our water? There was a payout after the taking, maybe worth half of what they'd lost if you were an honest insurance company, and lots of people just flocked into New Center when it rose up from nothing, hanging around the bars and the stores and the Indian Agency. Harleigh's family was already into beef and drove their herd up onto the shelf, where the grass was poor and there wasn't a tree standing to slow the wind down in the winter, and stuck it out.

Danny Two Strike, who's been head of the tribal police for some years now, has them pulled over across from the boat ramp. It's Fawn and Ella Burdette's grandson Dickyboy and a white kid he doesn't know, got an old wreck of a Mustang that must have been something in its day. Fawn is leaning back against it, looking at her feet when he gets out to talk with Danny.

"Chief."

"Chairman."

It's a routine between them, kind of a joke between old teammates a little surprised to see where they've gotten to. Danny was shooting guard when they got
to the state quarterfinals his senior year, his basketball sneakers the only shoes
he owned, with Harleigh a forward and the leading rebounder.

"What we got here?"

"Oh, speed limit violation, paraphernalia in the back seat, and what feels like
ten or twelve ounces"– Danny wiggles a large Baggie filled with loose marijuana
for him to see– "in the glove compartment. Don't carry my drug scale with me,
so I can't be precise."

"Fawn driving?"

"Says he just give her and Dickyboy a ride."

"They were smoking when you pulled them over?"

"Nothing in their hands, nothing in the air, but they were feeling no pain."

"You test the town kid?"

"Had him walk the line and he didn't do so good. For what it's worth."

"So there's no charges on my stepdaughter, is there?"

Danny jerks his head for them to step away further from the sulking teenagers.

"I talk to you for a minute?"

They move closer to the boat ramp, and seeing it puts the idea back in Harleigh's
head. I mean, why not? That cruise him and Connie went on for their honeymoon
was a floating gold mine. Nice food, nice scenery, but pretty soon you're all bored
enough to park yourself at one of their betting tables and throw away some serious money. 'We are now beyond the one-mile limit,' they'd announce over the
PA system, and the dice would roll. Hell, if we promised to stay in the part of the
lake that's surrounded by the reservation, and remind them how they drowned
our only hospital when they built the dam and never made good on replacing it–

"So what's the deal with the thumper trucks?"

Danny is with the bunch that would like to drain the lake and start growing
squash and beans again. Danny burns sweet grass on his patrol car dashboard
before he makes the rounds and wants all signs on the rez to be in the Three Languages as well as English. Danny is a constant boil on Harleigh's ass at council
meetings.

"They send sound waves into the ground that bounce back up and tell what's
down there."

"I know how they *work*. What are they doing here?"

Harleigh nods toward the lake. "Federal government stole all the mineral rights under the water, on what used to be most of our land. But we still hold em on dry ground."

"You remember that mess when we were kids."

There had been a quick oil boom-and-bust in the '80s, the Arabs monkeying with the prices, and another one way back in the early '50s, when the first well up in Tioga come in. Some people made out pretty good, but not many of those were enrolled with the Three Nations.

"They got whole new ways of bringing it up, Danny. If we play this right."

"Drilling is drilling. They cut roads, they use water."

"And we make sure they pay as they go."

Danny does not look mollified. Danny got a chip on his shoulder and his favorite word is 'no.'

"The council gonna vote on this?"

Danny and old Teresa Crow's Ghost and some of the others think you can beat them with Spirit, that you can just be true to the land and it will take care of you. Good luck with that.

"We'll take it up," says Harleigh, starting back toward the Mustang, "when I decide to call a meeting."

By the time he gets there Will Crowder has pulled up and gotten out of his patrol car. There's four counties that overlap with the reservation, which is bigger than Rhode Island but only got a few thousand people living on it. Will is the sheriff that bothers to come on the most. Some of the others, if it's a white perp and not a big deal, just call and say we're too busy, let im go.

"We meet again."

Harleigh shrugs, jerks his head back toward Danny, following. "Roadside powwow."

He leaves Will to deal with the white boy and opens the passenger door to his pickup, calling to Fawn.

"Let's go."

"Can you give Dickyboy a ride?"

"In the back."

The kids get in and Harleigh patches out, thinking about the cruise idea. Be a nice wrinkle, especially with the rush that's likely to be coming soon.

"Slick truck," says Dickyboy. Harleigh has the Sierra Denali out today, with the wood trim and premium leather and, most important to Connie, heated front seats.

"Thank you."

Dickyboy is a good kid, smart, but has let himself get fat like so many of them. Don't burn many calories playing video games at the casino arcade.

Fawn checks her cellphone before speaking, still not looking him in the eye. "You mad?"

"I can't believe he pulled you over for that piddly shit."

"Dylan was going ninety."

Harleigh gives her a look, holds it for a moment.

"Dylan."

"He figures he can get away with anything on the rez."

"He might be right. But if I go into one of their towns and roll through a stop sign."

"You don't ever roll through stop signs– "

It's true. Fawn goes on about how 'strict' he is, but really it's discipline. Harleigh does two hundred crunches a day. Harleigh doesn't eat fry bread. Harleigh could still out-rebound half the players on the high school varsity.

"He didn't try to outrun Danny, did he?"

"No. We just saw the lights flashing and I told him if he got me in trouble you'd come after him."

Harleigh has to smile. Fawn is a hot number and knows it, dresses sexy, lots of eye makeup, and generally knows how to work the system. If she just wouldn't antagonize her mother on purpose. He looks past her to the lake. Not much moving out there, this time of year.

The view if you're cruising on the water is pretty, but nothing exotic. Maybe if the boat had a glass bottom, he thinks, and you could see those houses that we lost. Underwater Indians, it could be, View the Lost Civilization. But of course tourists would want arrowheads and earth lodges, not some old truck farms. Luxury fishing tournaments, though, sure, and The World's Only Truly Floating Crap Game. He'll have to talk with the casino people about it.

"You know, smoking weed doesn't make you smarter," he says to Fawn and her friend, because he knows he's expected to say something. "It just makes you *think* you are."

"THE PICTURE THAT HAUNTS me," says Mr. Wiley Cobb, sitting on a crate in his barn with a tractor transmission taken apart and laid out in front of him on a tarp, "is my livestock mired in one of those oil slicks. Drowning in it."

There's nowhere convenient for Sig to spread his papers, so he is leaning against stacked hay bales in a neighborly fashion, hoping there aren't any bugs crawling onto him. "You mean like the La Brea tar pits."

Cobb grins. "We had that illustration– covered two pages– in some book back at school. Biology? Earth science? Big hairy animals stuck in the goo."

"I been to the place itself. Pretty impressive. They got a whole wall covered with nothing but hundreds of skulls of the dire wolf."

"What's a dire wolf?"

"Something we're awful glad went extinct and we don't have to worry about it any more."

The farmer laughs. He'll be closable, this one, neither suspicious nor overeager, just needs a little groundation on the realities.

"If you don't have oil slicks on your property now, Mr. Cobb, I'm afraid we won't be able to supply any. The hydrocarbons we're talking about are bound up in shale rock, and we're guessing that the principal strata are near two miles down from the surface."

"Two miles."

That always impresses them.

"To get to it, first we'll have to drill vertical, way, way down, and then go *sideways*."

"But when it comes up– "

"We don't have gushers anymore, Mr. Cobb. The process is a lot more like twisting the water out of a wet towel than jabbing a knife into an aerosol can. And that oil turns into *money*– the last thing we want to do is go around spilling it in the dirt."

"So my well– "

"Your water well is just a little pinprick in the earth compared to what we'll be digging, and believe me, the production folks don't want a thing to do with it. The only water coming up will be what they've pumped down there themselves, drilling mud it's called, and it keeps the bit from overheating, brings the cuttings back to the surface so the bore doesn't clog up."

"I've heard about gas."

"Oh, they'll be gas too, but that's expected, that's a *good* thing. We'll either flame that sucker off real quick or bottle it and add what it's worth to your royalty.

Most of your shale plays mostly produce gas, but what you're sitting on, Mr. Cobb, is unique."

"I've always thought so," says Cobb, standing and rubbing his butt to under-line the joke.

Sig chuckles. "You know what puts the most bad gas, the climate-killing stuff, in the atmosphere?"

"What's that?"

"Pig farts. Cattle burps. You find a way to capture the methane that comes off a medium-sized herd in one week and we could heat every building in your little town over there for a winter."

"So it's all the cows' fault."

"Not all. If we could get the Chinese to stop burning coal and buy more of our product it would do some real good."

You have to step careful out here with the global warming idea, some of the locals equating a belief in it with Satanism and the Red Menace.

"They don't have oil?"

"They're perched on some awful rich strata, don't worry about the Chinese. Only their technology tends to lag a couple centuries behind ours. Thing is, a collateral benefit of this find up here will be our government getting to tell those desert sheiks to go take a hike."

Cobb strolls over to his well-stocked, immaculately organized tool bench. "So you're saying that it's my patriotic duty to sign up with you?"

"All I'm saying is you got a tremendous opportunity here, Mr. Cobb, while it lasts."

"The oil gonna go away?"

"There are a bunch of factors that go into the Company's decision to bother with alternate-source energy– which is what your rock way down there represents– or not. Worldwide price fluctuations, changes in environmental regulations, compet-ing oil sources, and– well, have you heard of the Rule of Capture?"

"That's a law?"

"As solid as shale rock is, Mr. Cobb. The oil and gas molecules can *migrate*– otherwise we couldn't harvest them."

"You're saying they've got a way of draining my– "

"I'm not a geologist or an extraction expert, Mr. Cobb, only a lowly landman. I deal in acreage and potential. And to tell you the truth, the Company keeps me on an awful short leash. You've heard today's offer, and I promise you it will hold until midnight, no matter what I hear from Houston."

"In that case, Houston," says the skinny, balding character in his sixties who appears in the open barn doorway, "we have a *problem*."

Cobb does not seem thrilled to see him. "This is my neighbor, A, J. Niles. He got the spread that runs over by the tribal lands."

"Ah. I've spoken, very briefly, with Mr. Niles on the phone."

"I saw your car parked out front, figured it was you."

It's a Ford Fusion rental. Up here you definitely want to go American-made. Not too luxe or they resent you for a profiteer, not too modest or they figure the Company is cheap and will lowball them.

Niles steps in toward Wiley Cobb. "You get a Pugh clause in there?"

"What's that?"

"I'm not sure, exactly, but without one they can screw you."

This is the prick the Three Nations chief warned him about, the one who cut him off on the phone. This will be fun, but Sig chooses to hold onto his ace for another moment.

"He talk to you about access?"

"You mean the road."

"You sign up, they can stick a road wherever on your property they want. Dozens of roads."

"That is all negotiable," says Sig, calmly, crossing his arms to wait out the onslaught.

"And water– they can suck up all your water and pump it down the well for this fracturing business."

"Not without consent and compensation."

"Me personally," says A. J. Niles, "I'monna sit on my acres till the price shoots up. Hell, this salesman right here'll be back offering ten, twenty times what he wants you to sign for now."

Wiley Cobb looks impressed. Sig raises his hand, waves it gently.

"May I ask– what acres are those?"

Niles gives him a pitying look. Love to play poker with this asshole. "A hundred fifteen of em, snug up against the rez over there."

"Ah. And you bought this property from Jim Willis."

"I did."

Sig tries to make his frown of concern seem genuine and not ironic. "So I'm guessing that Mr. Willis didn't tell you that when *he* bought the land from a Mr.– was it Liedecker?"

"Fritzy Liedecker," says Cobb, helpfully.

"He didn't tell you that Mr. Liedecker had retained the mineral rights?"

Sig would love a snap of Niles's face right now to use as a screen-saver.

"Liedecker died three years ago."

"Aw– I'm sorry to hear that. To pass on without enjoying such a windfall."

Niles is beginning to thrash now, the shore suddenly impossibly far away.

"You're sure of– "

"I'll have to get back to the county courthouse, see if there's anything record-ed on where I might locate his heirs."

"His girl Darlene lives in Rapid now," says Cobb, a fount of information. Niles looks like he wants to strangle his neighbor. "That's his oldest. Then there's Bud, who went to Minneapolis."

"But they can't let you drill if I don't– "

"See, that's the *rights* part of mineral rights. Mr. Liedecker was a man of some foresight, thinking about his children's future. Grandchildren?"

"Darlene got three, for sure," Cobb offers eagerly. "Bud, I haven't kept up with."

There's no point in burning them worse than you have to. Leaving a bad taste. The state has got some language down for surface owners– notice of drilling ops, damage and disruption– and this guy will be a real pill, but that's for the hardasses who come after Sig. He lays his best look of commiseration on A. J. Shit-outta-luck Niles.

"I'monna put in a word, Mr. Niles, if it works out with the heirs, keep the operation and whatever access they need to build to get to it as far off from your home– I assume you got a lovely house there– as they possibly can. And you might consider renting a patch of your surface land out for a man camp or a trail-er park. Be a shame not to profit *some* little bit with all your neighbors getting fat from this deal."

Sig pats Cobb on the arm on his way out. "You think my proposal over, Mr. Cobb, and I'll do my best to swing by later this evening before I have to go back."

"You're leaving?"

A. J. Niles has changed color, choking down too much to be able to interfere any more.

"Got some folks in Oklahoma I got to see, bright and early. Some soon-to-be-very-wealthy folks."

HE DOESN'T LIKE TO look at Connie when she's ripshit angry. Her eyes get too big and her jaw comes out and she brings her shoulders up like she's set to paste you one. And Fawn is just playing her, raising her voice but relaxed through it all.

"If I don't hang out with my friends," she tells her mother, "there's nothing to *do*."

"It wouldn't hurt to do some of your school work."

"Says Miss Dropout of 1999."

"Fawn," ventures Harleigh, then wishes he hadn't, the look they both give him able to singe hair off a hog.

"How bout this," Fawn continues, "how bout I don't take rides with anybody if I can have my own car?"

Connie makes a noise halfway between a snort and a yelp.

"Because you're so re*spon*sible, like you showed today."

"He bought *you* one."

Fawn is able, even happy to call him Harleigh, or even, in formal situations, 'my stepfather,' but when the feathers are flying it's always 'him.'

"I have a driver's license."

"After you flunked the test twice. In a place where you got to drive for twenty miles to find something to *hit*."

"You're just jealous cause I have *friends*."

"When did you get to be such an asshole?"

It isn't meant as a question.

The thing is, they're more like sisters than mother and daughter, Connie's mom taking Fawn for several of the early years when Connie wasn't so together. They argue about borrowing each other's clothes now and even like a lot of the same bands. They're both traffic-stoppers and know how to get what they want out of men. Connie has to skate extra careful in the don't-get-pregnant-yet conversation cause it can sound like having Fawn so young ruined her life, which it didn't. Staying with Joey Drags Wolf would have, but he had the common decency to get himself incarcerated before he could cause any more trouble.

"Everybody," says Fawn, fixing her mother with a look but careful not to move any closer, "says I take after *you*."

"You are grounded, young lady."

"Fine."

So Fawn goes off to her room to sulk and complain about her miserable parents to her friends on her personal cell phone. Harleigh guilted one of the big providers into setting the rez up with broadband just last year, and so far the response has been mixed, though everybody under twenty-five is hooked on it. Connie turns to look at him.

"What?"

"You weren't much help."

"Just here to back you up, darlin. We already had some words in the car."

"The way she talks to me."

"You never said nothing like that to your mother?"

"That doesn't make it right."

"No, it doesn't." Harleigh steps in to kiss her on the cheek and pivot for the door. Get your footwork right and there's nobody can block you. "I got trouble at the pens."

He's a good ten yards from the house before he hears whatever she picked up this time crash against the wall. Connie never breaks anything she likes, which is a useful hint around birthdays and anniversaries. And for some reason she resents him stepping out to deal with council business but won't object if it's for the animals.

Harleigh leases two hundred fifty acres from the Three Nations and runs cattle, grows some hay and alfalfa. The mineral rights stay with the People, but he can put up any kind of business he wants on the leased land and the profits are all his. There's some non-enrolled who lease land as well, whites from Yellow Earth or other towns on the periphery, but Harleigh has put a cap on that without making too much noise in the council. No use in revealing the master plan till it's well on its way to working.

Arne is waiting next to one of the wind fences with a couple two-year-olds that aren't thriving.

"You want to take a look at their shit?" Arne is Norwegian on one side, like a lot of folks in the enrollment, but got the Arikara genes.

"Just tell me about it."

"Watery, kinda green. Stuck some fresh hay under their noses but they barely sniffed it."

"Gut worm, most likely."

"They had it when they's calves."

"What we use then?"

"The pour-on stuff. Worked pretty good."

Harleigh sighs. You cut corners, sometimes you get away with it, but if you don't–

"Give em the drench, then. Worms get used to the same meds, they'll never go away."

Albendazole. The name of the main worming ingredient. You can bet the original cowboys pushing longhorns up from Texas didn't need a damn chemistry degree.

"And be sure to keep their heads down when you give it, put that tube– "

"Right down the esophagus." Arne is a real find, steady, got a feel for the animals, and a hell of a worker. He drives Fawn and the Otis girl into the Yellow Earth high school every morning, picks them up when they can't find some pothead fellow student to do it.

"Yeah. And then when the new grass comes up, start em over by Bachelor Hill, not so many old pats laying around to breed the larvae."

Cattle are basically machines– grass in, gas and cow flops out, milk or meat depending on what you breed them for. Long list of what can go wrong with them, of course, but most of it fixable, and a cow will put up with a good deal of discomfort– having a tube jammed down its gullet on a regular basis, for instance– without much fuss. Horses can be stubborn or flighty, but if they're real bad you just get rid of them. Crowbait. But with *people*, in this modern world, each one you got to handle in a different way, and even that depends on the situation. Harleigh has seen former chairmen of the Three Nations who spent all their time trying not to make enemies, and they never got a damn thing done. Others got too far ahead of the accepted opinion, even if their ideas weren't bad, and got voted out real quick. But folks want a leader, they're herd animals at heart, and if you put up a strong enough front, put your ass out on the line for them, they'll follow you anywhere.

Even over a cliff.

Arne is nodding and stroking the hair on the muzzle of the two-year-old he's holding, but it's clear he's got something on his mind.

"Anything else?"

Arne shifts the ball cap on his head, looks sideways at Harleigh. Arne deals out words like he's got to buy them on credit. "So we got oil coming, or what?"

No keeping it back now.

"Where you hear that?"

"It's all over the rez."

It never ceases to amaze him, what with all the space and so few people to fill it, how quick gossip can travel.

"It's being looked into. Exploration stages."

"Gonna be good?"

Arne is missing a bunch of teeth up front. The dentist at the clinic is only in three times a week, and don't get Harleigh started on people opting for food stamps instead of the commodities and then buying candy bars and soda pop with them. Operation gets up to speed like he hopes, he'll soak the oil companies for a real hospital and a full-time cavity driller.

"Let's put it this way," he says to Arne. "Things work out, you'll be quitting me to work for some service outfit, make a bundle for half the work."

"I wouldn't quit you for that."

Harleigh has to smile. It's nice to hear, but that kind of old-school loyalty is part of the problem.

"You know, Arne, how when we brought the casino in, folks had stars in their eyes about all getting rich."

"It's half empty over there."

"That's cause we don't have enough *people* up in this part of the world. To run a business, you got to have customers. But if the oil thing hits like it should, we'll have em up to our ears."

"Good for the casino."

"Good for everything. What we're looking for here is *sovereignty*. You know what that means?"

"When you got your own country."

"Exactly, but what use is having your own country if your belly is empty? So this time, if they want our minerals they play our *game*, which includes paying us what they're worth."

"People here get rich, just like the white man."

"The smart ones do, Arne. The smart ones do. And the way white folks get rich is to look out for Number One, which fosters competition and initiative and a whole lot of other things we could use a lot more of around here. They sure as hell didn't make any fortunes giving it away in a potlatch."

Arne tugs on the bill of his cap, thinking this over. "So when these oil people come," he says, "first thing is, I'll ask you for a raise."

Harleigh smiles and thumps Arne on the shoulder. "That's the idea, buddy. Find the highest bidder."

CLEMSON DOLLARHIDE WATCHES THE salesman do a lap around his den, looking over the paintings.

"All the same artist?"

Though technically he says he's buying, not selling, the fella is still a salesman. Do you out of something in the friendliest way.

"'Artist' might be pushing it some. They're mine."

Mostly landscapes with cattle, done in oil. The sky above the prairie at different times of day, different moods.

"Wow, really? Incredible detail."

"It's a long winter up here."

"I bet. So the thing is, Clem– you mind if I call you Clem?"

"Nobody else does."

"I stand corrected. The thing is, Mr. Dollarhide, several of your neighbors have already signed leases with the company."

"I got over four hundred acres."

"Four hundred and twenty-seven," smiles the salesman, Zig or Sig, something like that.

Clemson nods. "And most of those folks got as much or more. It's not like we're jawing over the backyard fence together."

"What I'm getting at is that they've made an investment in the future," the man says as he sits down across from Clemson. "While at the same time doing their bit to free our country of its dependence on foreign oil."

If he'd been busy he would have just sent the fella away, but he drove all the way out here, and what the hell– give him a workout.

"Foreign oil don't run as good as ours?"

"It's not the *oil* itself, it's the political entanglements, military adventures, whatnot, that come with it. But that's only a collateral issue, the main point being that you are sitting on what could be a sizable fortune, Mr. Dollarhide."

Clemson shifts to look at the cushion of his chair. "All these years, huh? Right under my keister."

The salesman appears to have heard that joke before. The man understands by now that they are sparring, but doesn't know he can't win.

"Whatever you choose to do with your mineral rights, this area is going to be transformed. A great deal of industrial traffic, wells popping up on the horizon, new businesses in Yellow Earth, new people."

"Not on my horizon."

"Pardon?"

"Wells. There won't be any popping up on my horizon. Even if Jake Wiltorp has said yes, I can't see that far."

The salesman shuffles his deck, deals a new hand.

"Perhaps if I give you a better idea of the numbers involved."

"Shoot."

"The drilling and stimulation of the well is an expensive process."

"How much you figure one might run you?"

"It's not unusual for a well in this type of play to run over a million dollars."

"So they're figuring there's a good deal more than that due to come out of the hole."

"Exactly."

"And they'd sink, what, a dozen holes on my property?"

"That depends. We'll make seismic and geological surveys."

"Let's just say ten, make it a good even number."

"Fine."

"And you were offering what?"

"I am authorized to offer you fifty dollars an acre– that's only the signing bonus."

"You said it was four twenty-seven I'm on, didn't you? That'd work out to twenty-one thousand, three hundred fifty dollars."

The salesman stares at him for a moment, catching up with the mathematics. "That's correct. Have you received other solicitations in the mail, Mr. Dollarhide?"

"None that I've read. So if you can get me to sign up for fifty an acre instead of, say, a hundred an acre, you already saved your company twenty grand."

The salesman smiles again, almost enjoying this. "A market value for these things quickly establishes itself. We hope to have our lessors feel they're in a *part*nership."

"So there's usually some kind of percentage of profits from what you drill, too."

"You've been studying on the internet."

"I was sitting on this same fortune back in the '80s," he tells the salesman, "when the last batch of wells were drilled."

"This promises to be a much more successful phenomenon, Mr. Dollarhide. The technical advances we've– "

"Just to keep the numbers simple," he interrupts, "let's say, conservatively, that you pull two million in profit from each of your wells."

"It could be much higher than– "

"Stick with me here. Ten wells, two million dollars profit each well, and what's the percentage you been authorized to give out?"

The salesman has settled back into his chair now, understanding that Clemson holds the reins of this particular wagon. "Twelve and a half percent," he says quietly.

"Anybody ever get fifteen?"

"As I said, these things fluctuate with the market, which has several dynamic factors that affect it."

"I'll take that as a 'yes.' Ten wells, two million a piece, twelve and a half per-cent– " even Clemson has to pause a moment to calculate. 'Show your work,' old Miss Jutress used to tell him in class, but it was so much more fun to show off and do it in your head. "Why that's two and a half million dollars."

"So if we should drill more wells, or profit more from each, you could easily– "

"Whereas if it was a *fifteen* percent cut– royalty? That would come out to an even three million. Why, you could be saving your company a half million dol-lars today, you do your job right. You work on commission?"

The salesman is openly grinning now, not a bit embarrassed. "I wish. But I think your calculations give you an idea of what a financial opportunity we're offering here."

"Don't want it."

"This is only a preliminary meeting of course. Some rights owners choose to gamble, hope that with time both the bonus and the royalty the Company is willing to pay increases."

"Don't want the oil business on my land. Don't want to see it, don't want to hear it, don't want to *smell* it."

There's a good dirt road off the highway that crosses his property, of course, and they'll be after him to let them use it for a short cut to their wells on the Wiltorp place. Might even get the state or county to try to force access. Bring it on.

Tina comes in from school then, offering the fella a moment to get his face back together.

"You look like you run all the way from the bus."

"The wind is murder today," she says, unwrapping her scarf. The wind is al-ways murder up here– his wife used to say it blew people's brains out, which explained a good deal of their behavior.

"This here's Mr. Rushmore. The fella who carved all those presidents' heads on the mountain down by Rapid."

"I wish."

"This my granddaughter, Spartina."

The salesman stands to shake hands. "Pleased to meet you."

"Mr. Rushmore says we could be millionaires."

Tina looks at the man with some interest. "Jason Cobb says there was a guy– "

"That was me," smiles the salesman. "Mr. Cobb and I were able to come to an agreement."

Tina looks to Clemson, more resigned than eager. "No way, José, right?"

"You know how I feel about it."

She nods, crosses to the big painting over the mantel, and points to a spot on it for the salesman to look at.

"You see that one cow, it's pointed in the other direction from all the others?" she says. "That's Granpa Clemson. Nice to meet you."

The salesman waits till she goes off to her room. "Beautiful girl."

"*Compet*ent, too. Had her in the 4-H back when I was still doing the dairy. Won something every year with her show calves."

"Is she hoping to go to college?"

"Last I heard she was going to be a supermodel. Don't know where the school for that is."

The salesman gets up, adjusts his jacket. "You know, it could be worked so that our operations are nowhere near your home. You've got enough space."

"It's the money."

"As I said, terms are, in the long run, negotiable."

"I, we, get money because my great-great grandfather was so weary of tramping around the country that he parked himself on this piece of ground, not knowing that– "

"Think of all the work that's gone into this ground, Mr. Dollarhide."

"I don't need to think about it, every time I bend over I got three compressed discs do the reminding. But that was the life we chose, people found a way to make a living from this sorry patch of land."

"So consider this a kind of compensation."

"That kind of money, it doesn't *mean* nothing. I don't need that. Don't de*serve* it. And neither does Tina."

"So you're willing to deny her."

"It isn't *hers*. And I'll tell you what– we get attacked again, whoever the new

enemy is comes marching onto our territory and the country needs fuel to fight
em? Government can come get it. For *free.*"

The salesman, Rushmore, holds out his hand in parting. "Mr. Dollarhide, it's
been a pleasure. If your philosophy should evolve or your financial situation alter,
you have my information."

Clemson can tell it's going to be painful to stand, and chooses not to show
his visitor the twinge.

"Thanks for your time, Mr. Rushmore. You do a good pitch."

He can see the fella drive off in his rental car through the den window, which
is buckling a little with the wind. The money would have been something when
Nora was sick, but it wouldn't have saved her. Clemson tries hard to think of
something he'd like to do with all those millions. Ten thousand, sure, there's
repairs that could be done. The heating bill wouldn't be a worry. But millions.
After Ted and Alva were killed he'd sit with Tina and watch her favorite shows—
she didn't ever like to be alone then— which was mostly singing competitions,
fashion deals on MTV, and the latest profiles of the rich and famous. He never
wanted to be any of those people, or live in any of those places. And a few of
them had even *earned* what they got.

Tina comes out and sits in the chair the salesman just left.

"You know what an iPod is?"

"Computer thing?"

"It's a bunch of stuff. Computer stuff, you put all your music on it, carry it
around— it's like smaller than those things— cigarette cases?"

"Expensive?"

"Couple hundred dollars."

"And everybody's got one."

"Pretty much."

"So you could share."

"That's not the point. We've got like a museum of obsolete technology around
here."

"You mean the record player."

"Starting with."

"It's a nice piece of furniture."

"That I can't carry in my pocket. Even if it worked."

She is a beautiful girl— would have been in any era— and he has to stay on her
to keep the makeup to a minimum. Let your natural good looks shine through.

And he feels bad for her, stuck here with just him, but none of the others had their lives together enough to be taking on an orphan girl, even if she was blood. Alva's family, not that she wasn't a pearl, but half of them are wearing orange suits and living off the county. And his daughter Jennifer, her three got enough learning disorders and behavior problems to keep a mental institution busy, and her always the nervous type for whatever reason, married to that slacker.

"I'll think about it, Tina."

"I'm joining the Fashion Club."

"Is that wearing or designing?"

"A little of both. It meets after school so I'll be home later."

"The bus."

"One of the girls in the club will drop me off. She's a good driver."

He nods. It hurt when she said she didn't want to do the calves anymore. 'I'm tired of smelling like cowshit,' was the exact declaration, and there was a whole sudden campaign for clothes that 'weren't embarrassing.'

"These pod things," he asks her, "they break easy?"

"It's more like people lose them cause they're small. But I wouldn't."

He gives her the nod that is just encouraging enough. They don't fight. She just gets quiet and then you hear the wind and it can be worse than being alone. Tina is looking past him, out the window in the direction the salesman drove.

"I know this is your place," she says, "and I totally get it that it's your decision about the oil."

"It will be yours someday."

She looks hurt. "Oh, Granpa. What would I do with a farm?"

THE SIGN OUTSIDE THE motel says 'American Owned and Operated,' which means the Patels have made it this far north and somebody assumes you give a shit. Free Wi-Fi, breakfast bar, lovely view of the parking lot and the highway beyond it. Sig showers, using his own soap that he's not allergic to, and changes into his casual selling outfit. Never know who you might run into. He runs his story for why he's not driving back to Oklahoma or Texas or whatever he told people over in his head, just in case, then steps out. Not so much traffic that he can't just stroll across the highway to the Arby's.

Sig orders and sits by the front window, shuffling leases on the little table after he wipes it with a napkin. Have to get out early tomorrow before the tom-toms start beating the news. There's only one other customer who's passed up the drive-thru option to sit and eat inside here– and damn if it isn't Ginny Sloan, two empty tables between them, grinning and wiggling her fingers at him.

"Passing through?" says Sig.

"Said the kidney to the stone."

Sig leans back and adjusts the Brown Sugar Bacon deal in front of him. The girl behind the counter had red glue-on nails long enough to eviscerate a bull elk. Put her in a new dress and get her a hostess spot with one of the steakhouse chains that will be hurrying in and she's good for 50K a year. Sometimes Sig feels like a man from the Future.

"Who you pitching for?" he asks.

"The Swedes."

"You're shittin me. Here?"

"They like this field."

"They do any mapping or are they just tagging after my bunch?"

"They say they know what's down there."

"How much do they want it?"

"Enough to yank me out of Pennsylvania."

The Swedes are big. Not as hyper and reckless as Aubrey's outfit, but they can sling some hefty numbers if they want to. Sig considers inviting Ginny to his table, but she'll just start in again on how you can't get a decent salad in these godforsaken oil patches.

"I'm starting at fifty an acre," he tells her.

She laughs. "It's not your money, Sig."

"They hire me cause I'm careful with it."

"This rock pays anything like what they hope," says Ginny, "*careful* is out the window."

"Anybody can wrap up a lease if they throw enough money at it," says Sig. Ginny worked for Aubrey for a while, buying anything with a fart's worth of gas beneath it, but apparently there was some personal problem, an attitude adjustment improperly completed, maybe some sloppy ownership research. "To do it and maintain your company's economic advantage requires a *salesman*."

"And that's why you're a legend, Sig," smiles Ginny, turning back to her Roast Turkey Farmhouse Salad. "*Bon appetit.*"

BULLETINS FROM THE BLACK STUFF

Could the Bakken be the next big play?

Some very swift moves on the Energy chessboard this week, as Big Oil zeroes in on shale deposits in the Peace Garden State. Advances in stimulation technology make the formations here highly attractive, and the land rush is on!

With crude at $115.46 a barrel, and auto juice skyrocketing over four dollars a gallon at the nation's pumps, this may be the time to stop futzing and start fracking.

Wherever you go, go with all your heart – Confucius

EVERY DAY THERE ARE more of them. Most only stay five to fifteen minutes, watch the equipment move around, speculate with their neighbors about what exactly is going on. Maybe cause they're a full week ahead of any of the other rigs being thrown up in the area and right off the highway, and this whole play has been dormant for decades. Plenty of folks here who never seen a drilling operation up close, don't know that from a safe distance it's a bit like watching paint dry.

But today there's a good two dozen hunkered in and somehow sensing that the real deal is about to kick off. Some are standing and some sitting on the hoods of the cars and pickups they've pulled onto the shoulder, not going anywhere till they see an event worth talking about. Upshaw doesn't pay them much mind till the sheriff's car pulls up.

He tells the boys to hold for a minute and climbs the ladder down from the platform. The wind is already a bitch and the locals say it just gets worse. Have to keep that deck clean, keep people from sliding off it. The sheriff steps across the field to the edge of the pad to greet him.

"Are they any problem?" he says, jerking his head back toward the peanut gallery. "Cause I can move em to the far side of the road."

"They're welcome to stay, it's totally safe. We don't even have the blowout preventer on yet."

The sheriff frowns at the word 'blowout.'

"That like a safety thing?"

"Yeah, but while we're just spudding in there's not enough pressure to need one. We're working with the wide bit today, get down past your aquifer and establish the surface hole, throw some casing in and cement it." Back in Texas there's schoolkids who can recite the whole routine for you. "We'll let that cement firm up for a day, test it, and if everything's jake we pop on a BOP and get on with the real drilling."

The sheriff nods as if he understood it all. "So they're not in the way."

"Long as they stick clear from the access road. As for danger, if one of these suckers does blow it'll go *up*, not sideways."

The sheriff tilts his head to see the top of the derrick. "Like a rocket launcher."

Upshaw smiles. "Let's hope not. Anyhow, they want to stick around, we're just about to break ground on YE Number One."

He walks back to the rig and shimmies up the metal rungs, aware that his crew is watching, that they've got nicknames for him and think he's old and grumpy, think that somehow they could run the drill string in and out just fine without him. He felt the same way when he was their age and roughnecking in Oklahoma, just as full of the same shit. He can hear Dizzy's boombox playing something hyper, like guitars in heat clawing at each other, way up on the monkeyboard.

"We under arrest?" asks either Ike or Mike, no nameplate on their hardhats like he asked, so impossible to tell them apart.

Upshaw settles behind his controls. "Just wanted to know when the curtain comes up," he says, starting to lower the kelly drive. "Let's not keep em waiting."

They'll go down eight hundred feet before they put the casing in, taking no chances with the water. The bit augers into the flattened prairie dirt and he can hear applause from the road, a little crackling of it over the machine noise. Ike and Mike turn and bow to the onlookers, and then horns are honked and people whistle.

Must be a bunch of leaseholders, thinks Upshaw, or life here is awful damn slow.

He's LOOKING IN THE rear view mirror again. Clink Roberts, who broke him in on the rigs, always said 'What's happening, what's bound to get you into trouble, is always in *front* of you, and that's where you got to keep your head.' But that was before, and now even though he's barely over the speed limit and got the road near to himself, he can't help but look behind.

Buzzy swings off the bypass onto I-35 north of Dallas and eases into the passing lane. He loves to roll as long as he possibly can without shifting gears, going with the flow, and if he's going to make this run without sleep it won't hurt to play a couple mind games to keep him on his toes. It's been a long time. When Terry packed it in and deeded him the truck he wasn't sure at first, all that bad karma waiting at the wheel, but where else can he pull down the kind of money they say is just calling out his name up there?

"Goodbye hemorrhoids, goodbye kidney stones, goodbye huffing diesel eighteen hours a day," said Terry, who is on his second wife and for some reason wants to keep her. "You take this sumbitch and get up there, send me a couple grand every month till we're even."

Terry had a little hotshot rig he run around Houston with, oil fields, construction, whatever, and then got the Big Truck Fever and borrowed enough to move on up to this Western Star 4900. And no sooner had it on the road when his butthole decided to quit the business.

"I'm not talking the itchy ones, just remind you they're with you mile after mile," he'll tell near-strangers if they hold still long enough, "these little bastards *hurt*. Doc said they could lead to complications, and that's one part of my body I don't want *complicated*."

He tried cushions, he tried ointments, he tried twisting one way or another till his back started to spasm, but there wasn't nothing for it but to get off the road.

"So it's up to you, Bro," he said when he showed up at the door dangling the keys. "Whatever you went through before, that was none of your fault, and the thing to do is jump on back into the saddle."

So he's *Waking Up with the Wolf* in the northbound lane, Lisa playing lots of Reba this morning, which is fine with Buzzy even if she is a holdover from the Old Man's generation, him and Terry getting a nightly dose of Reba and Dolly and Merle and Hank Junior while the Old Man emptied his toolbox tinkering with that quagmire of a pickup truck, popping rebuilt engines in and out of it like it was ever gonna be more than something you'd run to the dump with. He'd crank up the radio, only part of the heap that still worked good, wrestle with the plugs and valves for a couple hours and then slam the hood down, crank her up, and go out 'to put some juice back in the battery' when really it was out to Dusty's Place, and the only juice he'd allow past his tonsils come from the tequila fruit. And then home in the deep dark, caterwauling the same damn song–

> I'd like to settle down, but they won't let me
> A fugitive must be a rolling stone

–when the Old Man was near the most settled man you'd ever want to meet, forty years in the same house, same job, same Punch and Judy marriage. Ate pork chops on *Mon*day, goddammit, and don't put it out of order.

"Only good thing about boot camp," he'd always say, "you knew when the fucking horn was going to blow."

Whatever it was he done in Vietnam, and even Ma never heard more than the tip of it, it kept him nailed down snug in West Texas the rest of his life.

Tim McGraw, who the Old Man said he could tolerate, sings that "It Felt Good on My Lips." PLX will get you out of Texas and through a good deal of Oklahoma, where you can pick up XXY, and after that Buzzy will go with his mix tapes. He can't deal with the CB chatter unless there's weather or some slow-down to reckon with, and those endless Louis L'Amour stories Terry used to listen to would just put him to sleep. Got to stay alert the whole way, even if 'alert' hadn't helped any when his load started sliding.

Buzzy drinks coffee, still hot out of the thermos, and powers through what's left of the Lone Star State. You got to watch your fluids, know which ones will stick and which run right through you or you'll be stopping to tap your bladder every damn hour. Terry had one of these plastic deals, something like a vacuum cleaner hose with a little tank attached, but since he rolled alone you still had to get your John-son out, do your business, and tuck it back in while shifting gears and staying on the road. Pretty much the definition of Unsafe at Any Speed. The trick is to watch your intake and develop stamina. Before the accident Buzzy was an iron man, only stop to take on fuel or change loads. 'If you ain't in a hurry,' Clink used to say when he was racing around the oil fields, 'you sure as hell ain't making any bread.'

Welcome to the Sooner State. Buzzy is not so sure about the whole *idea* of Oklahoma. They taught in school how once it was the Indian Territory, and he figures they could have let the Indians keep it as long as they picked it up and moved it, all 236 miles to the Kansas line, somewhere else. That one time he tried to get a drink in the state on a Sunday they stared at him like he had an ant-ler growing from his forehead. And it looks like something you'd stick the poor Indians with, just flat and scrub and nothingness, like the most pitiful stretches of Texas and nothing but. They got all those tornados here because the wind gets so fucking bored it needs to spin in circles just to stay awake. Carrie Underwood now, who escaped from somewhere around here to get on *American Idol* and onto Terry's garage wall in her cowboy hat, prairie skirt, and boots, warbling her "Cowboy Casanova." Girl sounds like she looks, which is not always the case. Buzzy's sister Jessye sounds like a goddam country angel when she sings but looks like a Russian lady shotputter. On steroids. The Old Man always moaned how he didn't get no football players for boys, and he sure didn't get any cheer-leader in Jessye. Only one with brains in the family though, got into UT and kicked butt. Sang in some outlaw chick kind of group, too, popular in the Austin clubs, covering Patsy Cline and dressing like biker sluts. She got more tattoos than Buzzy now, which they don't seem to mind at the heart clinic.

"In my day," the Old Man said when she come home with the first bit of ink on her, a pretty tramp stamp with some Oriental writing around it, "a woman with a tattoo was either in the *circus* or peddling her ass."

"In your day," Jessye come back at him, which she could do like nobody else, "tats only come in one color, Varicose Blue, and it was either 'Mom,' that anchor offa Popeye's forearm, or 'Property of Hell's Angels.'"

A guy in a Trans Am comes up fast from behind and Buzzy eases over to let him go by. Nobody on my tail today, no matter how many times I checked the damn straps. Just let me worry about what lays up ahead.

It would have to be drill pipe for his first trip back. It is half the damn work available, true, but it's back there now like a loaded rifle, and if he'd been carrying still Buzzy would be hammering his lungs with Camels, one after the other. The long haul drivers, when they talk, got their opinion of what the worst load is, with swinging beef, HAZMATS, and anything you got to put a tarp over always high on the list. Buzzy moved a house once, creeping extra-wide down the highway with Terry blinking away behind him in his Chevy, and it near drove him crazy. Everybody and his mother in law piled up on your tail, looking for a spot to pass, people honking. Should of hired a damn ox team to pull it.

Drill pipe is the worst.

Buzzy has been operating behind the dashboard since he's fourteen, before beer, before girls, before he had to *shave*, goddammit. Just head out of Floydada, what direction don't matter, and blow some air, run down some roadkill, keep that ribbon of highway flying under your wheels. Didn't nobody in the world but Americans drive for the hell of it like that, except maybe some oil sheiks and they do it in Beamers or solid gold Caddys or some such shit, and they sure as hell don't run listening to Toby Keith singing "Courtesy of the Red, White, and Blue."

Another damn Sooner.

He passes a string of extra-longs hauling those wind turbine blades, well over a hundred foot, look like something out of a *Star Wars* movie. Trying to put us all out of business with that wind and solar, and you got to wish them luck. Hell, if I could just leave this rig outside for a couple days, soak up the sun, then drag a battleship halfway across the country with it– good Lord. Owner-operators be happy to say fuck you, Mr. Texaco, and keep the difference in their pockets. And then if they could work on some kind of electromagnetic ray that would vaporize all the weigh stations–

By the time Buzzy has put the Okies in his rear view mirror he's got his first mix tape in, which is all duets, guys and gals, Lee Ann and George, Trisha and Garth, Conway and Loretta, Rodney and Emmylou, George and Tammy, Johnny Cash and Pam Tillis and that Allison Krauss with whoever's waiting next in the hallway. He's even got the Nancy Sinatra one about Jackson that the Old Man used to quote when he'd give Ma a hard time, only Buzzy has never been to a Jackson yet worth running off to, starting with the one in Mississippi. The voices run together nice, and with so many of the women singing about what a dog their last man was, it's good to have a guy on the track to get his licks in too.

A little Volvo zips off the entrance ramp and disappears up his butt. Always wanted a bumper sticker that said 'If You Can't See My Mirrors, Dipshit, I Can't See *You*.' Buzzy speeds up till he can spot the clueless sumbitch, then passes a couple more civilians to put some distance between them. If you're not a hemorrhoid, get off my ass.

Thing is, you got to really *drive* the rig, stay with it, not sit there watching the phone poles strobe by like it's a damn video game. Sure, you can get by for hours with your mind on automatic pilot, but when a situation pops up you'll be too slow to deal with it. He decides to stay north through Topeka and come on to KC from the west. He tears into the first of his PowerBars and washes it down with Nitro2Go, which he's grown to like the taste of. Back in the day, he was a coffee and amphetamine man, jacked up to the eyeballs and then crashing between jobs, then staying on that same diet after the accident when there weren't any more jobs. Wonder he never got popped for DUI. Blew the marriage, blew the house, got his nose rearranged a few times in bar fights, but never was on the wrong patch of road at the wrong time. Not that he'd been sensible enough to worry too much about it. It wasn't for the Program and Terry staying in his corner through it all, he'd still be sitting in the Loser Locker feeling sorry for himself and abusing whatever substance came to hand. Buzzy's back is starting to complain and he decides he'll hold out till the Farris truck stop on I-29 outside of St. Joe. Good to have something to aim for.

It is so easy to slip into a hole, and so damn hard to dig yourself out. The Old Man, he found a cozy spot about halfway down and just stayed there, while other fellas Buzzy come up with– well, there's more than a few dead or lost for good. Seems like things that used to just come natural are now actual work, like how an old rig can't make the grade anymore. Like the Old Man at the end, laboring just to get another breath. Like how Buzzy can't remember a ten-, twelve-hour stretch on the road seeming like such a death sentence before.

But here he is, how many wasted years later, back on the move with a load of pipe on his flatbed, like God or whoever it is in charge of the whole deal saying,

'Here you go, son. You get another shot at it. Sorry for the interruption.' All right then, one solid year with his nose to it, maybe two if the play holds up, and he'll be back in the game for good. Sober will be tough, hell, it's tough already, but you figure that's a nice hunk of change not left on a bar counter or going up your nasal cavities. And money, *real* money like this promises to be, changes every-thing, thank you very much Cyndi Lauper. The women, God love em, pretend it's not such a big thing in how they look at you, but just you stop bringing it home and see how long they stick. Get ahead a little ways, Buzzy figures, and he'll have something righteous to roll around town in, and it won't be a goddam pickup truck. Get his teeth fixed, maybe lose a few pounds, pimp up his look a bit, you never know what might happen. Maybe get Terry up with him, start their own field services outfit, let some other chumps do the driving and the scut work. Just got to keep your hand upon the throttle and your eye upon the rail.

It's still bright enough that they haven't turned the lights on over the pumps when he pulls off the interstate. The kid fills his tanks up while Buzzy checks the cinch straps, ratcheting them to where they won't budge anymore, then tucks it in near the back of the lot, avoiding the stock haulers, and strolls to the Big Rigs Family Restaurant.

They got George Jones coming out of the system when he walks in, low brick walls separating the table areas, lots of flowers, the real ones that come out of the ground, and it's near full so he sits at the end of the counter. Good deal of Mexican stuff, which he doesn't trust north of San Antonio, on the menu since he was last in here and the place had a different name. Buzzy orders quick, chicken fried steak, baked potato, salad with the blue cheese to give it some heft, and heads for the Men's. He arranges himself on the throne, closes his eyes, and there's still road fly-ing at him. George is piped in here too, mooning over some woman who's got the wanders. These places by the interstate never close, just change people all day and all night, like Vegas without the gambling. Sometimes, long-hauling in the dead hours, you pull off the highway attracted by their lights, find a couple human be-ings rattling around inside who'll look you in the eye, and it'll near make you weep.

Buzzy throws cold water on his face, mashes it dry with pull-down paper towels, and comes out to give the room a better look. Good number of truckers, some eating together, some that look more like salesmen or customer service agents. Road warriors. And then like the name says, there's families, some trav-eling and some probably locals from Wherever, Missouri, this is. The big river is just off to the west for a lot of the trip up 29, but you don't feel it much.

Buzzy takes his time eating, orders pie for dessert, decides he likes their coffee better than what comes out of the machine at his neighborhood 7-11. The Beast is out there waiting for him, of course, but he's hoping the tingles will shake out of his fingers before he has to go back to it. He's forgotten that, and the vibrations in Terry's rig aren't near as bad as what he used to put up with, but it won't let him relax. The waitress is blond and powerful-looking and friendly enough, though she's always on the move. Now there's a job he don't envy. He watches her take the order from three fellas come in together without writing a thing down, and it's not that short a menu. You figure the minute a table clears out she forgets who was sitting there, like traffic going southbound while you're going north. You'd have to be a prodigious asshole or have a seizure or something to make an impression when there's this volume of trade flowing through. Buzzy pays in cash and leaves a nice tip. That's another thing to get done up there, get his credit situation straightened out. Terry has lent him his Fuelman card for the next three months and that should get him a toehold. Lots of situations, you walk in without plastic and you might as well have 'Leper' printed on your T-shirt.

It is night when he walks out of the restaurant, moths the size of flapjacks flittering under the lights. Buzzy checks the straps again, fires her up, and hooks into the stream of ruby taillights flowing toward the Promised Land.

There's cloud cover and maybe rain coming and a crosswind that makes him glad he's rolling with a low profile. Seen dry van trailers turn into sails in this kind of wind, lift the rig right off the highway. Night is different, especially with no moon or stars, just your headlights burning a tunnel in the black and you powering into it. Even when the lanes are full you're more alone, more likely to get ambushed by your own thoughts.

Buzzy tries a couple of his mixes till he settles on one Jessye give him last Christmas– 'not that you deserve it, you sorry sumbitch'– a lot of different colored people singing about Jesus. After a bit the words, which can sometimes put him to brooding about Ma's doomed campaign to make good Baptists out of him and Terry, kind of ease back and it's the *feeling* in the voices that takes over, they sure can do that, the colored, and Buzzy feels tears running down into his stubble. Shit, he can't be that tired. He's met some truckers over the years who grease-gun their faith into every cranny of their lives, but they mostly been guys who fucked up way worse he ever done. Drugs you got to pump in with needles, prison time, violence, all kinds of heavy business. If Jesus really did lift them up he pert near got a hernia doing it.

But, Lord, wouldn't it be nice if it were like in the songs, somebody looking out for you on the highways and byways, a great good place to go to whenever you finish your Last Run. There was one old boy in Lubbock, name of Eugene when he was promoting the gospel, though the tat on the back of his left hand told he'd been known as Pit Bull when he rode with the Bandidos OMG, who did a whole rap about how he passed out after a party one night and woke up with his house afire. How Jesus had spoken to him personally, spoken softly despite the roaring flames and cracking glass, telling him which way to crawl through the blinding smoke and find the open window to safety. How that calm Voice had saved him, and how he, Eugene, who had been freebasing on that night and was probably responsible for the fire, had dedicated the rest of his life to serving his Savior. And he really meant it. But if Eugene hadn't still been a scary, bullet-headed, no-neck pile of muscle somebody like Buzzy might have asked him why Jesus, while He was at it, hadn't clued Eugene's old lady and two kids in on the path out of the inferno. Slipped His mind? Wicked sense of humor? His eye was on the sparrow?

Still, the singing is great, it lifts him, if that is possible, past the lights of Kansas City, on past Omaha, the traffic thinning out to a few lonely rolling islands following the thread of highway in the black night, Buzzy forgetting his own story, till a hard, gut-wrenching jolt of wind pulls him back.

The boys in the yard had loaded the drill pipe for him, like always, looked fine to the eye, never a problem before. And he always made sure to check the cinch straps whenever he stopped, ratchet the slack off and keep the load bundled tight, only he was long-hauling on a schedule and hadn't stopped yet when it happened. It was night, like this, not too much moving when the engine changed tone and he felt a little surge forward and then sparks and flame in the mirrors as near half of the eighteen-thousand tons of drill pipe he was carrying slid back onto the family in the VW Golf who'd just drifted in behind him. He got his rig off to the side and ran back and there was nothing to do for it but keep his back to the burning wreck and try to roll pipe off the road before anybody else crashed. He spent a night shaking in jail, and then there was people in uniforms grilling him till Terry come up to take over the rig and had a friend drive him back home. The TV at the truck stop where the friend stopped for a break showed photos of the family– Vince was the father, just home from the Gulf War, Natalie was the wife, and Melissa and Kimberly were the girls. Lawsuits like crazy, but none of them touched Buzzy, he didn't even have his license suspended. Relatives went after the service company, where the real money was. The boys in the yard got fired, then hired on somewhere else within the week. The pipe got rounded up and delivered where it was meant to go. Buzzy had a hard time swallowing for a year or two.

> Precious Lord, take my hand
> Lead me on, let me stand–

You want to believe that it's just a thing that *happened*, an accident, and not part of who you are. You want to believe that nothing like that will ever happen again, at least not to you. But it's never going to leave, it's riding with him now, and all the dope in the world couldn't chase it away. And that cocky kid who was before the pipe come loose won't ever be again.

When the mix is over he lets the night just *be* for a while, no soundtrack to try to fill it up. Somehow, creeping up on Sioux City, he starts trying to do the math about how much oil you got to burn through to put in a well to drill for more oil. How many truckloads of whatever, each trip burning diesel to and from, how much to drive the drill assembly a mile or two underground, how much do those gangs of pumper trucks they need for the fracturing guzzle, then all the trucks to break it down and move the pieces to the next pad. And how the whole deal rests on it– electricity, transportation, plastic the computers are made from, heat for the dumbasses who live up in the cold places. You work around the oil patch for most of your life and it seems like there's nothing but that, that it's always been and always will be. But then you figure all them cowboys that come before Henry Ford and how people still lived a full life, at least to them it seemed so. And what was it– horses and grass? Squeeze a little grease out of a chunk of whale and run a lantern at night? Shit must of fallen off wagons back then, too, logs maybe, and killed people. But it wasn't so *explosive*. The Old Man did a whole demonstration for him and Terry and Jessye once, like he was the redneck Science Guy, on how it was only just a series of controlled explosions that moved the pistons that cranked the engine that made the machine roll forward. *Boom boom boom boom boom boom boom*– a whole damn war going on in there just to drive around the block. Whereas horses are just born to run, natural, they like it so much they'll do it with a tobacco-spitting hunk of cowboy and fifty pounds of Spanish leather piled on their backs.

Not that Buzzy ever rode a horse.

The night stretches on into South Dakota and Buzzy is really feeling it, taking deep breaths and popping his eyes and starting to talk to himself some.

He's never nodded off at the wheel and he's not about to goddam start on this trip. The energy drink don't seem to be doing much for him, so he decides to think on something raw to get the adrenaline pumping, and that always leads to Tara Beth.

So maybe she took the 'in sickness and in health' part to just mean the flu now and then, cause she sure bailed quick when he needed her support. And no, things weren't a hundred percent before the accident, but compared to most guys he can think of he was a bargain. Didn't slip around on her, if he come home drunk he just fell out on the couch without a fuss, paid the rent on time. But there was always some idea in her head, maybe from TV or the movies, of how it was sup*posed* to be, and to that he couldn't measure up. Always had that less-than-expected attitude, even when he'd take her out some place. And it wasn't like she'd turned down any millionaires or *People* magazine Ten Sexiest Men to go with him. After a short while together they got to be Is That All There Is? on her side of the bed and This Is Life, Darlin, Get Used to It on his, and never moved off their positions. He could tell that being married was important to her, to how she felt about herself and how she was around her friends. It just didn't have to be to *him*. And then one morning he comes home, fucked up, sure, but he never spent the whole night out before, not once, and there's half the furniture and appliances gone, must've rented a damn U-Haul, and it's written on the back of a *shop*ping list she never got to the store for. I mean, five years of marriage, use a fucking clean piece of paper. You Know Why, it said. Goodbye, that's all she wrote. She'd even took all the photographs and the video of their wedding party, like erasing that any of it ever happened. They're always talking about feelings, women, but you got to have ESP or something to pick up on their moods, and when it comes down to the crunch they can cut you dead without a twinge of emotion. Let your guard down, show a little weakness, and they're gone with the wind.

Buzzy grabs one of his mixes at random and jams it into the slot, cranking the volume up as loud as he can stand. But it's just noise, cause the only song he wants to hear, the only true one, is another from the Old Man's era, Johnny Paycheck before he shot that fella and made his trip up the river–

> *Take this job and shove it*
> *I ain't workin here no more*
> *My woman left home and took all the things*
> *I been workin for*

Buzzy grinds through to daybreak, crosses the ND line and cuts west on I-94, and suddenly he's got company. More flatbeds hauling casing. Three lowboys carrying thumper trucks with their extra wide tires. Thirty-ton winch trucks, tankers, a convoy with various pieces of drill rig dealt out between them, little knuckle boom cranes and their big brothers, coil-tubing trucks, fracking-pump trucks with their huge rusty muffler units mounted on top and Kenworths and Peterbilts and Freightliners and old beat-up Macks and by the time they all take the US 83 exit at Bismarck it's a goddam army on the move, Buzzy getting his third wind from the energy of it all around him, till they slow to a crawl on the four-lane and he realizes he's already late to the party. Just *look* at all these people. Twenty miles short of the Three Nations rez he sees a new painted sign for Gil's Park 'N Snooze by the side of the road, but it looks to be only some open space in a field, behind a row of storage containers with cots lined up in them. Be sleeping in the rig for a spell. Buzzy cranks his window down and calls across to the white-bearded character driving the drop-deck semi in the next lane.

"Hey Buddy– it always like this?"

"This time of day, sure. You new?"

"Started up from Houston yesterday morning."

The old man lifts his Drill, Baby, Drill cap in salute. "Sonny," he smiles, "welcome to the Wild West."

HARLEIGH PUMPS HIS OWN, then goes in to palaver with Chuck for a minute. Everybody's business, personal and professional, gets hashed over at the station, so a visit here is basically a campaign stop.

"Mr. Chairman! How they treating you?"

Chuck is tall and amiable and has been here so long you can forget he's not enrolled, not any part anything Native. He sells all the usual convenience store junk, accepts food stamps, and carried rifles till Elmer Reese killed his ex-wife with one he'd bought here.

"I got a feeling we're on a winning streak, Chuck."

Harleigh pays the amount on the pump in cash, adding some buffalo jerky to the tab. His new theory is that chewing it in the day will tire his jaw enough to keep him from grinding his teeth at night. His dentist in Yellow Earth, Dr. Goldschmidt, says if it works he'll publish a paper in the ivory drillers' medical review.

"Yeah, I heard you're about to be an oil baron."

"Not me personally, but it is about to get pretty lively around here."

"I seen some dozers and whatnot go by."

"Making pads for the drill rigs. You want to start the whole process absolutely level."

"So nothing rolls off the platform."

Harleigh smiles. Chuck comes to the open meetings even though he doesn't have a vote, takes an interest. After the Elmer Reese thing he joined up with the Domestic Violence ladies, helping at the shelter.

"Figure this– let's say when you start drilling down you're a quarter-inch off plumb," Harleigh explains, indicating a diagonal with his hand. "Now you go down two *miles*."

"That far?"

"Sure, if that's where your hydrocarbons are hiding out. Imagine how far that wrong angle has taken you from your target."

Chuck pauses, trying to do the math in his head. "You might be off the rez altogether, tapping into somebody else's oil."

"They done a good deal of that on purpose, back in the old wildcatting days. Slant drilling. 'Oh, I'm sorry, did I suck up all your oil? How careless of me.'"

"Must have been some uneasy neighbors."

"Believe it. Lots of little wars were fought. But nowadays they send a *tool* down the hole, it's like the GPS on your phone, tells you the exact angle your drill pipe is set at."

"So you go straight down."

Chuck gets busy opening boxes of cigarettes with a cutter. He's good about not selling them to minors, most of the vendors on the rez are, but the kids got much worse habits than tobacco. Just in the rack in front of the checkout counter there's enough sugar and grease to stop an elephant's heart.

"You go straight down till you penetrate the shale layer," says Harleigh, "and then you start to deviate your angle, inch by inch, till you're moving horizontal through the rock."

"That part is tough to imagine." Chuck arranges packs and cartons on the shelf behind his counter. Harleigh's father burned his lungs out smoking Old Golds, which you don't see around much anymore. His father would quote the catch phrases while he lit up– 'Made by a tobacco man, not a medicine man' and 'It's a treat, not a treatment'– and swore he needed them to 'get the gunk out' from his lungs. His lungs which failed him so young.

"I mean I get it how a plumber's snake can bend sideways in the trap under a sink," says Chuck. "But that far beneath the ground– "

"It's not just pipes and pumps anymore, Chuck, it's *science*. Space-age stuff. Once they gone as far horizontal as they want in a couple different directions, they hit that shale with a jolt of water at high pressure– it's got two miles' worth of weight piled up behind it to start with– and it makes these cracks in the rock, where the oil bleeds out and runs back into the pipe."

"No wonder I'm pumping it for four dollars a gallon."

"Oh, it'll go down some, Chuck, once we start rolling. But never so much it won't pay to drill here."

"So I should be getting ready for a lot more traffic."

"You'll get a workout," says Harleigh as he exits, with his jerky in his shirt pocket, "just keeping your beer cooler filled."

There is a white fella at the pumps with a two-gallon plastic gas container he's just filled, staring out at the empty prairie. Harleigh doesn't see another vehicle anywhere.

"You hitch to get here?"

The fella turns– late twenties, buff, starting to bald a little but has got his hair short enough you don't notice it so much.

"Walked."

"Filling stations can be few and far between out here."

"Tell me about it."

"Which way you parked?"

The young man points west and Harleigh nods to his pickup. "Get in," he says. "I'll run you over."

So Brent Skiles, that's his name, puts the jug of gas in the bed and they take off across the rez, Harleigh knocking ten miles per hour off his usual speed so the kid doesn't get the wrong idea.

"I feel like an idiot. Not only do I run out of gas, but I leave my cell phone at the motel so I can't call my wife to come get me."

"Vacation?"

"No, actually, we're up here scouting business opportunities, and I thought I'd take a look at your three tribes here."

They pass some of the little, low government housing, concrete rectangles with the usual debris of life spread out on the yards around them.

"How you like it so far?"

"People been awfully friendly. I expected they'd be– I don't know– like more– "

"Hostile?"

Brent grins. "That sounds bad, doesn't it?"

"I'd venture that historically, unless you were a Sioux warrior who made a wrong turn somewhere, this is one of the least hostile communities you'd ever stumble across in North America. Not many places you get three different tribes, different languages, different cultures, can manage to iron things out enough to function as a united front."

"People marry across the tribes?"

"Oh, sure, plenty of that, we got a long tradition of bringing new blood into the mix, white or Indian. It's more how you live and who your family is that people care about."

Brent nods. "Yeah, me and my wife got a mixed marriage– she's Baptist and I was raised Lutheran."

Harleigh smells the gas fumes from the back. He rolls his window up and punches the button for the fan. "So you're looking for work?"

Brent gives him a quick appraising look.

"You must know about the oil play that's coming here."

"Oh– I heard some talk." This is the beginning, thinks Harleigh. It's going to be like the Oklahoma Land Rush in the movies, people racing, crashing into each other. But this time it doesn't end with us losing our land.

"I've got a friend who's a friend of a geologist who did a probe up here for some people. He says from the readouts they got it's the real deal."

"So you're a roughneck?"

Brent laughs. "Hell no."

"You look like you do some kind of physical work."

"CrossFit. I toss a truck tire around for an hour every morning, box jumps, power cleans, lots of squats."

"So you're what, a drilling engineer?"

"You know, with all the technology they've got to throw at it these days, oil and gas exploration is still high-*risk*. Jinxed wells, environmental lawsuits, international price fixing– to me it's a lot of potential headaches, and you need like mega capital to even get started. No, you look at the people who make sure money on any boom, going back to the California Gold Rush, it's the ones who provide the goods and services to the crazy prospectors."

"I hear you."

"I've got some trucks down in Texas, hoping to set up an oilfield services company somewhere it's not all sewn up already."

"This would be the spot."

He seems not to hear. "So I'm looking for the ideal space to stage it– good access to the highway, surrounded by drill sites."

"Seriously– plenty of opportunity here on the reservation."

Brent cuts a look to Harleigh.

"You wouldn't have to be a member?"

"I think you'd find we're offering better terms and lower taxes than Yellow Earth or any of the outside communities."

"But there must be special rules and regulations."

"Nothing too fancy."

Brent seems to consider, nodding his head. "Still," he says, "I'd need a partner, who was, you know, in the tribe. One of the tribes. Knows the rules, knows the players, can guide me through it all."

Harleigh hands him one of his cards, his name above the arrow shaft and his office information printed below it. Brent seems impressed.

"You?"

Harleigh nods, keeping his eye on the road.

"You're the Chairman."

"For at least another two years."

"Get outta town! I'm on a reservation bigger than some *states* and I happen to hitch a ride with the chief– I mean the Chairman– of the whole deal!"

"Don't be too impressed."

"No, I *am*. It must be a hell of a job."

"I read this story," says Harleigh, "about a tribe down in Mexico, where every year the elders choose a new head man. And once they got him picked, they sit him in a chair and for a whole day the former chiefs all sit around telling stories about what a wonderful guy he is."

"Good gig."

"Only the new man is sitting bare-assed in the chair, which has a hole cut in the seat and is situated directly over some hot coals they keep fanning. So all day long his ego gets a massage and his ass and balls get blistered. Just a reminder of what the job really is."

"Ouch."

"You get serious about this company," says Harleigh, "you come look me up."

"Aren't there rules against you being head of your council and– "

"I got elected cause folks seen how well I run my cattle business. And I've been thinking about oil services already– the whole slew of things these outfits are going to need when they get up and going and prefer to subcontract."

"Can you hold a lease?"

"The mineral rights on the rez are complicated, got tribal ownership, individual ownership– but the collateral stuff, hell, we try to encourage the entrepreneurial stuff whenever we can. People got to learn to do for themselves and not wait on the government to bail em out all the time."

Harleigh slows as he sees the Vette ahead on the side of the road.

"That a ZR1?"

"Bingo."

"What year?"

"'92."

"Good Lord." They stop and get out of the pickup. The Corvette is red with a black top and looks like it's speeding just sitting there.

"Not your best pick for fuel efficiency," says Brent with false modesty.

"But it can *fly*, right?"

"The thing is, the faster you go, the more the aerodynamics push you down to the road, increase the efficiency."

Harleigh takes a slow walk around the beautiful machine. Idaho plates, another thing you don't see much on the reservation. "We got a couple stretches out here," he says, "no traffic at all, you could let her rip."

"I had her up to 175 once, not a tremble. You should drive it some time, I think your legs will just fit."

Harleigh holds out his hand to shake. "All right, got to run, Brent, but you think about this service company idea. As many trucks as you can find, I got drivers on the enrollment, good ones, who can handle anything you put on the road."

"Been a pleasure, Chairman. You'll be hearing from me."

Brent empties the gas can into the tank, watching the pickup grow smaller in the distance. He caps it off, pulls his cell phone from his boot. It vibrated twice during the ride from the filling station, almost made him jump.

It's Bunny.

"Yeah, darlin, it's looking good. Made contact, and he's everything they say."

There is a prairie dog standing upright in its hole, maybe twenty yards from the edge of the road, staring at him. He's spent a couple afternoons out on Cooter Landry's flatbed setup, with the bass-fishing swivel chairs and the beer on ice and his Remington .22, whackin em and stackin em. You hit them anywhere but dead center they'll do incredible flips before they flop to the ground.

"Will do, darlin," he tells his wife. He's feeling pumped, the endorphins flooding into all the places they ought to be. This Harleigh seems he might even be some fun to hang with. "See you in twenty."

CARPET HOLDS ON TO the nasty stuff. People spill drinks, puke, drop their used safeties, which at least means they're not clogging the toilets with them. Vic wanders the linoleum floor, probing for bubbled spots, trying to think with the hammering and power-tool whine on every side. You start up from scratch like this and you've got to be a bit of everything– politician with the local authorities, recruiter for the girls, accountant, contractor, and worst of all, an interior fucking designer. Button-tufted bonded leather banquettes are running a hundred twenty bucks a lineal foot. Some shit called Makrolon is less likely to scratch than acrylic, as if the slobberers at the tip rail won't put up with wood flooring under their fantasy babes. How these people get his cell number is a mystery, and they won't stop. Did he know that armless club chairs in real leather allow for greater customer density without sacrificing the Wow Factor? That a free-standing stage, lit from below, enhanced the atmosphere of interaction? Well the stacking chairs he just hauled over from Walmart don't have any arms, and the main room that used to be the American Legion bar is dinky enough to force the hardhats and the hos to interact whether they like it or not. So carpet, yeah, there's a guy lying on the floor stapling strips from what was on the floor of the post-Katrina club he ran in New Orleans, with a repeating pattern of those mudflap girls who glow magenta when you throw the black lights on, to cover the sides of the little stage that sits flush to the wall. The stage is up three feet, just over table-top height, so when the girls crawl backwards and wiggle their moneymakers the boys don't need to strain their necks. Had to explain that to the building codes guy before he got down to serious business and asked how often Vic was going to change dancers. And yes, hockey puck lighting alongside the stage ramp is what the girls are used to, continuous tread would only confuse them. They're not fucking stewardesses.

Vic watches the guy on the ladder bolting in the top sleeve for the pole and hopes he measured right. Nice high ceilings in these old buildings, so even three feet off the floor the pole can go up a ways. He's put the stage over the section of floor that was really scabby, probably leakage from the old Legion bar, and had the electrician add two more outlets. Other than that it's just slap some paint on the wainscoting, yellowed from the years when everybody smoked, and hang his good-luck disco ball, veteran of a dozen clubs, when these clowns stop waving their Makitas around. It's a *strip* bar, not a fucking gentleman's club.

The ladder guy– kid, really, looks like he's just out of high school– drops a plumb bob from the ceiling collar and gives it a little jerk, the point of the bob marking the soft wood flooring. Spike heels will do a number on any surface, but black paint is cheap, and that's what Sundays are for. The sheriff steps in.

"I was hoping you'd stop by," says Vic, heading for him with his hand extended. Youngish guy, doesn't look like too much of a tight-ass. "Vic Barboni."

The sheriff shakes his hand without much enthusiasm, looking around. "I thought you were opening this Saturday?"

"Oh, we'll be open, all right– just kind of a taste of things to come. Mondays are actually are our second-best night, the regulars all come to see who the new girls are. You need to see my paperwork?"

"No, the mayor told me you're all insured and permissioned, you and the fella next door."

"Next door?"

The sheriff deadpans him. "In the old pharmacy. Liquor license just come through this morning. Gonna call it 'Teasers' I believe."

Which means they're a week, maybe two behind him. Fuck.

"I'll have my own security, of course," says Vic, "but it's a comfort knowing you and your boys are out there for backup. How big's your department?"

"There's me and one patrol deputy per shift, plus always somebody on the phone."

"For the whole *coun*ty?"

"Wasn't enough before," says the sheriff, "won't be near enough for what's coming."

"Damn."

The kid is on his knees now, power-drilling holes for the bottom support. The sheriff raises his voice over the noise.

"I don't want anybody *selling* out of here," he says. "And if your girls are making dates, it better be for off the premises."

Vic holds out his hands to indicate the room, filled with workmen and construction stuff. "Not enough *space* here for hanky-panky, and I ride tight herd on the girls. The drugs, I got you– my boys keep an eye out for who's visiting the john a little too often. As for fights, well, they are called *rough*necks."

"You close at twelve-thirty."

"Twelve-thirty *sharp*."

Vic sneezes into his handkerchief. The sawdust and the plaster dust on top of what seems to always be blowing outside–

"How many entrances?"

"Just one for the customers. Right now I'm thinking it's that side door, we'll have a fella on, somebody they take serious, looking out for weapons." He grins at the sheriff. "If only we could make them check their *att*itude at the door."

"The less I hear about this place, the happier I'll be."

"I hear you." This is how I must make the girls feel when I lay down the law, thinks Vic. Like the fucking vice principal. "Listen," he asks, hoping to divert the offensive, "is there an ATM machine in this town?"

"One at the bank."

"They said it's down."

The sheriff shrugs. "There's Bismarck down the road."

Vic ran Boobie's Palace in Fairbanks for three years, steady money in a full-nude, full-liquor, full-contact state till the weather and the bare-bones nature of the town finally got to him. This will be a challenge, and now with some sleaze-bag setting up right next door–

"Three deputies," muses Vic, watching a pair of the workmen try to carry the bar counter in from the front without denting it.

"Two right now," says the sheriff. "Had one quit yesterday, sign on with one of these oil service outfits."

"You people don't get paid enough."

"Public servants."

The sheriff goes then. The best you can hope is that they're not some kind of bedrock Christians, or gimme gimme cops like some he could name in New

Orleans, and that they're actually competent when you need them. Vic has asked the police to arrest one of his own employees more that once. The lighting guy from Dallas calls, lost on the highway with a van full of LEDs and stage spots, and the kid is pulling the brand-new pole out of its long box when a biker comes in, something like a smirk between the sides of his Fu Manchu moustache.

Familiar mug, but there have been so many.

"Odessa?" says Vic. "Okie City? Reno?"

"Daytona Beach," says the guy, turning sideways to show off his name, running down his left arm in flaming letters.

"Scorch."

"How you doing, Vic?" asks the bouncer. One of the good ones. One of the best.

"Up to my neck, as usual. We open Saturday."

"Don't look like it."

"Hell, we'll sweep anything that's still loose under the stage. What you doing here?"

Scorch shrugs. He was a real find, totally up front about his time in the joint, never looking for a fight, a natural born drunk-whisperer.

"I got this buddy, Brent, he said there's money to be made."

"He ain't lying to you. My oil patch connections say it's gonna be a whopper."

With Katrina it had been the cleanup crews, a lot of them Mexican but good spenders with some tequila under the belt, then the pipeline in Alaska, and Florida just a magnet for horny guys with laps that needed sitting on.

"What's your plan?"

Scary-looking fuck, Scorch, you think twice about messing with him if you've got half your brain cells still functioning, but smart. Knows the racket.

"I figure I'll run three, four girls a week to begin with," Vic says, "pay their way out here, maybe even a base salary, let them keep fifteen out of twenty on the lap dances. Then when the full boom hits and we're turning riggers away at the door I'll charge the girls a club fee, maybe two hundred a night, as many as want a crack at the floor, and they keep whatever they can hustle."

"Plus you always got the cover charge and the liquor."

"This won't be a mixed-drinks kind of crowd, but my bartenders will keep pouring, yeah."

"Security?"

"I've already brought on a couple muscle-heads, look like they won't trip on their own dicks. I got a little phone-booth private room back there that'll need a watchdog, got the floor, the door– you interested?"

"How much you paying?"

He was good with the staff, this Scorch, if memory serves, kept his hands off the girls, and if he was slinging anything on the side he was so discreet it never got back to Vic. One less headache if you got a guy like that keeping a lid on the place.

"What say I give you a two-hundred-a-week bump over the other guys, have you run the whole deal? Hire and fire if you have to, set the tone."

"Sounds good."

The kid is jockeying the extendable pole into the fixed sleeves, twisting the chrome till it's tight as it goes. They're only one door down from the Amtrak station, right on a main drag, plenty of parking. A beautiful spot. The kid jumps up, hugging his knees around the pole, sways side-to-side, then steps away to look at it. Solid as a rock. Scorch grins his devil grin.

"Kind of like raising the flag, ain't it?"

THE CIVIL WAR DID it for Lincoln. For TR it was surviving his 'crowded hour' on San Juan Hill, and the Depression and Second World War made FDR. This is far from a national arena, of course, but you got to ride the bronco you draw. Senator Prescott Earle, Governor Prescott Earle– why the hell not?

"The mayor is acutely aware of what's going on."

Jonesy from the next room. Father a state trooper, mother a hospital administrator, she was fluent in Official by the eighth grade.

"The companies are still only in their exploratory phase now, but the mayor is preparing a projected impact report for the next city commission meeting."

She can sling it with the best of them, Jonesy. 'Projected impact.' As if you can know who's going to get squashed by the meteor and who's going to escape. Or better, into whose pockets all this money is going to fall–

"I will inform the mayor. We appreciate your call."

Jonesy has been appreciating over a hundred calls a day since the big outfits took their landmen off the leash. Press raises his voice to call to her–

"Get the Frack Out, or Drill Baby Drill?"

They leave the door half-open to spare their tonsils. "Just a concerned citizen. Wondered if there was oil under city hall."

"That would be something, wouldn't it?" Press gets up to stretch his legs, wanders in to Jonesy's domain. She coaches soccer and works with a half-dozen team photos behind her head. "Which one does my three o'clock rep again?"

"He's from Case and Crosby. Mr. Rushmore."

"Texas?"

"Texas, Oklahoma, quite a bit in Pennsylvania lately, oil sands in Canada."

"Behave themselves?"

"When they break something they tend to settle."

"Deep pockets."

She stops working the computer keys, leans back. "It's a popular stock with aggressive investors."

Jonesy is Wikipedia with legs. Maybe three or four years older than he is, blushes if you make her speak in public, but capable of tearing you a new one over the phone. Every mayor should have one.

"You got that list of what we need?"

She hands him a printout. "First column what we need, second column what would be nice to have."

Unless Planning and Zoning jump the corral they should be in pretty good shape when things start popping. State might help with traffic, but they're pretty slow on the draw, so the phone calls will keep rolling in. How long it took Mrs. X to drive to the Walmart. The trick is not to get suckered into one fixed contract with these operations, just keep the communication open, let them know that ground given can always be taken away.

"He's here, you know." Jonesy taking off her reading glasses to look up at him. "Sitting in the lobby. I said you were talking to somebody from the EPA."

Press grins. "Throw a scare into them."

"You *did* actually have a conversation with them a month ago, with a Richard Cosgrove," says Jonesy. "In case he inquires."

Richard Cosgrove. Dick Cosgrove. Remembering names has become the toughest part of the job. When he's got Brewster running interference for him at a function, Brewster whose hard drive is not cluttered with thirty-five years of politics, names come easy.

"Oh, hello, Mrs. Johannsen," says Brewster at volume, three feet in front of him, and then it all comes back. The four sons, including the one they tried to get into West Point who's in Canada now, working for their rail system, and dear departed Soren, who used to raise prize bulls—

Dick Cosgrove, EPA.

"What have I got, five minutes– ?"

"He didn't seem to be in a hurry."

"Give me two and send him in."

Press steps back into his office and crosses to the window. The east-west stuff has already started to pass right under his nose, the state highway making a dog-leg around city hall, sixteen-wheelers stopped at the lights, spewing exhaust. The old timers are already complaining about how busy it's gotten, the same ones who want him to attract business, like there's a– what– hormone? Some smell you could set off and they all come running. Well it's been here all along, right under their feet. He crosses to pull the street map down, poses in front of it, choosing a concerned but confident frown. He hears Jonesy behind him.

"Here's Mr. Rushmore for you, Mayor."

Press turns as if interrupted from deep thought to face a guy who looks like he should be selling Hoovers to '50s housewives.

Find out what people want and make them think you're going to give it to them. It's always easier with the office holders if a couple of them are personally sitting on a mineral deposit, but neither the mayor nor any of the committee members are big landowners. A couple of the guys with businesses will do well– the hardware guy, the one with the diner, at least till the big chains can throw some competition up. But Sig gets the impression that Prescott Earle is less interested in cash than *credit*.

"It looks like you folks will be staying awhile."

Apparently Earle is not going to sit down behind his desk, so Sig gets comfortable as he can on the arm of the leatherette chair. "That's our hope. The initial outlay is so expensive, you need wells that keep producing year after year."

"Any idea of the population numbers we're looking at? I know it won't be families coming in at first."

"It's not so much how many workers we'll employ," Sig tells him, "it's how fast they show up. Expect a bit of shock and awe from your constituents."

"The trucks."

"All our company-owned tractor-trailers have ECMs– that's a speed governor– in their engines for highway use. And if they pick up a ticket in town, we make sure they pay it." No need to get into the subcontractors.

"It's the volume."

"We'll be happy to consult with you about alternate routes wherever practi-
cal, or even some kind of loop around town if state funding can be tapped. But
today I'm only authorized to talk to you about where we're going to *put* all our
people."

"Workforce Temporary Housing," says the Mayor, planted in front of the wall
map of the town as if posing for a campaign photo.

"'Temporary' might be quite some time if we're lucky. And you've presently
only got a couple hundred units available, I figure, counting your private-home
folks willing to take on boarders– that'll disappear in no time."

"So you'll want to build."

"*Build* is too grand a word for it. We have access to integrated housing systems
that are extremely portable."

"Not trailers."

"No wheels on these babies." Sig points past the mayor to the map. "You're
fortunate to have so much unoccupied *space* here in Yellow Earth."

Western towns tend to be on the airy side in general, but this burg has clearly
had some hard times, six or seven warehouses that look to have been barren
since the first Bush, empty lots sprouting weeds–

"I have to warn you we have some pretty strict ordinances on the books. And
I was just chatting with my friend Dick Mosgrave at the EPA."

"Costs and benefits," says Sig, holding up a hand. The main drag looks like any
godawful commercial strip in America, then some decent old wooden houses
with actual trees growing next to them, the railroad tracks and the flood plain
of the Missouri to the south of town– not a candidate for heritage preservation.
"People in your area, in your city, are going to benefit, at least financially, a great
deal from my company's activities. But of course there will be some inconve-
niences, and some allowances will have to be made. Once you prime the pump
of private enterprise– "

"We can't just roll over."

You *can*, of course, and it's been done even in states where nobody wears
cowboy hats or eats crawfish. But nobody wants to admit that's what the deal is.

"One of the positive reports I've been able to relay to headquarters, Mayor, is
that Yellow Earth has a highly functioning local government. Most of our headaches come from people who *don't* have their act together."

The jury is still out, but it never hurts to get them thinking they're a vital part of the team. The mayor has lifted his chin, waiting for something specific to bat around.

"This is going to be a *process*," says Sig, "and I've found it's always good policy to show the public some of the workings of that process."

"You mean press releases."

"Maybe," says Sig, cocking his head to study the mayor, "and I'm just iffing here, maybe we could make a proposal, then you make a counterproposal that is slightly less generous, slightly more restrictive, then we could gradually come to an agreement, all in the public eye."

"Open hearings."

"Open for the edification and– let's call it *pacification* of the public's worries."

"Chill them out."

"–but with the end result previously agreed upon."

Prescott Earle takes a moment to chew on this one.

"You mean we make a private deal?"

Phrasing is everything in these preliminary bouts. Nobody wants to get filthy rich anymore, they want 'wealth' to manage. Nobody is just plain honest, they're 'transparent'–

"We make an agreement away from the noise and anxiety that our particular kind of invasion can engender. You and your committee will have what's in the best interests of the town in mind, of course, and we'll have our side of the story to represent. But standards are set, tolerances, guidelines. A mutually beneficial agreement. Then we publicly make a much more aggressive proposal, you people shoot it down, then we go back and forth a few volleys before we settle on what we've already agreed to. Your constituents are reassured that their mayor is holding the line for them, but the result is something guaranteed to be fair and reasonable."

Sig stands before the mayor can yea or nay the proposal, his hand out. He's not the detail man on housing, just there to plant the seeds. "It's going to be a wild ride, Mayor, but we want to be sure *you're* the one in the driver's seat."

When the door closes behind him it's clear the secretary has heard it all.

"So this is shale oil," she says. It sounds like an accusation.

You never want to alienate the secretaries. With a keystroke they can put you at the end of the line, and half the time they've got a better sense of the big picture than their bosses.

"And quite a bit of it, if we're fortunate."

"I grew up in Rock Springs."

"The Green River formation. Before I got into the business."

"I was fourteen when it hit."

"Mid-'70s."

She has taken her glasses off to look at him. Wyoming gal, maybe a barrel racer or calf roper– some kind of jock, certainly, from the squads of sturdy-thighed girls on the wall behind her.

"We had the crowd who built the Jim Bridger plant."

"The mighty mountain man."

"That was PP&G. Then we had Bechtel throwing up housing, and the soda ash people, and finally the shale oil came and went."

"It's still there. We have new technologies."

"Our sewage backed up and two of my friends got strung out on cocaine."

Not slipping any junk pitches past this one. Sig nods and raps his knuckles on her desk. "The very purpose of my visit. Never too early to start planning."

"You want to put man camps in town."

It isn't hostile, exactly, just a little I-know-who-you-are.

"Some of our employees do bring their families."

"I remember trailers out in the middle of nowhere."

Wyoming Gal clearly knows it's time to head for high ground, while her boss still thinks he can surf the wave. Not so easy to tell people their town is being kidnapped.

"There will be quite a bit of that. But the men will come into town one way or the other. If they already dwell here you won't have them on the highways."

"Under the influence."

"I imagine you have your local over-indulgers." Keep the tone pleasant but don't give ground. "We're discussing a matter of scale."

"Do you imagine," she asks, "that the other companies will want the same sort of concessions you'll be asking from Mayor Earle?"

"The good ones will." He gives her the hundred-watt smile and makes for the exit. In the old movies men had hats to put on when they left a room, a period to dot at the end of their final word. "You have to remember, I'm just the advance man for all this."

The secretary puts her glasses on and goes back to her keyboarding, muttering behind his back in French.

"Après moi, le déluge."

IT SMELLS LIKE COFFEE, which you'd figure, and there is a lot of noise from out front. On *Friends* and the other TV shows coffee shops always have a nice even buzz, sort of like the cafeteria at school but with more of the boys and girls sitting together. This sounds like what Tina imagines goes on in the boys' locker room, shouting and joking and hard laughter and all male voices.

"Spartina," says the manager, reading off the form she's filled out with her official information, Annie's cell number for a contact, "you understand that this is a part-time position?"

"Yes, sir."

The manager graduated from Yellow Earth High maybe two years ago, a red-haired boy with something wrong with the way he walks. KENNY, it says on the nameplate pinned over his shirt pocket.

"We won't be paying in to pension or welfare or any of that."

She only got her Social Security number yesterday, after the big hunt for her birth certificate without Granpa Clemson knowing. What her parents were thinking of with 'Spartina' is anybody's guess, the best the internet can give her is that it's a kind of grass that grows in saltwater marshes. It's what Granpa still calls her when he's mad at her or disappointed. Like if he knew she was getting this job–

The idea is that she'll do the 3 to 5 part of Annie's shift so Annie can keep running the school paper but still put some money away for college. Annie choked on her SATs and is worried she won't get any financial aid, even though she's always nailed down straight As.

"The job is basically like being a bartender– mixing drinks, running the register, bussing tables– only there's no alcohol involved."

Kenny is sweating, looking nervously toward the noise out front. He hasn't made full eye contact the whole interview, even though he is standing and she is sitting, the both of them crammed in among stacked bags of coffee beans and roasting and steaming equipment that has yet to be uncrated.

"The main thing is to be *fast*. These guys are in a hurry, they got their jobs to get to, and they're not, like, *patient*."

It was some kind of birth defect thing, his funny walk, not an accident. Made it kind of uncomfortable to watch him struggle down the hall, him having to throw the one leg forward instead of just stepping.

"And while you're still like, pro*b*ationary, we'll pay Annie and she'll pay you."

Annie says she's getting fifteen dollars an hour, which is pretty good when you figure a year ago there were lots of grown men in town who couldn't find anything for minimum.

"How long will I be on trial?"

"If you don't quit in the first week you're pretty much home free," says the manager.

"Kenny!" somebody shouts, a woman's voice. "We need you!"

"So are we good?"

Kenny kind of sneaks a glance at her as he says it. Maybe he's shy. Shy with girls.

"When would I start?"

"Uhm, do you think you could stay and help out now for a bit? We'll call it training and then tomorrow you'll start getting paid."

It will take some careful storytelling with her grandfather, but pretty soon she'll have the iPod and the phone and won't have to do everything through Annie.

"No problem."

Tina stands and realizes she is a head taller than Kenny. He finds a blue apron with the logo on it hanging from a hook, hands it to her.

"Welcome to Havva Javva."

THEY'RE IN THE COMMUNITY center, more than the usual suspects watching from metal folding chairs as Harleigh struts in front of the screen, microphone and laser-pointer in hand. Teresa, uneasy, drifts at the back of the room. She's seen the maps before, knows every bitter fact, but wonders where he is going with this.

"Our original lands," says Harleigh, swooping three big circles over the map with the glowing red dot. "Overlapping– sometimes peacefully, sometimes not, always shifting with the patterns of weather and game, yielding to the river whenever it needed to adjust its course."

Another slide comes up, an irregular red patch against the tranquil green of states, territories and countries.

"In 1870 this southern part of our lands is taken by presidential executive order, and the reservation is established. This isn't *punishment* for anything, just the federal government doing whatever it wanted to do. They put the Indian Agency in the old fort."

The view changes and Harleigh turns to his audience. Teresa can see that he's loaded the house with his supporters, something new on the docket he must need approval for.

"And let us remember that while this is taking place, several of our men are risking their lives, guiding General Custer in the Black Hills and into the Little Big Horn country. It always pays to cooperate."

Chuckles from the history buffs in the crowd.

They always tell about the scouts who went with Custer, and about Sakakawea and her baby, and the men who left the rez to fight in Cuba or the Philippines or France or Germany or the Persian Gulf or wherever the government needed bodies at the moment, but they never include Teresa Crow's Ghost on the list. Or Ted Drags Wolf or Leon Bender, who went with her to fight at Wounded Knee and got there too late to sneak past the FBI agents and vigilantes, who were arrested at a gas station in Kadoka and were shuffled from jail to jail for over a year before the vaguely worded subversion charges were finally dropped. The first time she explained it all to Ricky, who must have been ten or eleven, he looked at her like she was a crazy woman.

"You thought you were gonna, like, what? Beat the US government?"

"Anything we've still got today that's good," she told him, "came because we stood up then."

"We don't negotiate with terrorists, Mom," he said, shaking his head. Ricky's father had already made tracks to become a career Marine, who still never writes or calls his son but casts a very long shadow.

The red dot wiggles on a spot next to the old river. "In 1884 the Indian Agent decides that living in Like-A-Fishhook Village, where the Three Nations first came together for protection and the strength of numbers after the great smallpox wasting, was interfering with our 'progress.' He had our cabins and earth lodges *burned* to persuade us to move up the river and start farming like the white man farms. Within two years the Village was abandoned."

She sees Ricky in the front row. He's been dodging her on the phone, and the one time she got him at home he put the little ones on to say hello to their grandma, as if they don't stay with her three times a week. Teresa can read her boy like a book, and he had that 'I know you don't approve but I'm doing it anyway' look when he passed, coming into the meeting. Send him all the way to Grand

Forks for an education and he comes back spouting consumerist homilies like a corporate shill.

"Eighteen ninety-one," says Harleigh over the microphone. "The Dawes Allotment Act goes into effect. The Nations can no longer own the land commu-nally, but must assign hundred-sixty-acre lots to individual male heads of house-hold and eighty-acre lots to unmarried males. And somehow, in the switchover, we give up two-thirds of the original reservation area." The red patch suddenly shrinks as a new slide appears. "Furthermore, these allotted lands can now be sold to white speculators or settlers, and worse, they are subject to taxes that are manipulated, leading to foreclosures."

Harleigh is an activist in his way, a product of the casino era. The People were always traders, middlemen, toll-takers on the river. But there was a collective spirit, a balance that was always foremost in the minds of even the most merce-nary leaders. Harleigh's worldview, and her son's, if she is willing to admit it, was developed watching *Who Wants to Be a Millionaire?*

The slide changes and yellow blotches appear on the northeast section of the red patch, as if it's diseased. "Nineteen oh nine," croons Harleigh, "the Native American Ripoff Act– I'm sorry, the Enlarged *Home*stead Act– is passed by Con-gress, opening up the prime grazing quadrant of the reservation to outsiders. You could get off a boat from West Podunkistan or East Transylvania, wander out here, throw a few spuds in the ground and claim up to three hundred twenty acres of our land."

An American flag replaces the map. "Nineteen twenty-four, we trade our sta-tus as wards of the government to become citizens of the United States of Amer-ica. The Bureau of Indian Affairs, however, is not abolished."

A portrait of a smiling Franklin Roosevelt, sitting behind a desk, replaces the flag.

"Nineteen thirty-four, Congress passes the Indian Reorganization Act, with-out asking if we want to be reorganized or not. The idea is to have us govern our-*selves*– unless it interferes with the federal, state, or local plans of white people."

The next slide is of a trio of men standing with the old river at their backs, their wives and children sitting on the ground wrapped in blankets. Teresa rec-ognizes her Uncle Carl and her father's best friend, Wiley Burdette. She remem-bers playing on the banks, remembers the grownups working in the fields, re-members the trucks– thousands of trucks, rumbling past to feed the huge dam they were building.

"Nineteen forty-four, the Flood Control Act is passed. Eminent domain is threatened, and General Pick's workers invade the reservation. The dam is completed and over one hundred fifty thousand acres are flooded, virtually all of our farmland, and half of our people are relocated– meaning everybody managed to get out before they were drowned."

There is a buzz of reaction as the new slide flashes on the screen, the old river gone, the lake like a snake bloated with a swallowed rodent appearing in its place, new little towns dotting the map upstream.

"We are paid money for 'land readjustment,' the funds distributed on a per capita basis. Today over 57 percent of the land on what's left of the reservation is not owned or controlled by the Three Nations or our enrolled members."

The screen goes black, then the lights come up and Harleigh steps to the front of the platform, scanning his audience. He works a room better than any chairman ever has, Teresa will give him that. Looks good in the outfit, nice sense of drama, a voice made to narrate nature documentaries.

"A little reminder of our long history with the federal government," he says. "And my question to you is– are these people we want to be in *business* with?"

Some laughter at that. Harleigh and the tribal business council control only about an eighth of the land on the rez, but members who hold private tracts almost always follow their lead.

The women Ricky calls the Front Four are here, taking up an entire row, each one more substantial than the next. They are related to everybody and not to be trifled with. They are both church ladies and the keepers of tradition, hosting bake sales, judging beadwork and Eagle Dance competitions, and voting as a block once they've made their minds up. Teresa went to high school with the oldest two, who always regarded her involvement with AIM as proof of loose morals and hippie inclinations. But they can be reasoned with and can see beyond the needs of their immediate families. They are watching Harleigh with their arms crossed over their chests, waiting for the pitch.

"I think you all agree with me," says Harleigh, on the move again, keeping his rhythm tight like a good evangelist, "that the answer is *no*. We want to be in business on our *own*. *Sovereignty* is the word, people, the right and ability to steer our own course that we lost starting back in 1870. That's a long time of getting kicked around by the federal government. So why'd we put up with it so long? Well, no matter how brave our warriors were, their army was a hell of a lot bigger than ours, and besides that, we didn't have two Indian-head nickels to rub together."

Harleigh drops his voice to a more intimate tone. "You see, folks, sovereignty is kind of a pipe dream when you got an empty belly. But that don't have to be anymore. Cause the federal government left us a couple loopholes. By their own rules we get to decide that gaming is legal, even if the state that surrounds us doesn't. And– and this is gonna turn out to be even more important– when they pushed us up on the shelf where the forage is sparse and the farming's no good, they forgot to steal our *min*eral rights."

Another reaction to this, Harleigh nodding his head as he struts parallel to them all. "That's right, that's right, we got something they want, and this time, I am here to tell you, they're going to pay what it's *worth*. We are sitting on millions, maybe billions of dollars worth of shale oil. When Saudi Arabia tells the world to jump, the world asks 'How high?' Well from now on that's gonna be the deal between the Three Nations and the oil companies and the federal government of the USA!"

Applause now, and Teresa realizes that the horse is not only already out of the barn, it's running full tilt across the prairie.

"If we want our sovereignty, we want to control our own lives, we got to get out and compete in the white man's world, to be in the *real* deal, not the Special Olympics, where they've shunted us off to for so long. Beat em at their own damn game! Which is why I'm so happy to announce the formation of the Three Nations Petroleum Company, which will be overseeing the development of our tribally held energy assets!"

The lights go down again and a color-coded chart appears on the screen. "This is what it looks like, people," says Harleigh, peppy as a game-show host. "The executive board is your elected officials, serving with no increase to their mandated salaries, and the stockholders are the enrolled members, man, woman and child, of the Three Nations. We're all in this boat together, folks."

Lights up again, the audience abuzz, already spending their billions. Teresa calls out from the back of the hall.

"What about all the trucks, Harleigh?" she calls. "What about oil spills and what gets into our drinking water?"

Harleigh smiles. "I was wondering when we'd hear from you, Teresa." A ripple of laughter. She's on the council, the always-dissenting voice, the entertainment portion of the public hearings.

"Drilling for oil can be a messy business, and those are all important matters to consider. It's why I've appointed us a director of environmental vigilance– Rick McAllen. Ricky, stand up and show yourself!"

Applause and some knowing laughter as Rick stands and turns to the people in the folding chairs behind him. He doesn't meet Teresa's eye.

"As this process swings into action it's gonna get pretty busy, lots of moving parts, and so if you've got concerns about the impact you go see Rick, he'll have a direct line to the oil companies involved, and we'll get things sorted out. There is accepted industry practice, of course, and we'll make sure these people don't cut any corners they're not cutting over in Yellow Earth and the surrounding counties."

"Why wasn't any of this run through council first?" Teresa again, stepping up into an aisle to be heard better.

"We've got so many forms of land ownership here– tribal land, homestead land, fee patent land– and these oil-lease people are *sharks*, believe me. Too many of the council were missing, didn't have five for a quorum, and it was thought we had to make a move before individuals started agreeing to leases they weren't empowered to sign and muddying up the legal waters to where we'd be left holding the bag again when it come to cashing in on this bonanza that's about to happen."

Harleigh is the master of not finding council members when there's something big he wants to ram through, but the truth is people love having him as chairman. Her Uncle Carl, who held the position as a fill-in for only a year, said it aged him ten.

Harleigh is smiling at her, eyes sincere beneath the brim of his silver-banded Stetson. "There is a *timing* factor involved with this kind of oil play, Teresa. You saw the slide about the dam."

"I was there when it happened, Harleigh."

"Well, you may not hear the roar yet, but the big gates have already been opened and the water's pouring in. You either get on the boat with me, or you go *under*."

"IT'S A LITTLE LIKE squeezing a pimple."

Noises and faces of disgust. Do kids still have pimples? The teacher with the cobalt blue eyes gives him a smile. Was it Miss Gatling? Old Man Gradenauer, administering Physics to his own high school inmates like a dose of purgative, had been born without a humor gene. 'Needless to say,' he would intone, and then say it in the least interesting way possible.

"There's a buried deposit, pressure is applied, and it's forced to the surface."

"So it wouldn't come up on its own?" asks the teacher. Mid-thirties, braids, which you'd expect maybe from the Art Department but not American History, whatever that means these days. Great smile. With a bonnet she'd look like the girl on the raisin box.

"With liquid or gas," explains Hardacre, "the deposit is often already subject to a good deal of geological pressure, but *trapped* beneath the surface by something like cap rock or a salt dome. In that case we just drill in to relieve the pressure and up it comes."

"Like opening a bottle of champagne," says the Eager Beaver in the front row, no doubt president of the Science Club.

"Same principle. There are leaks in the surface crust sometimes, which is how ancient man discovered this black, sticky stuff that burned really well. In Los Angeles you have the La Brea tar pits."

"Which, if you know Spanish, it means the the tar tar Pits," says Mr. Wizard.

Hardacre smiles. "We prefer to tap into deposits be*fore* they reach the surface and are polluted by the bodies of Ice Age predators. And these days we've gone well beyond the Jed Clampett method of oil discovery."

Even the teacher doesn't get the *Beverly Hillbillies* reference.

It's been over twenty years, but walking in here today he got the old feeling in his stomach. *My time is not my own, my life is not my own.* He was good at the subjects he was interested in, didn't cause any problems, and still felt sentenced each school day for a crime he'd never committed. They must have new cleaning products by now, but this place even *smells* the same.

"We can read rock strata, we take core samples, we send vibrations into the earth and end up with something like a seismic photograph of what lies beneath."

"This is for fracking?"

The teacher again. Could be married, which is just too much trouble. Though the flesh might be willing, his stress threshold is low.

"Ah, the F-word." This gets a laugh from everybody. "Hydraulic fracturing has been around since the late forties, and it's really only an extension of traditional drilling techniques."

He goes to the blackboard, hopes the chalk doesn't squeak. "In a shale oil deposit like the Bakken, the oil and gas lies not in pockets or pools but in individual *mole*cules, trapped inside strata of rock. You've heard of getting blood from a stone? Well our method is only slightly less difficult than that, and until lately it was prohibitively expensive."

He decides not to get into oil price fluctuations and the Machiavellian scheming of OPEC, a field of conflict above his pay grade and not pertinent to geology. He draws a ground line and a stack of strata beneath it.

"Let's say our shale rock is down *here*. What we've got to do is drill down to just about this depth, it can be more than a mile deep, and then gradually angle the pathway of the pipe and begin to drill trunk lines hori*zo*ntally." He curves the dotted line indicating the drill hole into the layer of shale. He's got them now, the seeming impossibility of this task always impressive. "But not only in one direction– we fan out in six, maybe eight, maybe more channels, really penetrating that strata. But now, how do we get those molecules out of the rock?"

"Explode it?" calls a kid by the window.

"You're right, in a way. Back in the early days they tried *dy*namite to crack the rock, and besides stirring up a lot of fear and superstition, it didn't work out too well. What we use now is basically forced *water*– you ever put the palm of your hand over a garden hose that's running full blast? You know how it pushes and then sprays all over the place if you let up a bit? Well, we ram tons of water with a few things mixed into it to make a kind of sludge into that narrow drill hole, into those even narrower horizontal channels, and what happens? Thousands of tiny little *cracks* all along the length of them, like streams feeding into a big river, and when we pump the sludge out those cracks start to weep oil and gas molecules, which make their way down into the channel, then back to our vertical pipe and up"– he follows the flow back, dotting with his chalk– "right into the tank of your dad's Jeep Cherokee."

Simple enough for their level and basically true. He tries not to let Mr. Wizard, hand rigid in the air, catch his eye.

"So where does the ecological disaster part come in?" A pretty girl in the back row, kind of Indian-looking–

"That's not a very polite way of putting it, Jolene." The teacher is just there on the sidelines, arms crossed, smiling, no indication that she prepped them for an ambush. If he'd had her in class he'd have spent the whole period fantasizing, no matter what the unheard subject, hormones overwhelming intellect. Watching her mouth, the way she moved–

"Whatever human beings do on this planet in order to sur*vive* has its side effects," says Hardacre, taking a step toward the class and dropping his voice into the patient-but-firm register. The Company has him do two or three of these in every community about to get the works, and he can glide calmly past desperate hope and open hostility.

"Farming entails the use of fertilizer and the loss of prairie grass, the cattle business has impacted the rain forest, the Missouri River has been dammed nearby and no longer flows wherever it wants to. The ideal is to have the benefits far outweigh the drawbacks, and do what we can to minimize collateral damage."

What he can't tell them, what he is probably too jealous of to share, is the fascination, the satisfaction, sure, call it the *joy* of orchestrating the entire carnival, holding the geological formation and the vast array of knowledge and machinery used to get at it in his mind, with the power to put it in motion. Because it isn't two separate things, prize and seeker, but a single, complex organism, the oil as useless under the ground as blood spilt on a slaughterhouse floor. He sometimes feels like he *is* the organism, a creature conscious of every process running through its body– respiration, alimentation, digestion, drilling, casing, fracturing, extracting– each with its own character and quirks, depending on the individual well, no clones in the energy business. He can't tell them, because it doesn't translate into words exactly, the feeling– treasure hunters must be addicted to it– how even with all the reassurances of technology that the hydrocarbons are really down there, when that drill pipe starts to shiver and talk, and the rush of it, the *rush*–

"How about earthquakes?"

The Indian girl again. Probably got a list written in her open notebook, a litany of complaint–

"I'm against them."

A good laugh this time. He steps away from the blackboard.

"As a geologist I've been following the seismic problems they're having in Oklahoma quite closely. I assure you that the depth and layout of the strata up here is totally different. Those rumblers are most likely caused not by fracking but by wastewater injection wells– after we've used the sludge to crack the shale it has to be *put* somewhere. Here we'll be drilling those wastewater wells into a sandstone formation about five thousand feet down, like having a big sponge under you. And we're nowhere near any fault lines."

"But there's radioactivity." Mr. Wizard this time, oozing with information.

"Very good point. As you may know, most radioactivity is not man-made– it exists in the sun's rays, it's present in the Earth– radon gas being the most obvious example. The geologic formations that contain oil and gas deposits generally also include what we refer to as NORM– Naturally Occurring Radioactive Materials."

"Which you bring to the surface."

The Indian girl, an edge of accusation in her voice. You don't expect an eco-kid out here in God's Country, but there's probably even vegetarians now. Better than being totally clueless–

"As part of our process, yes. And because they are displaced and *concentrated* in that process, they now become TENORM– Technologically En*hanced* Naturally Occurring Radioactive Material. Now the amount and potency of those wastes varies enormously from formation to formation. We haven't drilled here enough yet to know how hot our produced water is going to be."

"Doesn't the EPA monitor it?" The teacher now, voice of authority and rational thought. Beautiful eyes. Miss– no, it was Mrs., wasn't it? Mrs. Gatlin. Too bad–

"The EPA has no legal authority over the UIC– that's Underground Injection Control– associated with fracking. It's commonly known as the Halliburton loophole."

"So you can just pump it wherever– ?"

"We make every effort to deal with our wastes responsibly." The Company line, and true within the budget limitations applied to each well. He can't tell anything from their high school faces, the children of ranchers, cattlemen, shopkeepers. Interested, semi-conscious, chemically sedated? Whatever, they deserve a warning, however cushioned in Company-speak.

"But up to now," he says, "no one has had the desire or the political will to slow the industry down long enough to figure out what the risks truly *are*."

She catches up with him, looking a little embarrassed, after the period bell has rung, kids scuttling down the hallway like fracked energy molecules. She'd said the big thank-you and had the kids applaud– nice old-school touch– back in the classroom.

"There's something I wanted to ask you– you know– not in front of the students."

He's been more cautious the last few years, a little more upfront about what the contract is and isn't. In the early days the guys called him Randy Heartbreaker and he supposes he deserved it, a couple bad parting scenes, one stalker who luckily was not computer literate and lost track of him quickly. You're there to open up an oilfield, two years max, and then move on. That's the deal. It helps that most of the assignments are located in the armpits of the universe– Coral certainly didn't show any interest in following him to Yellow Earth, North Dakota. He thought El Paso was funky back in his UTEP college days, but this–

"My husband Tucker?" she says apologetically. "He's been out of work a long time– business venture that didn't pan out. Can you think of any– "

"I'm not in HR, and– quite honestly– the people around me are all highly trained technicians."

"Of course."

No, she's not after your telephone number. Hubby needs a gig.

"Is he in fairly good shape?"

"He jogs. Or he used to a lot, before he– it's depressing, being without a job for so long."

"Well, the work is very physical, but once the rigs start going up he could make the rounds. They're always looking out for"– no, don't say raw meat– "for hard workers. But it's not for everybody."

The smile again, the cobalt blue eyes. He knows they sell contacts that color, but hers look like the real thing.

"I'll tell him. And thanks for your honesty– you know– with the class."

He smiles back, not so much catch-and-release but look-and-forget-about-it.

"When we're up and pumping have them come out for a guided tour."

"I'll do that."

And then I'll be gone.

THEY DO THE INTERVIEWS in the Veteran's Hall. It was a five-and-dime that closed down in the '70s, now with a large front room for receptions and speakers, the walls armored with patriotic mementos, with the bar and pool tables through a door in the back. Tuck notices that every other job applicant steps back there to compare notes and lift a few instead of returning to the street. The military has somehow managed to do its business without him, too young for Vietnam, where his father served in the First Signal Brigade, and otherwise engaged during the First Gulf. Butch Bjornson, two folding chairs ahead of him in the waiting line along the wall, was in that one, and Tuck wonders how collecting for deployment-related chronic fatigue syndrome is going to sit with the Company personnel scouts.

"This is all for show, you know," Hollister Ekdahl, a seat after him, leans in to mutter. "They're gonna bring all their own people up from Texas. Just don't want the natives to get too restless."

"No, these operations, when they do them, are so big," explains Tuck, who spent the night researching the Company online, "there's all kinds of jobs where you don't need experience. Why ship somebody in when we're right here, hungry for work?"

They were living in Rapid, just getting by, when Francine got the teaching post in Yellow Earth. Otherwise, what, are you kidding? Tuck poked around for a few months, nothing that paid enough to justify taking orders and punching a clock, then borrowed money from his dad and took over the diner on 11th. Good location, some diehard regulars– the folks who had it before just wanted to retire. He was full of ideas. Redid the décor, added some new wrinkles to the menu, replaced the greening hamburger photos in the window with '50s-style painting and lettering, hired a brace of teenage and young-wife waitresses to flirt with. It was fun at first, playing the proprietor, called over to explain the new dishes as if they were something exotic, trying to be avuncular yet firm with the parade of clueless kitchen staff. But finally huevos rancheros did not find favor with the locals, content to eat drive-through Egg-Mc-fucking-Muffins and Triple-Bypass Burgers from the chains, the diehards probably moving their morning gabfest to here at the Vets for all he knew. And a month ago it was either ask Francine to borrow money from *her* father or cut bait. So the fella who bought it cheap just stepped in the shit with this oil boom coming, now remodeling the place into a cutesy coffee joint that will be a goldmine if he keeps the girls in tight T-shirts hopping and the retired farmers from parking their carcasses there all day.

There are two folding tables set up, two interviewers, and you bring up the form you've filled out. The guy Tuck draws, curly hair and glasses, barely looks up as he scans the employment and health history.

"No oilfield experience?"

"No." Tuck is about to say 'No sir' but the guy might be younger than he is and it rankles. He hasn't been out with his hat in his hand for years. In fact, maybe the hat would have been a good idea– the guys like Butch wearing UND or John Deere caps look a lot more roughnecky than he feels at present.

"Commercial license?"

"No. But I could get one easy enough."

Tuck doesn't know if this is true, but they should know he's ready, willing, and able.

"Construction?"

"Oh sure. Bit of this and a bit of that."

Francine despairs of his lack of handiness around the house, but he has held the other end of the two-by-four more than once, run a power saw, nailed in nails. They must have some kind of training for new people.

The curly-haired guy frowns and turns the form over to scan the other side, and Tuck glances back to the waiting men. Quite a few older than him, even. The state has been losing population, with cattle easier to raise away from the wind and weather you get up here, no industry to speak of, and the fact finally sinking in that farming this bleak prairie is a sucker's game. If it wasn't for Francine's job–

"We'll give you a call," says the interviewer, setting his form on top of the pile of those who've been patronized ahead of him, "if anything comes up."

Tuck stands, takes a step toward the back, then reconsiders and heads for the street. It's ten in the morning. If he's not just going back into bed like yesterday, what he needs is coffee.

It's A TOWN THAT she considered when she first got to Yellow Earth, on Route 1 just south of Bonetrail, at least a hundred animals, with the mounds starting about a football field's distance back from the county road, no drilling apparent on the horizon yet. The shooters are set up just in from the shoulder, and Leia is pulling up in front of their van before she can think of a reason why.

They have a card table laid out with ammunition and other hunter stuff she can't identify, with the taller one standing to look through a telescope-looking deal on a tripod and the one in the desert camouflage and earmuff headset sitting on a camp stool with his rifle propped on some sort of fold-out support to steady the barrel.

Camo Guy fires and Leia sees something fly in the air out in the colony.

"Nailed im," says the Spotter, extra loud to be heard through his buddy's ear baffles. "Judges'd give you an eight for altitude."

"Only an eight?" says the Camo Guy, still sighting through his scope.

"It flew but it stayed pretty intact."

The Spotter notices Leia's shadow on the ground next to him and turns.

"Hey, we got a spectator!"

The Camo Guy glances over without shifting from his firing position. "If she's a game warden give her the rap."

"We got permission from the rancher," says the Spotter, not lowering his volume. "Course he oughta pay *us* for every rodent we whack."

"Whack em and stack em!" cries Camo Guy, looking through the scope and panning the rifle slightly. "Got another one."

He fires and there is a distant geyser of sand.

"Shit."

"I'm not a warden," she says. "Just curious."

Spotter lights up. "Well you come to right place," he says. "I'm just a weekend hobby shooter, but L. T. here is a killing machine."

Another shot. "Took his head off!"

"But what were you aiming at?"

"Cut me some slack, Jack. Crosswind's already dicking with me."

Spotter turns back to Leia. "It's best to shoot early in the day," he explains. "Wind picks up, you want more fps– that's your bullet speed– to compensate, and these Super Explosives we're shooting will start to come apart."

He senses her lack of comprehension.

"The jacket's a lot thinner, so the twist starts throwing off bits of metal."

"They don't just stay down in their holes?"

"You mean the p-dogs?" He points a finger at her. "Good question. Lemme show you."

He bends to look through the telescope thing, panning it, adjusting a knob, then calls out to Camo Guy. "Two o'clock, three hundred fifteen yards– we got a cluster!"

Spotter steps to the side and waves Leia forward. "Take a look."

"I see em," says Camo Guy. "Here comes a cluster-fucker."

Leia just has her eyes to the lens, three juveniles and an adult female in and around the crosshairs, when the rifle barks and one of the juveniles is lifted spinning in the air, intestines flying raggedly from its little body, landing in the dry grass several yards beyond the mound.

"Helicopter!" cries Camo Guy. "More to come!"

The remaining prairie dogs freeze for a moment, either stunned or unable to comprehend their cohort suddenly disappearing, then the adult and one of the juveniles turn to touch mouths–

Another rifle bark and the female explodes in a red mist, the bloody rag of her remains tumbling backwards. The other two whirl in place, alert, but don't retreat into the burrow opening. Leia steps back from the rangefinder.

"She blew up."

"Just 50-grain Hornadys, real fur-friendly, easy to find. There's other loads might give you even more splatter but they're more expensive."

"If it doesn't splatter," calls Camo Guy, finger easing onto the trigger again, "it doesn't *matter*."

He fires and another juvenile flies into the air, the only survivor finally scurrying underground.

"So do you, like, go out and collect the bodies?"

Camo Guy laughs, lifting the rifle, which is also camouflaged in Desert Tan and looks more like a machine than something Daniel Boone would carry, to change out a black metal box on the bottom of it.

"You hear that, Shakes? She wants to know if we collect our trophies."

"There's not enough left to stuff or tack up on the wall," says the spotter, Shakes, with a shrug.

"Scavengers'll take care of em sooner or later," adds L. T. "Might have to spit out a couple bullet fragments. Hell, I shot one last week, biggish son of a gun, and you could see daylight through the hole I drilled. Like a Wile E. Coyote cartoon."

"Except with blood."

"So this is not considered overkill."

She sees something change in the Spotter's eyes. "You understand, Miss, that these are *pests*. Like as not they got the plague."

"And tearing them apart is part of the fun of it."

The toothy smile loses some of its wattage.

"You don't shoot."

"Never took it up."

Shakes steps to the card table and lifts the rifle leaning against it. "This is just an old Savage Model 12 my wife give me when I turned forty," he says, propping it on his hip, "while Lyle is operating something more than a varmint rifle. I find em with the Leupold laser tech and he uses the mil dots in his Bushnell to zero in. But even with the optics, at this distance it takes a degree of skill."

"They don't even run into their holes."

"Not unless a hawk flies over." Camo Guy, L. T., is back in shooting position. "Dumb little fuckers."

Shakes is staring at her, eyes traveling up to the streak in her hair. "You wouldn't be a vegetarian, would you?"

"Let them eat kale!" calls L. T.

"No."

"Animal rights activist?"

"No."

"I asked a liberal once," calls L. T., eye back on his scope, "'What is it with you people, ignorance or apathy?' He said 'I don't know and I don't care.'"

"What I don't get," says Leia, "is the fun in it."

Shakes makes a face. "Hey, whatever brings you out from under your rock."

He holds the rifle out toward her. "You like to try?"

"No thanks."

"Afraid you'll like it?"

"I've run over a couple on the highway," she says. "Didn't do anything for me."

"But that's an accident. There's no marksmanship."

"So shoot targets."

"I do. But it's not *hunting*."

"I always think of hunting, you got to go find something in the woods or up in the mountains." Her father would come home from a weekend stalking deer with beer farts, wet clothes and no trophy. "Something that can run away or charge at you."

"Hunters are the greatest conservation group in history."

"Like the ones who gathered to kill the last flock of passenger pigeons."

"If they'd known– "

"They *knew*. It was advertised in the newspapers, 'Last chance to shoot a passenger pigeon.' That was the attraction."

Shakes holds his hands up as if surrendering. "Don't look at me, I wasn't there."

"Look who's come up to join the party," says L. T., and fires. "Nicked him pretty good."

Leia looks back through the rangefinder. The juvenile is lying on its back, rear legs twitching spastically.

"You gonna finish it?"

"Ammo's not that cheap. He'll die soon enough." L. T. is scanning through the scope again.

"It's not like they're endangered."

"Borderline," she says to Shakes. "And they're a cornerstone species. If they get scarce a lot of other creatures go hungry."

"Well I just laid out a buffet for them other creatures." L. T. fires again. "Prairie dog on a cracker."

She pans the rangefinder. The little town is in full swing, prairie dogs grazing, grooming, kissing, display-fighting as if no danger was present. Maybe they're right, she thinks, maybe any creature so clueless doesn't deserve to survive. If the lesson of the Dust Bowl wasn't enough, the acidification of the oceans, carbon dioxide increase in the atmosphere, the melting of the ice caps– the *planet* will survive, even thrive, if they all disappear tomorrow.

"I spose it is a little bit more like bowling than going after mountain goats in the Rockies," says Shakes, fucking with her now and enjoying it. "But some days you just got to *kill* something."

BRENT IS A BIG thinker, always has been. And willing to take the headaches that come with it, willing to take the risks. It was Brent who pushed Wayne Lee along from misdemeanor to felony status, Brent who counseled him to get something beyond a quick thrill from his transgressions.

But Yellow Earth?

They're in some kind of coffee place, not one of the big chains but trying to look like it, that's been thrown together in the last week or two. Trucks lumber down the main street, which is also the highway, just outside the window, while an annoying bell tinkles every few seconds as somebody steps in or out. Mostly in. He gave up on the line at the Walmart earlier in the day, and forget about the drive-thru lanes at the couple fast food places. The town doesn't have enough service people, goods, motels, *anything*, to deal with what's hit them. The barista girls behind the counter are still consulting a laminated drink chart on the wall to fill anything but the simplest order, and there are locals, farmer-looking characters in down vests and crew cuts sitting behind their overpriced cups of joe and looking around with a kind of amused bewilderment, like they're at the freak tent of some old-time carnival.

Cute girls, though.

"There's thousands of dollars," says Brent, swirling his Mochaccino Motherfucker or whatever it is in the bottom of the plastic cup, "*hun*dreds of thousands, wandering around up here looking for somebody's pocket to jump into. *Idiots* are making fortunes, and we're not idiots."

"But there's nothing *here*."

"Here is only where the money lives, where you make your killing. Where you *spend* it is your business."

"So you want me to drive for you."

"Some of that, yeah, some back and forth grinding the gears. I mostly got tribe members on the regular payroll, but you can do my special delivery business. "

"And I get paid."

"More than you ever made running a truck in your life. Guys who got their CDL-B license a week ago are set to bring down eighty grand in a year."

The taller one, definitely. Wayne Lee likes the way she moves. There's a word for it–

"That's just your base salary, of course." Brent looks around the noisy, packed room, standees crowded at the counter and just inside the door, nobody paying attention to them. "You remember in Texas how we had that problem with cash."

"Not showing enough legitimate income."

"I got this company with the chief– the Chairman– of the tribes up here, minimum regs, dozens of contracts, and people too busy drilling and raking in the moolah to look at the books."

"Where would I live?"

"I'll find you a place. And then you'll be making runs to El Paso and back."

"For product."

Again Brent glances around. He's starting to lose some hair but has kept up with the Mr. Universe routine, almost busting out of the T-shirt he's wearing.

"What we've still got in inventory down there won't last a week in this zoo. You'll have to resupply."

"And on this end?"

"I'll get you started with oilfield contacts and then– hey, you're good at making friends. It's a customer-service job, dude, and nobody does it better than you."

"I don't know a soul in this town."

The tall one, the one he's positioned his chair to watch, comes over to them.

"Fellas, you see we've got people stacked up, you're gonna have to order something else or free up the table."

She's even taller up close, a single braid over the shoulder, skin like new snow that nobody has stepped on yet.

"Sorry," says Wayne Lee, reading that she is TINA on the little nametag over her left breast. High school still? "Brent here said we should leave, but I bugged him to hang so I could look at you some more."

And she blushes. Can't have had this job for long if a strange guy can nail her like that.

"No, really. Brent's been trying to convince me to stay in town a while, and he wasn't doing too good till I saw you."

Tina fights back a smile. "Can I get you anything else?"

"No, thanks, we'll clear out." Wayne Lee stands. They can tell if you're lying, just tossing grenades into the pond to see what floats to the surface. But look them in the eye and drop an honest compliment–

"You full-time here, Tina?"

"I fill in a couple hours after school." She is already removing their cups.

"I'm gonna have to develop a taste for the bean, then. My name's Wayne Lee Hickey, the muscle-bound guy here is Brent, and it's a pleasure to meet you."

He starts out then, don't push it, leave em laughing.

Brent mutters at the door. "Still thinking with your dick."

"You know those sticks the water-well guys used to carry around?"

"Divining rods."

"Mine was starting to wiggle."

"Yours was threatening to bust through the zipper. I'm betting sixteen, and you'd better check the age of consent law up here."

They step out into the wind and the truck exhaust and he gets a last look through the window. *Coltish*– that's the word.

Brent steps to block his way, spreading those iron-pumping arms out wide.

"So what do you say?"

The answer is pretty much his personal motto, tattooed on his left shoulder in what the inkster called Blackletter Font.

"What the fuck," says Wayne Lee.

IT'S ALWAYS A BIT of a chess game with the Chairman. First off, there's maintaining your physical space, not that he's ever actually made a move, but it feels like if she ever gave him the slightest hint she was open to it–

"So I thought this was settled with the boat, Ruby," he says. "Our gaming compact specifically states– "

"*'The Tribe is furthermore authorized to conduct gaming on navigable waters within the exterior boundaries of the Reservation, limited to excursion boats offering food service, where passengers may board and unboard only from the Tribe's marina co-located with said casino…'"*

"Cut and dried."

"Though 'unboard' isn't really a word. And 'co-located.'"

"What's the hold-up?"

"That's only your agreement with the state. It still has to be approved by the IGRA."

"Why would they have a problem?"

"They have go through the whole deal. Minimum Internal Control Standards."

"Can't we just tell them that nobody not approved to work in the regular casino will be used to– "

"I've filed all the details with them. It just takes time."

If you don't hold the fort, Harleigh will have you post-dating documents, jumping the gun left and right. Some of her job here is to save the Chairman from himself.

"I got some good friends over there," he says. "I'll make a couple phone calls."

"That might help. Now about this lease situation– "

"It's a rat's nest."

"I'm aware of that."

Ruby lays a land-title map of the reservation on the desk between them. The whole western half is a jumble of blue, yellow, and red rectangles with no discernible pattern.

"Tribal land, allotments, fee-simple land, government trust land," she says, waving her fingers over the rectangles.

"I know, I know, and the kicker is that any oil outfit wants a certain amount of *e*lbow room to drill. The people who hold these little three- and four-acre plots– "

"Swat Gilchrist's bunch are buying them up."

The Chairman stops to consider this. It isn't often Ruby knows something cooking on the rez before he does.

"Swat has a *bunch*?"

Swat is their top man at the casino, who was a good enough hitter to get pretty far in the minor leagues before he came home. He can run percentages for you without ever looking at a calculator.

"Badlands Petro. He brought some New York investment firm in to back it, and the company has been tying up leases left and right."

"It's an oil company?"

"If flipping documents makes you one."

Harleigh chews on this for a minute. He's sitting under her wall photos of Wilma Mankiller and Shirley Chisholm, looking a lot less sure of himself than they do.

"We can't really step in, can we? If the land is individually held."

"No matter how it's held, if it's within the reservation boundaries the BIA and the BLM have to okay the contract."

The Chairman has his parody versions of the acronyms– Busting Indian Asses and the Bureau of Looting and Mugging– but looks pleased at this information.

"So we're off the hook. It's up to the Feds."

"Who've got way too much to deal with on their teeny budget, even without Congress threatening to shut the country down again– "

Harleigh grins. "People think Indian politics is bad, they just got to look at Washington."

"So you're not worried about Swat?"

Harleigh looks out at the few cars creeping along the New Center main street, tilting his head the way he does when he's strategizing.

"Swat's uncle Les had my job before you come here. Les was doing some skimming, getting federal money for jobs that didn't really exist, giving people a title and two-thousand dollars a month while he kept the other *six* that had been mandated. Got his nuts caught in the wringer, of course, and he tried to get his nephew to claim some transactions, explain away all these checks kicking money back to his personal account. But Swat sat there on the witness stand and told the truth."

"Convicted?"

"Embezzling, misapplying and converting tribal funds, knowingly and willfully making false material claims– guilty on all counts."

"Pretty heavy for the nephew to be the one to– "

"Swat's a good boy."

"With a head for numbers."

"That's why we put him at the casino."

"But his involvement with Badlands– "

"If he didn't have an important job on the reservation to wave around, sitting on all our casino money, the New York investment people wouldn't have listened to him. And if he wasn't a popular young fella around here who can impress folks with his contacts in the white people's world, they wouldn't be sending their leases his way. That's capitalism, Ruby. Hell, in Washington– "

"In Washington people get indicted."

"But rarely convicted, not if they've got smart lawyers."

"Not if they got smart lawyers and *listen* to their advice."

"What are you advising me, Ruby?" An edge to his tone.

The job pays really well and there's never a shortage of things to do. Lots of good people here, with less of a defeatist attitude than many of the places she's worked, plus she's not related to a soul on the reservation, no barefoot cousins coming to her for redress or advantage. She'd like to hold on here at least another couple years.

"I'm just reminding you that I am principle counsel for the *Nations*, not for you or any other individual, elected official or not."

"I understand that."

"So when we're discussing the oil resources here, I represent the interests of the enrollment, and not– "

Harleigh holds up his hand and begins to quote, "'*WHEREAS, The Constitution of the Three Nations generally authorizes and empowers the Tribal Business Council to engage in activities on behalf of and in the best interest of the welfare and benefit of the Tribe and the enrolled members thereof–* ' We're on the same side, darlin.'"

On the other hand, there comes a point where you've got to cut bait and paddle away. Ruby grew up in a hut with a dirt floor. She didn't live with indoor plumbing till she went to college, tended bar to make ends meet during law school, clerked for a federal district judge in California. She won't have trouble finding another position if she puts the word out.

"There's a lot of money at stake here, Mr. Chairman. Crazy money. People do crazy things."

"You know the Wounded Knee story?"

"Teresa Crow's Ghost told me."

"I mean the *first* Wounded Knee, the massacre in the snow."

He must have been a good teacher, good school principal, way back when. The energy, the sense of conviction–

"I know the history," she says. "I've seen the photographs."

"There's a part of it doesn't get told too often." Harleigh sits back in his chair, full storyteller mode.

"When the Ghost Dance started moving up from Nevada, tribe to tribe, there was a young Sioux named Plenty Horses, who'd just come home from the Carlisle School."

"I had relatives who were there."

"Yeah, they took kids from all over, pretty much every tribe. Anyway, Plenty Horses had been there six years, didn't much care for it, mostly they sent him out to work on farms. But six years is a long time in a young man's life, he come back to the new rez they'd just stuck his people on, and he couldn't fit in no more. His Lakota didn't sound right, and his old friends and family treated him like an outcast."

Ruby knows the treatment. Her first week back in the pueblo, whenever she'd been off at school for a while, it was 'Oh, look who decided to come pay a visit' and 'You haven't dyed your hair blond yet?'

"So he's there when the massacre happens– not in the line of fire, but right in the middle of the whole build-up and the killing. And two days after Big Foot and all those people are murdered, he walks up behind this cavalry lieutenant during a parley and blows his brains out."

This part she didn't know.

"From behind?"

"If he'd come head-on carrying a weapon he couldn't have got so close, could he? Now Plenty Horses thinks he's made it as a martyr, right, he'll be hanged by the US Army and the tribe will honor him as a warrior. He'll be a legend. But those photographs you've seen got published back east, and the word come out that it was just some jumpy soldiers overreacting and then getting blood-hungry, killing everybody in sight. So the army got an image problem, people's jobs are on the line, and they got to go into damage control mode. It wasn't a misunderstanding or a flare-up of tensions, they say, it was a *war*. A real short one, granted, but a bonafide war, and as such Plenty Horses is just an enemy com*bat*ant, not a murderer, and it's not long before he's cut loose again, just another poor broken soul on the rez who speaks better English than most."

"I'm struggling to make a connection here, Harleigh," she says. "The army hasn't been called in here yet."

"What I'm getting at is that if they want to *nail* you they'll always find a good excuse. But if you got something they need– "

"And that would be?"

"The company I'm mostly dealing with, alla these outfits, got good friends in DC. Why you think the EPA is forbidden to butt in when it's oil extraction? Cause Mr. Cheney and some other heavy hitters in the Congress got busy for their friends at Halliburton. The big folks want something to happen, a lot of the formalities get pushed aside."

"Misuse of influence."

"As long as Swat doesn't go dipping into Three Nations' money, he's got the right to operate in the free market."

Indian Law, her favorite professor used to say, was to the regular law what Ozzy Osbourne was to Justin Timberlake. Regular law refined itself as it went along, attempting to be clearer, fairer, while Indian Law was eight-tenths Greed and two-tenths Guilt, not evolving so much as jerking desperately this way and that like a hooked fish in a small pond.

Ruby holds her hands up in surrender. "So we're not overseeing the lease agreements."

"Only on the land the Nations hold in trust. But even there we got TERO regs, we got fragmentation of heredity."

"What?"

"Somebody with an allotment dies and their estate goes to twelve different people."

"I think that's termed 'heirship.'"

"Airship?

"'Heir' with the silent 'h.'"

"Well it's a beast to deal with. There's this hundred-percent-signature require-ment, which means a lot of parcels can't even be considered for drilling because there's one sorehead."

"That's a federal statute."

"Which I want you to get them to modify."

The Bureau of Indian Affairs has been everybody's whipping boy for so long they are almost numb, but there are some sensible people there and they know they no longer hold all the cards.

"To what?"

"Say eighty, ninety percent. That would take care of most of the problems we got right now."

"I'll need some strong language from the business council."

"You write it, we'll put our names on it. This is high priority, Ruby, we don't want to get left behind."

When she passed the bar exam Ruby felt like a warrior, with the Law a so-phisticated weapon she could use to defend her people. Lately she thinks about how any weapon, left around the house, can just be trouble.

"We're talking about a layer of rock that's a zillion years old, Harleigh," she says. "The resource isn't going anywhere."

"But the conditions where it makes money sense to drill *into* it might not last."

"Ah."

"These things, it's like a fever comes over the buyer, and it can pass like a fever too. You don't want all these regulations, these impediments, in the way when the action is hot."

"They were put there for a reason."

"They were put there so the white people could say, 'See? We're not gonna steal anymore.' After they figure they've took everything of value."

There is no arguing with that. The same professor used to say that in Indian Law the preliminary statements are always made with rifles and sabers.

"I'll get on the phone with Kayla at the BIA today," she says. "Make it sound like they'll take the heat for losing our people a truckload of money, tell her to start thinking about how to work an amendment."

The Chairman flashes her the full smile. If she was enrolled in this outfit it would be hard to resist him on Election Day.

"Atta girl, Ruby," he says. "We're gonna win this round."

HISTORY IS A MINEFIELD. Vet your sources, get your facts as straight as you can, lead your students toward some sort of understanding, some sort of *synthesis*, and before you've taken three steps you've trampled on somebody's worldview or regional pride. Francine wanted to call it American Civilization for that reason, to recognize that 'history' was an always contested collection of viewpoints, but it got to the Board of Ed and there was screaming. Really– *screaming*. Quoting the Am Civ syllabi from a couple Eastern colleges, invoking the scarewords of talk radio conspiracy theorists, she was accused of revisionism, defeatism, advocating "loser studies."

Francine goes over her notes as she waits for the Lunch Over bell to ring, hunting for incendiary phrases. The idea, the *theme*, if you like, of her teaching is to get them to understand a mind-set, that essential American belief system that assumes that one should always have more, take more, *be* more. With God's blessing.

Tucker has got it, of course, got it bad. He never tires of telling the story of how his dad, a gangly kid with a box of carpenters' tools, 'took a shot' and founded a successful lumber company, so successful that he sold it to a chain when he was fifty-one years old and went fishing for the rest of his life. How the timing was right, sure, and a natural disaster or two that jacked up the price of two-by-fours didn't hurt, but mostly it was a question of having the *balls* to believe in yourself, to plunge in and be ready to accept the consequences.

Tuck has done more plunging than accepting. And now this romantic idea of being an oil rig worker, excellent short-term money if he can get hired on, but leading to what? There's a mural of the Lewis and Clark expedition that runs the length of the second-floor hallway, and the one time Tuck passed it he pointed to a figure dragging a canoe near the end of the procession, a rangy explorer wearing what looks like a whole skunk on his head. "That's me," he said. "Those were the days."

If only he could find something. Like the good-looking geologist who talked to her class, confident, in love with his subject, a man with a mission. Yes, that kind of commitment probably means time away from his family, if he has one, but the time he does spend with them isn't a constant complaint, a stew of sour grapes and self-recrimination. Even if Tuck had some engaging *hob*by that would get him out of the house–

Mondays she avoids the teachers' lunchroom. Hearing about everybody's weekend, the who-just-signed-a-lease news. Each week she tries to start her seniors out on a specific quest, a historical thesis to be tested, and it pays to prepare the challenge. This week it will be two teams, one half of the class representing General Crook and his Treaty Commission, and the other representing the Sioux, both the 'progressive' American Horse faction and the 'irreconcilables' who sided with Sitting Bull. Few of the kids are Native American, or at least few are claiming it, but there are plenty more Indians just down the road to empathize with. She needs to explain how taking half of the remaining Sioux land was vital to the Republicans' political agenda of the day, allowing them to admit Dakota Territory as two states and add four new senators to their majority–

"Mrs. Gatlin?"

It's Jolene, one of her favorites even if she's on the timid side. Francine wonders, if they had been classmates, if she'd have been cool enough to seek Jolene out for a friend, Jolene from the reservation, with clothes that make her look like an apprentice nun, Jolene who's probably not allowed to stay out late or wear

makeup, who's here because her IQ tests were off the charts and because Elise
Donovan who teaches over at the Three Nations school waged a campaign–

"Yes?"

"I'm sorry to bother you on your recess."

Recess, I love it. As if we mill around and punch each other in the arm a lot,
play keep-away with each other's lunch bags–

"What can I do for you?"

"Uhm, it's this." she holds up the old library paperback, *Bury My Heart at
Wounded Knee.*

"Pretty upsetting, isn't it?"

"The thing is, my parents– "

Jolene's people are some sort of Christian, hard core, she knows that much.
Every now and again in class a subject will come up or a word be spoken and she'll
see the panicked look on the girl's face– I shouldn't be hearing this. But hey, if you
don't want your kid exposed to public debate, don't send them to public school.

"They saw it."

"And?"

"Uhm– they don't approve."

She assigned it to Jolene thinking it would connect with her background,
help her understand how her people got where they are–

"Have they *read* it?"

"No. But they've read a*bout* it. It's on a list."

It's on a bunch of lists, most touting it as required reading if you want an
introduction to our westward expansion, but belief is belief.

"You know, honey, there's nothing in there that's a challenge to anybody's religious faith."

The panicked look.

"Faith in country," says Jolene.

"Ah." She is careful not to say, 'But they're *Indians!*'

She is pretty, Jolene, got the wide cheekbones and the coloring, you could
think she was Mexican if the reservation wasn't just next door. Rides in with the
Indian princess Fawn, who probably talks Jolene into writing her papers for her.

"I mean I read the whole book, like I was supposed to, but now that they know–
can I not write the report on it?"

The girl is not hers to win or to lose. You want to give them *something*, though,
the courage to make up their own mind some day, the sense that knowledge

might make their life better, not just more complicated.

"What did you think of it?"

Jolene ponders this for a moment. She is a thoughtful girl.

"I've seen some of the movies they made out of the stories in it on TV. Where they never have a real Indian play the chief? I think the stories in the book are more interesting." She gives a little self-deprecating shrug. "There's two sides."

Tuck only lasted three chapters and tossed the book aside. "Unless we're ready to give the whole country back," he said, "why dig all that business up?"

"All right, Jolene, can you think of any book that's, you know– germane to what we've been studying– that they *won't* have a problem with?"

She shyly produces another well-worn paperback, a Laura Ingalls Wilder called *The First Four Years.*

"She and her husband lived in Dakota Territory when they were first married," she says.

"So you've already read it."

"A couple times. I know having babies and just trying to farm is not really history, but– "

"It most absolutely *is* history, young lady, and don't let anybody tell you it's not. You just have to find a perspective to come at it from, a way of tying it in to the bigger picture."

Jolene looks relieved. She's not going to flunk, or be made fun of–

"Well, you know how you talked about how the railroads sold people on the idea of settling out here, and how some of it was sort of exaggerated, and at first the people couldn't sell their crop until they figured out how to mill the bran out of the winter hard red wheat– "

"You should be teaching this class, Jolene."

"I thought I might write how her and her husband had that, like, American Dream you're always talking about? And how many of those people failed."

He bangs things, Tucker. Doors, drawers, anything he puts down. She always knows where he is in the house, punctuating his disappointment with kicks and slams.

"You mean their crops failed."

"Well, yeah, a couple times, and there were fires and she lost a baby."

"Did they stop loving each other?"

Jolene again stops to consider. "From what she says in the book, I don't think so. But they had to leave the Territory."

They could go back to Minnesota, be near his parents' money. Maybe he'd resent her less if she was unemployed too.

"Then what you're saying is that their *crops* failed, but they didn't."

Francine can tell that this is a totally new concept to Jolene Otis, a little smile playing around her lips.

"I guess not. Wow."

Today I have opened a mind, thinks Francine, at least a tiny bit.

Then the Lunch Over bell rings and the hordes descend.

IT CERTAINLY ISN'T VEGAS.

Of course the structures never look their best in the daytime, no colored lights or mega-screens to pimp them up. This is a particularly unimpressive stand-alone at the side of a dreary stretch of road in a state he was hoping never to have to visit.

There are machines the minute you enter the lobby, good, but nobody is playing them and one is dark. Fitz's rule is you fix the damn things right away or get them off the floor. Your drummer overdoses and dies, you get a new drummer, you don't haul his corpse out onto the stage for everybody to gawk at.

The girl at the desk is clueless.

"You said it's a suite?"

"For Fitzgerald."

More scrutinizing of the reservations, the girl swinging her head back and forth to read.

"And the name is– ?"

"Fitzgerald. It's comped, so it might not be in your regular file."

"There's only one place to look."

"Then it should be in there."

The girl frowns. "The manager's on his break."

As if the world stops.

"Are all your suites booked?"

Again swinging the head. "No."

"Then book me into one," says Fitz, the drive even longer than he had imagined and his back killing him, "and we'll sort the rest out later."

"Welcome to Bearpaw!" she shouts when he is almost out of earshot.

From the lobby to the rooms you have to walk through the casino, good again, but somehow it lacks that 'hot damn, we're here' feeling. It's the usual Friedman-style layout, a maze of gleaming slots on a carpet with a squiggly, color-clash design under a low ceiling like a giant, futuristic Tiffany lamp. A bluish glow predominating, but capable of switching to red at night. Maybe twenty people scattered at the machines, half of them sitting at slant tops, the combined boops and beeps and MIDI theme songs sounding a little anemic in the big room. He hopes this is considered way off-hours. He hears a cheesy roll-up as he passes a middle-aged woman hitting for maybe twenty dollars on Lady Godiva, quarters rattling down as the machine pays out. The woman's expression does not change, her face dappled with LED light as she waits with finger poised to continue play. You need these people, the hard-core slot feeders, need lots of them. They usually have two, maybe three machines they've bonded with and on crowded nights wait jealously till one of their favorites is unoccupied. Or just turn around and go home.

The suite is pretty standard, with a view of the lake. Fitz never reads the online babble, the gushers and the haters, before he consults on a spot. Especially with casinos there's the sore-loser factor, and then the posts stay up forever. Things can change for better or worse. More often for the worse.

Fitz finds his way to the Bison Room, following the bearpaw marks on the floor. There is the general manager, young guy, who has some kind of jock name, Thump or Bump, something like that, and he remembers the white guy, Purdy, chief operating officer of the casino, from one of the mid-sized spots in Oklahoma, Cherokees maybe. And then there is the tribal chairman, who looks like who you'd hire for a poster of the twenty-first-century Indian– tall, handsome, got the slightly graying ponytail and a belt buckle big as a dinner plate.

"Harleigh Killdeer," says the Chairman, rearranging the bones in Fitz's shaking hand. "Appreciate you coming up to see us."

They are paying him to be here, but it's nice to be appreciated, even if it doesn't last much past his first observation. People pay you to consult, they deserve truth with the varnish off.

"This our GM, Swat Gilchrist, and COO, Tom Purdy."

Swat, that was it. Baseball player, or maybe a boxer, though his face is unmarked. Another poster-boy Indian.

"The steaks are legendary in here," says Purdy, who must have screwed the pooch pretty bad to end up at this remote outpost, or maybe they bought him away with a big bump in salary.

"You feed a lion one of those slabs," says Fitz, nodding toward a wall placard proudly featuring something bloody and four inches thick, with a ball of herbed butter sitting on top of it, "he'd sleep for a week. Any bison on this menu?"

"You know, we usually have it, but our supplier has been awful spotty, so we have to run it as a special."

Fitz orders the walleye, imagining the omega-3s like little miners ready to go hack away at the plaque the doctor tells him is clogging his arteries, and notices that the other men just stick to Starters. He's never actually seen a Pheasant Popper, but likes the idea.

"What we're looking at," says the Chairman once the waiter has left, "is a sudden influx. You've probably seen it in your bailiwick when a new field opens up."

"What stage are you at now?"

"Leases are still closing, a half-dozen outfits have just begun the conventional drilling."

"The lull before the shitstorm."

"And we'd like to be prepared for it."

"You had a chance to look around?" asks the COO.

"Enough."

"What'd you think?"

Any operator willing to ask him that in front of his employers deserves it with both barrels. On the reality TV show this is where they'd cut to a close-up of the guy's face as the sweat beads start to pop out.

"First thing, you need to teach your people to *smile*."

"My *people*," the Chairman jumps in, choosing to read this as an ethnic generalization, "smile plenty when they want to."

The great thing about being the pro in the room, the Answer Man, is you don't have to tiptoe.

"But that's not the job, is it?" he says. "The job is to make the guests, the players who are going to leave all their money behind, feel good about it. Saying no with a smile is usually better than saying yes like you could give a shit one way or the other."

"We can work on that," concedes the operator.

Fitz jerks his head back toward the casino. "When the oil workers get here, you'll want to stay open twenty-four-seven for a bit instead of just doing it Fridays and Saturdays. Look at your expenses, look at your profits, see if it makes sense."

"That means lots of new hires," says Swat, who is sitting back in his seat like he owns the place, a show-me look on his puss.

"Exactly. And whether they come from your enrollment or not, they've got to be well-trained and well-paid– a step higher than you're paying at the present. Once the thing really hits, even the burger chains will be struggling to keep people behind the counter, the local contractors will lose their best workers, the gas stations– they want to stay in business, they'll have to step up to the plate and so will you."

"You think the oil workers will gamble in the daytime?" The Chairman now, who's got a authentic-looking arrowhead for a clasp on his string tie.

"These fellas will shower up, crash for a few hours, then be ready to party hearty, no matter what shift they're on. And forget about free drinks on the floor," the operator's eyes lighting up at this, "they'll come to you well lubricated."

"We were thinking more poker."

"They can play poker with each other at the bunkhouse, man camp, whatever. Here you got the lights, the noise, the machines. You might want to swap out for some of the more babe-centric themes, the more boobs the better– your biggest rival is going to be the titty bars in Yellow Earth."

"There aren't any t– "

"Don't blink, there will be. What's your RTP on the slots?"

Swat seems to be the numbers guy. "Between seventy-five and eighty percent."

"That's awful tight."

"And it's a long, long ride," he smiles, "to the next casino."

Fitz nods. Like a lot of the Indian spots they have more jobs than they can fill from the enrollment, but the place is so far from the beaten path that attracting competent people–

"We've got over six hundred machines," says the Chairman, hopefully.

"And you could do with a lot fewer of the old three-reel jobs. These kids from the rigs, a lot of them are online gamers already, they like to multi-task. Throw a lot of bonuses and jackpot levels and animation at them, they eat that shit up. Five, six, seven reels, lots of scatter symbols and multiple playlines. Put your cheap slots and sitdowns in the corners for your first- and fifteenth-of-the-month regulars, let em dole out their government checks a nickel at a time like always without getting in the way."

"Blackjack?"

"Blackjack and craps, sure, if you've got dealers who can run a good crisp game. Keno if you don't take up too much space with it. Remember, this whole place should feel like it's on amphetamines, without the side effects. It's got to be *magic*."

There are people who really understand the odds, understand how it works, and still enjoy gambling, or 'gaming,' as the Industry likes you to call it now. But Fitz is not one of them. For the rest it's just magical thinking, which is to be encouraged. In his floor-boss days Fitz explained to folks many, many times how an eighty-three-percent Return To Player rate does not mean they are guaranteed to get eighty-three-percent of *their* money back from the machine. They'll get more or less, usually less, and some lucky sucker, and don't get me wrong, it might be you, will walk off with the bulk of it. If you knew you could feed that flashing bastard for three hours and at the end be sure to walk away with exactly what you put in, guaranteed, why would you bother? But that's just rational, and as successful politicians and Vegas casino owners know, rational doesn't hold a lot of interest for most people. They'd rather have their betting systems or favorite colors or lucky machines or some other angle, and God love em if they think it's fun while they empty their pockets. Most pathetic are the streak-chasers, no matter what the game, but drawn like moths to a flame by the roulette wheel. Every time they slap a chip on a number they're asking 'Do you love me, Jesus?'

And Jesus lets the ball stop where it will.

"So basically you're saying keep doing what we're doing," says the Swat kid, "but do it a lot better."

The dynamic of this situation is clear to Fitz– Swat a little sore to have his mastery of the situation questioned, the COO just trying to put up decent numbers and not let the place slide into grunge, and the Chairman with a half-dozen other agendas. Not unfamiliar at the rez casinos, with jobs to give out, anti-gaming Christians to mollify, social programs hungry for funding, and old grudges dying hard. Whereas in Vegas or Reno it's simple– separate the players from their money in the most entertaining and cost-effective method possible. This Harleigh has got a mission, you can tell, while his GM and operator wish he'd leave more money in the business instead of getting visionary with it and placating the tribe members.

"The thing is, we don't want to lose our regular folks," says the operator. "Down-staters, people who drive in from Montana."

"Never complain about a crowd on your floor."

"True."

"But you might have to raise your rack rates in the lodge. Housing's gonna be a bear if there's nothing more to Yellow Earth and your New Center than I've seen, and you don't want the drill jockeys living here. Or sleeping in the parking lot– keep your security people on that."

"And what about the yacht?" says the Chairman.

Fitz looks out to the lake. Nothing but a little fishing dock and empty water. "You've got a yacht?"

"On order," grins the Chairman. This is obviously his baby, and just as obviously a point of contention between him and the other two. "Ninety-six-footer, one of those two-story jobs."

They are famous for magical thinking themselves, of course, the Indians. Just sing this and dance that and give up the white man's hootch and before you know it the buffalo will be back, and not just on the menu. But most of the people Fitz has dealt with on the casino end of the tribal government have been fairly grounded, dollars-and-cents types. Harleigh's got an evangelical gleam in his eye.

"Capacity?"

"I figure we convert the bedrooms into casino space, we could get a hundred fifty head in there."

Both Swat and Purdy look away.

"You want to run gambling on it?"

So this is it, an ass-covering operation. When anybody kicks at a council meeting he can say 'we consulted with an expert in the field.' The Chairman doesn't want advice, he wants absolution.

"Sure," says Harleigh, showing his perfect teeth. "Just for the Players' Club members at first, then if it catches on– "

"We'd stay inside of the reservation boundaries," adds the operator.

Fitz shakes his head. "You'll have to redo your Class III agreement. The NIGC, the state."

"We got Ruby on it already."

"Ruby's your lawyer."

Again the proud-papa grin. "Comes out of Yale. She's a mix of little tribes, but none from up here. Ruby Pino."

"She'd better be good."

"The gal doesn't take any prisoners."

Fitz looks out the window again. "There much else to see on the water?"

"Not really," admits Swat Gilchrist. "It's an Army Corps of Engineers kind of a deal."

Fitz makes a cross with his fingers, as if fending off a vampire. The men laugh. "Keep those people away from me."

"I figure they stuck this big-ass lake on us, cut the reservation in two," says the Chairman as his Pheasant Poppers arrive, "the least we can do is make the sucker pay off."

THE BOYS ARE EATING it up, the skinny white kid and the fat Indian kid, eyes sliding past Scorch every time the door opens for men to come in or out, offering a good see-through to the pole humpers on stage. Who knows how long they been getting their rocks off out here, fifteen, twenty seconds at a time.

"You don't even have a fake ID to try on me?"

"No sir."

'Sir' is a new one. "That's fucking pathetic."

The white guy is definitely cruising behind something, his eyes all pupil, and the Indian kid looks permanently pissed off.

"I mean, I know it's a little slow in this burg, but beaver hunting in the alley– "

It's wider than an alley, delivery trucks able to drive between the clubs to get to the back. Vic decided to use the side for the main entrance to cut down on the fights with the crowd coming out of Teasers next door, or at least keep them out of public view. Teasers had been a drugstore that died in the '80s and Bazookas was the old Legion post turned evangelical storefront, a race between the carpenters and wiring guys to see which could open first.

"There's not much to do."

When the door isn't open the white kid can't keep his eyes off the tat on Scorch's neck, the flaming skull he got when he was in the Outlaws in Tampa.

"So, what, people grow their own weed on all these farms?"

The boys relax a little, understanding now that he's not going to kick their asses or call their mommies.

"A couple try," says the Indian kid. I wedge him in the doorway, Scorch thinks, nobody gets in or out. "It's not, like, a really long growing season."

"But kids can get baked if they want."

"Pretty much. If it's just, you know, something to smoke."

The problem with Beavis and Butthead here is they didn't grow up in the culture, never seen some punkass snitch taken away in a body bag.

"You think you could hook us up with something better?" asks the white kid.

"Better?"

"Ecstasy, ketamine, rohypnol, GHB, coke."

"What did you, Google that shit?"

The kid shrugs. "Stuff I'd like to try. And we got lots of friends who, you know— like to try stuff."

Scorch remembers being outside in the alley looking in, everything the adult world got to do cooler, more fun, more dangerous than the kid world. And he got early admittance, held with lifelong cons at the Okeechobee CI until his trial, sent back there for another year when he aged out of juvenile. Welcome to the rest of your life, fucker.

"So how bout it?"

Persistent little prick. Brent's lightweight surfer-dude buddy, Wayne Lee, will be bringing it all up on his Texas runs, and Brent says he promised him the drillers and the drivers, leaving Scorch with zip besides working the door at Bazookas. Pay is good for this kind of gig, Vic waving off his arrest record, but compared to what other people are knocking down in the oil patch–

"Suppose I could hook you up," he says. "How do I know I could trust you?"

Neither has a snappy reply, so Scorch one-hands the white boy around the neck and lifts him off the ground.

"This is how," he answers for them, glancing down the alley to be sure no new customers are coming his way, then bringing the boy's reddening face close to his. "Because nobody who's ever fucked with me is alive to brag about it."

He puts the kid down. His knuckles are still raw from beating on that pipe pusher the other night, and Vic says he can't wear MMA gloves on the job– too much provocation for the wildasses who come in.

"There's almost no cops in Yellow Earth," says the Indian kid. "Even less on the rez."

And they got their hands full. The deputy who came by to get Scorch's version of the last incident said he was doing twelve-hour shifts racing all over the county to deal with truck accidents, fistfights, overdoses– "It's Saturday night every day of the week," said the badge, who didn't look much older than these two.

"I'll think about it," Scorch tells them. "Meanwhile, stay the fuck off of my porch."

Jewelle's music, Lady Gaga doing "Just Dance," starts to play inside as Scorch watches the two walk back out to the street. They probably got uncles, brothers that he can connect with, get some real action going here. Brent will make sure he gets whatever product he needs. Brent likes to keep all his options open. Scorch steps back into the club and there is a cheer from the cranked-up drillers and drivers, Jewelle in her hard hat and yellow safety vest, wrapping her long legs around the gleaming silver pole as the mock-up derrick behind her gushes inky liquid in appreciation.

And it really is Saturday night.

THE WAVES DON'T STOP. It makes sense, of course, it's the ocean, but still it's the thing that impresses him the most. There is a steep drop-off from the sand and then it levels and you have to time it right getting in and getting out or get smacked by one of these big waves that keep piling in.

At home the wind, even in the worst season for it, gives you a break now and then.

Not that they aren't fun to wrestle with. Lots of screaming, amusement park screaming, from the tourist kids, skipping up and back on the wet sand as if to taunt the waves, catch me, catch me, and the people already in bobbing to keep their heads above as the big ones roll in, and twice now he's been thrown up against Brent's wife.

Bunny.

Never actually seen a bikini like that in real life, and she's not the only one on the sand and in the water wearing one, and you have to try not to stare. When in Rome, or here I guess, when in Waikiki.

The hotel actually only has this pretty narrow strip of beach that it claims, Diamond Head off to the left and a boardwalk that goes along in front of the other beach hotels starting just to the right, and he had pictured something longer, unbroken. Bronzed women riding white horses in slow motion along an endless stretch of white sand. Not that he's kicking.

He's glad Brent loaned him the goggles, no telling what kind of beating the salt water would deal to his eyes, even if he probably looks funny in them. No photographs, please. Harleigh ducks under and leaves his feet, frog-kicking down, pass-

ing all that blond whiteness of Bunny and heading parallel to shore. His Granpaw
Pete told him how the river Indians were expert at holding their breath underwater,
hiding from enemies, and he used to practice in the reservoir when he could stand
the cold. This, this bath water, doesn't make your testicles shrink but it's hard to
stay under. Buoyant, he can really feel it. He goes under again and kicks toward
the boardwalk side. No old farmhouses under this. Something looming, a bloom
of green to one side near his head and he realizes it's a turtle. Up for a breath and
then following it, webbed flippers stroking, a huge green turtle with what looks
like an island of green ferny stuff growing on its back, wavering behind as it swims.
Harleigh swims after the turtle till it moves between the mass of bodies directly in
front of the hotel, then he stands, taking a gulp of seawater as a wave breaks at just
the wrong moment. Like his mother always said, keep your mouth shut and nothing bad will come into or out of it. He coughs, spits, feeling it halfway up his nose.

"You okay?"

Bunny, who has been hovering close with the idea that Indians can't swim.
He wants to tell her that's black people, that Indians only drown because the Big
Water Snake gets jealous of their amphibian ability and pulls them down.

"I saw a turtle," he calls over the shrilling of the tourist kids and the boom of
the waves, holding his hands wide apart to indicate its size.

"Really? Wow!"

Bunny is an enthusiast. At first glimpse Connie identified her as a cheerleader
for the Timberwolves, which turned out not to be true but pretty damn close.
Tyler Junior College, dental technician program, part of the 'Apache Cheer.' And
yes, a couple of the girls on the squad were actual Apaches.

"It had stuff growing on its back."

"Like fungus?"

"More like camouflage."

Bunny smiles. If she had gone the dental route her own teeth would have
been her best advertisement. Harleigh has cautioned his wife to quit calling her
'Miss Doublemint' or she's likely to say it out loud where Bunny can hear.

"You're right," Connie said before she crawled under the sheets in the fantasy
of a hotel suite. "'Bunny' pretty much says it all."

Connie, who has never been west of Butte before and is afraid of flying, is
down with a killer dose of jet lag, and Brent is off mentoring Fawn through a
surfing lesson. Fawn had another of those bikinis, must have bought it online
cause nothing like it was ever sold in Yellow Earth, and you could see that she

was excited that her natural coloring made it look like she'd been out tanning for weeks. Harleigh thought it was too much, Brent treating her to the trip as well, but Connie reminded him what happened the last time they left Fawn home for a week. And what the hell, how many kids on the rez get to go to Hawaii?

"You think poor Connie is okay?"

It was bad for her on the flight, not just takeoff and landing but the whole thing, hours and hours of it, and Bunny starting every approach with 'Oh, you poor thing' didn't help any. But you never know with women, the Big Ladies and Teresa Crow's Ghost act like they can't stand each other and the next thing you know they're conspiring together to heat his britches over something.

"Yeah, I should go check," he says, lifting the goggles off and hoping they haven't made raccoon rings around his eyes. "Don't want to get too wrinkly in here."

Harleigh leaves her hopping in the surf and makes a rush with the incoming wave till he's up the steep part of the beach. There's a little footwash deal before you unlatch the gate into the hotel pool and he gets most of the sand off. The pool is big and roundish, some kind of white tropical flower painted on the bottom, with lounge chairs and little tables and sun umbrellas all around it. Couple women doing the thing where they lie on their stomachs on the flattened chairs with their top straps unhooked. Kids already splashing in the pool, climbing on and flipping off inflatable floating animals of different species. Harleigh shakes his head, still not sure he's allowed to be here.

It is a Junior Ocean Suite on the twelfth floor. All-white interior, balcony overlooking the ocean and the pool down to the left, Connie a lump of misery curled up on the giant bed.

"How's the toothpaste model?"

"You're awake."

"I felt like something was pressing me down into the mattress. Like I weighed a thousand pounds."

"You look better."

"I feel more or less human. What time is it?"

He moves the cat-squasher of a book Brent gave him to read on the plane– whatever he sees in this Ayn Rand babe is a mystery to Harleigh– to reveal the digital clock, not that Connie could read it without her contacts in.

"Bout eleven." He steps into the bathroom. There are people on staff at the reservation with offices smaller than the shower stall. He calls out as the perfect spray shoots down. "You think you're up for lunch?"

"I doubt it," Connie calls back.

"He's an awful nice guy."

"Keanu."

"Kapuni. Kapuni Barnes."

"That you met at the conference where?"

"Phoenix, I think. The first time."

Harleigh steps back into the bedroom, toweling off. He's never touched a towel so thick, so white. A shame to get it dirty. Connie is sitting up now, frowning.

"The Hawaiians usually come if the conferences are in the West."

"Don't *look* at me." Connie has linen wrinkle marks on her face from sleeping so hard.

"You look better."

"When people say 'You look better' it means you been looking *worse*. It's like saying 'Hey, you lost weight– '"

"You should eat."

"If I am ever hungry again, I'll get something by the pool. Or call room service."

Harleigh pauses in dressing himself. The lunch place Kapuni chose has a Hawaiian name and he's not sure how swanky it is.

"What did Bunny wear in the water?"

"Some kind of two-piece thing. Hey, I saw a turtle." Harleigh shows her how big he thinks it was.

"In where you were swimming?"

"Of course."

Connie makes a face. You can get her into a swimming pool if she thinks it's clean, but the idea of putting her head under 'in the stuff fish pee in'–

"Harleigh," she says, looking around at the suite, at the louvered panels, the ocean sunset paintings, the complimentary fruit and macadamia nut basket, "how do you think he can afford this?"

"He's been successful in the business."

"Driving trucks."

"Owning and managing trucks that service the oil fields. It's a niche business. He must be good at it."

"But he's not investing in the– "

"He's putting in his time and his experience. I can't tell you what a bit of luck it was running into him."

Connie slumps back down to her pillow, not looking satisfied with his explanation. "You look good in a Hawaiian shirt," she says. "Who would have thought."

Harleigh steps out of the elevator and crosses the lobby. From what he's seen so far, the hotel seems to be a Japanese wedding factory, women in tight business outfits carrying clipboards and ushering bridesmaids and family members and even the brides in their meringue-pouf dresses this way and that, chairs constantly being rearranged in the tropical jungle of a courtyard. He weaves through three different clusters, trying to avoid appearing in any of their group photographs, and makes his way to the pool bar.

Bunny is there, looking fresh and blond and as if she'd never been in the water, parked behind a long frothy drink with a pineapple wedge impaled on the rim of the glass.

"Milkshake?"

"Piña colada. You can barely taste the rum."

"That could be dangerous."

The bartender wanders over and Harleigh orders a simple Scotch on the rocks, hoping it doesn't come with fruit hanging out of it.

"How's poor Connie doing?"

"Poor Connie," he says, squeezing in beside her, "has gone back to sleep. She should be fine by tonight."

"It usually doesn't hit me till the second day. Not that I've done that much long-distance travel."

"Where'd you and Brent go for your honeymoon?"

"Mexico. This place called Zihuatenejo? It was like a Club Med thing."

"I've never been to Mexico."

"Really?"

"We've had delegations come up, from their tribes."

"Right, those are Indians too."

"Still a high percentage of the population."

"I just don't think of them as– you know– riding horses and having teepees and all that."

"Hundreds of nations, hundreds of cultures."

"Even our Apache girls weren't from the same– whatsit– band?"

"They live in a dry part of the world. Hard to sustain a big concentration of people in one spot."

Bunny pulls her pineapple loose and takes a nibble. "Brent is so pumped about the company. I don't think I've ever seen him this excited."

"It's going to be terrific."

"You know, we're partners too. You and me."

The bartender sets Harleigh's drink down.

"A lot of our end of things will be in my name. Some kind of tax advantage Brent figured out."

"So you're a silent partner."

"Not so silent. I end up doing a lot of phone work. Whenever a little honey is called for."

Harleigh has explained to Brent that at first there won't be any contracts directly with the Nations. Let them get established in the field, a couple jobs under their belt and the going rates set before they compete for that work. Brent will run the trucks and Harleigh will be out scaring up opportunities, besides his role in the initial financing. He and Sig Rushmore have worked out a sweetheart of a deal, the Company advancing funds against the royalties from Harleigh's fee– simple land leases, not only allowing him to capitalize ArrowFleet but guaranteeing them a year's service contract the minute they put rubber on the road. 'Synergy,' Sig called it, and Harleigh had to look it up when he got home. A terrific idea, kind of scientific and business-oriented at the same time.

"The trick will be growing at the proper rate," he tells Bunny. "You don't want to be caught without enough trucks, but if you get ahead of the play– "

"Brent said it's like surfing. You have to know just when to get off the wave."

It reminds him of Fawn.

"You think they're okay?"

"Oh, they're fine, Brent just phoned me. It's a beach up the coast a ways. The traffic is a beast here."

"Yeah, that was murder coming in from the airport."

She has a simple, thin dress on, just white. Anything else would be gilding the lily.

"I hope she didn't take too much of a beating. Fawn's never been much of an athlete."

"It's more balance and focus than strength. I bet she did fine."

He puts the drinks on his room tab, having insisted they'd do their own incidentals, and gets up to go. Brent is taking the girls to his favorite sushi place for lunch, and Harleigh has a twinge of wishing he could see Fawn pretending to like raw fish.

"So we'll meet you here at seven."

"Right after the hula exhibition."

More wedding parties arriving, the young Japanese men in their tuxedos looking all alike to him, stepping out of rental limos under the carport, smiling and occasionally making those little half bows to each other. Must be some kind of wedding package. They tried one at the casino, a discounted suite with a hundred dollars' worth of gaming tokens complimentary to the bride, but it never caught on.

The sun nails him the minute he steps out from the shade of the hotel tower, and he wonders if walking is such a great idea. There's a soft breeze and heat isn't sharp like the Badlands summer, but he's sweating a bit already. Harleigh hurries past the ABC store on the corner, where they have the killer malasada donuts he shouldn't even be thinking about, and wades through the tourists with his downtown map in hand.

This part of the island has been pretty thoroughly colonized. Lots more Japanese, which would have started Granpaw Pete into his reenactment of the Battle of Okinawa, lots of big tall blond Dutch or Germans or Swedes, the usual American white folks, and even a few blacks who look like they just stepped off a golf course. Harleigh turns right on Kalakua Avenue and realizes he's been here before. Houston? San Francisco? It's all the same stores that crop up wherever the gold-card crowd stays, some kind of comfort zone for them, like McDonald's for people with too much money. The idea that shopping is something you might do for fun, like hunting or playing basketball, is still a wonder to him, and he has to smile as he watches the ladies– they are mostly ladies– pop from one air-conditioned boutique to the next with their classily-bagged purchases bouncing against their legs.

Hey, only a matter of months before Gucci and Hugo Boss hit Yellow Earth.

The place with too many vowels in its name turns out to be a little hole-in-the-wall up by the canal. Kapuni is already at a table, and starts laughing when he sees Harleigh.

"What?"

Kapuni has to push his chair way back to get his belly clear of the table and stand. "You look more *kanaka* than I do. Welcome, bra."

Kapuni gives him a shake and a thump and they sit. There are other Hawaiians, even bigger than Kapuni, and some smaller Asian people at the tables, none of them looking like tourists.

"Yeah, folks on the street were kind of looking at me."

"They think they just saw you hugging a ukulele in one of the hotel shows."

Harleigh looks at the menu posted over the service counter. "So is this where you get that poi stuff?"

"I don't go near it." Kapuni pats his belly. "You know what the plastic surgeons take out when they do a liposuction? That's pretty much what poi is."

"With us it's Cheetos and Coca-Cola. We got fifteen-year-olds with diabetes already." He can't tell what half of the stuff listed is. "What should I get?"

"Can't go wrong with the basic plate lunch."

Harleigh and Kapuni and a couple Lummis from Washington State got good and lost in San Francisco one night, looking for their rental car for a solid hour before they figured out it had been towed. Kapuni declared that his doctor forbade him to walk uphill, and they had a hell of a time getting a taxi that could fit them all.

"I just walked from the hotel."

"Brave man."

"I like to see what's going on– you know– on foot. How do you feel about all this?" Harleigh waves his hand toward the outside.

"Waikiki? I wish I had a percentage of it."

"But, like, culturally."

"It's just not *ours* anymore. "

An older lady comes and they order, Harleigh noticing that it's '70s R&B on the sound system instead of the Don Ho stuff in the hotel lobby.

"Tough place to give up," he says.

Kapuni shrugs. "We didn't have the massacres that your outfits on the mainland did, at least not with the white people. Mostly we were killing each other, district against district, island against island, till finally there was kind of an empire under Kamehameha– more like the Aztecs and Incas and that crowd. Only then the first white sailors come with their diseases and then the missionaries, who converted most of the royalty, and then the Americans just decided to take it– it was a *steal* more than a war."

"Same deal with my Three Nations. Not that there haven't been some battles along the way."

"If the timing had been different we might have fought back, like the Maoris."

"And now– "

"We're five, six percent of the population. Filipinos and Japanese both got at least double that, and there's *haoles*– "

"The white Hawaiians."

"If you're all white, you're not a Hawaiian," says Kapuni. "No matter how long your family's been here. We managed to keep a few nice patches of land, our story is being told a lot better, but we don't run anything."

The lunches come, Harleigh's kalua pig plate with macaroni salad, rice and cole slaw and Kapuni's shoyu ahi poke bowl, with a couple cold Longboard Lagers.

"Looks like real people food."

"Can't beat it."

"Where was it that your bunch brought the dancers to the conference?"

"Seattle."

"That was something."

"Beautiful women wearing grass and flowers, what's not to like?"

"There's just a vibe here," says Harleigh, "and I may be way off, but you get the feeling things were never that desperate, just living day to day."

"No winter."

"For a start."

"Pretty good ownership and irrigation systems for farming, always surrounded by edible fish."

"So people were fighting– ?"

"Because people fight. Too many kings, too much testosterone, a warrior culture." Kapuni shrugs. "No going back now. I heard you come into some kind of mineral bonanza."

"As a matter of fact I'm here on a business deal."

"Don't tell me there's oil under *us*."

"No."

"Cause that would be the end. I mean there's days, maybe I been stuck in traffic where the H-1 meets the Pali for an hour, I look over toward what's left of the Ko'olau Volcano and say 'Let er *rip*, baby. Time to let the lava flow and start this sucker over from scratch.'"

"But it's *dead*, right?"

"Dormant. Like my sex life at the moment."

Harleigh lifts his beer bottle to toast. "May we rise again."

"And again and again," says Kapuni, clinking his bottle against Harleigh's. "To the survivors."

By the time he gets back to the hotel, damp and beer-dozy, Connie is ready for action.

"We've only got four days here," she says. "I can't believe I missed half of one."

"You needed to sleep."

She's wearing a dress that she looks great in that he's never seen before, probably bought it for the trip, and has the guidebook open.

"I want to see this Iolani Palace."

"I need a nap."

Connie watches him peel his shirt off. "You're leaving me alone?"

"What caught up to you just caught up to me. Remember we got dinner downstairs."

"So what am I sposed to do?"

He lays the laminated downtown map over her guidebook, points to Kalakua. "Bear left out of the hotel, you can look at all the stuff we'll be able to afford a year from now."

"I don't want to shop without Fawn."

"She's not back?"

"They went out somewhere. Her and your partners in crime."

Harleigh gives her a look and steps back into the bathroom for a cool-off shower. "They give a tour of this hotel every couple hours. Lots of famous people stayed here."

"Elvis Presley?"

"I wouldn't be surprised."

Connie appears at the door just as he's about to turn the water on.

"None of this is real, is it?" she says. "It's all just Disneyland."

The dream is one of those that keeps building on itself, one section opening up to another. There is a part of it that is him and Bunny underwater, only they can breathe there and twine together like river otters, and then there's a battle, which he later figures comes from the big mural on a wall they passed of Hawaiian warriors chasing their enemies off a cliff, with Brent all greased-up and tattooed and being the chief in charge of the slaughter, and then it's back home on the lake only it's black and shiny and he's running from dogs and mounted killers through the prairie grass, dogs yipping behind him as he sprints naked and bleeding and finds an opening in the earth to dive into and listen to them thunder past, safe for a moment till he realizes he's in the crawlspace beneath some old house, some busted farmer's lone outpost and the weeds that are growing up are growing up right through his body, which is only bones now with a little bit of blackened flesh attached, like after you chew through a plate of ribs.

And then it's time to wake the hell up.

The restaurant downstairs is supposed to be the only five-star joint in Hawaii, which leads to a lot of jokes about how the only place with a star in Yellow Earth is the Texaco station out on 2 that went out of business but never took their sign down.

Everybody is dressed up, with the women looking like a million bucks and Harleigh in what Connie calls his cattle baron outfit, drinking mai tais just to go along. The second one tastes pretty good. The room is nut brown with beautiful cane chairs and lots of carved panels and waiters in brown jackets and blue ties, their table overlooking the bay, with a line of torches alongside the edge of the beach. No Hawaiian shirts in here.

"When they tapped into the deep stuff in the Eagle Ford," says Brent, who has been telling old Texas wildcat stories, "oil was at ten dollars a barrel, gas under two bucks for a thousand cubic feet, and I'm working my tail off and still losing money."

"It was a nightmare," Bunny adds. The table isn't that small but somehow her leg is pushed up against Harleigh's.

"Then the prices start to shoot up, but I've got these service contracts, right, that I went into long-term so's I could be sure to keep my people working. Lesson Number One– you got to stay as lean and mean as you can. We were out there running this equipment– some of it was like museum pieces, there was so much demand– and we're still tied to our old rates."

"But you honored your agreements."

"Yeah, and the dinosaurs kept lugging their carcasses around when there wasn't enough to feed them."

The menu is in both French and English, with a Menu Dégustation to start off and lots of little side dishes like squid ink sausage that Harleigh wouldn't eat on a bet. He's learned what abalone is and sniffed at Fawn's caviar and ordered the duck, figuring there's only so much you can do to a quacker in a restaurant kitchen.

"You can learn a hell of a lot from the animal kingdom," says Brent.

"My stepfather," says Fawn, who sits by Brent, looking five years older than she is and drinking some complicated cocktail without the rum, "is a big deal in the Speckled Eagle Clan."

"Right, right, your people have been doing it for centuries. And what it boils down to, whether it's sports, business, whatever, is survival of the fittest."

"Dog eat dog."

"More like big dog eats little dog's bowl of Purina."

They laugh. The waiter comes with another round of drinks, Harleigh not so sure he finished his last one. He's always had this idea that the white people do so well because they figure to do it *alone*. No clan, no tribe to back them up, to share and share alike, just that hot focused eye on the prize all the time and let the slackers fall by the wayside. Hell of a way to live, but it's how the game is run these days.

"You've got to be opportunistic," Brent continues. "Look for your opening. A wolf pack doesn't just charge after a herd, they follow around the edges, pick their spot."

"Pick the right victim," says Connie.

"You've got it, you've got it. That's why it's so important that we're setting ArrowFleet up at the very beginning of this Dakota play. When oil doubled and gas tripled in Texas, if I could have adjusted my prices to it, when there were operators begging for trucks– " Brent shakes his head. "Not that I didn't make a killing, but it could have been a *massacre*."

They came up with the name together, Arrow for Harleigh's connection with the Nations and Fleet for the idea that they'd be quick and efficient with their remuda of haulers and specialty vehicles. Brent has already showed him the logo he worked up on a computer program, and Harleigh can't wait to see it rolling by on the side of one of their trucks.

Brent raises his drink for a toast and the others follow suit.

"Ladies and gentlemen," he says, "to the *victors*."

STAGE TWO

STIMULATION

THE FIRST BOOM HUGGED close to the superhighway of the era, the Missouri River. Frenchmen came west from the Great Lakes, or, in the employ of the Hudson Bay Company, down from the north, while a Scotsman working for the Spanish paddled and portaged from the south with his entourage. Empires were staked, proxy wars waged, tribal alliances fought for or purchased in pursuit of the fortune promised from the slaughter of flat-tailed rodents.

The Native people had lived beside the animals for years, fishing the ponds they dammed, studying their industry, taking a certain number of them each year to roast in the skin and feast upon, favoring the tender meat of the tail. But when it was explained by the advance men of the great northwest companies that the pelt alone was currency to acquire guns, powder, knives, axes, kettles, objects of utility and beautification, their harvest intensified, the competition to control the supply and movement of skins suddenly fevered and violent.

In a common method of extraction, young men would climb out over the snow-covered dams to the mounded houses, so similar in shape to the earthen huts of the people the French called the 'underground Sioux,' and chop into them from above, killing any winter-plewed adults they found hibernating there, while other men walked the banks, stomping the ground to discover the hollow escape washes dug underneath by the beavers. Drowning or a hard knock on the skull, so as not to damage the fur, were the preferred methods of killing.

With the goad of competitive trade and the fear of nearby enemies being suddenly able to outgun them, hunters now began to skin the creatures and leave the carcasses for scavengers, the kits often killed or left to starve as collateral damage, and it became common to see a beaver missing one of its paws, twisted or chewed off to escape the metal traps that increasingly replaced the deadfalls and surrounds of the Native people. River traffic increased exponentially, some tribes setting up tolls, while easy firewood and edible game receded further and further from the banks.

A number of lucrative support industries flourished during the boom— suppliers of canoes, pirogues, keelboats, traps, guns and powder, trade goods, liquor, women. Certain of the river villages became known for commerce, gambling and prostitution, with the attendant murders, domestic violence, disease, and increase in infants born blind. Some investors from across the great ocean became wealthy in the trade, and a few of the shrewder, or luckier, beaver men on the ground were rewarded for their risk and effort. But more common was the experience of the *coureur de bois* who braved treacherous rivers, hostile tribes, blizzards, near-starvation, and the rigors of daily life far beyond the sound of church bells, only to return home with a string of canoes piled high with bales of pelts and discover that during his years of absence, fashion had changed in Europe and the price of felted beaver sunk so low the skins barely merited the shipping cost. More than once, in an attempt to counter a surplus and the resulting trade inflation, warehouses in the eastern port towns were ordered emptied, bales of pelts coated with pitch and set fire to, years of bloody striving gone up in acrid flame, the smoke and nauseating odor hanging over the inhabitants for days.

News of fashion, war, and shifts in economy traveled slowly in those days, and so the bust was not abrupt. The trapping around the tributaries of the big river steadily played out, unattended dams deteriorating and ponds draining to leave spongy meadows and bogs, the trade activity moving steadily northward and westward, till in the area later known as Yellow Earth, it was a rare, rare event to stand at dusk and witness the wake of a beaver spreading across the smooth water's surface.

NINE THOUSAND FEET DOWN, making hole a joint at a time and hoping the weather holds out, warm enough still that only Hurry Upshaw, the driller, and the latest worm, Tuck or Buck or Schmuck– take your pick– are wearing heavy stuff under their rig togs. They're not into the lower layer of the shale yet so it's quick drilling, not much more than twenty minutes till the kelly drive is nearly to the deck and it's time to add to the string, Hurry shutting the mud pumps down and winching the drive up as Ike squeegees sludge off the outside of the pipe with a rolled towel till the kelly-saver sub is clear, Mike steering the break-out tong over to clamp on and kicking in the heavy slips to hold the string steady in the hole and Hurry spins the rotary table to break the connection before lift-ing the kelly clear for Ike to walk it over to the joint waiting in the mousehole, Mike quickly swabbing dope on pipe threads before Ike clamps the makeup tong on the mousehole pipe and Mike sets the chain, wrapping it just below the box of the joint. Ike guides and Hurry stabs the kelly-saver sub pin into the box, lets a bit of weight press down as Mike throws the chain, whipping around the sub to be immediately pulled taut and the connection torqued solid with cat-line and tongs. Mike and Ike back away with their tools as Hurry hoists the kelly assembly and new joint up into the derrick till the bottom end hangs clear, Ike waltzing it over to the standing pipe and the connection dance is repeated, thread dope, tongs, and chain, the satisfying scrunch of married steel and then Hurry sends the string down again till the kelly bushing is jimmied solid into the rotary table and the bit meets strata and the mud pumps thrum back to life– drilling ahead. Tulsa, the motorman, is helping with cleanup and the hoisting of the next joint from the V-door down into the mousehole, which somebody more competent than the local hire Pluck or Fuck would be doing instead of off dumping hundred-pound sacks of bentonite into the mud flow.

"Fella's got emergency room written all over him," said Diz on the guy's first tour, and Hightower, the tool-pusher, has told them to take it easy on him till he knows his asshole from the annulus, which might just be never. The pre-tenders before him all left the field with concussions or mashed fingers or that rash that looked like raw hamburger, as if anybody could be fucking allergic to oil base.

But they are making hole and Hurry hasn't screamed at anybody all morning, and it's neither cooking them on the metal deck or freezing them with that Cana-dian dick-shriveler wind they know is coming. The hole is a gassy son of a bitch, of course, one nasty kick while going through the top shale layer that had Hightower on site for half a day reading gauges and Gleason throwing kill mud down the hole, but that's always a sign the well is likely to pay off. You draw your check the same whether it does or not, but nobody likes humping pipe into a disappointment.

Drilling, even in this soft stuff that cuts so quick, is a pretty relaxed rhythm, entire minutes where there's nothing weighing a couple tons swinging around trying to decapitate you, time to scratch your nuts or fart or ignore the NO SMOKING signs plastered everywhere. Dizzy has the new worm tending what little is needed with the mud pits, and Hurry won't invent jobs that don't need doing like some drillers you could name, while Tulsa keeps all the machinery roaring and screeching. Good rig so far, for one of the better companies. Some of the shit they've seen thrown up on this patch looks more like a set for an OSHA disaster tutorial.

Tuck climbs onto the platform, safety mask pulled down around his neck, blinking and coughing.

"Didn't I tell you not to dump it into the hopper all at once?" says Tulsa.

"Lot of dust."

"Which you just huffed into your lungs. You take a shit tonight, it's gonna come out like a hunk of lead."

"What do I do next?"

Tulsa sighs. This is the fourth roustabout hopeful this month. "You remember where you put that shovel?"

"I do," says Tuck. He's not a kid, with good focus, a willingness to work, and no oilfield skills whatsoever.

"You remember which end of it you hold onto?"

Tuck just waits.

"Follow me– we got some trenches need digging over by the tanks."

Mike and Ike are veteran floorhands, pushing twenty-five, not related though constantly taken for brothers. They hire out as a team, were both wide receivers for their high school teams, which met in the state Class 5A quarterfinals in McAlester, both drive ramped-up GTOs and rarely utter a sentence unrelated to pussy or its many permutations.

"I think we getting close here," says Mike, eying the few joints of drill pipe left on the rack. "This bitch about to pop."

"Bout goddam time," Ike agrees. "We been givin her the shaft most of a week now."

They are blond, still thin and rangy, dancing around each other and swinging the huge orange tongs in place with never a bump or a stumble, chain flying within inches of Ike's head when Mike throws it singing around the pipe, imperturbable even wet-tripping in a windstorm.

"Not that I'm complaining," says Mike, centering the end of the next joint over the mousehole, "but a man gets tired of screwing the same damn patch of ground."

Tuck tries to remember to bend his knees as he digs. He dragged the new-bought coveralls around the yard a couple times and had Francine wash them without soap the night before he started, but still looked like a model from a Carhartt catalogue when he reported for work. Three days on the job and they look just like the other hands' gear, dirt and oil ground into the fibers, hanging wet against his skin. The driller hasn't let him any closer than the edge of the platform yet, so what he's learned about what goes on there is off shaky You-Tube videos, but he's starting to get a handle on circulation. He had no idea of the amount of energy involved with forcing fluid in and out of the hole, water thickened with clay and chemicals and who knows what to cool the drill bit and push the cuttings up the outside of the drill pipe and do more mysterious things while it's down there, a specialist named Gleason consulting data in the doghouse and sampling what flows out from the shaft to determine just what and how much of it to add, a range from weak tea to brownie mix pumped in from the tanks and something similar flushed out into the mud pits to sit till the cuttings have dropped out, the liquid waiting to be refortified and recycled through the system. New water comes in regularly on tanker trucks, and Tuck is clueless as to where it all comes from or where it goes to live when it's too fucked up to reuse anymore.

Somebody else's problem.

Tuck's problem is getting through the tour without wrenching any part of his body so bad he can't show up the next morning. He's tried going to bed extra early, lying there trying to discover a joint that doesn't ache, but even with decent sleep seven-to-seven is a long day, the sheer relentless noise of the whole operation like an assault on his soul.

Tuck stabs and lifts, stabs and lifts, not sure what the ditch he's digging from here to there is supposed to drain and it's clear any question he asks at this point will be considered a dumb one. "Pay attention, do what you're told, and stay the fuck out of the way," was the extent of his orientation from Hightower, and he is doing his best to follow that advice. Hell, if he was dropped into Francine's classroom and told to explain North Dakota history he'd be just as lost– every job takes some breaking in. But these oil-patch characters are like a cult, got their own language, their own sense of humor, know what to do before it needs doing. The pay, if he can stick for a month and be taken on as a full-time hand, is through the roof, and he's never seen guys hungrier for extra hours.

"Food sucks, nothing to fuck, nothing to do," one of the twin deckhands, Ike or Mike, immune to the charms of Yellow Earth, told him. "If you ain't asleep you might as well be getting paid."

Upshaw flushes the hole and shuts the pumps off at something over ten thousand feet and confers with Hightower in the doghouse, the bit cooling to await their decision. Time for lunch. Mike and Ike, Tulsa, Dizzy and the new guy sit on a stack of planking by the pre-mix tank, eating what they've brought. The Okies both have steak and cheese sandwiches prepped at the man camp where they're staying, and decide to fill the worm in on the big picture, passing the baton so quickly that Tuck loses track, if he ever really had it, of which is Ike and which is Mike.

"Your average toolpusher got a lot of decisions to make."

"There's *finesse* involved in the process."

"–cause out here stimulation happens *after* drilling– "

"–so you start with your entrance-hole diameter– "

"–which best be able to accommodate the gauge of your tubular– "

"–and then you'd better evaluate the downhole environment– "

"–particularly important if it's gonna be a deflocculation– "

"–and keep an open mind while you're still just spudding in, cause the deeper you go, the tighter it *gets*."

"–so you just keep screwing away at that bore hole– "

"–controlling your rate of penetration– "

"–unless you're off dumping into a Golden Throat hopper– "

"–which is a whole nother job description."

"Always sure to have your BOP– "

"–that's a blowout preventer– "

"–linked into the process. Don't wanna spritz off before it's time– "

"–well-site fluids sloppin all over the place– "

"–and then when you're coming out the hole– "

"–you're gonna *know*, see, whether this deal is gonna proceed to *pump*– "

"–or it's just another P and A– "

"–that's Plugged and Abandoned."

"Any questions?"

Tuck waits an appropriate beat, deadpan, then asks the difference between a mousehole and a rathole, and they begin to hope he makes it through the week without permanent bodily injury.

Hurry Upshaw comes out from the doghouse to holler that they'll stop drilling at this depth and send the diagnostics down, so the whole string has to come up.

"Here's where we find out," says Ike or Mike to the new guy, "whether we gonna fuck this bitch *side*ways or not."

Tripping out. Pipe is flying out of the hole, Ike and Mike twisting off three-joint stands that Dizzy, safety-strapped up in the crow's nest eighty feet from the rig floor, plucks from the elevators suspended from the top drive and tucks into the monkeyboard fingers, the new man guiding the bottom end, twelve thousand pounds of steel tightly racked into the stand as the string comes up, up, up, Diz leaning out from his belly-buster cable, jerking his head in rhythm to Anthrax blasting from his boombox hung from a derrick strut and loving it, top of the world, a real-life Spiderman pulling down thirty-five smackers an hour. Hurry is an artist with the draw-works and you can't hear him curse or yell up here, even without the music going, Mike and Ike are double-teaming the connections, and from the top you can see Tulsa over fixing a shale shaker and the north-south highway and two sorry-ass farmhouses and at least eight other rigs in various stages scattered around the horizon. The Bakken is rockin'.

The sky above and the mud below, thinks Dizzy. Rack em up and keep the fluids coming. Hurry Upshaw makes more money and gets to push the buttons and yank the levers, but drillers have to stick with the hole pretty much 24/7 and answer to the toolpusher and the Company and deal with flakes like himself who get off on the circus-act part of the job. Dizzy has only ridden the Geronimo cable down once, during a mandatory safety drill, but it was so much fun he's tempted to quit the derrick that way all the time. They hit a couple doglegs coming up, something shifted inside the hole that snags a joint, but nothing that doesn't hoist free. There is a kind of music to the procedure, a rhythm, and it's always a little bit sad to have to return to Earth. The top of the stack is only swaying a little bit in the wind today, no clouds in sight, and he can't think of a place he'd rather be. Down time is tough, though, nothing but scruffy deckhands with deep voices shuffling around you in the cafeterias and public rooms, the awkward calls to home, the generic high-plains-nothing of a town if you do bother to drive in. Girls waving their titties at him just make him lonelier, and you don't want to strap into that derrick climber still wrecked from the night before. But tripping out in decent weather is as good as it gets.

The stands stack up one by one and the sun dips, getting dark earlier now, just a few fingers above the horizon when the cable outfit arrives and starts unloading their gear. Tuck is running on fumes by the time the bottom hole assembly finally comes up, Mike and Ike pulling the drill bit and collar off the bottom of the last stand, barely space left for it in the rack. He teeters on his feet, not comprehending at first as Mike and Ike pass him to leave the platform, as Dizzy starts his descent from the crow's nest, that this tour is over. He's survived again. Other men clang up the metal stairs as he wanders toward them and he feels a sudden pang of jealousy.

"Welcome, gentlemen," shouts Hurry Upshaw to the arriving crew. "Do not fuck up my hole."

RUBY WISHES IT WASN'T in the Three Nations' office. Even the casino would have been better, and maybe more appropriate, given the way she feels about Skiles. But as many times as she's explained to the Chairman how important it is to keep reservation business and his new private venture absolutely separate, he insisted on the signing being on his home court.

"If he was bringing more cash to the table, I might feel different," Harleigh told her this morning with a wink. "But as it is, a little reminder that we're not exactly *equal* partners in this thing isn't a bad idea."

She's laid all the paperwork out on the desk, called Rick McAllen, who is a notary, in from the next room. Two new pens, one black ink, the other blue. The Chairman loves a ceremony, but thank God he hasn't insisted a photographer be there to immortalize the occasion.

"Articles of Organization, then Operating Agreement, then your Application for Name Registration," she says. "Three copies each."

The LLC is Skilldeer, and they've chosen ArrowFleet for a trade name. Nice moniker, and Harleigh has proudly showed her the logo. She at least got him to go the limited liability route instead of a straight partnership, convinced him that no, she couldn't be registered agent for the company, and they'd have to hire a third party off the rez. Tougher to get him to agree to personally pay for her hours on this, twice having to threaten to stand down as counsel for the Nations. "We need a *fire*wall here," she told him, "cause this has got conflict of interest written all over it."

Not that the Chairman hasn't thrown his own money into the tribal pot a few times when the Feds have been slow with payments, not that he hasn't finally appointed and hired good people to run the casino. It's just that he doesn't think white people have to put up with regulations too, that this is all some special form of harassment.

"Lookit all this, Brent," he says to Skiles, eying the stacks of forms. "Like they heard we got hoop dancers over here and want to see how many they can make us *jump* through."

Skiles is wearing what look like expensive workout clothes and is squeezing a tennis ball as if to crush it, constantly switching it from one hand to the other.

"They want that tax money, Chairman. Lord forbid we make a dollar and they don't get their thirty cents of it."

Harleigh won't have to deal with the S-corporation rules at tax time, and if something goes wrong, his ranch, or whatever you call his setup there, and other personal property can't be attached. It's all gone so fast she's only had time to make sure there really *is* such a person as Brent Skiles, who indeed had a service company in Texas and owns some trucks. She thought of asking Danny to get one of his county sheriff cohorts to do a background check, but it seemed a little aggressive. Just cause she doesn't like the guy–

Rick is just behind the new partners, crimping next to their signatures with his notary seal.

"Ought to work with one of these," says Skiles, wiggling the tennis ball. "Does wonders for your grip."

"His grip is just fine," says the Chairman. "All that practice pinching pennies."

Ricky is a CPA and did accounting for the Nations, stepping in twice a day to warn about overruns, before Harleigh shifted him over to Environmental.

There will be a few on the council to wrinkle their noses over this. Rick's mom, Teresa Crow's Ghost, for sure, Danny, maybe one of the others not sitting on a deposit. Most of the drivers for ArrowFleet will be enrolled members, of course, and they'll gas up on the reservation, saving a bit of sales tax. 'I preach entrepreneurship every damn day of the week,' the Chairman has told her, 'the least I can do is provide a good example.' And yes, the white companies out there wouldn't blink to cut the same corners. Business is business.

"These go to the secretary of state for processing," Ruby tells them. "But as soon as your DBA comes through you can at least start making bids."

Two of the companies drilling on reservation land have already promised to subcontract ArrowFleet for some of their hauling, and she'll have to ask one of the others to please hire someone else, Phil Enterlodge maybe, to keep up the pretense that there's competition. The Chairman will never withhold a permit because a driller won't book his drivers, she's sure of that, but Skiles makes the hair on the back of her neck stand up. She's never run into a wolf in the wild, even back home when she was a girl, but she imagines you get the same edgy feeling.

Harleigh signs his declaration of personal assets, turns to shake with his new partner. Skiles stuffs the tennis ball into the pocket of his track pants and pumps the Chairman's hand.

"ArrowFleet is on the *road!*" he crows. "Let's make history, buddy."

SUBJECT A, REAR QUADRANT

OB/D (ogling behavior, demonstrative)

Body parts employed: Torso, head, facial features, hands

On departure of acne-scarred but passably nubile teenage waitress, Subject tilts head sideways in exaggerated manner, eyes fixed on hindquarters of aforementioned overworked service person, attempting to bug them out in imitation of gawking cartoon wolf, lips forming the tight circle of a 'W' (as in 'Wowser!') while flexing both hands forward, fingers and thumb slightly curled as if to cup her callipygian wonders within them to administer a hearty squeeze. Enacted in conscious display for the benefit of Subject's cohorts.

Subject B, rear quadrant
  MG (moronic guffaw)
  Body parts employed: Lungs, diaphragm, glottis
  Reacting to cohort's gesture, Subject makes loud, plosive, braying vocalization ac-
  companied by expulsion of minute droplets of popular mass-produced hops beverage
  that spray well beyond subject grouping to next table, eliciting AS (annoyance stares)
  from several males.

Subject C, rear quadrant
  GF (genital fondling)
  Body parts employed: Left hand, package, facial features
  Also regarding barely legal hashhouse underling's posterior, Subject reaches below to
  briefly palpate entrousered penis and testicles, while narrowing eyes and pursing lips in a
  'wincing' expression, meant to indicate lustful appreciation rather than pain or discomfort.

Leia only eats at the diner if her spot is available, in the front left corner, back to the room but able to observe it in the mirror. To cut down on hardtail intrusions she always wears her UC Boulder sweatshirt with the hood up, as if the draft from people coming in the door is bothering her. She has not been hit on this much in her life, and considering the sudden male/female imbalance here and the blunt and primal nature of most approaches, it is not flattering.

Subject D, front right quadrant
  GC (gesturing with comestibles)
  Body parts employed: Hand, arm, vocal apparatus
  Subject, in between bites, continually waves uneaten portion of double bison burg-
  er, dripping copious gouts of house-special BBQ sauce, simultaneously chewing and
  vocalizing in an insistent monotone, never returning food item to rest on the plate it
  was delivered upon.

Subject E, front right quadrant
  N (nodding), C (cutting)
  Body parts employed: Head, neck, hands, wrists, fingers
  Subject nods head in continuous affirmative display, meanwhile manipulating im-
  paling and cutting utensils to divide cooked food item, possibly a 'chicken fried steak'
  (gravy makes specific identification impossible), into smaller and smaller sections.

It is imperative, of course, to distinguish behaviors from mere *states*, such as the mindless stupor the guy with the frighteningly large belly at the near end of the counter has lapsed into, staring slack-jawed into space over the remnants of his stuffed pork chop and smashed potatoes, exhausted from his shift perhaps, or merely rendered semi-comatose by the energy-sucking process of digestion. And when assembling an ethnogram it is important to avoid rushing to hypothesis without constant and ever more focused observation. Mental snapshots (or in this technologically enhanced age, video recordings) of a subject's activity, taken at five-minute intervals, must be compared to the field results of other researchers, must be placed within a broader context, before they may be interpreted as typical of a species. Just because the present customers appear to be a herd of belching, loudmouthed, nut-scratching yahoos (as they appeared to be yesterday and the day before and the day before) does not preclude the possibility that some unnatural setting or circumstance has exerted an undue effect, like caged bonobos at the zoo.

Leia picks at her Weight Watchers' Special, which involves cottage cheese and iceberg lettuce, and writes into the scan sample book at five-minute intervals, hoping the appearance of work and concentration will discourage any roughneck able to see beneath the hood in her reflection and ascertain that yes, she possesses human-like features and a vagina. If the hood comes down they always say something about her streaks, having to do with Cruella De Vil or various woodland animals and leading to they are really sexy and would you like to see my truck? It is illogical, perhaps, to wear your hair in a style not commonly seen locally if your purpose is to remain unnoticed, but perhaps it will eventually work like the coloration of the ladybug (*Coccinellidae*), whose black spots on shiny red carapace and vile taste mitigate against predation. Stay clear of the one with the yellow stripes, she imagines the verdict, she'll bite your head off.

But eating alone back in her room or in the rental car has its limits.

Subject F, front left quadrant
  OO (obscenity overload)
  Body parts employed: Wrist, right index finger, vocal apparatus
  Subject, close but only partially visible, spews a colorful and highly detailed vocal account of recent drill rig interactions using curse words as nouns ('As if I give a shit'), verbs ('trying to fuck me where it hurts'), adverbs ('he's got to be fucking kidding'), adjectives ('the cocksucking kelly drive'), what the Catholic clergy label ejaculations ('Holy fucking shit on a shingle!'), and, when euphoniously desirable, as an expletive infixation ('For-fucking-get about it'), accompanied by an insistent thrusting forward of the right hand index digit toward his cohort. An EPM (expletives per minute) score of twenty-three was registered, twenty-eight if euphemisms such as 'Hershey highway' and 'choking the monkey' are included.

Subject G, front left quadrant

RG (ruminant grazing)

Body parts employed: Hands, wrists, fingers, maxillary and mandibular musculature

Subject relentlessly chews mouthfuls of coleslaw and chicken fingers (anatomically improbable but ubiquitous on regional menus) with an expression of slight perplexity on his face, as if the over-masticated food might provoke a thought or even a response to his cohort's obscene screed.

Her room, in a private house formerly occupied by elderly cat-lovers, comes with kitchen and bathroom privileges, a parking spot out back, and a view of the now nonstop traffic on the main road through Yellow Earth. The owner insisted, before the boom exploded, on a one-year lease, which he is now trying to break– smaller rooms are now going for three times the rate. Solo field work is often a challenge, with difficulties of language and culture, inclement weather, local mistrust or even sabotage of long-term studies. But this has been a special kind of hell, what was meant to be a year of quiet observation turned into a kind of furtive survival test at the edge of a combat zone, a bait-and-switch no more expected than finding Bobby Fisher (a Nabib tiger snake and particular favorite of her boyfriend's) coiled in her underwear drawer back in Boulder.

Then He comes in.

Pretty much true to pattern, ten of two, heading straight to the counter. The height, the walk, the slightly haunted look, the casual but professional glance around the room.

Subject H (for Hunk)

LG (looking good)

Body parts employed: I can't get past the eyes.

Subject sits on counter stool and <u>*removes hat before speaking to waitress*</u> *(97 percent of other males present eating with lids still affixed, with the logos of college and professional sports teams, heavy equipment manufacturers, or beer brands most common on their crowns). Swivels to observe room after making order, as previously observed, wearing badge but without gun (more often termed 'pistol' or 'sidearm' by militaristic local hardtails).*

There is always plenty of display in the diner, but so far no overt aggression– punching, biting, clawing, assault with eating utensils– while she has been inside. Maybe he keeps the gun locked in his patrol car, the one she keeps a hopeful eye out for whenever she's on the road. The one she fantasizes will stop one day as she is watching the coterie, the Sheriff coming over to sit on the hood of her Ford Escape and get to know her.

It doesn't seem judgmental, his gaze, or censorious, just a mildly interested inventory of the players in the room, always crowded now with pre- and post-shift workers scarfing down their meals and leaving piles of crumpled cash behind, putting the waitresses through twenty questions and tipping big. Leia's cyberstalking has come up with only a name– Will Crowder– and so far no wife or children, just some mentions as arresting or investigating officer, some high school sports triumphs further back. He looks to be what she hopes is no more than ten or twelve years older than she is, broad at the shoulder, narrow at the hip, and surprisingly soft-spoken, at least the one time she got close enough to hear.

His eyes connect with hers in the mirror for a second, no more than that, then move on. He has a pair of sunglasses hung on his shirt pocket but doesn't wear them in here, hiding nothing.

The trick with an ethnogram is in dividing up what can be only a partial and possibly random record of behavior into a meaningful pattern, all in an attempt to *know* the focal organism, to understand how it will likely react in a given situation, to understand its passions and priorities. The most common downfall is, of course, projecting assumed or desired motives onto the individual, what Professor Blake called 'wishful narrative.' One must remain alert but detached, observe and record without seeking order or connection.

But he looks like he might be *nice.*

THE WIND OUTSIDE MAKES the aluminum sides of the data monitoring van boom and pop. One of the techs offers Harleigh a pair of earplugs.

"I'm used to it," he smiles, holding up a hand.

"Really, put them in," says the tech, who has his own already in place. "We haven't started yet."

It feels more like being in Mission Control for a shuttle launch than anything to do with drilling. Hardhats hanging on pegs on the wall while their owners, wearing communications headsets, sit at data screens droning information to the rig hands outside at the valves and connections, Randy Hardacre standing behind to orchestrate the whole deal. Harleigh's head nearly touches the ceiling as he crowds back into a spot where he hopes he won't be in the way.

"Pressure check," says Randy, and the men at the screens call out numbers for their pump groupings.

Harleigh has been watching the frack spread come together, unavoidable, as it lies between his house and the tribal office in New Center. It was fun to see the progress as the drilling rig was assembled, Harleigh invited to say a few words before they spudded in the first rez well, using the extra-wide bit to cut into the soft ground. The working of the drill string was pretty much what he'd seen in movies– roughnecks building stands of pipe then lowering them into the hole, cranes swinging more pipe around, no way to know if it was going a hundred feet down or two thousand. Then– it seemed like it happened during lunch one day– the rig was gone. Nothing much happened for a week, Harleigh seeing a coyote sniffing around the pad, and then the new armada arriving, first to widen the flat area around the hole, then the positioning of the tanks, and then the water trucks, a steady rumbling procession of them that backed up onto Route 23 from time to time.

Today the spread reminds Harleigh of the painting he has of bull bison standing shoulder to shoulder in a circle to defend their cows and calves from a pack of wolves, only these big beasts are all facing inward toward the well-head. Dozens of frack pumpers with only inches between them, clustered in a row and backed up to the rear of an identical group, hoses snaking between them. Chemical storage tanks, sand trucks, frack blenders, a phalanx of water tankers, the monitoring van sitting in the lee of some serious tonnage in case something blows loose when the pumpers throw down in unison. Driving up and seeing it he felt like there had to be a rocket somewhere, ready to be blasted off to Mars.

Randy Hardacre frowns at something he is watching on one of the screens.

"Okay, back off, everybody. Bring them down." He points to a readout. "We've got to swap this one out, Larry."

Larry gets talking with his people outside, and the other techs sit back to wait for the valve to be replaced. The geologist comes over to Harleigh. Harleigh has read all the literature, feels like he's got a pretty good handle on the process, but must look like he needs some reassuring.

"We've got a hell of a lot of protection between your aquifer and our operation here," says Randy. "Surface casing– that's steel pipe encased in cement–

then production casing inside of that, a couple different diameters with more cement around them."

"Kind of like a fella wearing three condoms."

Randy smiles. "And for the same reason. To prevent the migration of fluids."

"Don't want any of that. So when you pump the water down– "

"It's more like a kind of goo by the time we mix everything in to send it down. But yeah, we'll go through four, five million gallons of water just on this well."

"And when it comes back up?"

Harleigh has walked around the lined pit they dug for the drilling mud, wondering how long the sludge or whatever will sit there, whether birds will want to land on it or not.

"Well, we recycle it as much as possible. But eventually– ever work in a fast-food joint? You can only dip so many fries into that grease before it gets brown and funky, then you got to throw it out and start with a fresh batch."

"And what you throw away– "

"We don't *throw* anything, not since the mid-'80s. We'll produce something near a barrel of brine water for every barrel of oil we pull out of here. In Pennsylvania we used to ship it to Ohio, but unless our friends up here in Canada want it– "

"Not likely."

"It'll sit in the spoil pond here till we can truck it or pipe it to an injection well."

"Those Class II jobs that cause all the earthquakes."

Hardacre gives him a tight smile.

"Seismically not very likely here. You don't have the granite substrata where it can cause trouble."

Harleigh shrugs. "Folks keep asking me if something's going to blow up."

"Sorry, nothing we do is that dramatic."

Larry calls over to say they're ready for a new pressure check, and Hardacre returns to the row of computers.

Harleigh has gone over the injection sites he okayed on the rez with the EPA and the state people and Teresa Crow's Ghost's posse, with her son Rick right there, flipping the charts for him. Doesn't look like anything can go wrong if the Company can just get the stuff there without any spills, but you'd think the reservation ground was Teresa's backside and anything you put on it or poked into it capable of making her jump. None of the founding spirits– First Coyote or Lone Man or Woman-Who-Never-Dies– bothered to make any electrical power or diesel fuel, but people act like it just magically exists for them to use. The wind, okay, that was set up back in the First Times, but you still got to throw up a row of those giant pinwheel things and run a lot of cable to get anything out of it.

"Let's bring the pressure up," says Hardacre to his techs, "nice and easy."

A noise that is not the prairie wind starts to build then, and Harleigh pushes the rubber plugs into his ears. It grows and grows till it's like the world's biggest helicopter has landed on the roof, cranking its rotors and shaking the planet. Randy bends down, pointing to readouts on the various screens, talking close to the ears of the technicians. Then the noise begins to back off, retreating to a constant but bearable level.

"That's it?" Harleigh says, aware that he is nearly shouting. Hardacre smiles.

"First step. We just cracked that section, now we send in the proppant– we're using sand on this job, but sometimes it's little pieces of ceramic."

"The cracks are only that big?"

"Yeah, but there's a huge network of them by now. We go back along our horizontal drill shaft, close off a section, blow holes in the pipe for the frack gel to go out and the oil to come back in, working our way back to the vertical hole. The smaller the area we're hitting, the more pressure we can put on it."

The racket is building up again, and Randy mimes to Harleigh to cover his ears with his hands. The lady at the clinic in Bismarck who tested his ears said hearing loss at his age was mostly due to shooting guns, listening to rock music, and being around loud machinery. Well now I got all three he thinks as he presses his palms to his ears. He has a picture in his head of the fracturing gel racing down the vertical pipe like a giant fist in an old *Popeye* cartoon, making a quick undercut loop when it hits the angled tubing and speeds horizontally into WHAM! a block of black shale that shatters like ice under a sledgehammer. And then starts to bleed, oily black blood seeping through every spidery crack until it fills the pipe and starts to rise toward the surface. He'll ask the Company if they have a cartoon like that he could show to the schoolkids and the worrywarts, one that is clear about just how far under the surface, how far beneath any of their USDW– underground sources of drinking water– the whole operation is.

Granpaw Pete used to tell the creation story about how the First People lived underground and sent somebody up top to take a peek and see how nice it was, but only half of them made the choice to come up and live on top– 'so remember you got plenty of kin percolating beneath your feet.' Pete was one of the Storytellers and always had a posse of anthropology students following him around with tape recorders. He said he was at the very last *okipa* ceremony, remembering torchlight in a big earth lodge and men hanging from cords wedged behind their chest muscles. Or maybe he'd just heard about it. He had a way of looking through you that could give you goosebumps, and was said to have dreamed the flooding of the good land thirty years before the Army Corps of Engineers made it happen.

There is a moaning outside, a wail louder and mournfuller than any he's ever heard the mighty prairie wind give out. It's the pumper turbines all going full tilt at once, thinks Harleigh.

Or it's Granpaw Pete.

"IT'S NOT LIKE I won the lottery, dude," says Brent. "It *is* a fucking lottery. There's just over four hundred elk licenses this year and like twelve thousand guys applying, plus if you've struck out before, your name shows up more times– the more years you signed up and whiffed, the better your chances."

"But you nail it on your first try." Wayne Lee drives the Camaro like he always does, like it's a fucking stock car race.

"Not only that, I got an 'any elk' tag. Two-thirds of the guys who scored have to whack something without antlers."

There's a light rain and some wind, typical funky Dakota weather, but the forecast has it clearing up. Wayne Lee already has the orange vest over his camo outfit.

"So this Okie from Muskogee– "

"He's from Drumright, west of Tulsa, and he's looking to stick a dozen wells on the rez."

"And you want the service contract."

"At the least," says Brent. It's been a bitch setting this all up, feelers out to ranchers in the E 2 unit, non-resident permits for Mutt Miller just in case they run into a game warden with a hard-on, salting the mine far enough ahead of time. He needs Wayne Lee for a buffer, make it all seem like guys just out having fun. "What I want is for Mutt to go away convinced that nothing happens unless I put in the word with Killdeer."

"So he depends on you."

"So he sweetens the pot a little. Maybe puts me in for a percentage of one or two of the wells."

"He'd go for that?"

"Hey, when I told him I got an elk tag he was the one who hinted he'd like to be the trigger man."

"Not a stranger to a little larceny."

"More of an old-fashioned wildcatter than a corporate type. You'll like him."

Mutt Miller is parked by the post office across from the Catholic church in Grassy Butte, pretty much all there is to the town. Wayne Lee swings in and honks lightly, pausing a moment for Mutt to get back into his crystal red Caddy DTS and follow them to the ranch.

"Give the guy a break," Brent says to Wayne Lee. "Keep it under eighty."

"My only problem with this state is not enough *curves.*" Wayne Lee glances at the speedometer, probably for the second time in his life. "That and the weather and the food and that there's nothing to do and not enough women."

"You ever been to Oklahoma?"

"Arrested in Okie City for a bar fight."

"Maybe keep that one under your hat."

They swing over and up past Medicine Hole, then hook left onto Gap Road. The rain stops, and by the time they pull off by the east gate into Jesse Gilmore's place there's a bit of early-morning sun peeking through the clouds.

Mutt looks like a catalog ad, wearing Bone Collector camos new-bought from Scheel's in Bismarck, silver hair curling out from under an Oklahoma Thunder gimme cap. He looks like some actor Brent can't remember the name of, played a lot of generals.

"Fellas."

"Looks like a good day for it, Mutt. This is my buddy, Wayne Lee."

The men shake hands and Mutt pops his trunk open with the remote on his key ring.

"What you pack for me, Brent?"

"Remington 700 with a Leupold variable scope," says Brent, lifting the case out of the bed of the pickup. "Shoots a thirty-ought-six."

"So I'll be good for what distance?"

"It's a tack-driver from way out, but I wouldn't try anything past four hundred yards. Tracking wounded elk is an acquired taste."

"That you never acquired."

"Exactly." Growing up, Brent always had the Marines in the back of his mind, but his second state jail felony nixed that option before he got properly motivated to sign up. He's read the Corps training manuals though, put himself through

an equivalent to Basic without the top sergeant growling in his ear, and feels like
he could do pretty well anywhere you dropped him on the globe with a can-
teen, decent rifle, and K-bar knife. Mutt, on the other hand, brags about shooting
wolves from a helicopter up in Alaska.

"Pull your tailgate, down, Wayne Lee," the old boy says, "I need to show you
fellas something."

It is a muzzleloader, a Knight Mountaineer, that he lays out with great reverence.

"Damn," says Wayne Lee, "we're heading out with Jeremiah Johnson!"

"He used an old Hawken, and this here's an inline job." Mutt spreads all the
loading gear out on a blanket. "I'd like to do it traditional, flintlock or cap-and-
ball, but those old grizzly hunters had too many misfires."

"Inline or not, we'll have to get awful close to put a bull elk on the ground with
black powder," says Brent, as if getting close will be a problem.

"That's the sport of it," says Mutt, tamping powder down the barrel with the
rod. "It's all about the stalking."

He pushes the bullet into a sabot and rams it down, makes sure the safety is
screwed out. The cap will go in at the last moment, so you can carry it loaded.
Mutt pulls some Saran Wrap over the muzzle and fastens it down with a rubber
band. "In case it rains again."

"Keep your powder dry," says Wayne Lee, who has never hunted in his life.

"Keep your powder dry and your nose to the wind," sings Mutt.

The idea is for Brent to carry the center-fire rifle and Mutt his muzzleloader,
pretending that he and Wayne are only along with Brent as spotters. They both
hang binoculars over their necks while Brent unlocks the gate and pulls it open.

"Gentlemen," he says, "let's go harvest a monster."

"Harvest, hell." Mutt carries the Knight without a sling. "I'monna *kill* the sumbitch."

Jesse Gilmore has provided Brent with a map of the property, a hundred twenty
acres of it okayed for hunt-through. Brent has planned for a bit of hill and dale
that will bring them to lunchtime before he heads straight to the spot where the
animals are supposed to be hanging. He's got dinner reservations at the hotel in
Yellow Earth and does enough cross-country in his workout.

"Rancher says we'll need to go in a ways before there's likely to be any action,
so it won't be silent running right yet."

The game people schedule a couple informational meetings for tag winners, public invited, and he met Jesse there, bearded dude with a help-I'm-drowning look in his eye. The spread belongs to his parents, who are in Florida for the winter, and it turns out he got paranoid about flyovers while doing prescription drugs one night and burnt down his own patch of home-grown and quite a bit of innocent ground cover while he was at it. Happy, then, to take product rather than cash for the whole setup.

"You try for a tag too, young man?" Mutt asks Wayne Lee.

"No sir. Only way I'd ever get an elk is to chase one over a cliff on my dirt bike."

"Not very sporting."

"Try it some time. There's never a good high cliff around when you need one."

"You work with Brent?"

Wayne Lee nods. "Dispatch vehicles, fill in as a driver when needed."

"You look like you're in good shape. Rig workers make a lot more than drivers."

"Skating up on that platform in a seventy-mile-an-hour gale with a half-dozen pieces of equipment that can knock your brains out swinging around."

The oilman smiles. "It can get a little hairy, now and then. That's the fun of it. I done some roughnecking when I was your age."

"And still got all your arms and legs."

"Been electrocuted twice, which I don't recommend, but other than that it was an excellent learning experience."

They come over a rise and see a stand of trees ahead, a creek running behind them. Jesse warned that there'd be some beef cattle wandering around, not cold enough yet for them all to be gathered at the pens, and so far a couple rabbits and a pheasant have flushed out ahead of them. It all looks pretty much the same in every direction, flattish and yellow-brown, and Brent understands why Jesse might want to alter his consciousness on a regular basis. He said he'd been married and living in Rapid, but that had turned into a real disaster and he needed a little porch time to get his head together. Weed smokers always have a plan– the fuzzier the better.

"Brent asked the chief about hunting on his reservation," says Wayne Lee, opening his end of the pitch. "But they only get two tags a season. Can you imagine that? All those Indians– Native Americans, whatever– and only two of them allowed to bag an elk."

"*Wapiti*," says Mutt, putting the accent on the first syllable. "The proper name is wapiti, from the Shawnee word for 'white butt.'"

"And you don't have em in Oklahoma."

"We're lousy with elk. Indians too."

"No shit. I thought you'd just have a lot of jackrabbits, like Texas."

"We even got a couple mountains, you look hard enough." Mutt calls up to Brent, who is playing the pathfinder today. "You ask the chief about that thing I mentioned?"

"He said it's under consideration."

"A moody bunch, those redskins," says Wayne Lee, trying to help out. "But Brent plays the chief like a violin."

"I'm a quarter Cherokee myself."

Wayne Lee stops to look Mutt over. "Yeah? Which quarter?"

Mutt laughs. The great thing about Wayne Lee is that he seems like more of a lightweight than he really is. At least when he's straight.

"The thing with Killdeer is he doesn't like to be pushed," says Brent. "You can bring him around, but it takes some finessing."

"My outfit's got a whole pile of finesse sitting in the bank."

Brent's turn to laugh. He's right about this guy– not afraid to push the envelope here and there.

"The thing about elected officials," he says, "whether you're talking Washington DC or the Three Nations, is they always got to have denia*bi*lity. So maybe it's a favor that gets done for a third party who the official owes for something else, and the chain of evidence is impossible to establish."

"You been watching cop shows."

"I been working at the edge of oil and gas for a number of years. Seen how laws get passed, how other laws get enforced selectively."

"I'm sure we're gonna be able to work something out."

Which means Mutt has talked as much business as he wants to for the day.

"What's the biggest thing you ever put down?" asks Wayne Lee, picking up the vibe.

"Brahma bull," says Mutt. "Must of gone two thousand pounds easy."

"He got a disease or what?"

"Broken leg. A little rodeo at Guthrie, I was buddies with the vet, and he give me the honors. Got a thick skull, your brahma, so I put one through his eye."

"How was the rider?"

Mutt considers as he strolls with the muzzleloader held low. "Well– we didn't have to *shoot* him."

Mutt, it turns out, is not in terrific stalking shape, so Brent calls lunch a half hour earlier than he planned. The trick to the white hunter thing is to give the client the feel of a chase even if the trophy is a cripple that never wanders from the same half-acre patch of terrain. He's stopped several times in good downwind positions to have them glass the surroundings, started to whisper and signal instead of talking out loud. They sit on a shelf of rock on top of a middling ridge, the sun countering the nip of the wind, and eat the sandwiches Wayne Lee bought at the Supervalu in Watford City. Mutt drinks two beers and takes his boots off.

"Haven't had time to break these in," he says. "Left all my usual gear back home."

"I lived in Colorado, I used to break in new boots for other people. Had my flyer on the info wall at REI."

Mutt looks at Wayne Lee's feet. "What are you– ?"

"An eleven. But I could go a size smaller or two bigger, just pull on more pairs of socks."

"Pay worth the blisters?"

"Not bad, considering you just go about whatever you were up to anyway. And it was easier on the nerves than my previous employment."

"Which was– ?"

"Pharmaceutical escort service."

"He means a drug mule," says Brent.

"I had a regular truck run going from McAllen to Monterrey and back. Took on some extra cargo."

"He was young and stupid," Brent interjects, not wanting Wayne Lee to get bragging on their shared history. "Now he's just stupid."

"The thing is, I was never uptight crossing the border. But making the pickup and paying off– damn. Lots of crazy *pistoleros* down there, looking for an easy score. You ever been?"

"Got enough Mexicans back home. Seems like everywhere there used to be a Chinese restaurant now it's Burritoville. Stuff don't agree with me like the chop suey did."

"Too spicy?"

"Binds me up. Alla that cheese."

"They go a lot lighter on the cheese south of the border."

"I'll trust your word on that."

Mutt looks all around, nothing moving but weeds in the wind. "It ain't pretty," he says, "but there sure is a *lot* of it."

"You should check out Teddy Roosevelt Park while you're up here," says Brent. "Got some variety to the landscape."

"But no hunting."

"Oh, there's a load of elk get shot over there, just not by hunters. The staff and a few volunteers culled a couple hundred out of the herd, a lot of them females and juveniles, just a couple weeks ago. Ecological balance or some shit like that."

"Park rangers shooting wapiti."

"They get used to tourists so they're not people-shy. You can walk up and shoot most of them from a couple yards away."

"Execution style."

"I guess the meat goes to charities, once its been checked for the wasting disease."

"Probably the healthiest thing those people eat all year," says Mutt. "I saw a fella at the Cenex in Tioga the other day, Native guy, trade his food stamps in for Pringles and Little Debbie Donut Sticks."

"The white man killed their buffalo," says Wayne Lee, his face solemn, "but at least he brought them reconstituted potato flakes."

Mutt goes to take a leak then, and Brent scoots closer to strategize.

"Should be only fifteen, twenty minutes from here," he says, keeping his voice low. "I got no idea if this guy can shoot or he expects to take the elk out with his breath, so be ready for anything. If you see the herd with your glass give me the nod so I can be the first to spot it."

"Brent Skiles, master of the bush."

"That's the idea. He wants to negotiate with the game, he's got to go through me."

Mutt comes back then, face a little red from the beer or the pissing, and picks up the Knight.

"Onward, gentlemen," he announces. "I hear the call of the wild."

Technically it's against NDGF rules to provision or bait anything you're hunting, but they cut a lot of slack to private property owners. Jesse says he's been laying out elk candy for two weeks, and sure enough, there's a small herd in front of the gappy thicket of trees right where he made the X on the map.

Brent comes to a sudden halt, claiming to have a 'feeling' before he lays out on his belly with the field glasses to his eyes. Mutt is already putting the cap into the muzzleloader, screwing the safety to off, as if they're only seconds away from the moment of truth.

"Check em out," Brent whispers, handing the binoculars over. He exchanges a look with Wayne Lee while Mutt scans the herd.

"I see three bulls," says Mutt, louder than he probably should. "Awful nice racks on them."

"There's a six-by-six looks to be in charge. That's who we want to go for."

Mutt brings the binoculars down. "You bring a caller?"

"Nope, but Wayne Lee does a pretty good cow-in-estrus."

Mutt grins.

"Bugling won't do us much good when they're on their feed like that. We'll just keep low and work our way closer."

Wayne Lee carries the muzzleloader, giving Mutt both hands to steady himself with, managing to get his head low while his butt remains stuck up in the air. They ease from clumps of bunchgrass to a sprouting of chokecherry bushes, laying down to glass the spot and be sure the herd hasn't moved. Mutt has begun to sweat and breathe hard, and Brent wonders if his heart is okay. They're two football fields away when the cover gives out, nothing a chipmunk could hide behind left between them and the browsing animals. Wayne Lee looks like he's gotten excited about the hunt, golden eyes big and shiny, always up for anything that feels like you shouldn't be doing it. The whispering helps.

"We can try to move around to the left and risk spooking them," Brent whispers, "to get you a shot with the Knight. Or we can stay back here and hit him with the Remington."

The muzzleloader has iron sights on it, Daniel Boone style, and Brent doubts Mutt can hit anything past fifty yards. Mutt adjusts his binoculars, takes another gander.

"It looks awful far away. Even for the Remington."

All hat and no cattle, as his cellmate in the Hightower Unit used to say. Brent guesses that Mutt is more exhausted than nervous, that it's been a long, long while since he's had to climb up on a drilling platform.

"Tell you what," he says. "See that mess of chokecherry over there? High enough for you to get up on one knee for a good shot. We'll move over there and dig in while Wayne Lee works around to the other side of those woods, make a little noise– just a little– and see if he can goose that herd a little closer to us."

"You gonna be shooting in my direction?" Wayne Lee is fearless to the point of stupidity, but this is not his world.

"Find yourself a nice thick hunk of elm and stay behind it."

Wayne Lee moves off first, and Brent is relieved to see he's taken the muzzleloader with him, not just to keep it from getting underfoot but because Mutt packed enough black powder in it to re-sink the *Maine* and he doesn't want to be anywhere near when it goes off. He carries the Remington and Mutt follows him, on hands and knees, to the edge of the little cluster of chokecherry, growing about four feet high but insubstantial enough to see through easily.

"Get the feel of this baby," Brent says, making sure the safety is on and giving the Remington to Mutt. Mutt brings it up, points it at the herd, squints through the sight.

"My guy is blocked by a couple of the young skinheads."

"If Wayne Lee can flush them, he'll come clear."

"He's sure *tall*er than the other sumbitches."

The big bull is raking his antlers against the bark of a tree, the sound coming, faintly, after the sight of it, like dialogue in a dubbed kung fu movie. Mutt is breathing shallow and fast through his mouth, and Brent wonders what he's killed besides a crippled rodeo bull at point-blank range.

"The Plains Indians," he says, hoping to calm the man, "would bury themselves in whatever the ground cover was and wait from sunup till sundown for their game, if that's what it took."

Mutt's shoulders relax a little. Better if he shoots and misses than if he hits it where it can't kill. Days getting short this time of year, tracking will be shit pretty soon.

"Must have had their cell phones on vibrate."

Still in a good mood. Tranquilizers in the elk bait, thinks Brent, that's what we needed here.

Mutt, waiting comfortably on one knee, has just laid the rifle carefully on the ground beside him when there is a distant explosion and the herd scatters. They are in ten different places, all of them out of range if not out of sight, by the time Brent gets the field glasses up.

"What the fuck?"

Then Wayne Lee steps out from the woods and waves his hat. Not in triumph.

It is another huge bull, tongue out, head skewed sideways with its antlers jammed against the bole of a tree, hair at the base of its neck column slick with blood.

"I was just coming in here," says Wayne Lee, his voice still a little shaky, "and I run right into it. Like, it could have gored me with those prongs."

"You were walking with your finger on the trigger." Brent has the Remington in hand now, making sure Mutt doesn't shoot his idiot friend with it.

"I don't think so."

"Then how did it get there?"

Wayne Lee looks like he's trying to recreate the moment in his head. "Self-defense?"

"I shouldn't have left the safety off," says Mutt. It is a statement, not an apology.

Brent tears the appropriate month and day from the tag provided with his license and fixes it to an antler with the rubber band holding the remnants of blasted Saran Wrap at the tip of the muzzleloader. He thinks he can see black powder burns on the huge animal's chest. Make a note not to do any armed bank robberies with Wayne Lee Hickey.

"There's still pretty much light– you think those other ones went far away?" Wayne Lee knows he has fucked the pooch six ways from Sunday and is wearing his best innocent-little-boy look.

"You know why they call it a once-in-a-lifetime license?"

"Oh. Right."

"It doesn't refer to the *elk's* lifetime," adds Mutt, who has squatted down to look in the glazed eye, tilting his head this way and that like he's searching for his reflection.

"What do we do now?" Wayne Lee staring at the dead bull with something like awe. Like he might have to bury it.

"Mutt and I," says Brent, standing up, "are going to walk the ten minutes to the ranch house and have a drink or three. While you," and here he unsheathes his Outdoor Edge skinner and hands it to Wayne Lee, "are going to stay here with the kill."

Wayne Lee looks at the knife in his hand. "You want me to, like, gut it or something?"

"Just sit here with it. If a pack of coyotes or a bear shows up, use that to cut your throat."

MOST OF THE OILFIELD songs are country, which don't do a thing for your dick. Even when the lyrics are racy, it feels like that top button is always snapped, like it hurts to have those words come out of the same mouth that honors God and Mama and the Red, White, and Blue. Even rockabilly, which has some backbeat to it, doesn't work on the pole. And most of these young ones out on the rigs now are metalheads anyway– if sound was drugs they'd be blasting meth into their ears all day long.

She's hot, can't stop, up on stage doing shots

Theory of a Deadman on the attack, Jewelle goes up and down the chrome like a squirrel in heat, what Unique calls the aerobic part of her act, as the mud men and valve jockeys and tool pushers up at the rack whoop and wave paper money in the air.

Grab her ass, actin tough
Mess with her, she'll fuck you up

The trickiest thing about the outfit was figuring out how to keep the hard-hat from falling off when you're hanging upside down. She's simplified the routine over the years, though guys down from Wasilla say the marital aids on the tool belt are still a legend. Jewelle leaps into a front hook spin, then slides down, down, down into a wide-leg squat that becomes a split, showing them almost everything.

You know what she is, no doubt about it
She's a bad bad girlfriend

She slow-motion dives onto the floor now, dragging her crotch like it's on fire and she has to rub out the flames and it hurts so good. They have the nipple law here in North Dakota, meaning only the little bump itself has to stay hidden. Jewelle uses a pair of butterfly bandages, careful to make an X and not a cross, on each, and they come off easy with a little baby oil and don't cause a rash. She leaves the one-dollar offerings lying for now and crawls forward for titty tips– the regulars know to flash the denominations so she can see them before she'll go squeezing anything between her boobies. There are so many men in the club these days it's gotten pretty competitive, and she'll panther-slink right on past a line of fivers to trap a twenty or a fifty. There hasn't been any cheating yet, like that awful month back in Anchorage when the good three-color printers hit town and guys thought it was funny to stuff counterfeit bills in your panties.

Jewelle loves the feeling of the bass line throbbing up through the boards when she slithers across the stage, easing her into the Zone that makes the whole deal bearable, at least for her twenty minutes out front. The strobe lights are good too, with what's staring up at you never something you want to take a long, cold look at, and the free-form nature of her pole routine, songs in different tempos– never putting her couple dozen moves together in exactly the same way– keeps it in the moment instead of seeming canned. Until it's time to collect the tips she doesn't really focus her eyes at all, trying for what Mr. Tanaka at the dojo calls *mushin,* willing the drillers and Vic and Unique and Oxana and Yellow Earth and all the huge, gouging machines out there on the high prairie away and just becoming the music and the movement. Leaving the state of North Dakota for the state of No Mind.

But the final crawl is prelude to the next hour's action and you have to pay attention. Tuck's sweet, dopey, just-shaven face is the last thing Jewelle sees as her music fades, pushing her elbows in to hold her breasts around his fingers for an extra long moment and giving him The Look before backing away with the twenty on board. Tuck is the gentleman in mind when Vic added 'A Gentlemen's Club' on the awning and spiffed up the VIP Room, promising the kind of hassle-to-profit ratio you're always hoping for whether you date or keep it all in the club.

Jewelle casually sweeps up her singles, smiling and greeting some of the rack rabbits as Eddie comes up on the sound system, asking for the boys to show her a little more love. Whoops, applause, some more grudging Washingtons thrown in her path. DJs are a new wrinkle Vic has added since the Bakken patch started to really percolate, replacing the need to slip your own CD in the player behind the bar and hustle to beat your music to the stage. But now Eddie can cross-fade songs, cutting them short when there are lots of laps waiting for a workout, and any guy who brings a stopwatch into a club will have his ticket punched. Jewelle dumps the tips, loose and uncounted, into her lunchbox, snaps it shut and pushes into her floor shoes. Sultana is on now, one of the new girls, who is paying Vic well over a hundred a night just to work his spot and still kicking a piece of her lap dance revenue back into the staff pool. No complaints though, not with the place running twenty-four hours a day, six days a week, with a seemingly inexhaustible flow of oil workers dying to spill their pay for a little gab and grind.

He usually hangs back for a while, Tuck, while she does two or three table dances, monitoring the action from a distance but not in a creepy way. Some guys just like to watch, okay for the house with cover charge and drinks, but nobody a girl should waste her time on. Tuck just takes his time.

"I'm all yours, darling," says a hefty guy with a walrus mustache, spreading his arms out wide. Jewelle gives him The Smile.

"What's your name, handsome?"

"Chester."

"I've had my eye on you, Chester. Grab the loops and we'll get it on."

Vic has put these handles that come off of health club machines onto all the chairs, something for the boys to hold onto while their zippers are getting polished, and keeping the really little ones from sliding out from under you.

Sultana's music is way too techno to keep up with, so Jewelle leaves out the dance part of the deal and just begins to writhe, snakelike, rubbing her tits and belly against his front fat till his damn Bucking Bronco belt buckle pops out from his gut roll and she has to retreat, twisting around to ride em cowboy with her cheeks a while before finishing with the butt shiver she learned from Marvelous Marvella in Reno. Sultana's songs top out around two and a half minutes, so even though Chester gives her a swat on the backside as she hops off, it's a good quick twenty. She passes on a table of gesturing guys who've just climbed off the deck without changing, like she's going to park her bare bottom on their sweat, dirt, and oil, and instead throws an arm from behind around the neck of a guy in geek glasses, who looks like he reads seismic charts all day, sitting with another guy who could be his twin. She pushes her bumpers up so one rests on each of his shoulders and whispers hot into his ear.

"Give a girl a ride?"

"How much is it?"

He's pushed his chair out from the table to make room, so she's been invited.

"Twenty for a song."

"With this stuff I can't tell where one stops and the next starts."

She swings around and mounts him, sliding her fingers gently down his arms and placing his hands on the seat loops. "Neither can I, honey. I'll just go till you make me tingle."

She starts moving and before she can ask the ride his name, his twin, bending his head sideways to get a better view, pipes up.

"I had one in Houston," he says, "biggest rack you ever seen. I think they were real, too. Some kind of Mexican."

"This one's nice," says her guy.

Sometimes it's shyness, sometimes they're just rude, but fine, you don't have to come up with any patter.

"Andy says that in Toronto you can touch them wherever you want."

"For like, the same amount?"

"Yeah, but it's– you know– Canadian money."

Jewelle wriggles close and hits his lenses with hot breath, steaming them up.

"I can't see."

"Yeah, but do you *feel* this, baby?"

"And then in Mexico," the twin continues, "like in TJ? They're all for sale."

"Andy worked in Mexico?"

"Nah, just a weekend trip. If I had my choice, I'd go to Thailand."

"No tits to speak of, those girls."

"But they know how to treat a man. I had one of those massages once, like just rubbing the muscles without any extras, and it got me so hard I nearly lifted off the table."

"A cultural thing. Like trained to be subservient."

"Yeah. I had one in Oklahoma once, from somewhere else over there, Southeast Asia, said she came off one out of every three dances."

"All night long?"

"That's what she told me. She had those nipple piercings– kinda scary– and tattoos everywhere."

"You don't have any tats," says her guy, pushing his crotch up.

"I'm an ink virgin," she says leaning back. There's talk of building a sport complex here in Yellow Earth but for now she has to do her ab crunches in the tiny living room of the rental house, with Unique and Misty stepping over her to get to the kitchenette. Jewelle got here early enough in the boom to snag a motel room, but then one of the maids got a look at her work gear and ratted to the management, some kind of Christians, and they put her out. Like suitcases crammed with her stuff and out in the *street*. The house is expensive and too small for the three of them but you can park behind it so guys who scope out your car have a harder time stalking.

She braces her hands on his shoulders and does a belly-dancer roll. "Plus the drawings are so beautiful these days, I could never make my mind up."

She's the only dancer here who doesn't have at least a tramp stamp or a little something on the ankle. She went overboard on her first implant and has downsized since then, wincing in sympathy every time Unique lets her DDs spill out, what the criminal who owned the first club she ever worked in used to call 'sweater meat.' That shit catches up with you, healthwise, and right now only her knees are a problem. Somewhere else she might go for a skateboarder theme and work some kneepads into the act, but guys here can't get enough of the oil worker stuff. "*Here's a gal who's set off more gushers than ExxonMobil–* " Eddie shouts for the intro, and they holler and stamp their feet. "*Got to push a lot of pipe to make Miss Jewelle pay off!*"

"I hear they just got a new batch next door," says the twin, and Jewelle decides the song is over, leaning close to thank her guy and pluck a twenty from the wad in his shirt pocket. Another girl might have had something smart to say, but snappy comebacks to clueless guys never make you anything extra. Tuck is waiting for her.

"Miss Jewelle," he always says, obviously liking the sound of it, "you think I could tempt you into the other room?"

She takes his arm, leans up against him. "Aw, baby, I thought you'd never ask."

There's an art to bringing a good payer like Tuck along. It's all fantasy, of course, even in hard-core porn you've got your space vixens and horny genies and love-potion plots, but in the VIP Room the fantasy is that it's *real*, that only state laws, cruel fate, and a wide-awake bouncer are preventing your perfect union.

Tuck shells out the entry fee and leads her through the beaded curtain, holding her hand, then Scorch, buzzed from the floor, opens the soundproof door. It was a storage room for liquor when Jewelle first hit town, but now it's another little world, low lights, slower, softer music and plushy chairs with plenty of room to maneuver. Jewelle is one of the girls who will come back here during the few slack times to douse the upholstery with anti-bacterial spray, and Vic will throw the black light on a couple times a night to check for suspicious stains. Lady Pamela, who roomed at the house till her tricks started showing up there, bragged about pushing the envelope when Otto was on duty, snoozing, but she's over at Teasers now, and Vic has switched from red pleather to black velour on their work platforms.

"I've missed you," says Jewelle. Tuck is up to twice a week already, but it's Wednesday and she's wriggled on so many clients between visits it seems like a long time.

"Me too," he says, sitting on the chair furthest from Scorch's throne. The other love seat is unoccupied, which Jewelle prefers. Some of the girls think it's a contest, outmoaning you and shooting looks to your client, and the illusion of privacy just gets harder to maintain.

Beyoncé's "Naughty Girl" is playing as she climbs aboard, Tuck wearing some kind of loose jersey pants he must have bought online because they sure don't sell them next to the Iron Boy rack in Yellow Earth. The client is learning– save her butt some wear and tear and get himself a closer rub. Amazing how many of these guys, titty bar veterans all, still come in with their Levis and trucker's caps and wonder why they're not feeling the magic.

Jewelle starts to move, slow and easy, and her bottom is telling her this boy isn't wearing underwear.

"You happy to see me?"

He smiles. "Always and forever."

"Rough week so far?"

"I seem to be getting the hang of it. Only got chewed out three times today."

"Those rigs are noisy," she says, slowly swinging her head to brush her hair across his chest and throat. "People have to yell to be heard."

"They haven't fired me yet."

Tuck is a local who's caught on with a drilling crew, dumping big sacks of different stuff into the mix they send down the pipe, and wants to be accepted by the old hands. She's never asked, but he feels married, and she hopes he leaves his ring in a good safe place.

"You're too cute to fire."

She pushes up high enough to let the side of her bare breast slip along his shaved cheek, almost accidentally. These long VIP sessions you have to deal it out slow, build some tension. Uncle Marvin, the only thing she ever knew to call him, back in Anchorage, used to do a running commentary on the state of his erection, with a nonstop flow of faster-slower, lighter-harder, that's it, that's it, no, over to the left a bit– but Uncle Marvin was good for a cool twenty thousand a year if you were "his girl."

"Aw, that feels nice."

"Feels nice for me too, baby."

The track switches to Nine Inch Nails' "Closer," which a lot of the younger girls like. Jewelle turns so her face is down by his knees, just moving her ass in front of his face for a bit. He's hard already, probably got a rubber rolled on in the men's room. What's that Boy Scout motto– Be Prepared? If he is married, his wife probably still does the laundry.

He is more than a bit of a Boy Scout, Tuck, waiting out in front to walk her to her car when her shift was over– *you know, just to be sure you're safe*– till she told him it was absolutely forbidden and he might get her fired.

Jewelle twists around, shoulders on his knees, her legs over his shoulders, and rubs her bottom up and down his chest. He's taking deep breaths now.

"You talk to Jasmine over the weekend?"

It takes her a beat too long to remember that Jasmine is the daughter she's told him she's supporting, back with grandma in a FEMA trailer in Ketchikan. Some of them want to be gallant, to help save you from ruin.

"There was something messed up with the Skype," she says. "I could hear her but I couldn't see her."

"That's tough."

She tries to remember what grade she said Jasmine is in now. It's either Jasmine or Jocelyn, and she's grown over the years, must be nearly out of junior high, since part of the story is getting pregnant when she was fifteen.

Which she did, but that's real life.

"You must be saving some good money, working here."

Some idiot reporter came through and talked to a girl, high on whatever, who claimed to be making three grand a night dancing in Yellow Earth, when even the full-service gals don't make half that. It hit the wire services and for a couple weeks the tips really suffered, guys busting their nuts on the platforms unhappy to be outearned by somebody shaking their moneymaker in a nice warm club.

"I got to pay a flat fee to work here," she lies, "tipouts to the bartenders and bouncers, and you wouldn't believe the rent they're charging in town." She spins around and leans against him back to belly, whispers hot in his ear. "But when you come in I love my work."

She's got him hard beneath her now, into a rhythmic, gentle grind, with an eyeline to Scorch on the throne. She gives him a subtle nod, holds up a finger. Should be able to keep him on the edge for another minute–

"They asked me back," says Tuck, voice a little strained. "The highway department. But what they're paying– "

"They shouldn't have let you go."

Jewelle had been fired from her first job, a little dive in Wasilla with no dressing room and a circular bar around a cockpit where she'd peel her school clothes off and dance in bra and panties for fifteen minutes, having to sit on the floor and tug her jeans back on when the music stopped. The owner, who later did time, wanted her to turn pro and she wouldn't so he threw her out and things got rough with her mother at home. She was glad to be rid of the place, but getting fired is never good for your ego. Owners are starting to ask her how old she is again, and it's not because they're worried she's not legal.

She swivels again to face him, lifting off it long enough but not too long, and goes back to the slow grind, looking him in the eyes.

"This is getting me really hot," she says. "Look what you're doing to me."

She knows girls who can fake all kinds of things, including some who aren't really girls, but she's the only one she knows who can blush on cue. It just takes a little imagination— what if this guy isn't a pincher or a poker, a squirmer or a humper, a poor deluded soul so goggle-eyed over having a live woman who's not his wife moving on his lap that he'll believe anything, but somebody real. Somebody real who wants just her. She can feel the blood coming up her neck and into her face, Tuck out of words now, taking deep breaths and holding them, pretty flushed himself. There are men, probably lots of them out in the oilfields and here in Yellow Earth, who don't go to strip clubs, who send their money home to their wives or save it hoping to meet somebody special some day, who don't pay women to fuck them or dance naked for them or lie to them. But Jewelle, pepper spray in her pocket when she leaves the club, is not going to meet those men at Bazookas.

And if she did, what could she say, what could she do, that didn't feel like part of the racket?

Tuck is just about there when Scorch's meaty hand clomps onto his shoulder.

"Sorry, folks," he says, "that's all she wrote. House rules."

Jewelle gives the bouncer a hurt look but swings off Tuck and perches on the arm of the chair, placing the palm of her hand on his chest.

"You're not going to forget me are you?"

Tuck pushes up in the chair to make his erection a bit less obvious. "Can't imagine how I'd ever do that."

She kisses him on the cheek. Vic asks for a seven-and-a-half-hour shift and she's only three into this one. "You're a lifesaver in this crazy place, Tuck. Don't be a stranger."

Then Scorch swings the door open and the floor music crashes in.

"ARE WE GOING TO be rich?"

As after-doing-it questions from Connie go, this is not bad, with not nearly so many landmines to avoid stepping on as 'Do you really love me?'

"We're already pretty well off."

"For the reservation."

"For the state, hell, maybe for the whole country. I'll get Doris at the office to run some statistics for you."

"You know what I mean."

The trick is to figure out where this is leading and head it off if it's nowhere good. "We'll have more money than we do now, sure. Cash money."

"Like Beverly Hillbillies rich?"

"You want to move to Beverly Hills?"

"Stop."

"And live next to some Kardashians?"

"Aren't they like part– "

"That was Cher." Harleigh starts to sing, softly–

> *"Half-breed, that's all I ever heard*
> *Half-breed,*
> *How I grew to hate the word."*

"Stop!"

"You used to like my singing."

"I used to *drink*."

Harleigh has to laugh. Connie's been sober so long she can joke about it.

She rolls her head on the pillow to look at him. "You think people will resent it?"

"Everybody in the Nation is gonna do well out of this."

"But not as good as us."

"Because I took some initiative. I told you, we're not making it from the oil, we're making it from the services company. And then the residences when we get them up."

"Man camps."

"That's how you call it if you want to scare people. Like saying 'Indian reservation.'"

"Lots of strangers in the community."

"Oh, they'll keep Danny and his people hopping, all right. Have to coordinate with Crowder, all the other county sheriffs. We got to hope they leave most of their trouble back in Yellow Earth."

"The bright lights of Yellow Earth."

"The lights are on their way, I guarantee you. So what you gonna do with your half of the loot?"

Connie punches him in the arm. "There's things we could do."

"Like what?"

"You know I want Fawn to go to school."

"She's in school."

Harleigh surrendered and agreed to send her in to Yellow Earth instead of the rez school, not a great political move.

"I mean to *college*. "

"Where the work will be harder and the temptations that much tougher to resist. Fawn doesn't want to be in a classroom anymore, honey."

What Fawn does want, besides to ride around with cute boys and get high, is a lot tougher to nail down.

"Remember when she wanted braces?"

"Because of some character she'd seen on TV. She's got perfect teeth."

Connie shifts the rest of her body toward him. A mess of coyotes set up their yipping outside, but it's the wrong season for there to be calves to worry about.

"It's all *legal*, right?"

Connie has the worried look now. One of women's favorite occupations, thinking up troubles that haven't even started yet.

"I got a Yale-educated lawyer says everything's fine."

"Lawyers go to jail."

"Not less they get greedy and go into politics they don't. As an enrolled member of the Three Nations I have the right to run any enterprise that is– "

"But you got an in with the Company."

"I should hope so. That's called *bus*iness, honey. Ask Mr. Cheney."

"Isn't he in jail?"

"Not that I've heard of."

"I thought he was supposed to be."

"You're getting him mixed up with that Watergate deal, honey. Look, anybody else on the rez wants to get into oil services, I'll be only too happy to– "

"Like Phil Enterlodge."

"I haven't done one thing to block Phil doing business."

"But you got all the Company jobs."

"Because Brent and me got our act together."

"And the Company figures to keep the Chairman of the Three Nations happy."

You can't say it's not true, but if they didn't deliver, the Company would drop them like a hot rock. You look at the big picture, how much the Nations will be taking in from the leases– anything he makes on the side is peanuts.

"They'll be so much business," he tells his wife, "Phil's gonna do fine."

Also true, but the look doesn't leave her face. Connie won Miss Three Nations back when, but had to give it up after the driving drunk and without a license. As if Nora Hejdstrom who got the crown was any Girl Scout.

"I saw the boat today," says Connie, looking up at the ceiling now. "Ship, whatever you call it. What's it gonna be named?"

"I was hoping to call it the *Hot Streak*, but somebody told me you're not supposed to change the name of a vessel once it's been christened. Bad luck, which we definitely don't want tied to a floating casino."

"It looks funny."

"That's cause only half of it's *here*, Connie. The top will be shipped up separate and then they'll put it together."

"By your service company with Brent?"

"No, *boat* people that do it all the time. ArrowFleet is just gonna haul oil stuff around on trucks, do cleanup. I'm more worried about the legal end of the Class III permissions than if it's gonna fit together and float or not."

"If you're gambling, what's it matter whether you're on land or water?"

"Jurisdiction. Get more than a mile out to sea in most countries and you can break out the dice."

"And if you lose real bad I suppose you can take a dive and swim for the bottom."

He laughs. "Not at our casino, honey. 'Everyone's A Winner.'"

"That is so not true."

"Well at least *I'm* a winner. I got you."

She eats that stuff up, Connie, knows he means it, but you got to deal it out a little bit at a time.

"So what's it called?"

"What?"

"Your little ocean liner there. What name did it come with?"

They'll have to make a story about it in the literature, explain the superstition, maybe even give it a romantic past of some sort. Reclusive zillionaire sort of a thing.

"*Savage Princess*," says Harleigh, shifting his arm, which has fallen asleep under her. "It's called the *Savage Princess*."

IF THEY WANTED TO chanrge rent for the parking lot, something reasonable, most guys would be willing to pay. Ten dollars a night, even twenty, whatever. I mean here it is, it's just empty otherwise, and they keep the floodlights on in any case. And the guys have been good about it, clearing out at least a half hour before opening time in the morning. *Attention Walmart shoppers–*

Buzzy has gotten used to the lights, used to rigs rumbling in and out all night. Plug the bunk warmer into the cigarette lighter, crawl into the rack and take off whatever you're going to take off inside the sleeping bag, make sure the cell is powered up and within easy reach. Levi, in the Peterbilt he usually parks next to, got one of those diesel-fired cab heaters cost near a thousand bucks, got extra insulation, even got a cable TV hookup, but he's from Green Bay where the weather is shit all the time. Like up here. Wind gets going at night it doesn't just whistle, it *shrieks*, and it's only getting colder.

Two bars on the phone, not bad, and he's set the ring tone full volume. Three or four service outfits jobbing him in now, never know who's going to call or when. Take this load here, drop that one off there. The GPS helps some but there's not exactly addresses to aim at out in the fields, more like just roads with numbers and a derrick or feed silo now and then for a landmark. West Texas can be that way, roads so straight and featureless you got to fight not to zone out and drift off into the chaparral. Used to be if you slept in your truck in winter you were idling the engine to keep warm, burning up fuel and smoking up whatever lot you were parked in. Now these rigs with 'hotel accommodations'–

Of course there's a sight of difference between real *sleep* and just having your eyes closed while your mind keeps jamming gears. Tomorrow he ought to go inside the store– they must have some kind of stationery section– and get him a notebook, start writing down when he goes to sleep and when he wakes up. You want to average eight– okay, maybe seven– hours of sleep in a twenty-four-hour day, or what's that– fifty-six in a week? But laying in the bunk with the phone by your head, itching to ring–

Vern the night guy taps on his window and Buzzy rolls it down.

"Sorry to bother you," says Vern, who's getting the same Walmart minimum as the inside workers and has some asbestos damage in his lungs, "but I seen you weren't quite tucked in yet."

"No problem."

"How'd you do today?"

"Fair. Traffic's getting worse, and I get paid by the load, not by the hour."

"Tell me about it. My twenty minutes ride into work has come to be forty. And then prices going up, everything but gas."

"Hey, we can always drive down to Bismarck, right?"

The merchants got you over a barrel here, and if Buzzy wasn't making crazy money it would piss him off. What the fuck, everybody gets healthy–

"I got bad news." Vern has got that hollow-eyed look, gets out of breath just crunching across the snow from the store to the rigs in the lot.

"They gonna start charging us?"

"It's over."

At first he thinks Vern means the drilling, but that's crazy, the amount of pipe and waste he's been hauling, there's no end to it in sight.

"They made a decision– I'm going to have to start clearing the lot at ten."

"*Who* made a decision?"

"I figure it must have been the store and the city together. Worried about liability."

"But we just park here and go to sleep."

"Maybe the folks who rent rooms in town put some pressure on it."

"They're all filled up! That's why most of us are here."

Vern holds his arms out in a gesture of resignation.

"Where they expect us to go?"

"Any place you can find where it don't bother nobody. You got the whole county."

Good spots to coop are a hot topic in the diners and take-out places, but most are either full-up crowded or there's signs been posted by the time you check them out.

"I heard about some guy got jacked out on Route 15."

Vern nods sadly. "Yeah, there been some robberies. Mostly equipment when nobody's around, but, you know, get a herd this size you're gonna attract some *wolves*. Might be what the store is worried about."

Buzzy looks out the other window. Maybe two dozen rigs, some pickups, couple passenger cars– an average night. Makes the place seem friendlier when it's closed, less abandoned.

"When's the order take effect?"

"You got till Monday. Tell you the truth, I'm gonna miss you fellas. Not much to do here nights."

The other great thing about the lot here is the easy walk to Little Caesar's or

Doc Holiday's Roadhouse. Pizza is the best workday food, easy to eat a slice at a time while you're driving, and sit-down meals are a luxury, usually grabbed while the loading is in progress. When the weather's not too bad he tries to roll with the windows down, suck some of the French fry smell out of the cab.

"If I was younger, and healthy," says Vern, looking off toward the main drag, the usual nighttime parade crawling through town, "I'd be out with you boys, raking it in. I worked on the big dam, you know."

Buzzy knows, he's heard the story a couple times now, but an actual conversation up here is too rare a thing to get picky about.

"Just a pick and shovel man, wasn't married yet, living from payday to payday. Jesus, we had some times."

"I'm trying to hold onto a few bucks."

"That's the way to do it. If I'd socked away a bit more from them gravy days I'd be sittin in a lawn chair down in Florida somewhere instead of freezing my butt in this parking lot."

Buzzy tries to make a deposit every couple days, with a surprising number of his jobs paid in cash, and a couple times it's been clear he's actually doing the work one of the regular outfits has contracted for and are just too busy to cover. Don't want to be carrying a wad of the green stuff if you get hijacked–

Vern sighs, taps the side of the truck. "Well, I got to go spread the word. When you run into any of your brothers of the road, let em know."

"Bye, Vern. Take it easy."

There are some spaces up by the Fuel Stop north on the Canada road. There are warehouses you can tuck in behind at night, got security lights, though he's been rousted from these more than once. There are motels, some of them thrown up in the last couple months and little more than shipping crates with water and power.

Or he could just forget about sleep.

DANNY TWO STRIKE LIKES to cross the Missouri at Washburn, then take the smaller roads that follow the river down, easing through Mandan on the west bank to the Fort. He rarely has business in Bismarck, and there's nothing much to see from the highway unless corporate food and hotel chains fanning past give you a sense of warmth and well being. He remembers the first time they drove from the rez all the way to Fargo with the kids, Tavaughn being so excited to see a Pizza Hut– "Hey, there's another one!"– and having to explain what a franchise was and just how off the beaten path they lived. He passes the refinery, then the little stretch of residential on Collins Avenue, aware of the river even when it's not visible. He wonders if it might be something magnetic, like how geese migrate, because you can blindfold him, spin him around a dozen times and even if he can't stand straight when you stop he can point where the river is, east, west, north or south, ever since he was a little kid. The Storytellers probably have one to explain that, or can make one up.

The guy at the park entrance takes a look at his car, what he's got on as a uniform, and waves him through. Works with nearly everybody but the FBI. A tour of the fort is just leaving the visitor center, white-haired geezers and their wives eager to see the house General Custer and his Libby lived in before he left for the Little Big Horn. Danny did the whole thing on a field trip in junior high, mooning around an excitingly stacked period laundress who explained everyday life at Fort Abraham Lincoln, then teaming up with Nate Flies Away to torture one of the young docents dressed as a Seventh Cavalryman.

"My father took your brother's scalp," Nate said to the play soldier, who couldn't have been more that twenty. "I'll sell it back to you for five bucks."

Nate, who pulled what they called a Dying While Intoxicated in the tenth grade, after he stole a Department of Transportation pickup and tried to make it do a hundred.

The woman behind the counter says Winona is at On-a-Slant Village with a school group.

He wouldn't mind living in the Custers' house– big covered porch, spacious kitchen, buffalo head over the fireplace– a replica (or so they guessed) built by dollar-a-day CCC workers during the Depression. He wonders if there were any Sioux or Cheyenne on the crew.

There are six of the earth lodges where there used to be close to ninety, looking like giant prairie dog mounds from a distance. Danny can see the Heart River, just about to join the Missouri, through the trees. There's not a soul on the village plaza, but smoke rises from the center hole of the biggest of the mounds, and he guesses his ex has brought her captives in there.

"On-a-Slant Village, or *Miti-ba-wa-esh*," says Winona, whose pronunciation of Mandan always bit the big one, from inside, "was the southernmost of sev-

eral villages on the banks of the Missouri River, beginning in the late sixteenth
century."

Danny has to duck slightly as he steps through the tunnel of tree boles that
form the entrance. There is a cook fire crackling low on the center of the floor,
scores of elementary school kids and a few teachers sitting on benches facing
Winona, who explains from a low wooden platform. Danny is relieved to see
she's not wearing buckskin.

"By the time the first white trappers and traders arrived, over a thousand people lived here– hunting, fishing, farming, making valuable pottery, curing and
decorating animal skins. This was a busy, successful commercial river town, like
St. Louis or Cincinnati in later days, set behind a protective moat and palisade
and built on a gentle slope leading to the highway of water just to the east."

Danny eases behind a support column, back in the shadows beyond the fire
and away from the sunlight spilling through the entrance.

"These lodges were mostly built by the women, placing layers of willow
branches, grass and soil on a frame of cottonwood logs, providing protection
from the elements in all seasons. Cool in the summer, warm, if you kept the
fire blazing"– she indicates the paltry little effort on the floor– "throughout the
harsh Dakota winters. In each of the smaller lodges around us perhaps a dozen
people lived together, most of them closely related, while a lodge of this size
might be used for village meetings or ceremonies."

Winona is Upper Yanktonai and not Mandan, something she never let him
forget. The passionate nomads of the plains, not some bunch of sell-out river
traders who burrowed in the ground. *You people*, she used to say, when something she didn't like went down on the rez or with his family. As if Standing
Rock, or particularly her hometown of Cannon Ball, was America's Model
Community.

"It was a happy, productive existence. But in 1871," says Winona, lowering
her voice, "something appeared that destroyed that life and led to the demise of
On-a-Slant Village. Does anybody know what it was?"

"White people?" pipes a little blond girl with Princess Leia braids coiled
around her ears.

Winona smiles. "Well, they had something to do with it, but I'm talking about
a deadly disease– *smallpox*. Who here has had a smallpox vaccination?"

Several of the little kids look on their shoulders and arms as if to check, and
most raise their hands.

"Well, back in 1871 on the upper Missouri River, smallpox vaccination was virtually unknown. Follow me and I'll tell you what happened."

Danny catches up to her, striding ahead of her flock, halfway to the next lodge.

"Excuse me, Miss."

She is not surprised to see him. He took her call in the car this morning on the way to a domestic, too pressed for time to strategize long distance. Danny isn't happy to leave his staff to deal with the usual mess, but it's a rare day that Winona will admit the kids might need a father.

"I just started this tour."

Winona was an RN at Medcenter One until a month ago, when Shaneekwah's rashes and allergies got so bad that she decided she must be bringing bugs home from the hospital and quit. This can't pay as much.

"Give me the short version, then. You're worried about Tavaughn."

"He quit the Rodeo Club."

"It was probably pretty lame. Bismarck."

"He quit it for *Thespians*. That's like– "

"–a drama club, so what?"

"He's almost the only boy in it."

"Better odds if you're a horny adolescent."

"The boy who got all the leads last year before he graduated, Jerome? He was like that guy on *Hollywood Squares*, the one in the middle box with the snarky comments."

"You're saying our son is going to grow up to be Paul Lynde."

Winona looks back to be sure the fourth graders and their minders are not too close. "You know what I'm saying. Not that there's anything wrong with it."

This is typical Winona. With her half-German and his half-Irish the kids came out light enough that she decided to give them names belonging to inner-city hoop stars with a chance at the pros if they avoid getting shot in a drive-by, 'just to be sure people don't think they're white,' and then moves to fucking Bismarck, where she can barely make the rent even with what he sends above the court mandate, so Tavaughn can go to the best high school in the state. Who tells white people they're condescending, while correcting the grammar of everybody, especially his family members, on the rez. And he's supposed to be psychic about which way she's going to break on every issue, like that's the way anybody but an idiot would feel.

"If there's nothing wrong with it, what's the problem?"

"Don't you want to *know*?"

He doesn't especially like the idea. Some of the behavior, not the sex part, which he *really* doesn't want to think about, but the acting out in public, all that phony behavior–

"Okay, if he wasn't a celebrity," he says as they stop by the next earth lodge, "Paul Lynde would have had his nose busted on a regular basis."

"He's home by three– Thespians doesn't meet on Mondays."

He's never actually been in the house when Winona was present, just dropping in when allowed in her absence or waiting in the car outside to pick them up.

"Okay– I'll check it out."

"Smallpox," Winona intones, turning to face the muddle of children as they catch up to her, "sometimes known as the Red Plague, is a communicable disease that can cause blindness, scarring, deformity, and death."

He has to go back up to Mandan and cross the river on the Interstate to get over to Bismarck. It is a capital city without a skyline, much easier to drive through than Yellow Earth these days, and he only gets lost once before finding the little house. Tavaughn is on the floor watching a video with lots of screeching cars when Danny steps in without knocking.

"Surprise," he says, smiling more than he feels like so it doesn't seem like a bust. Tavaughn puts the road warriors on mute and sits up.

"Something wrong?"

"Naw. I was just, you know– in town."

"Cool."

Danny sits on the couch, which feels uneven, and looks at the screen.

"Is this Two or Three?"

"It's the fourth one they've made but it's the sequel to the first one."

"So– faster and furiouser."

"They just whacked Letty."

"The Latino girl."

"Yeah."

Danny nods. He doesn't follow movies much, but hears the plots to the mainstream stuff from Jimmy his deputy who keeps saying 'and then– and then– ' like an eight-year-old, continuing even when Danny pretends to be looking at paperwork.

"School going okay?"

"It's fine."

"Where's Neek?"

"Girl Scouts."

"Since when?"

"Since forever. Keep up."

"She's what– making lanyards?"

"Who knows what they do over there. Not my world."

"So she wears the uniform and all that."

"Mostly just T-shirts now. They do good deeds and build their leadership skills."

Shaneekwah was born only a little before Danny and Winona split up for the final time, and has always been shy with him. He should have fought more at the custody thing, but Winona cornered him outside.

"Think really hard," she said, "about how you'd get through a day on your own with a four-year-old and an infant to keep alive."

He wasn't seeing anybody then, not that any of the women he was vaguely interested in would want to take on child care as part of a relationship, and couldn't imagine the day she was proposing. Neek gives him shy, yes-and-no answers on the phone once a week.

"How's her skin?"

"Pretty good. She's on meds."

He reads the names of the medications on the doctor's bills, looks them up online. Some of it is pretty scary.

"You still roping and riding?"

"Uh– no, I quit that."

"Oh. So a sport– ?"

"Nope. Season's already half over."

"So you got time on your hands."

The bald-headed guy is holding somebody out the window by their feet, threatening to drop him.

"I'm doing drama."

"You mean like plays?"

It's good to have the TV on, somewhere for their eyes to go. His old man would take him fishing and tell him stuff, the two of them watching the lines on the water, now and then reeling in and recasting–

"We do one full-length play and one musical."

Danny tries not to frown. Tavaughn is as off-key a croaker as he is, which leaves dancing in the chorus–

"So you're into that?"

Tavaughn turns to look at him. "I know it's weird, but I like the idea of– like– being other people."

"In the traditions," says Danny, hoping to reassure him, "when you take on the spirit of an animal for a ceremony– "

"It's not like hopping around inside a dead buffalo– not that that's not cool for, you know, when you're doing like a roots thing and all. In a play you're playing a *person* who's not you, even though you've figured out where he's coming from, and the audience gets to watch that person in action."

"No car crashes in it though."

"Not this one."

You don't just come out and ask this shit. He'd leave it where it is, only Winona will call him later and expect a detailed analysis.

"How things back home?"

He loves it that Tavaughn still thinks of the reservation as home. He's spent more years here than he did up there–

"Oh, pretty bad. The usual."

"People making money on that drilling?"

"A few that made the right deal or got lucky, sure. Not that it's made them any smarter about how to spend it. And the money that trickles down to everybody else– well, we've got our hands full."

A couple of the boys Tavaughn would be hanging with if he'd stayed are in real trouble. Dickyboy Burdette is still showing up at school but his grandmother says he almost never comes home, the Menke brothers are heading for prison and none too soon–

"I play a guy named John Proctor."

"Who's that?"

"He's a farmer back in pilgrim days and people start accusing him and his wife of being like Satan-worshipers and witches."

"Wow."

"It's the lead character."

"Hey, congratulations. So, witch hunt, I take it this is not the musical."

"Later in the year. We're doing *Legally Blonde*."

"You won't be getting the lead in that."

Tavaughn at least got the raven hair, which he still wears down to his shoulders.

"I might just do tech. Lighting and props."

Danny makes a snipping gesture. "You gonna cut it?"

Tavaughn shrugs. "Probably. I'll wait till the performances though. There's hardly any other Indian guys at Century, and the hair is like a chick magnet."

Danny has to smile. Love to catch Winona so far off base once in a while. Chick magnet.

"You got anybody special?"

"Not this week."

Cocky son of a bitch.

"You go to the football games?"

"Sure, everybody does."

The Century Patriots have a quarterback, Wentz, who can throw it all over the lot. "I might come down for a game."

"Great."

"And your show– you'll send me the dates and all?"

"I'll forward you the stuff from our website."

Danny is fully online now, Marjorie Looks for Water coming over to the office and getting everybody up to speed once Harleigh got the rez wired.

"Terrific." Danny stands up. "I better push off now, get back to the crime wave."

"Good to see you."

"Gimme five."

They slap hands, Tavaughn not getting up from the floor.

"And say hi to your sister."

"Will do."

He's halfway down the steps when the mayhem resumes inside, gunfire and screeching brakes. He'll have to tell Ruby that his son got the lead in the school play.

USUALLY WITH A LAUNCHING you want the boat to be in the water, but who can wait?

Rick has told Harleigh a dozen times that there would be a hell of a lot more people coming if it wasn't so cold, but Harleigh got so jazzed when he came down and saw the thing put back together there was no holding him back. So it's maybe three hundred bundled up around the presentation space, the mammoth yacht and the near-frozen lake beyond it as a backdrop. Noreen Birdbear is doing her celebrated hoop dance– she's won competitions– and no matter how many times he's seen it the mechanics of the thing are too quick for him to follow. Rick loses track at a dozen of the bright red plastic hoops, spinning, flying, rolling, Noreen flicking them with her feet up from the ground and into the ever-shifting combinations, a horse and rider now shape-shifting into a sea creature then spreading into a butterfly that becomes an eagle, the drum and chant steady while Noreen crow-hops around the circle the tribe members have left open. He recognizes the reporter from Bismarck, one from the Yellow Earth giveaway and the woman from *Indian Country Today* in the crowd. Harleigh will try to spin this all to the positive and Rick will try to back him up, but if they talk to some of the downers here– like his mother, standing with arms crossed and frowning past the swirling hoops like her gaze could set the *Savage Princess* on fire– it's going to be another controversy.

How exactly it became Rick's job to get the damn thing here overland is a mystery, you'd think if it's going to be a casino operation they'd be the ones to do the scutwork. It's only passed through two states from Lake Superior to here, but each has its own regulations for transport, speed limits, road access limits, insurance requirements, permit schedules and deadlines, tolls and tariffs, generating a rat's nest of paperwork and a least a dozen phone calls a day, not to mention the emergency drive to Bemidji to argue the extra-wide procession out from the clutches of an overzealous highway patrol lieutenant. Of course the boat was too tall, or whatever the nautical term is, even on the lowest lowboy trailer, to fit beneath many of the overpasses on the route. The people who sold it to the tribe took care of removing the superstructure and the 'flying bridge' and radar gear, the stuff that sticks up at the very top, and shipping it on a second crawling, gas-swilling rig, but the crew they sent here to get it shipshape again arrived at the casino hotel two days before the boat and proceeded to act like sailors on shore leave. At least the casino boys were the ones who had to clean up after them.

Noreen finishes to well-earned applause inside a kind of giant ball she's woven from the hoops, then somehow she's got them all hanging from her arms like coils of electrical cable and is skipping out of the circle. Now it's Storyteller, who coached Rick's baseball team in junior high, taking the podium.

The microphone setup is working fine, and Storyteller can speak in his easy, familiar manner, like he's home with his feet up on his Barcalounger recliner, a Bud Lite in hand, filling you in on which lures the bass are biting.

"At one time," he says, "long, long ago, the People lived underground."

It was Rick's favorite thing as a kid, when his mother would sit by his bed at night and tell him the stories. Stories not just from the local tribes but ones she'd heard all over the country while doing her political work. Most were traditional creation stories or why Coyote sticks his tail beneath his legs or Raven stole the morning, but sometimes there would be battle stories as well, the Indian side of the movies you saw on TV where Charles Bronson played Blue Buffalo of the Sioux or Captain Jack in the Modoc war. The tales didn't all make sense, totem animals never known for cold calculation, but the lights were out and his mother's voice was deep and soft and he'd nod off to sleep feeling safe because you can't ever fall when you live on the back of the Turtle.

"It was dark underground, but there was just enough to eat, and people wondered about the many vines that hung down from overhead. One day there was a pinpoint of light from above– one of the vines had broken through to the earth-plain and was letting a thread of sun penetrate into their world."

Rick sees Harleigh standing to one side of the yacht, hands on hips assessing the crowd, and drifts in his direction.

"There was much debate among the People, as always"– a laugh of recognition at this– "but one young brave became weary of the talk, and began to climb the vine that was letting the light through, his bow and arrows lashed to his back in case there were monsters to deal with above."

It is a truly beautiful thing, the boat, a ninety-six-foot Hargrave, sparkling white double-decker hull, two thick bars of anti-UV-ray-tinted observation glass running fore and aft, the giant craft looking sleek and speedy even up on the chunky wooden blocks.

"When the young man crawled through the opening to the earth-plain, it took his eyes a long while to adjust to the blinding light– which was only the warm sun above. When he could see well, he discovered that he stood on the bank of a mighty, swift-running river. And then a monster came running toward him, a big-headed shaggy monster, which he brought down with a swift and perfect shot from his bow and arrow."

Harleigh looks disappointed with the turnout.

"I can't believe we can't at least slide it into the water."

"The Coast Guard."

"We're not operating the yacht casino, we're not *sailing* it, we'd just whack it with champagne, slide it into the water and then tie it to the dock."

"The dock we haven't gotten permission to build yet. And then have to haul it out again the minute the ice starts forming."

Last year he'd had to talk Harleigh out of the idea to ignore Daylight Savings

Time on the rez. People here have enough difficulty showing up on time as it is, he'd argued, without confusing them even more.

"I still don't see how the Coast Guard gets involved. We're not a *coast*."

Coast Guard are a minor nuisance compared to the Army Corps of Engineers, who oversee all water access and have been busting his balls about the proposed dock– ·

"The young man was very hungry from all his climbing," says Storyteller. "So he cut meat from the shaggy monster, which he decided to call *ptí-i–* buffalo. It was the best thing he'd ever eaten."

"I explained to you how once a boat gets to that size– "

"But we're not taking it off reservation land."

"The lake," says Rick, knowing that Harleigh is fully aware of this, "and the river it is part of are controlled by the Feds. As long as we keep the boat on shore we can do whatever we want with it." He sees his mother approaching, braces himself for the cold front.

"So the young man climbed back down the vine, always easier on the descent, bringing a robe made of the monster's hide, and told the People about the wonders he'd experienced. There were many more hours of debate, but finally it was decided that the People would migrate up to this bright, warm world above, to fish in the mighty river, to chase and kill and eat the shaggy monster."

"Hello, Teresa. Beautiful day for it, no?"

Harleigh has mastered the art of greeting his enemies with a smile. Rick has been working on it, but his face or his voice always betray him. His mother doesn't even meet his eye, homing in on the council chairman.

"How much did it cost?"

"They're really excited about the upside at the casino," says Harleigh. "Besides the gambling, it will be available for rentals– a party boat kind of thing– weddings, business retreats, birthdays for rich kids– for a thousand a day. Seats a hundred fifty, plus standing room in the bow and stern and up on the top deck– "

"How much?"

The figure, if she ever gets it out of Harleigh, will not include the shipping, taking the top off and sticking it back on, the operating costs, the salaries of the certified skippers they'll have to hire–

"Next financial report, it'll all be laid out for you. We had kind of a time-sensitive bargain situation, so I had to make a move."

The only bargain Rick knows about is that the owner threw in the dry-dock blocks for free. For two and a half million it was a small gesture.

"So the young man led the way, and one by one the People began to climb the vine up to the new world. A couple dozen of them had made it to the earth-plain and were marveling at the winding river and the warm sun and the huge herds of the shaggy monsters whose meat would feed you and whose hides would keep you warm, when a very large lady, a little too fond of her fry-bread– "

A big laugh here, the audience imagining the woman trying to climb–

"–tried to make it to the earth-plain, and the vine snapped and sent her hurtling back into the underground. There was no other way up, and from that day our People have been divided, a few here on the surface, never forgetting those many left behind under the ground."

Warm applause, Storyteller saying a few good luck blessings in the three languages, and Harleigh uses the opening to hurry away from Rick and his mother.

Rick has been aboard the boat, all shiny surfaces, tidily arranged cook space and bathrooms, everything smelling new though it's been in service on Lake Superior for at least two years. He wishes every member of the tribe could come aboard and take a cruise, sit in the cushy leather seats and look out the high-tech windows and think, 'We deserve this, this is *ours*.' As his mother always says, the important battle is for hearts and minds–

"The government and the Army Corps of Engineers took our river away from us," says Harleigh from the platform, his voice rolling outward with microphone-amplified echo. He lifts an arm to indicate the massive white vessel behind him. "And now we are taking it *back*."

Enthusiastic applause, though Rick sees that some, maybe one out of ten, are not clapping at all. 'They don't trust anything that's new,' Harleigh is always saying, 'and don't trust a word you say unless you hire two white men in suits to come out and back you up.'

Teresa Crow's Ghost sighs. "Oh my people, my people," she mutters, and walks away without acknowledging the presence of her son.

THEY NEED TO OUTLINE the town before they can destroy it. GPS for location, setting boundaries with the 'total station theodolite' (sexy-looking surveyors' equipment), then going old-school to hustle around with wooden stakes and yellow tape. The p-dogs pop up to watch from time to time, and Leia records their man-warning chitter from across the highway despite the traffic rolling in between. For what– evidence? To present to whom?

In some states there are volunteer relocators, out with a water truck, pushing soap suds into holes till the dogs splutter up (Jeff used to call it 'fracking for *Sciuridae*'), mostly soft-hearted suburban moms who greet the refugees with towels and eye drops and often have a dozen or so back home digging up their yards and making the neighbors nervous. But not up here. At school her thesis advisor was a major ferret-head, vital in the eleventh-hour conservation of the species, and Leia was in thrall to him for a couple years. A man with a cause, not too old, good cheekbones, not that anything unprofessional happened despite her efforts to emit the appropriate pheromones. Professor Chad had a source for the live prairie dogs that Leia and his other student minions would toss into the preconditioning enclosure and then take notes as the long, lithe apprentice ferrets darted out of their burrows or PVC pipe snuggeries to streak after them, pinning the befuddled creatures against the wood and chicken-wire walls, rolling around and breaking free, rolling around and breaking free, until they either succeeded in clamping the dog's windpipe shut long enough to suffocate it and drag it down into the burrow to feed on, or give up. More than a few times a rookie ferret, bred and raised in a university cage, would throw in the towel, retreat to lick its wounds, and at least one was killed by desperate bites from a p-dog while Leia and the rest of the team watched. Weeping and the gnashing of teeth in Ferretopia. She preferred the days when no live prey was available and she'd stroll in with several sections of sliced rat, dangling by the tails, calling till the young ferrets popped their little periscope heads out to snatch-and-go with their dinner.

The worst were the days she was instructed to jam a live p-dog right down into the ferret holes, the quick and violent yelping and thumping and wet tearing sounds that followed making her nauseous. Jeff always went sarcastic when she'd complain about it.

"It's a jungle out there, Babe," he'd say. "Deal with it."

Of course Jeff was in Herpetology, one of a half-dozen grad students her friend Melanie called the Slithers, and hand-fed an inexhaustible supply of wriggling white mice to his various snake and lizard test subjects on a precise schedule.

"You feel so bad for the poor little ground squirrels," he would say, accurate as to subfamily but condescending nonetheless, "why don't you study *them*?"

It had been a revelation to her, the one valuable thing to come out of the relationship, which ended with a screaming fight in their tent on a department field trip, attacking not only each other but each other's doctoral species, with Jeff labeling both the ferrets and prairie dogs as 'flea-ridden varmints' and Leia responding that 'at least they're homeo*thermic*!,' an observation that Jeff chose to take personally. It was at night during a wild thunderstorm, and they were stuck silently fuming at opposite ends of the air mattress, backs to each other, till the sun rose gently over the Rockies.

It has something to do with the shale oil, she knows, this marking, this vast yellow-taped rectangle that encompasses her target coterie and perhaps a dozen others. 'Destruction of habitat' is always cited as the principal cause of the sinking numbers of the prairie dog, for the near-extinction of the black-footed ferret, and she chose this spot because it seemed too remote, too firmly in the back-of-beyond, to ever be encroached upon by human endeavor. Rodential academics love to cite the vast Texas colony that lasted nearly into the twentieth century, a kind of Aztec Empire of the *Cynomys* that covered twenty-five thousand square miles and held more than four hundred million individual p-dogs. How many ferrets and eagles and swift foxes and coyotes must have feasted off that mass! You think *you* people dig holes in the ground, she mentally beams across to the Company men still pacing around the doomed colony, try to match *that*.

Iphigenia gives a nervous chirk and the dogs are suddenly up and alert. They spend over a third of their above-ground time scanning for predators, which must be incredibly stressful. No wonder the females are sexually receptive for only a half a day each year, and the males rarely live more than three years. Not tonight, honey, I'm worried something is going to eat me.

Whatever set them off seems to be a false alarm, and a half dozen perform the 'all clear' jump-yip in unison, leaping straight up and sprawling to the dirt like a line of demented cheerleaders. Leia has a stuffed badger back at the apartment, along with a kite that looks exactly like a hawk when flown, which she used in the early days of the study to elicit and record warning calls. Each was eventually permanently rejected as a threat by the coterie, who would jump-yip only minutes after she deployed them. You can fool some of the prairie dogs some of the time–

This is one of the days she misses Brandi. Not the greatest assistant, bit of a space-shot, constantly implying they were in some field biologist version of *Heart of Darkness*, but lots of times you just need another pair of hands, somebody to hold the subject's front end securely in a cloth wrap while you perform some operation on the back end. 'Too weird here, can't hack it' was the extent of the note she left on Leia's observation pad, her few belongings gone from the apartment, although she didn't clean out the half-eaten Weight Watchers easy meals in the fridge. Leia knows she should have informed the department to demand a new assistant or even pulled the plug on the study, but somehow the die seemed cast and she has gotten used to going it alone.

"So if this is the Congo," she asked Brandi at the Applebee's one night, "I'm like what– the guy who goes down the river and observes and narrates– "

"No, that's Marlowe," said Brandi over her fettucine Alfredo with a side of parmesan. "You're *Kurtz*."

The Company men are taking pictures of their handiwork when the Eradicator pulls up beside her in his death machine. He is a little bowlegged guy wearing jeans with mud-caked knees and a T-shirt and ball cap that both bear the logo– a skulking, coarse-haired Norway rat (*Rattus norvegicus*, originally native to northern China) with a thick red X drawn over it.

Everybody hates rats.

He steps over to Leia with a tentative half-smile on his face, eyes flicking up to check out the streaks in her hair.

"Humane Society?" he asks. "PETA? ASPCA?"

"I'm a scientist," says Leia, though lately she feels more like a crank or a stalker, one of those humorless zealots who send death threats to animal-testing labs. SCUMCUB, she thinks, the Society for Cutting Up Men who Cut Up Bunnies.

"Oh." He seems confused. "Geologist?"

"Biology," she says, nodding across the road toward the colony.

It takes a moment for it to register. "You study *prairie* dogs?"

Worse than that, she thinks– I used to live with a guy who kept pet snakes in his clothes drawer and named them after famous chess masters.

"I have a *grant*," says Leia, feeling she might be about to be ordered to move on.

"Wow." He looks at her with mild awe, as if he's never beheld a grantee in the flesh before. She is emboldened.

"You ride horses?"

She realizes the bowlegs have prompted the question, blatant profiling, but lets it stand.

"Not much lately," says the Eradicator, whose hat also bears a sewn-on tag announcing that his Christian name is Jerry. "But when I was a kid, yeah."

"You ever have a horse break a leg in a dog-hole?"

"No."

"You ever hear of it?"

He actually tilts up the back of his hat so he can scratch his head. Leia wonders if there were Nazis running the death camps as friendly and folksy as this Jerry.

"It's a story you always hear, yeah, but I can't say as I recollect anybody I *knew* that lost a horse– or any cattle."

"Cause the ranchers all claim– "

"Well, back when there was a lot more prairie dogs and a lot more horse traffic, people riding fast after buffalos and whatnot, I'll bet it was quite a problem."

Leia nods, points across to the Company men finishing up. "What's the deal over there?"

"That's for a platform. Drilling platform. They'll level all that off."

"With, like, a bulldozer– "

"Right. And the thing is, there's some kind of regulation that they can't just plow your animals under."

"They're not *mine*."

"–can't bury em a*live*, so we got to come and *gas* em first." He holds his arms out, looking a bit embarrassed. "Crazy, huh?"

"Gas."

Jerry nods. "We started out with carbon monoxide pellets, but with that you got to stand over it with a leaf blower to keep the gas down in the hole long enough to do the job. Hated that. Even with the ear protectors on I's pert near deaf when I come home at night. And then the *time* you got to spend per kill– it just don't add up. So this time of year we'll hope for a little precipitation and go with the aluminum phosphide."

"Which makes them bleed internally."

"No, that's Rozol. Nasty stuff– your predators and scavengers eat the varmints when they come out to die, and then *they* got problems with their coagulation. Like a chain reaction. Naw, this stuff just turns to gas when exposed to moisture, goes for their lungs."

"Effective."

"If you're thorough, plug up all the holes with newspaper as soon as you toss it down, yeah. Something special about this bunch?"

He is looking through the stream of passing pickups and eighteen-wheelers toward the yellow-taped rectangle around the hodgepodge of mounds, hands in his pockets. How to explain the implacable courage of Ajax, the Machiavellian sexual strategies of Odysseus, Niobe's strange fixation with the one-eyed Iphigenia, without sounding like a crackpot?

"It's my study group," she says. "You observe a specific coterie over time, through the cycles of mating, of birth and death, contraction and expansion of territory, and begin to understand their behavior."

Jerry nods. "I'm like hooked on *Animal Planet*, watch it with my kids all the time. Pretty heavy for them when that fella Steve bought the farm."

Leia finds herself nodding in sympathy. In grad school they'd all developed vocal impressions of the Crocodile Hunter, tried to inject a bit of excitement into the most wearisome lab chores by describing them in a breathless Australian accent.

"So once they're all gassed, you– what?"

"We come by a couple days later, pick up the ones that have wandered out of their holes– they tend to be pretty out of it, you can walk right up to them– and then the earth machines move in. I've mostly cleared for golf courses and shopping malls before, but this oil boom has got us hopping."

He looks her over again, eyes sympathetic. "Today I just come to scope it out, so we got a little bit to wait before– you know– the pellets go in."

"But no stay of execution from the governor."

It is not the most generous grant one could hope for, nothing compared to what the ferret crowd gets or what private donors throw at the whale and dolphin savers, but it is *hers* and she's made her stand out here on the high plains. The *Journal* tends to look askance at papers submitted that end with "And then they all got run over by a truck." If only it was the very last passenger pigeon, or some lovable furry critter Pixar had just made a movie about–

"I'm not really sposed to do this," says Jerry, handing her a business card from his pocket, "but there's this *guy*."

BURROW BUSTERS EXCAVATION SERVICE it says, with a cartoon of a cute p-dog in a work outfit and safety glasses holding some kind of vacuum hose.

"What he does is suck em out of their burrows, pretty much in one piece. Where they go next is up to you."

Earlier in the day she had examined the failed Poker Flats colony behind them, virtually a prairie dog ghost town now, with scat and nose prints around only a handful of the burrows and most others caved in or with cobwebs across the entrance. She studies the card–

"You know this person?"

Jerry shrugs. "My brother Jett," he says. "He's always walked his own road."

"THEY'RE LIKE GOING NOWHERE."

Fawn always has the nicest clothes, stuff from Bismarck or even Minneapolis, stuff she sends away for, but she'll go to the Walmart with them and try on outfits she wouldn't be caught dead in.

"Unless it's like, the army? They get to go places then, wherever they're sent, but they almost always come back to the rez and they're the same sorry-ass guys but with new tattoos."

"There's other tribes, aren't there?" Tina is fascinated with the reservation stuff, but cool about it. And she has a thing about yellow, which she shouldn't wear, not with her so pale. Fawn can pull it off, with her skin it looks great on Fawn, but she wears mostly whites and patterns you can tell come from somewhere else.

"You meet really good-looking guys at the powwows," says Fawn, turning to check her butt out in the mirror. The jeans she walked in with fit like a second skin, and these look cheap on her. "But that's like a *part* they're playing– old-time Indians. Nobody lives like that anymore."

"And your stepfather won't let you date other kinds of guys– like white guys?" Tina rarely tries things on if she's not buying, and after the iPod and the Nokia smartphone she won't be buying again for a couple paychecks. While Jolene– well, this is her chance to wear clothes her parents will never allow.

"He never put it exactly that way, but he's like Mr. Red Power, Red Pride, so I gotta figure– "

"He knows you hang with Dylan," says Jolene.

"Dylan is so wasted all the time, nothing you do with him could be considered a date. These are probably made in China."

"Or Turkey, or Portugal." Jolene was part of a sneaker boycott when she was in junior high back on the rez, and always has some product or other on her shit list. Jolene takes a lot of flak for being so serious, but she's cute and can be fun and is really loyal.

"Hey, they're called No Boundaries. Could be from anywhere."

"Are there any sweat shops on Indian reservations?" Tina again.

Fawn laughs. "Sweat lodges, but no sweat shops. Not that I know of."

"So the boyfriend thing," says Jolene, getting back to the subject. She's not allowed to date, kept on a really short leash.

"Well, my stepdad was cool with Dickyboy back in junior high. Before he puffed up."

"He's a good guy, Dickyboy. And he used to be— you know."

"He never met a carbohydrate he didn't like. Sure, his family's a mess, but that doesn't mean you have to stuff yourself." Fawn is wearing her striped top from Aeropostale, which they don't have one yet in Yellow Earth. There was some talk about a new mall being built, but since most of the new people are oil guys it probably wouldn't have any good stores.

"So if the rez boys are all losers and you can't date white boys," Tina continues, checking the time on her new cellphone, "how come we barely see you anymore?"

Fawn looks around, sees Marjorie Looks for Water squinting through her glasses at sweaters a couple rows over in the plus sizes, then gives them her wicked grin and crooks a finger. "Step into my office."

They got kicked out of the dressing room once before here, the lady saying there was a rule against three at a time but looking at them like they were lesbians or something, and Fawn keeps her voice low as she steps out of the tagged jeans and wriggles back into her own.

"There's this guy— he's like, *older.*"

"An oil worker?"

"Not exactly. He's my stepfather's partner."

An appropriate moment of awe.

"The guy with the Vette," says Tina, not totally believing it.

"The *married* guy with the Vette," says Jolene, already set to boycott him.

"Married to Dumb Bunny. Brent says that's basically over, they're like business associates now."

"If she's so dumb, how can she be— "

"There's certain things he can't have in his name. My stepfather's always doing the same kind of stuff. It's standard practice."

"And you're like— what?" asks Jolene. Jolene who is so cute but has definitely not had a boyfriend.

"Like *everything*. He's a grown man, he's gonna what– hold hands?"

Spartina definitely is not telling them about her and Wayne Lee. Not just that they haven't gotten that far yet, but it seems too much like bragging, showing off.

"You're like, being careful."

"As careful as you can be, under the circumstances. I mean, like try to get birth control on the rez or in Yellow Earth without everybody in the world knowing it."

"So he uses– "

"Pretty much always." The wicked grin again. "But there have been a couple panty-twisters."

Fawn's mother gets *Cosmopolitan*, which Fawn shows to her friends so they can squeal over the sex articles.

"So is he getting a divorce or something?"

"He says it's complicated. Like he's having this whole new house built, but it's in her name."

"Sounds like you should be careful." Sometimes they call Jolene the Fire Marshal because she is the first to tell you what could go wrong or what's already gone wrong or what went wrong in the past. Her parents are Pentecostals, but she never mentions Jesus as her special pal or tells her friends they're going to Hell or anything, so it's hard to know if she's a hardcore believer or not. They've never asked and she's never told.

"We're in love," says Fawn, and suddenly Tina feels sick to her stomach.

THEY MEET AT HARRY the Greek's on the way east out of New Center. Danny never could stomach lamb till the place opened, but the gyros here are killer. Ruby comes in after him and they do their usual friendly but businesslike hello, the chief counsel and financial adviser for the tribes and the head of the reservation police getting together to compare notes. Part of Ruby's campaign 'not to get mired down here.'

"Jurisdiction," he says after they've ordered. "The usual nightmare."

"You want the council to pass an ordinance?"

"If it would help. We got all these oil company guys living on the reservation now."

"Renting from enrolled members who need the income."

"*Want* the income."

"Same thing."

They smile at each other. Ruby intimidates people here without trying– Eastern law school, always with a full deck of facts and figures to lay on the table, her self-confidence. But Danny likes how smart she is, likes that what you get from her is a competitive spirit and not just attitude. He's had enough attitude for a lifetime from Winona, who was born with a chip on her shoulder that had nothing to do with being Dakota.

"One way or another," says Danny, "I think the word has spread that I can't touch these guys cause they're white, and the county sheriffs around us are too overwhelmed by the invasion to drive out to the reservation."

"The drillers are all white?"

"All the ones I've seen. Good-ole-boy kind of thing."

Ruby nods, considering. "When they had the Indian Territory it was the same deal– tribal police could only go after Native-on-Native crime. So every rustler, train robber, and bootlegger from the surrounding states moved in, spread a little money around so they'd be warned whenever a federal marshal with a stack of writs in his saddlebags rode through."

"The Wild West."

"And you've got one hand tied behind your back."

"Sometimes it feels like both of them are tied. Will Crowder makes an effort to cooperate, but he's got Yellow Earth to cover."

"I hear they got a strip club now."

"Two of them."

Ruby raises an eyebrow.

"So I hear."

"Any trouble at Bearpaw?"

"You know, for whatever reason, they're pretty well-behaved over there."

"Too busy having their pockets emptied."

Danny shrugs. "The whole gambling thing is a mystery to me. You got money to burn, get yourself an ex-wife and two kids."

"Poor baby."

He's never seen her in traditional dress, but Ruby is the most Indian-looking woman he's ever known, a poster girl for Red Pride. And the business suits look great on her. Pocahontas in pinstripes.

"How's life with Harleigh?"

She takes a moment to answer, scanning the room. A couple drillers who have discovered the place, a tourist couple being amazed by the food, Harry behind the counter.

"Between you and me," she says, measuring off an inch with her thumb and forefinger, "the shit is *this* close to the fan."

"That bad?"

"I advise, I issue warnings, I cite conflicts of interest. But he's a– you know."

"He's Harleigh."

"I would have voted for him if I was enrolled here. Looking to the future, dresses the part, talks a great game."

"Are we talking criminal behavior?"

She shakes her head. "Not even il*l*egal unless you apply standards that nobody else is operating by. But whenever somebody takes the role of advocate for his people and owns a private business affected by the decisions he makes for them– "

"That partner of his– "

"Golden Boy. Don't get me started on him. These days Harleigh keeps me totally in the dark about what goes on inside of ArrowFleet."

"Probably a good thing."

"And you've seen some of the mess the drilling people are leaving around."

"That's supposed to be Ricky McAllen's turf."

"Ricky only does what Harleigh lets him, you know that."

"So what are you going to do?"

"Honestly? I'm going to get out before any of it sticks to me."

The waitress sets their food down, asks if they want refills on the drinks. Danny has lost his appetite.

"And go where?" he asks when the girl walks away.

"Somewhere they've got enough money to warrant looking after, where the politics are reasonable."

"In Indian Country? Come on."

"I said reasonable, not perfect. Here I'm afraid all the time."

"Of going to jail?"

Ruby leans a little closer, lowers her voice. "I put the nix on this deal Brent Skiles wanted to do– a leasing scheme run through the tribe that would mostly benefit him. I insisted it go up in front of the council and told them– Harleigh and Brent– that I'd have to voice my legal reservations. The way the guy looked at me– if he had superpowers I'd be a pile of smoldering ash."

"And now you're scared that– "

"I read a thing where certain people can be in a room with a psychopath and just *sense* it, not a word spoken."

"Psychopath, wow."

"My skin gets all tingly when he walks into a room."

"You know, the same thing happens to me when I see you."

She smiles. You should have a license to carry a smile like that around.

"Anyway, I can't stay here."

"You want me to talk to him? Brent?"

"You mean *lean* on him?"

"Just as a, you know, *person*. My badge doesn't mean anything to him."

Again the smile. "Except you get to pack a pistol. You'd do that for me, wouldn't you?"

"Of course I would."

She looks at him then like she might cry. "Eat something. It'll get cold."

"Yes, Mom."

They eat their gyros and fries, silent for a little bit. There is not a lot of drama with Ruby, and she seems to like him for what he is. Winona had been all scalding or freezing, either fierce love or violent retribution– if Winona had tangled with a character like Brent Skiles there'd be blood by now.

"So what about us?"

Ruby sits back. "You could come with me."

"To wherever."

"Yes. That's an invitation."

The idea of it makes him sweat. He doesn't even really like to go to Yellow Earth or Bismarck– the idea of starting from scratch on a reservation where he's a stranger, a nobody, not even an enrolled member, no history, no family–

"Think about it, okay?"

"I will."

"The thing to get out of your head," says Ruby Pino, "is the idea that you're irre*place*able. You might be good at what you do, great at it even, but if you take a powder tomorrow, life will go on. Believe me, none of the places I've left has disappeared from the map."

He can't think of who on his staff is ready to step up and take over the job. But then he's not exactly got the reservation under control–

"Can I come over tonight?"

The council gave her the old Lundgren house as part of the inducement to take the position. He parks a couple blocks away behind the post office and walks around to her back door.

Ruby smiles. "You had better."

THERE'S NO ART IN the council room. Most of the walls in the other tribal spaces are covered with the stuff, heroic history pictures or traditional symbols and designs. A Lakota woman up from Standing Rock did a lot of it, beautiful work, and it's good for people not to forget what came before.

"I think we should talk about the People's Fund," says Teresa Crow's Ghost.

"It's not on the agenda." Doris takes the minutes on a legal pad and doesn't like to have to erase or cross anything out. A computer has been suggested, but she claims 'it's too easy for things to disappear' on the machines.

"I make a motion to discuss the People's Fund," sighs Teresa.

"Second," says Harleigh. Might as well get it out. "All in favor?"

He raises his hand even before Teresa and the others follow.

"I'm hearing complaints," says Teresa, "that the money isn't being distributed. And rumors that it's being invested in some risky oil venture."

Eyes swivel to Harleigh and Norman Ross, the treasurer.

"Not much risk in oil these days," says Harleigh. "Not from where we're sitting. Not if you got half a brain."

"So it's true?"

"The money is sitting in *escrow*, Teresa. It can't be touched without an amendment to our bylaws. But if you think you could double or triple it real quick, we're all ears."

"How come there hasn't been a disbursement?"

He shrugs. "Weather's still holding. I figure when the winter really hits, people got heating, car problems to deal with, Christmas– five hundred to a thousand bucks'll look pretty good then."

"That's what it comes out to?"

"Right now it's about eight-fifty if we include nonresident enrollees. Interest we're making is ahead of the cost of living increases, and there's wells left to be dug on reservation land."

"So it should go up?"

"Absolutely. Maybe we ought to release a statement every couple months, let folks know where we stand."

"It would keep the rumors down a bit."

Always good to have something he and Teresa agree on. She has stayed militant, whatever that means if you're not actually carrying a rifle, and is generally impossible to please.

"Doris, could you put a statement together? Norman can give you the exact numbers."

"And the disbursement will be?"

"Let's say second week of December. Next item?"

Doris scans down her list. "A petition to the council– request for closed hearing."

"Bring it on."

Harleigh has called the meeting because he's got a bundle of leases for approval, always best held for the end when the council members are tired and don't want to hear any more details.

Doris opens the door and Phil Enterlodge steps in.

This won't be good.

"What can we do for you?"

Phil won't look him in the eye, instead standing at the far end of the oval table and addressing the other six on the council.

"I am here regretfully," he says, voice a little strained, "on a matter that brings me against the Chairman."

Nobody says a word. They know Phil Enterlodge was his partner in the little gravel trucking business before the oil, that they'd split over Phil thinking he did all the work, and that he's had his own outfit for a couple years now, struggling to get by.

"I believe that Mr. Killdeer is in violation of conflict-of-interest rules."

They'd been friends once, and Phil was lawyer for the tribes before Harleigh hired Ruby Pino away from the Puyallups.

"And what might those be, Phil?" At least get the man to look you in the eye.

"Using your elected position to– "

"There is no rule prohibiting a council person from engaging in a business."

"I bid on the same service contracts you do."

"Which is your right in a free market."

"I beat your rate by five, ten percent all the time."

"Good for you."

"My people got more experience, more local knowledge than yours."

"You're getting colder, Phil."

"And I get *squat*. Oil people won't go near my outfit cause of yours."

"Competition, Phil."

"Because they know that if they don't hire your bunch their leases will be held up."

"I have never, ever interfered with a lease to bring more business to my company."

"Well they Goddamn well *think* you do!"

For a guy with a law degree, Phil never really saw the big picture. "I can't control people's perceptions," Harleigh says softly.

"But you don't do anything to change them, do you? And you're happy to rake in the dough."

"Tell me where something illegal has been– "

"It may not be illegal, but it is absolutely un*eth*ical!"

Harleigh turns to the secretary. "Remind me, Doris, do we have an ethics board?"

"No, sir, we don't."

"Well you have a *code*," says Phil. "I got a copy right here."

"Does it say who is meant to adjudicate any alleged violations?"

"If it's not the council I don't know who it is."

"Neither do I." Harleigh looks to the other council members. "I make a motion that the council, at our next meeting, consider the formation of an ethics committee."

"Second," Norman calls out. Always good to keep a rubber stamp nearby.

"All in favor"– hands go up. "Motion passes unanimously." He looks to Phil. "We thank you for your time."

After the meeting, leases approved with only a little opposition from Teresa, he asks Doris to find him a copy of the ethics code.

"I've got one in my desk," she says.

"When was it written?"

"*Ethics for Tribal Officials, 1936*." Doris has an incredible memory for facts but not much imagination. "To think they needed them way back then."

THE DOG-SUCKER ARRIVES ABOUT an hour before the killing at the back of
the colony begins. A yellow truck, the kind that used to come to clean out their
sewer back in Minnetonka. The driver hops out and strides over to Leia with
his hand out, grinning. His ball cap has a prairie dog wearing a safety helmet
on it.

"Jett Tutweiler," he announces. "And you're the Wildlife Girl."

"Behaviorist. I've got a grant."

He keeps smiling. "Right. So how many of the little buggers are we talking
about?"

"The sample is two dozen, but I'd like to pull as many as we can, give them some
neighbors."

Only a few of the p-dogs have stuck their noses out to see her this close, the
coterie reappearing to forage a couple days back after the three weeks of snow
and zero-degree temperatures. They don't hibernate, just hunker down in the
burrows and live off their stored fat, and the very old and the very young often
don't make it through the season. Leia has the cages piled at the edge of the
highway, a housing chart prepared to minimize the potential for fights between
cellmates. She points to the first hole.

"I thought we'd start here and work our way to the end."

"Sounds like a plan," says Jett, who manages to be bouncy even when he's not
moving. "I'll pull the rig over."

The traffic, a steady day-and-night rumble of pickups and sixteen-wheelers,
has not altered the behavior within the colony, and Leia has had to cross the highway to observe with a clear field of vision, the p-dogs gradually ignoring, possibly
even expecting, her presence. Odysseus has filched some out-of-coterie nookie,
mating with a couple bimbos from the west side during their annual half-day of
estrus, and if persistence is a genetic trait it will be well represented in future
generations. She's lost only one of the sample, Clytemnestra, to a ferruginous
hawk that lugged her just twenty yards before landing and proceeding to pull her
guts out, the other dogs pretty much burrow-bound for the rest of the afternoon.

The truck rolls up beside the first hole and Jett bounds out to deploy the thick,
green hose coiled at the side.

"I got a four-inch gauge here," he says, wiggling and pushing the hose down
the hole, "which might seem a bit narrow for some of the fat ones, but if they can
squeeze into these holes, they can fit through my extractor."

"It doesn't hurt them?"

The hose bows as if it's gone as deep as it can. "Not too bad, usually. They'll be going two-fifty, three hundred miles per hour when the hose spits em out, but I got the chamber all padded up with foam. You see them NASCAR fellas these days, they hit the rail going who *knows* how fast, and like as not they bounce right off. Beats the hell out of a couple hay bales."

He flips a switch on the side of the truck and it begins to thrum noisily, the volume steadily increasing till the hose twitches and there is a dull thud, like an old softball hitting a brick wall, from within the side of the truck. Jett waits till there is another twitch and thud, then another. He listens, wiggles the hose a bit more, then switches the machine off.

"You got you a couple."

Leia pulls on her rubber gloves, brings up a cage. Jett opens a little hatch next to the hose port.

"You gonna have to just reach in and feel around some, but they ain't too lively right after."

"Stunned."

"I figure them people say they were taken up in alien spaceships," says Jett, "feel about the same way."

It is Demeter, Psyche, and little Daedulus, no cuts, only Psyche seeming a little out of it once deposited in the cage. 'The Effects of Extraction-Induced Concussion on *Cynomys ludovicianus*,' thinks Leia, with before-and-after MRI readouts of their little walnut brains and her photo on the cover of the *Journal*. Careers have been made on less.

"What do people usually do with them after they're, you know– sucked out?"

"Varies." Jett is jockeying the hose down into the next hole. "I'm of the don't-ask-don't-tell persuasion, unless folks feel a need to let me in on it."

She had a story about an out-of-state habitat already set up and waiting for the evacuees, and is relieved not to have to tell it. She figures she'll wait till after he's gone to start with the translocation.

"Some folks that just don't want them zapped– like by the fella who pumps propane and oxygen down the holes, lights it with this remote spark-plug thing– "

"Crispy critters."

Jett turns from his work to smile at her. "Yeah, it ain't pretty to think about. Anyhow, there's folks who leave it up to me as to the disposal. Disposition?"

"The fate of the dogs."

"Right. I got a Japanese fella, buys the pups for twenty-five dollars a head, probably makes a killing over there selling them for pets."

"The Japanese are seriously into cute."

"And then with the grown-up ones, there's these folks who breed this kind of weasely thing."

"Black-footed ferret."

"That one. Which is like endangered so's they got to throw a live prairie dog in with em every once in a while."

"They like it better than thawed rat."

Jett has the hose jammed down another hole. "Whatever. Watch your ears."

He flips the switch and the huge vacuum groans, transporting another dog into the padded chamber.

It is perhaps the worst time of year to be doing this, the breeding cycle incomplete, several of the females pregnant, the animals reduced in bulk from scanty winter feed, predators extra hungry and on the prowl. A few of the females haven't come into estrus yet, and strange surroundings plus conflict with new neighbors might just hit the 'off' switch. This could be the prairie dog Trail of Tears–

"This is a deep one," says Jett, switching holes and dealing more hose off the spool. "I'm already down six, seven feet."

"They'll go deep, sometimes. There will be two, three, maybe even four entrances to a burrow and nobody's got exclusive rights to it."

"Kinda like a hippie commune."

She doesn't want to get into the infanticide and cannibalism, which disgusts most people outside the field, which disgusted her when she first learned about it. Marauding mothers killing and eating their own sisters, cousins, grandchildren, gaining protein and possibly, in the briefly bereaved neighbor, recruiting a future nursemaid for their own pups once they first emerge at six weeks. What happens underground stays underground–

"I always figure there must be a few stuck between in the tunnels that get left behind," says Jett. "But so far I gotten no complaints."

"There's a couple individuals I need." The extracted animals seem fine, testing the limits of their cages, Echo even nibbling the grass that sticks up through the bottom wire. "You need a certain number of mature adults to start breeding again, or the coterie won't be viable."

Jett nods. "Like in the Bible, where you start with just Adam and Eve, and then get Cain and Abel– but who was their wives?"

"Laverne and Shirley."

Jett grins and scratches the back of his head the exact way his brother does.

"Yeah, but where did they *come* from?"

It is not quick work, Jett placing and pulling the hose, having to move the truck every few withdrawals, and they've only accounted for half the coterie and a few outliers when the Eradicator eases off the highway, bumping over the hummocky ground past them, the brothers, who she realizes now must be twins, waving almost shyly to each other in passing. Jerry parks at the extreme rear of the colony and begins to sow his death pellets, sealing holes with wads of wetted newspaper, with a teenaged boy, maybe his son, to help with the task.

"Rained last night," mutters Jett, wrestling the hose into a particularly dog-legged hole, "you got me just in time."

"Did you two ever work together?"

"Oh, we had a lawn-mowing operation when we were in high school. People couldn't tell us apart or thought there was just one, used to call us 'Jimmy.' Made us some money, but when you got different philosophies of life"– Jett gets the hose past the obstruction, pushes it down till it's snug– "it don't profit none to force the issue. We get along fine Thanksgiving dinner and Christmas."

Odysseus is hard to get ahold of once he's in the chamber, shrinking back into the far corner beyond her reach, and Leia has to ask Jett for help. He pulls on a work glove from a back pocket, sticks his arm in up to the shoulder, makes a pensive face as he fishes around. Odysseus is bicycling his rear legs when he's pulled out into the daylight.

"Lively little feller."

"Odysseus."

"You got names for em."

"Easier to remember than B-13, B-14." Leia takes him from Jett, places him in an empty cage. "You see the dye markings."

"That must of took you a while."

"Field work can be labor-intensive. You need a lot of patience."

"So you, what– hang out and watch what they do?"

"Observe, record, analyze."

"And when they go down in their burrows?"

"You wait for them to come up."

Jett mulls this over, the boredom factor of the job striking him as it does most people outside the field.

"Could you get like a small camera down there?"

"With a light on it? Sure. But that would monitor only one spot in a whole network of tunnels. Like a security camera stuck in the drainpipe of your sink."

"Not gonna get great ratings from the home audience."

"So we have to assume a lot from their behavior when they're up top."

"And the rest of it is in the dark."

"We figure they sniff each other out, make noises. This bunch"– she indicates the holes around them, numbered stakes pulled from the ones they've already vacuumed– "have a special call for when they see me."

"They know who you are?"

"Same person, same clothes– I've recorded it. I set up to observe at daybreak and it's like 'There she is again.'"

"Wow." Jett turns the motor on and almost immediately there is a snick in the hose and a thap, slightly off-key, in the chamber. He flicks the switch, the noise dying, a frown on his face.

"Didn't like the sound of that."

Jett moves to the passenger side of the truck, digs under the seat.

"Not strictly my business, but this bunch doesn't have the plague or anything, do they?"

"No. I've been lucky. The fleas around here– that's what spreads it– don't seem to have been infected. But it'll wipe out a whole colony in no time."

"Don't tell my brother, he'll have it in a bottle."

Jett comes out with a long, pirate-looking telescope and some equally long salad tongs, as well as a flashlight, which he hands to Leia.

"Gonna need your help."

He props the trap door open with the telescope and Leia kneels to point the flashlight beam into the padded chamber. Jett bends to look through the tele-scope, swiveling it left and right, then reaches in with the salad tongs.

"Not exactly brain surgery," he says, probing with the tongs, "but I've gotten the hang of it with practice."

He seems to grab onto something with the tongs, pulling the telescope out to drop it on the ground and taking a few deep breaths as he looks at Leia.

"You take that flashlight and clear over to the far side of this patch. I'm gonna have to move quick."

Leia backs away, turning the flashlight off and watching him. When she stops twenty feet away Jett gives out something like a board-smashing karate yell and whips the tongs out of the chamber, flicking them hard past the rear of the truck.

It is a moment before Leia can distinguish the wrist-thick rattlesnake wrapped around the tongs, the serpent quickly uncoiling itself to flow straight and fast into the nearest empty hole. Jett is laughing.

"Rabbits, gophers, field mice, salamanders– they might be pissed off when you pull em out, but none of them's gonna lay a killer bite on you. But rattlers." He shakes his head. "You wonder do they kill whatever prairie dogs are in the holes they claim or make some kind of deal with em?"

Leia retrieves the salad tongs. "My next grant proposal– 'Viper/Ground Squirrel Cohabitation– Predation or Symbiosis?'"

Jett looks at her, smiling, but not the what planet did this geek come from? kind of smile.

"So you get paid for this study or whatever?"

"There's a living stipend included in the grant."

"That pays for rent in Yellow Earth?"

"It did before the boom started."

"Yeah." Jett looks back to where his brother is methodically poisoning burrows. "A rising tide lifts all boats– except for the ones it sinks."

She has often wondered about the possibility of a group consciousness, a mammalian version of what goes on in an ant colony or beehive, a kind of *knowing* shared by all the town residents and somehow passed from generation to generation. How long has this outfit been here? Since before the first humans arrived? The insect jocks posit that you can consider the whole colony as a single organism, individual ants something like cells with discrete functions and communication paths to other cells. And this colony, this organism that may have existed for thousands of years, is being eradicated. Does it know? Do those dogs still below sense that something incomprehensible is happening? That the end is near? And if she takes a cutting and transplants it, has she saved the colony or created something new, some monster of intervention, freaks in a zoo without walls? The department will certainly be inclined to throw her data out, to censure her misuse of scarce funding and her anthropomorphic meddling with life in the raw. She can shift her focus to the effects of translocation, of course, compile data on digging behavior and survivorship. One of her favorite words– "Mom, Dad, I'm taking a course in survivorship." A real study would have an elaborate preparation, the new host site carefully vetted and modified, wildlife officials notified. But this drilling is like a prairie fire, and you have to save what you can–

It will smell something like garlic when the pellets begin to react to the moisture in the holes, phosphine gas filling the tunnels and chambers quickly, the animals breathing it in, their lungs immediately edematous, rib cages pulsing as they struggle for air, mitochondria beginning to break down throughout the body, their hearts losing function–

"You have any favorites?"

The question brings Leia back to the task at hand, three-quarters of her cages filled to capacity, the late-winter sun already starting to sink, a stiff wind picking up.

"There's a certain– de*tach*ment– required if you're going to do real science," she says. "It's not like they're your pets."

"We raised cattle, beef cattle." Jett is forcing the hose down the next burrow. "Both me and Jerry did the whole 4-H deal with calves. Looked after their feed, cleaned their stalls, kept track of their weight gain. Mine was Ren and his was Stimpy."

"Excellent cow names."

"And we showed em at the big state fair in Minot. You groom em, right, make sure there's no cowflop hanging from their behinds when you lead them into the ring, you even got this stuff they use in theater to color people's hair, Streak N' Tips?"

"You put makeup on your calves?"

"Sometimes they'll have like a spot that don't look so good, more like a patch of scrofula than a regular marking– anyway, Ren won the blue ribbon even though Jerry had worked a lot harder raising Stimpy."

"A point of some contention."

Jett nods. "And then they grew up and joined the rest of the herd and we sold em to get et at the Ponderosa Steak House."

"Could you recognize them when they matured?"

"Oh sure. The markings are all a bit different. Not like your critters here, got to paint code numbers to tell em apart."

The oil workers, when they are togged out in their hardhats and safety vests, look pretty clone-like to Leia, and they've displayed a predictably narrow range in their mating behavior so far. And then there's Jett and Jerry, identical except for the species of rodent featured on their ball caps–

The sheriff's department car comes by then, slowing on the dirt shoulder of the highway, Himself looking out behind the authority-figure sunglasses and then hitting the gas and taking off with a whoop of siren, flasher strobing above as he kicks up dust blasting past the stream of inbound traffic.

"Will Crowder," says Jett over the sound of the sucking machine. "Good fella."

Will. She was going to cyberstalk him some more tonight, look again for any consumer reviews–

"The sheriff."

"Not on this side of the road. You did check in with Harleigh, didn't you?"

"Harleigh."

"The big honcho of the Three Nations. This is his land."

"Oh– sure."

She has assumed that nobody could protest removing animals about to be poisoned from land about to be fracked.

"I don't think they got like a prairie dog clan or totem or whatever, but Indians can be touchy about whatever's on the rez property."

She knows that one of the tribe's foundation stories begins with them living underground, that their traditional houses resembled prairie dog mounds–

Another thump, Ajax, if she has her dogholes straight.

Jerry and his assistant are coming closer, mass murder quicker than rescue.

"They have problems with their teeth."

"Pardon?"

He has to shout as the motor begins to whine, perhaps something too wide stuck in the hose. "Their *teeth*. I been told that afterwards, from the crash when they shoot in or getting a dislocated jaw or whatever, some of em get problems with their teeth. You'll want to look into that."

Leia has a set of ring pliers to pry their mouths open and caliper the cusps of their molars, the best way to verify age.

"I'll do that," she says, a bit put out that Sheriff Will didn't stop to investigate, "and send you the dentist bill."

"BLACK HILLS GOLD," SAYS Jolene facing the class, just barely loud enough for Francine to hear her in the rear. Public speaking is a skill no longer taught separately at the high school, but one she considers important enough to impose on her students.

"The Black Hills of South Dakota were originally the hunting ground of the Native American, principally those who used to be called the Sioux."

It is a constant effort keeping up with tribal nomenclature, as the Chippewa

become the Ojibway become the Anishinaabe (and even then some bands in
Canada are still using the old terms). Francine is not old enough to remember when colored people stopped being Negroes and became black, but was
around when they started morphing into 'people of color,' an inclusive but
sometimes confusing category. There aren't enough of them here in Yellow
Earth to pose much of an issue, though, and the few Native people she knows
well are likely to use 'Indians' a lot, as in 'they got some real crazy Indians down
on Standing Rock.'

"The Treaty of Laramie, in 1868," continues Jolene, "between the United
States and those Sioux who submitted to negotiations, gave them the legal right
to the Territory in perpetuity. But white Americans persisted in sneaking into
the area to search for gold. In 1875, in Deadwood Gulch, they found it."

The assignment was structured like a debate– Resolved: Fracking Is Both
Necessary and Beneficial– but the students were told to write out their argu-
ments first. There are some success stories in the school, two of her fourth period students bound for out-of-state colleges with no student loan hassle thanks
to oil-lease royalties flowing in. Fifty thousand dollars a month was one figure
she's heard in the faculty lounge. Most of the others have not been affected so
dramatically, and have chosen the direct approach to Francine's challenge, quoting their parents or articles about what's happening in town in the *Sky News*. But
Jolene has written a cautionary tale.

"Thousands of miners flocked to the new town of Deadwood, Dakota Territory, to seek their fortunes, not knowing or caring that they were trespassing on
somebody else's land."

You don't expect original research at this level, or even much original thinking. But something is revealed, some cogitation experienced in what they choose
to lift from Wikipedia, by how they shape or try to rephrase it. Antonia Kjarstad,
the oldest member of the faculty, says it used to be the *Encyclopedia Britannica*,
available in the library and possessed, in all its bulky authority, by some of the
more well-to-do families.

"The spearhead of the invasion was led by General George Armstrong Custer,
who guided over a thousand soldiers, scientists and fortune seekers onto the
Sioux land under the pretense of exploration and scientific inquiry. By 1876
miners had claimed land beside all the streams and creeks, practicing a form of
mineral exploitation called 'placer mining,' in which the power of the rushing
water is used to move and separate heavier gold flakes and pebbles from bottom

gravel. We now know how damaging this is to the environment, as the sluicing diverts natural flow patterns and dumps huge deposits of sediment downstream, putting tremendous stress on both invertebrate and fish populations."

Francine loves the fervor of the few true tree-huggers in her classes, their indignation at the crimes against the planet committed by their parents and everybody else who came before them. They are a minority here, surrounded by job-starved Middle Americans, which only adds to the romance of their position. She even has two vegans in her third-period class this year, in a state where beef is a religion.

"More geologically sophisticated miners searched for the sources of this washed-down placer gold, eventually discovering the hard rock deposits near what is now the town of Lead. The first of these bonanza mines, called the Homestake, supplied over a tenth of the gold in the world for the next century."

She hopes that 'geographically sophisticated' comes straight from Jolene and not some Wiki contributor. She is a quiet girl, never volunteers in class, but does her reading and aces the tests. One of the few Native kids in the school, one of the ones you hope gets away and doesn't come back.

"But as the gold was now ore-bound in solid rock, crushing mills had to be built to separate and concentrate the valuable metal, a process called 'free milling,' and then the concentrate was treated with mercury to further purify it. The discarded rock, or tailings, were often dumped carelessly near to the rivers and streams that supplied the power to run the mill, leaching mercury and arsenic, devastatingly toxic to human, animal, and plant life, into the water system."

The boom has been a godsend for Tucker, of course, and not just the paycheck. He was sleeping later and later after the diner failed and he had to sell out, then the layoff from the highway department—

'Hi– I'm Francine's anchor,' he'd introduce himself to new people, only half kidding.

He still grumbles some about the long hours, about his sore muscles, even about the 'bar time' he feels he has to spend at night to remain one of the team, but always with an undercurrent of pride, a man out in the world doing a tough job.

"But what of the original owners of the land? Their efforts to resist the encroachment of these destructive profiteers led to a series of armed conflicts, with the only major victory for the Native Americans being, ironically, the defeat and annihilation of General Custer and his Seventh Cavalry troop at the Battle of the Little Big Horn."

Most of the students have their glazed, receiving-distant-channels look on–
Dylan Foster has his head down in his arms, sleeping or stoned as usual– but a
few of the boys, including Kent Buckley, who is up next, are stiff and scowling at
this interpretation of events. Francine assigned no sides in the debate, just posed
the resolution, hoping for some democracy-in-action fireworks. Jolene plows on
in her near-monotone, eager to be off the stage.

"Chlorination and smelting, two even more resource-intensive techniques,
were brought to bear in the 1890s, and a pervasive culture of lawlessness, perhaps brought on by the numerical imbalance between male and female partic-
ipants in the gold rush, characterized the era. Stagecoach robberies, lynchings,
senseless murders, rapes, and prostitution went hand in hand with the get-rich-
quick hopes of the boomtown immigrants, a legacy of blood and misery that
perhaps outweighed the tons of shining gold that were eventually ripped from
the bowels of the earth. I'm told there is a popular television series currently running that documents these events"– and here Jolene looks to her teacher apologetically– "but we don't get HBO."

How much misery, thinks Francine, stepping forward to smile at the girl, out-
weighs a ton?

"That was excellent, Jolene. We have to think about the similarities between
our present situation and previous sudden-wealth scenarios. Kent, could you
share your thoughts with us?"

Kent, wearing his camo vest and army-green cargo pants for the occasion,
jumps up and takes his place at the front of the class, nearly hip-checking Jolene
as they pass. Kent is one of the influx of new kids, generally a really interesting
bunch, and one of the few whose father is actually on the rigs, as a toolpusher.
Mr. Buckley has rapidly gotten himself on the Board of Education, a constant
decrier of government waste and curricular subversion.

"Okay," says Kent, not looking at his paper, "let's start with this– a single NA-
SCAR entrant who finishes all five hundred laps is going to need at least a *hun*dred
gallons of gas for the race. What's the MPG on that, Dexter?"

Dexter, who the kids call Intel, doesn't look up from the Desert Storm tank
he's been drawing.

"Five miles per gallon," he says. "A lot less than a Prius."

Most of the students wake up enough to laugh.

"So then figure an F-16 jet fighter that flies from San Diego to Houston like
that"– he snaps his fingers– "gets less than *one* mile per gallon."

Jolene is sitting with her head lowered now, having had her say with no interest in a fight.

"We're not gonna run those babies on *switchgrass*."

IT IS HARD TO find a gap in the traffic even at night. Leia totters across the highway with the last of the bulky cages, four p-dogs crouching silently within it, a pipe-hauler honking as it catches her in the headlights, then makes her way across the stubble on the far side to where she left her flashlight as a beacon. She's breathing hard as she lays the cage on the ground next to the others, tossing a handful of oat clusters in through the wire. She hopes the livetraps are coyote-proof, as the coterie will be out here all night at the edge of Poker Flats, at least able to smell and hear each other. Jerry said the earthmover will come at sunrise to plow over the colony ground, and the animals left there, dead or dying, will be buried.

The wind has died down some, and Leia pulls her hood down and sits by Odysseus, in with Nike and Medea and one of the female juveniles. The sky is clear and jet black, the stars especially bright. Trucks rumble past and there is scuffling from the cage as Odysseus and Medea, ghostly white in the moonlight, kiss and cuddle. Leia shivers, staring at the river of lights on the highway, as alone in the world as she's ever felt.

THORA AND BOB DON'T come up from St. Paul that often, so Rick has to make an appearance with the family. When his father was still with them there was a rule– no politics at the table. That was for out by the shed, like smoking. Ma never obeyed it, of course, but at least there was somebody to call a timeout, somebody to change the subject.

Thora is pregnant again, and Ma gets Thora's two and his two busy trying to lasso the lawn furniture out back, whooping heard whenever there is a successful toss. Ma says she had to rope horses and calves before she went off to Carleton and got radicalized. Her father, who was council chairman for a while, ran cattle before and after the dam was bullied in, and in all the old photos looks like a cowboy with a sunburn.

"I suppose any money is better than none," says Bob, who is seriously white and sells Minnesota lakeside properties to people with second homes, and insisted his boys, Caleb and Isaac, go to something called a 'progressive' school, where they get evaluations instead of grades, "but all this truck traffic has got to wear on your nerves."

"They take whatever they can turn into money," says Ma, grinding pepper into the stew, "and leave behind the poison."

It would be easiest to just let her go unchallenged, let her chant the old refrains that have gotten the People nowhere.

"Truck exhaust," says Bob. His parents were Bible thumpers of some stripe, Church of Holiness, maybe, and though Bob has 'transcended all that,' he dresses like a Christian missionary out ringing doorbells.

"Truck exhaust, frack water, oil spills, flare-off gas, venereal disease," says Ma. It doesn't look like there will be anything to dip in the stew gravy, Ma's revelation about the insidious Fry Bread Plot, the white devils' sly campaign of genocide-by-carbohydrate coming to her just before last Thanksgiving. And cornbread is out till the Super Valu carries something other than Indian Head meal.

"That's a new one on me," Rick ventures. "I wasn't aware that drill pipe carried venereal disease."

"The men who bring it here do. I talked to Angeline who works for the Health Service? She says there's been a spike in the incidence."

It was the first sex talk he ever received, Ma on the warpath about old-time fur trappers giving the Ree women syphilis and babies being born blind. Put him off the idea of copulation for nearly a week.

"Teenage pregnancy?" asks Thora, who miscarried when she was sixteen, leaving her free to finish high school, get a scholarship, and meet Bob.

"Don't think those numbers can get any worse."

Ma doesn't care about marriage, as she is eager to tell you, just good relationships and responsible parents, *both* of them. When Thora was done mourning– she was only four months gone with the pregnancy when she lost it– Ma gave her the lecture about being ready to bring a life into the world, and she took it to heart. Ma's talks on the subject with Ricky were more like feminist cautionary lectures, with the only positive result a supply of several packets of condoms in the eleventh grade, great for display with the guys though they never saw action.

"Is this like a traditional recipe?" ventures Bob.

"My mother made it, if that's what you mean. Probably got it from Betty Crocker." Ma can deadpan white people better than anybody he knows, keep them guessing, and it used to be something he liked about her. She did go through a Native Cooking phase, hitting on the hunters for whatever their wives refused to skin and gut, but it went unappreciated. His father liked hot dogs, chili, macaroni and cheese, what he called Real American Food. He'd go on about how the People had always eaten what was most available, what was in season.

'And hot dogs are never out of season.'

Hard to say if him putting ketchup on everything Ma cooked was truly just a matter of taste or an act of aggression, but Rick and Thora would meet eyes when he'd whack the Heinz bottle with the heel of his hand, Ma freezing still in her seat, face blank, till he laid it aside, as if psychically absenting herself from the scene of the sacrilege. But it was his non-activism that really split them apart.

'Bunch of born-again Indians acting out,' he'd say. 'Only going to bring the damn federal government down on our heads again.'

He made a distinction between the federal government and the Marines, his stories conveying a grudging kind of pride at having survived all the chickenshit of Basic and the soul-killing Asian war that followed. How he and Ma, who'd proudly been arrested at least three times for protesting what he was up to over there, ever got past hello was never explained in detail.

'The reservation is like a greasy spoon diner,' he'd wink. 'Not too many choices on the menu.'

He'd say it to tease Ma, but it was pretty much true, and when Thora got over not being a teen mother she took a good look around at the possibilities and was soon in a freshman dorm three states away.

"Some people must have hit the jackpot though," she says now, laying out forks and knives. "The ones with clear title to their land."

"The Hansens, the Micklejohns," says Ma, tossing the salad. "Grover Drags Wolf. They'll be cash-rich till they burn through it. Dusty and Ray Wyatt have picked up and moved to California."

"It's the *Wheel of Fortune*!" Rick intones in an announcer's voice.

Ma doesn't look at him, ladling stew into bowls. "Who wants to sell out their neighbors, their People? When you make money that way, it isn't real."

"Funny," says Rick, "the stores around here all seem to accept it."

"Call the kids in," Ma tells Charlotte, who as usual has been keeping her head low and her opinions to herself. "We're ready to eat."

Isaac comes in with a rope around Caleb, then his own girls, wired to see their older, off-the-rez cousins, and they sit at the table. Bob mutters some New Age kind of grace thing, not so transcended as he thinks.

"I baked some five-grain bread," says Ma, indicating a tan brick on the table. "Ricky can slice it if you want some."

With a chainsaw, he thinks, remembering the last encounter with Ma's healthful baking efforts. Bob is staring warily at the bowl of stew in front of him.

"Mrs. Crow's Ghost," he asks, "does this have elk in it?"

"That's the meat. Fresh killed."

"But the wasting disease– "

"Colorado, maybe, but not up here. And it's most likely to be found in the brain, spinal cord, eyes, spleen, tonsils, lymph nodes."

The cousins make retching noises till Thora tells them to stop. She and Bob don't let them eat processed sugar. At home they have a juicer that reduces carrots, apples, celery, whatever, into an almost-drinkable pulp, making a sound like a drilling rig in labor. Bob holds a chunk of the elk on the end of his fork, hesitating to do the wild thing.

"Really, Bob," Ma reassures him. "I talk to the fish-and-game people all the time, I buy organic when it's available, I've even had the tap water here checked twice."

Their father would smack the ketchup bottle even when the stuff poured out freely on the first tilt.

"There's been no problem with the water," says Rick, an edge in his voice. "Not here, not in Yellow Earth, not anywhere in the formation. The shale is too deep here, and we never had coal mining shafts crossing underground at all levels like in Pennsylvania."

"When we drove in last night the flare-offs were blazing all around us. It was pretty if you didn't– you know– *think* about it too much." Thora always tried to be the peacemaker, though Rick knew their father already had one foot out the door.

Rick remembers using the construction site for the casino like a jungle gym, trying to hurdle the yellow caution tape and cracking up laughing when one of the guys would tangle in it and go down, remembers never quite succeeding in their mission impossible to steal a nail gun when nobody was looking. Kids are indestructible, he thinks, because they know so little.

There wasn't a big fight or an official divorce announcement, just their father packing to leave for the logistics base in Barstow and Ma staying in the house till the car was gone.

"You'll hear from me when you least expect it," he winked, which was true enough, until even expectation died. Rick laid a lot of blame on Ma for a while, at that age where whatever your parents do is purposely designed to ruin your life, but she was never easy to put on the defensive.

'Just concentrate on what kind of man you're going to be,' she'd tell him in the middle of one of his sullen accusations. 'Think about what you can do for the People.'

Ma is like the nagging conscience of the Three Nations, and tends to make people, enrolled members especially, feel like they haven't done enough. 'Your mom is a real powerhouse,' people used to say, kindly leaving out the 'how can you stand it?' part.

"This is really good, Ma," says Thora. "Even if it does turn our brains into mush in ten years."

The boys make zombie faces and noises till Bob gives them a look. He is okay for a white guy, maybe even more into the boys' 'appreciating their heritage' than Thora, who has stated she'd just as soon skip the whole Native American thing if it has to come with a loser mentality.

And somehow Ma always gives her a pass.

"You must have your hands pretty full, Rick," says Bob, steering elk nuggets to the side of his bowl. "How you bearing up under the invasion?"

Rick pauses a beat, in case Ma wants to fire the first volley, then plunges in.

"The most important thing," he explains, zeroing in on his brother-in-law, "is to establish the principle, once and for all, that how we handle our land, our water, our mineral wealth, should be our business and nobody else's. These oil and gas companies have learned to come straight to us without going through the state or the Feds."

"So you're the energy czar in these parts."

Ma is busy sawing away at the bread, thin slabs clunking down on the plate. Hell, you can slice marble in a quarry with the right tools–

"Harleigh Killdeer, our chairman, is more like the czar. I'm the– what would you call the guy who sorted out disputes back in old Russia– ?"

"Rasputin," says Thora. She always creamed him at Jeopardy!, absorbing non-sports-related facts like a sponge and able to spit them back out when prompted.

"As I remember, Rasputin was a pretty negative character. I'd like to think I'm serving the People."

"Serving them on a plate," says Ma, buttering five-grain for the boys.

Rick softens his voice, trying to condescend without getting dinnerware thrown at him. "My mother," he says, "believes the Spirit of the Shale Oil wishes to be left in peace. That if we drive the corporations from our land and stop eating Cocoa Puffs for breakfast the buffalo will frolic once again on the prairie."

There are two photos of Ma in the living room, one with Joan Baez, who for the longest time he thought was an aunt or a cousin, and another a year later, right after Wounded Knee, belly swollen, about to pop with him, headed for jail.

"My son," answers Theresa Crow's Ghost, who in remembrance of treaties broken has refused to sign her name to a document since she made her mark on a marriage license thirty-six years ago, "has not only drunk the oppressors' Kool-Aid, but has invented a brand-new flavor. It tastes like forgetfulness, with a hint of petroleum."

Thora smiles at her husband. She has a beautiful smile, pure sunshine, which is how she got away with being ironic so long before it was in fashion. "Way too many Indians," she says, "and not enough chiefs. No wonder we lost the continent."

The main course over, Thora gets the boys started on an epic five-hundred-piece puzzle of Custer's Last Fight she's brought along– irony again– then retires into the kitchen with Ma and Charlotte to assemble dessert and talk gynecology.

"It's all done by lease," Rick explains to Bob the real estate salesman, "so no land actually changes hands. That's key. People have been doing that for centuries here, renting out pasture land, crop land, taking a toll if folks hunt or fish on their property."

"But the whatever– tribal entity– has to have some say."

"We try to lay down some reasonable ground rules, looking out for everybody in the enrollment, even if they're not lucky enough to be sitting on something the oil people want. Like the Tlingits, or some of those other north coast outfits, they'd have a sachem or a council of elders to regulate the haul when the salmon run started."

"But salmon return every year."

"Oil is just a resource, like any other, and when it's all been pumped out, guess what? We're still here, the land is untouched or reclaimable, the grass grows, the river flows. But this time the world pays us the going rate for what they take."

"The going rate is dropping some," says Bob. "At the pumps on the way here, I couldn't believe we're back under– "

The women reemerge, announcing strawberry shortcake.

"Isn't it supposed to have that white stuff on top?" asks Caleb, frowning at his plate.

"Whipped cream," offers Rick, who used to get to lick the beater bowl.

"And what's that full of?" prompts Bob.

"Carcinogens?" ventures Isaac.

"Well, maybe not directly, but definitely a bunch of empty calories. Besides, it masks the taste of the strawberries."

"You two have picked *wild* strawberries." Thora is having the fruit with no shortcake, determined not to blow up the way she did with each of the boys. "With your grandmother?"

"They're too young to remember," says Ma.

"Red fingers," recalls the first one, wiggling his in her face.

"We used to make dye from berries," says Ma, using what Charlotte, when they are home alone, calls the 'tribal we.' "And we made it from some plants and flowers, from certain kinds of soil, from tree bark. You didn't take color for grant-ed, you had to work for it, you had to *plan*."

"We used to do all kinds of stuff the hard way," says Rick, who only accepted the damn environmental job from Harleigh to make his mother proud of him again, the way he'd enlisted during Desert Storm just to piss her off, and then never got deployed overseas. "We used to sit in earthen bunkers all winter breathing toxic wood smoke and ruining our lungs, and still nearly froze our butts off."

The kids all laugh at 'butts,' as expected. Ma has gone into her trance, shutting down her face, absolutely still.

Whack the bottom of the ketchup bottle. *One, two, three–*

"But now we have oil and gas heat, we have cars that can drive us all the way from St. Paul, we have *X-ray* machines," he adds, looking at his mother, a breast cancer survivor thanks to modern medicine, "instead of bark poultices and spirit chants. We have Nintendo– "

The boys look to their father, who shrugs, equally uncool–

"–and various other computer games that engage the mind and sharpen the reflexes. We have antibiotics. The world moves on," he says, his voice gaining power the way Harleigh's does at this point in the stump speech, "and if we have the courage, the *will* to move on with it, the sky is the limit."

Ma sits back then and looks at him, hands folded in her lap, conceding this round for the sake of familial harmony.

"When Harleigh steps down or gets kicked out," says Thora, pointing a forked strawberry at him, "*you* ought to take over this mess."

WAYNE LEE HAS BEEN places, even foreign ones. Spartina has been to Fargo to visit an aunt and three times to the capital for school activity trips. Wayne Lee has done things, many of them daring, some even illegal. He has given her a picture of himself on a surfboard.

"That's the point break at Rincón," he told her. "What a day. Perfect sets, not too many barneys in the water, we were really killing it."

Spartina has never seen the ocean. There is a ski resort just over in Mandan, but she's never even been on a snowboard.

It takes them a while to get off of the 2, the main road through town always clogged with trucks now. Her grandfather complains about the noise from the rumble strips they've put in, but he'd complain more if the drivers blew through as fast as they'd like to. There are lines of cars and pickups stretching out from the lots of all the chain restaurants– Taco John, Arby's, the Chinese buffets, Grandma Sharon's Family Café–

"Most of these dudes," says Wayne Lee as he turns his Camaro off onto Broadway heading east, "just cruise till they find the shortest line."

"We get men who come in with take-out sacks and stick them on the floor to eat out of while they drink coffee," says Tina.

"They're just there to check out you and your fellow Java Janes. They'd drink carbolic acid to stare at a nice set of legs."

"Our coffee is better."

"Might be, but that's not the attraction. *Órale, putas,*" he remarks as they pass a pair of bundled-up, short, dark girls talking on the sidewalk.

"What?"

"Working girls. They come up from Central America, follow the rigs."

"You mean like streetwalkers?"

"If you had streets here to walk without being blown away by the wind, maybe, but it's mostly online hookups now. I could show you how to make a date on that new phone of yours."

Tina giggles. "I don't want to make a *date.*"

"There's even a special app you could download."

"That's really gross."

"Human nature, darlin. Been going on since the caveman times." Wayne Lee is wearing a Cabela's cap and a down vest that are both kind of golden, to go with the Camaro and with his eyes. He shaves every day, unlike most of the oil workers who look like bikers or hillbillies with family feuds. She feels safe with him. Things have gotten intense in town– her grandfather says it's thirty thousand new men who've showed up, an easy hundred to every woman– and just this afternoon at work a trucker with a beard like Noah in the church pageant offered to buy the panties she was wearing.

"What you want to do," teased Wayne Lee when she told him, "is buy up a couple three new pairs, take the tags off and keep them in your locker or whatever you got in the back room there at work. Just wink and say you'll have to go to the bathroom, then come back and slip him one of those you never wore. Easy money, and it takes the personal aspect out of the transaction."

"That's disgusting."

"What do panties cost, anyway? The frilly ones? You want to think about your profit margin."

She could never talk so easy about sex with any of the boys at school, and so far there's been no– no *press*ure from Wayne Lee. He just seems to like being with her, being seen with her.

"Total ego trip," he says. "Any guy steering you around looks like a winner."

They've finally oiled the dirt road that runs past Jolene's house, promising to pave it on the Company nickel to make up for all the wear and tear, but that hasn't happened yet. The sheriff's car, silver with blue and yellow stripes, is idling on the shoulder. Tina turns her face away as they pass.

"On the scout for outlaws," says Wayne Lee, smiling. "Plenty of those in the mix here these days."

He says he works for an oil service company but somehow is always free to see her, before school, after work, whenever she's available. He took her out to Lonnie's Roadhouse once, a half-dozen violently tattooed guys greeting him with complicated handshakes and checking her out. He apologized afterwards.

"Not the right room for you," he said.

She's had to tell some tales to her grandfather, has invented a school club she says she belongs to, surprised by how easy it's gotten to lie to him. There's barely a boy in her senior class he'd approve of, of course, much less somebody older and out in the world already. He does a lot of painting in the winter and early spring, shut in by the weather, big rectangles of the prairie the way it used to look. She'll find him sitting at the easel with his eyes closed, not dozing but *seeing*, remembering.

"The cattle we had when I was a kid were more this color," he'll say, pointing to a small herd of brushstrokes he's laid down near the horizon, "before everybody switched to the more commercial breeds."

When they cross onto reservation land Wayne Lee pulls over and they switch seats. When Granpa still had the tractor and her legs were long enough to reach the pedals he let her drive it, so stick shift is second nature.

"Try to keep it under a hundred," says Wayne Lee as she pulls back onto the road. There's isn't a thing moving in any direction but a pair of hawks that might as well be painted in the sky, hovering nearly stationary over the field ahead, hoping to get lucky.

"I can't learn anything out here," she says. "It's all just straight lines."

"This isn't a driving lesson, it's so I can look at you instead of the road."

He says these things, Wayne Lee, that make her blush, and she can tell he means them.

"That's it, darlin, pedal to the metal. Even if we get pulled over, my man Brent got plenty juice with the chief."

His man Brent has been seeing Fawn, she knows, having sex with her somewhere while his wife is still in the picture. Wayne Lee has never suggested double dating.

It is fun to drive fast, drive fast in a car that was built for it, low and powerful and beautiful inside and out, with a heater that not only works but barely makes a whisper. Tina hits ninety and keeps it there, telephone poles whizzing by, Wayne Lee smiling slightly as he watches her.

"You think any more on what we talked about the last time?"

"Which was– ?"

"You going to college."

"You're just like my guidance counselor."

"I seriously doubt that. When do you start applying?"

"Pretty soon. It's expensive, though. Some of the schools, the ones that are hard to get in? Just to file a application it costs like– "

"All the more reason to give it some real thought."

"You didn't go to college."

"And I'm a pretty shady character. Any desire to join the military?"

"No."

"Hustle for the Mormons in Tahiti?"

"We're not Mormon."

"Then what other ticket you got to get out of Yellow Earth?"

"It isn't so bad."

"Cause you never been anywhere better."

"My grandfather *wants* me to go to school."

"Maybe just down the road in Bismarck."

"Anywhere that I want to go. That I can get into."

"Well, good for him then."

She slows and makes the turn for the lake.

"You'll do fine wherever you go, Spartina, so make it count."

She likes it when he says her full name, which used to embarrass her when Granpa said it in front of people, sounding old-fashioned and weird.

"Get yourself into one of those big outfits, kids from everywhere on the map. I used to hang on the UC campuses, it's like the United friggin Nations."

"You were taking classes– "

"Selling weed."

She keeps her eyes on the road. He laughs.

"You can't turn me in cause I already done the time for it."

"You were in jail?"

He shrugs. "County farm. Had to get in with the Aryan Brotherhood cause of the whole gang thing out there. You think those characters we met at Lonnie's were scary."

"How long were you in?"

"Less than a year, seemed like twenty. Prison time, it's like every hour is dragging a two-hundred-pound sack of shit behind it. In the work rooms they still had like the old clocks with the hands."

"Analog."

"Yeah, those. Watching that minute hand climb to the top like it's friggin Mount Everest."

"But you like California."

He grins. "Hey, me and the Beach Boys."

And then he serenades her with "Wish They All Could Be North Dakota Girls," making up lyrics, till they get to the boat ramp.

The cruiser, or whatever you call it, is still sitting there up on supports, tarped over.

"The floating clip joint," says Wayne Lee. "Except it's not floating."

"You don't like boats?"

"Hobie Cat, sloop, Sunfish, sign me up. I rode in a Rough Rider cigarette boat with some Colombian dudes once, all it needed was wings to take off and fly. That thing"– nods toward the *Savage Princess*– "is just a toy meant for a very big bathtub."

He undoes his seatbelt then, which is her cue to do the same. She loves the way he looks at her when they break to breathe, like he can't believe she's really there with him. The rest, the surprising tongue, him touching her more intimately every visit together, his breath hot on her neck, gives her what Fawn always calls 'tingles in the weewee,' and this time he slips his fingers into the panties the trucker in Havva Javva wanted to buy, and after he makes her way more than tingle, another surprise, she realizes they've fogged themselves in with heavy breathing.

"Engine," he says. "Defroster."

He watches her turn the car on, work the heater knobs, and she knows she's blushing again.

"You're almost there, darling."

"There."

"Ready for the whole deal. But you've got to tell me."

He's never said he'll come visit her if she goes to college, or how long he'll be in town, or anything about them together beyond the next time he messages her on her phone. But his willingness to wait for her–

"There was a way the Indians– maybe not these around here, but *some* Indians– used to catch eagles. Like for the feathers? A guy would have himself mostly buried, laying on his back, out where they'd seen eagles hunting, and after he was all camouflaged up they'd stake down a live rabbit or prairie chicken right over his chest. He'd spend a day, maybe two, laying out like that, watching the hawks and the buzzards and shouting them away if they got too close, waiting, got to know that rabbit pretty good. Finally, some big old beautiful bald eagle would swoop down and wham!"

Wayne Lee snaps his arms tight around her.

"The Indian would just fold that big bird in, hug it to death, and they figured not only was it good for the feathers, which carried a lot of power in their ceremonies, but some of that eagle's spirit passed into the man."

Wayne Lee's defroster works pretty well, front windshield first, then the sides and rear. When their condensation is nearly gone Tina sees that a car has pulled up next to them while they were making out, a red, sporty car with Fawn laughing in the passenger seat and Wayne Lee's muscle-bound man Brent, smirking and giving them a thumbs-up, behind the wheel.

She throws the Camaro into reverse, does a quick 180 and is back on the highway. Fawn has never kept a secret for more than five minutes in her life. But then, for whatever reason, Tina thinks of the intersecting circles they use to demonstrate sets and subsets in math. Her grandfather lives so far removed from any loop as to be out of the equation. Her heartbeat begins to decelerate—

"They must have come to take a look at that boat," says Wayne Lee, grinning.

It isn't the cleanest fraternity house he's ever been in. Getting out of Yellow Earth was extra impossible this morning, the water-truckers wise to the side roads by now, the dirt one he tried to duck them on almost impassable in the downpour, so he's late. Gene, who he wishes he could hire to absorb malcontents at the office, is already at the cleared table working motor skills with four of the more tractable residents when Prescott comes in.

"You missed breakfast, Mayor," says the counselor. "Justin's got kitchen duty."

This is a big deal, his son pitching in at the group home. The years of therapy and specialists, breakthroughs and regressions, from that first 'severely affected' diagnosis at the Ann Carlsen Center to the decision to place Justin here in Minot, have led to this triumph.

Kitchen duty.

The squat little Hispanic woman who cooks the first two meals nods to him, scouring egg from a giant skillet in the sink.

"Good morning, Justin," he calls, putting some cheer in his voice.

Justin looks at him, goes back to organizing the breakfast plates. This too is progress, after the early years where they thought he might be deaf, the long period where eye contact was received as intrusion if not threat.

The Home has a set of Fiestaware in all the colors, and Justin first rinses the plates in like-hued pairs before slipping them into the dishwasher in the same order. He has a dramatically negative response to odd numbers, to imbalance, so the counselors set an extra, unoccupied place at the table whenever the diners come out short of even.

"I was in the neighborhood," says Press, sitting in a chair out of the way, "and thought I'd drop by to see how you're making out."

Phyllis comes twice a week and Prescott every other Saturday. He tells her it's so Justin gets more visits, but really it's that the way she talks to him like he's still four years old is impossible to be around.

"You're looking good. Like you're getting outside a bit."

Justin is not a fan of the great outdoors, too many uncontrollable stimuli, but the counselors take them out en masse if it's not pouring like today. Justin is clean-shaven as always, doing it himself these days with the electric razor Press bought him, right half of his face, then the left. He wears the same outfit he settled on as a boy– tan chinos, solid-color blue shirt buttoned to the neck, white socks and Hushpuppy loafers. Once Justin had finally stopped growing, a couple years ago, Phyllis bought ten pairs of the shoes in case Hush Puppy should ever go out of business or discontinue the style.

He looks normal.

"I got murdered in traffic getting out of town. This drilling thing– you wouldn't recognize downtown these days."

Or approve, physical change one of the many banes of Justin's existence. Phyllis has kept up the rocketship wallpaper in his room for the always stressful holiday visits, has kept several pairs of chinos and a half-dozen blue shirts hanging in his closet. Once she tried to teach him to play checkers, but he kept snatching the jumped pieces and putting them back where they started. The set lies on top of his dresser in his room here, black discs on red squares, red on black, symmetrical. He likes the pattern.

"So good luck to me, trying to ride herd on all these new people," he says as Justin begins to separate knives from forks, forks from spoons. "You can push things through the council, you can meet with the Company reps and make as much noise as you want, but finally the law says folks are allowed to make their private deals. That's the free market, that's America."

He's not sure if the cook understands any English, and wonders for a moment if she might be somewhere on the spectrum as well. She goes up on her toes to hang the huge skillet to dry on a wall hook, then leaves the room.

"I like to tell the hotheads who come in to holler about some little regulation we've passed that steps on their toes, nibbles at their profit, to think of what would happen if those NFL teams took the field and there was no rules, no refs? Just get the ball and put it over the goal line, the hell with out of bounds, holding, illegal blocks and tackles, all that concussion protocol. There'd be fatalities is what, and the beer companies sure as hell wouldn't be buying millions of dollars worth of commercial time to peddle suds during the slaughter. I mean, what would happen to the *game*?"

Justin begins to load the segregated silverware into the washer. One of his favorite things at home was putting all the loose change into those paper bank wrappers. If there weren't machines to do it at the mint he'd have a job.

"So it's kind of like that old Dick Feller song– 'Making the Best of a Bad Situation.'"

Prescott listens to country in his car, Phyllis to fucking Jimmy Buffett in the house, and Justin to nothing, till a friend of theirs bought him a little folding-case record player, already an antique, and a stack of 45s. Out of all those records he locked onto "Yellow Submarine," playing it over and over, the yellow and orange swirls on the label going round and round on the turntable. The one attempt to interest him in the flip side, "Eleanor Rigby," induced Justin's noise, somewhere between a grunt and a cry, and a bout of spastic wrist-flapping.

"Maybe the idea that I ever had control of it, even before the oil, is just kidding myself. I mean what with crazy national politics, mass media, even the damn weather like today– you can't strong-arm that stuff on a city government level. So this tidal wave that's hit us, well, maybe here in Minot they were a bit more prepared, been dealing with all those men from the Air Force base for years, but it's just swept *over* us. The best I can hope for is to maintain a little decorum within the city limits, try to hit the Company people up for something that'll still be there when it all washes away. And believe me, there's never a boom without there's a bust. Gonna be a hell of a mess to clean up when they're gone."

Justin measures dishwasher soap exactly to the line in the plastic cup, pours it into the compartment, closes the door and hits the proper buttons. He'll stand before it now, watching the digital timer count down thirty-five minutes till the symmetrically arranged load is done, then pull everything out in his preferred order and put it away. When he was little and you took something from him, that damn Beatles record for instance, he would make his noise and keep staring at the spot where it had been, just staring for five or ten minutes. Prescott has had time to understand the logic of his son's mind. This is what I can *hand*le, this much and no more will not terrify me. His own life as mayor is such a minefield of decisions to make, situational hats to put on, performances private and public. His own life is exhilarating and unpredictable and will put him in an early grave.

You come here because you should, because you're the father, not because the young man acknowledges you or desires your company. Sometimes when Phyllis left them home alone together Press would give Justin a roll of bubble wrap and leave him in the next room, able to concentrate on work or watch a TV show with the constant *pop, pop, pop* reassuring him that the boy was safe and content. He'd take it away and hide it when he heard Phyllis in the driveway, Justin left staring at his own hands, thumbs poised to press the next plastic bubble.

"Anyhow," he says rising, "it's great to see you doing so well."

He knows not to try to hug his son. That had been the hardest for Phyllis, a baby who struggled to disengage from her arms, his indifference or aggression as a little boy. Justin would throw things, not *at* anybody or anything, but throw them, and hard.

"Your Mom will be by on Tuesday."

Prescott leaves the sack of toiletries with Gene and runs through the rain to his car. The other day counselor, Maurice, is out with a couple of the hardier residents making a wall of white-jacketed sandbags around the yard. Press has to set the wipers full speed and turn his headlights on, the sky darker now than when he left Yellow Earth. By the time he crosses the 16th Street bridge the Souris is flowing near up to the concrete, men in yellow-striped vests pulling barricade sections from a van, ready to block it off.

There's going to be a flood.

BULLETINS FROM THE BLACK STUFF

Everything's coming up hydrocarbons!

The Bakken boom's up to 4,697,000 barrels of oil this month, an all-time high, with sixty new rigs spudding in and now over a thousand wells producing.

Crude oil prices are rising, rising, rising from February's low of $35 for Texas Intermediate to a more-than healthy $79.89 per barrel. Hydraulic fracturing and horizontal drilling processes continue to be refined, which forecasts increased efficiency and $$$$$ for investors.

Regular gasoline holds at $2.64 at the pumps, but Americans are heading back to the highways.

Carpe oleum!

THERE'S NOTHING BENEATH THE surface.

That's what Brent says, and with all the oil people he talks to, including some of the scientists, he should know. So it's theirs for a song, fourteen acres, and he wants the house put up on the highest spot, though it's hard to tell where that might be.

Bunny follows him and the builder, who has come over from Montana or he'd cost more, as they make a circuit around the staked footprint of the house. They're moving fast, Brent so excited these days, she's never seen him more full of life, enjoying his success, and she's listening hard to throw in a little caution if his ideas start spiraling out of control.

Just a little caution.

"The thing is," he says, "I need this to be more than a house. It needs to be a *state*ment."

He's said that to her a dozen times, though never explaining exactly what statement it will be. The builder is saying "Uh-huh, uh-huh" a lot and nodding his head, but it's clear he's just waiting for Brent to get to something specific, something that can be turned into boards and stone and glass, which is when she'll get to throw in her plea for some normal spaces. Brent has read that book about the crazy architect so many times he probably thinks he could sit down right now and whip off a blueprint for something that would amaze people, that they'd drive for miles to see and take pictures of. But of course he said the whole point was to give them some privacy.

"Like living in a fishbowl," he keeps saying. "No, not a fishbowl, a shark tank. People pressing their noses against the glass, hoping to see you get eaten."

The glass is a big deal with him.

"You know the glass, like on a really loaded town car, where the passenger can see out but people on the street can't see *in*."

"Tinted," says the builder. "Tinted and polarized."

"But you can get it for big windows."

"Sure, if you want to pop for it. All of these things you're saying, customized features, are going to run you more."

"I want a lot of it. So we're not getting stared at, but every way you look, there's a view."

Of what? thinks Bunny. They're not near the river or the lake or the city or any other houses, and all she can see if she turns a full circle is a couple oil derricks in the distance.

"It does cut down on the *bright*ness of what you'll see outside. Which in the summer won't necessarily be a bad thing."

"I want a carport attached here," says Brent, pointing to a spot on the string that stretches between the stakes. "With room for three vehicles."

Brent likes people to see the Corvette, which is a beautiful thing, but now that he's bought it hates to leave it out under the weather. What the other two things in the carport are going to be he hasn't told her. She'd love a Miata, and has said so, but Brent says house first, then we'll deal with transportation.

"The pictures you'd showed me, Mr. Skiles," says the builder, "require materials not easily available up here, require lumber that's not in standard lengths, require some real skill in construction."

"Meaning?"

"Meaning I'm not going to be able to hire local framers, a bunch of kids to throw the usual box up."

"Of course not."

"And bringing in more skilled carpenters is going to add to the– "

"Fifteen miles down the road," says her husband, pointing, "there's a man camp on the reservation, I put all my out-of-state drivers in there, cheap, cheap, cheap, but they got a food court twenty-four-seven, they got cable."

"That could work."

If only once it's done it could be picked up and carried to someplace else, someplace wonderful, Monterey on the California coast maybe. Brent says the oil business is here to stay, that this will be their base to make trips from, like when they went to Hawaii. But that he's going to work it so a lot of the expense gets written over to the company, he'll have a room that's just his office, and that staying in the hotel with the prices raised up the way they are is stupid. And after the years of barely unpacking before they had to move on, this, whatever it turns into, will be a real home.

"A house, a real house, should say something about the person who lives in it," says Brent. He's got that tone in his voice that means a lecture, that means just be quiet and listen. "And most houses do, in a way, they say 'A loser lives here' or 'Somebody on government assistance lives here' or 'A man with zero taste and imagination had this stack of shit thrown up.' But when any of them out there look this way"– he says, waving his arm to indicate the prairie dogs and the coyotes and maybe an actual person standing on top of one of those derricks– "it's going to blow their minds a little. 'Is that a fort, is that a castle, is that a mansion transported here from the future?' Whoever lives in that place, whoever had it built, is something out of the ordinary."

"We'll need an architect," says the builder, "or at least a qualified draftsman, to draw up the plans."

"And somebody to do that computer thing," adds Brent, "so I can see it 3-D, move around inside a bit."

"That can be arranged."

"The important word here is *speed*. You see those rigs going up on the way? Those boys don't stand around with their hands in their pockets, they hit the ground running, build the rig, then move on to the next one."

"You can pull anything off if you're willing to pay," says the builder. Bunny can tell he's still feeling Brent out, wondering if he's for real or not. Brent is the realest person he'll ever meet.

"You come to a crossroads between speed and expense, my friend, you take the superhighway. These big oil outfits, once they commit to a play, they throw everything they got into it. The companies that try to sneak in on the cheap, that want to hedge their bets, they end up with zip."

Brent does the money things and has her sign the papers. He's explained to her how to make debt work for you, how once you owe a vendor a certain amount they have to give you more credit in hopes of eventually getting paid at least some of what they're owed, how everybody smart does business this way, including the federal government. He didn't go to college but he's studied it, studied it in the real world, and if it weren't for some freaky bad breaks– things nobody could have foreseen– they'd have made their pile of fuck-you money years ago.

"Have you ever built a gymnasium?"

"You mean like with a basketball court and all that?"

"More like a heavy-duty health club. I'll get you some photographs."

"Sure. But the special equipment– weight machines and all that– "

"Those I'll order myself, you just have to worry about the specs on the box. Any big worries?"

The builder looks around. They rode in in his pickup, Brent leaving the Vette at the side of the road, what seemed like a quarter mile away.

"Oh, power, water, cable hookup," sighs the builder. "You see where we are."

"Impossible?"

He shrugs. "Expensive."

Brent grins. "That's how they get you. 'Oh, come in and link up with us, be part of our system, it's so convenient.' You think the people who settled this region came here to join what was already established? No way. They were running away from that life."

Running away from *some*thing, thinks Bunny. Refugees. Or maybe their wagons broke down–

Brent steps back and looks at the empty space above the land with nothing under it, smiling, as if the house is already there. She loves it when he's on an upswing like this, when she doesn't have to hide or tiptoe around, like the air around him is likely to electrocute her. If this oil thing can just keep growing, if the music can never stop–

"Before any great thing is made, any great deed is done," he says, that voice coming back, "somebody, some indi*vid*ual, has to *see* it in their head. To have a *vision*, not of what already is, but what can *be*."

He stands there looking at the vision of what will be for so long that she can see the builder is getting uncomfortable, not sure if he should break into the reverie or not. Bunny raises her hand slightly to get his attention.

"Uhm– could I talk to you– about the kitchen?"

IT'S A FAIRGROUNDS LIKE any other, Ferris wheel, a few rides emitting heavy metal music and screams, food and drink stands. The 4th is on a Sunday this year, so Jewelle has the night off, wandering among the crowd under the lights, happy to be in a place with so many other females. She has an Italian sausage sandwich with peppers and a limeade, half a sugar-dusted zeppole, and moves to get a good bleacher seat for the fireworks. They had some at the little speedway the other night after the stock car races, but she was working, plucking scraps of red, white and blue clothing off her body and flinging it out at drunken, hollering oil workers.

She's come unpainted to the event, no lipstick, no eyeliner, her press-on nails in the little box in the club dressing room, a BOOMTOWN, USA cap over her pinned-up hair. She's been to these in other towns, tries to never miss it, a community event where you don't feel like such an outsider. It's great to see so many kids– they're off to school before she wakes up, not very evident on the wide, vehicle-rumbling streets of Yellow Earth. Still making them here, and many of these families look like they have nothing to do with drilling or fracking. The stands start to fill, a tall, nice-looking guy maybe close to her age, on his own, squeezing in next to her.

"Almost showtime," he says and smiles.

It starts with a single spotlight beam going straight up, then the "Star-Spangled Banner" comes on the PA system and people stand and take their hats off and many put their hands over their hearts as they sing along. A cheer when it's over, everybody settling back down, and *Pop!* a wiggly white trail streaking upward that *Bam!* bursts into a round, perfectly symmetrical ball of glowing green fragments. Another cheer.

She finds herself smiling as the barrage continues, leaning back shoulder to shoulder with the guy, who she can see, in the flash of the bigger, brighter explosions, is smiling as well.

"What makes the colors?" she asks nobody in particular.

"Metal salts, metal oxides," says the tall guy. "They're coating the little stars that are mixed in with the gunpowder for the second explosion, and when they're heated up by the blast, depending on what metal it is, they glow a certain color."

Jewelle gives him a look. "Are you a rocket scientist?"

He laughs. "Just a glorified rock jock. But I was fascinated by these things when I was a kid."

"So what was that one?"

"Yellow Chrysanthemum is probably sodium nitrate."

"That's what that kind is called?"

"They're named after the shapes they make as they spread out, and a lot are named after flowers or trees. That– that one's a Willow, see how they curve out then weep down."

"Gold and silver."

"Let's see– red is strontium, green is barium, copper burns blue. Then if you combine them you can get other shades, just like with mixing paint."

They watch in silence for a minute, the crowd oohing and aaahing the effects in the sky. They are addictive, of course, and you just want more and more.

"You said there's two explosions."

"One– that kind of dull thump before it shoots up– is powder in the bottom of the rocket, which is sitting in a mortar, which is just a narrow tube pointed up.

That powder is on a short fuse, but a *longer* fuse gets lit at the same time, which reaches the second ball of powder and the stars around it at a certain height, which makes the explosion we see. Pretty simple technology– people have been doing it for centuries."

"But you've got to be careful to make them right, to shoot them at the right angle."

"Oh, sure. A show like this is a lot of work."

"But just to be pretty."

"And awesome."

"Yeah, I guess so."

They watch as the fireworks fill the sky, the man telling her which is the Diadem and the Peony and the Palm and the Crossette and the Cake, which is just a mass of many Roman candles all at once. Then suddenly there is a towering oil rig before them, outlined by golden lights.

"And finally, on this Fourth of July," says a deep male voice over the PA system, "we'd like to celebrate a special form of Independence– the independence from foreign oil!"

With that there is a gusher of fireworks shooting up and spilling outward from the top of the derrick, building to a red, white and blue climax, the smell of gunpowder smoke in the air, the audience cheering solidly for the full five minutes of the eruption.

He walks her to the parking lot. His name is Randy and he's a geologist.

"Any hint that there's hydrocarbons lurking under the ground," he says, "they send me in to see how much and how deep. Then they have me stick around a while to develop the resource."

"So you travel a lot."

"Up to a half a million frequent-flyer miles. If I ever get a chance to go somewhere not for work, it'll be for free."

"They keep you busy."

"Are you from around here?" he asks, a cautious note creeping into his voice.

"No."

"Well, busy is good. If it's not a national holiday there's not a hell of a lot to do."

"No kidding."

"I mean for the young guys there's bars, a couple of those strip clubs downtown– Buzungas."

"Bazookas," she says. "I work there."

Not a hiccup of hesitation. "Yeah? Waitress? Dancer? Owner?"

"I dance."

"Good money?"

She holds her arms out. "Here I am in Yellow Earth."

"What kind of shift do you pull?"

"Little bit under eight. But it's pretty intense."

"I can imagine."

"You've never been there?"

He shrugs. "Not my kind of deal. You want me to come see you work?"

She doesn't have to think about it. "No."

He laughs. Very good-looking guy, and not nearly as– as *hungry* as most she meets.

"It's not like I'm ashamed of it or anything, I just– it's nice not to have to be *her* all the time."

He nods. "So you ever get a night off?"

"Sundays. And every once in a while I take a mental health day. I do a week or two here, move on to a club in Bozeman or Billings, then come back. They don't seem to have gotten bored with me yet."

"I never thought of that."

"What's it– familiarity breeds contempt? Like if tonight they kept sending up the same exact rocket, the same pattern and color time after time. You'd clear the stands pretty quick."

They have come to her car.

"So if I could get in touch with you somehow, you think you could plan a mental health night and have dinner with me in one of the area's many one-star restaurants?"

She smiles. "That could be arranged." She digs out one of her business cards. What the hell, he knows where she works.

He reads it. "Jew-*elle*."

"You just say 'Jewel,' like diamonds and rubies and all that."

"There should be a firework named Jewel," he says, smiling and backing away, the Ferris wheel still spinning its lights behind him.

It must have been at least an hour, she thinks, while creeping along in the line of cars leaving the fairgrounds, and I didn't tell a single lie.

THE CAR IS STILL following. Macario is tempted to just pull over here on the highway, where there are other cars and people to witness whatever they do, but witnesses won't stop these people. He could try to outrun them, get to the office, but his Ram complains if you push it over 95 kilometers, and even if he made it they'll be there after work, there tomorrow and the next day, like the weather.

Macario pulls off the highway onto the north road, his usual route to work, and the car follows. It is the same silver Lincoln that parked just across the field from him and the crew the last three days at the rupture site, the thin man leaning casually against it, smiling and waving whenever he caught Macario looking over. The area was a mess, the dirt over and around the pipeline soaked with gasoline, the hot tap done quickly and crudely. Just closing the line down till the tap could be welded shut cost the company a fortune, with removal of polluted earth and reburying of the pipeline yet to be done.

The *huachicolero* was wearing sunglasses and a canary yellow polo shirt with a gold-trimmed *piteado* belt, grinning like the proud father at a wedding.

"You know, somebody stealing from the gas line, the guy behind it is probably just over there," Macario said to the *federal* in charge of the site on the first day of the repair.

"Keep your eyes to yourself," said the *capitán*, pointedly not turning toward the road, "and don't stir up shit."

He'd always been aware of the dangers on the offshore rig in the Sonda de Campeche, all the moving parts that could kill or cripple a deckhand, the strong winds that could blow you off the platform, the possibility of a blowout. Nilda begged him to ask for a transfer, less pay maybe but safer, and when Celestina was born he agreed. What could threaten a mere pipeline mechanic?

The Lincoln pulls alongside and the *chupaducto* in the sunglasses signals for him to pull over. In the movies there are tricks to avoid this, cars and trucks that can fly through the air in slow motion, that can roll over and over and land on their tires and drive away at high speed. But this is San Martín Texmelucan and not the movies.

"Come sit with me," says the man in the back seat. "We need to talk."

Macario leaves his *camioneta* on the shoulder of the road and gets in beside the man and they drive away. Maybe Jorge or Hector or another one of his crew will pass the Ram and wonder what the story is. The one behind the wheel, who is young with a complicated design shaved into his short hair, keeps his eyes on the road ahead.

"It seems you are very good at your job, Señor Paredes."

Macario watches the news. The war that President Calderón has made on the *narcos* is going badly. The biggest groups, especially the Zetas, have been striking back, and not just against the army and the police. Massacres at drug rehabilitation clinics, civilians gunned down at parties in Juárez and Torreón, mass graves found in old mine shafts and on remote ranches– but so far it has been relatively peaceful here in the state of Puebla.

"I try my best," says Macario.

"You're too modest. We've read your employee evaluation. Your superiors at the Company have nothing but praise for your skill, for your industry."

Don Pánfilo, the territorial supervisor, rides now with a *guardaespaldas* at all times, a man who wears sunglasses like this one and carries a pistol where you can see it. The *narcos* in Chiapas have made a specialty of kidnapping Pemex employees, mostly managers, but that is for ransom. Pipeline mechanics are not taken because they have wealthy relatives or because the government fuel monopoly cannot function without them.

"What did you think of the *grifo* you plugged up the other day?"

Sometimes the bodies are found with a simple bullet to the back of the head, the victims forced to kneel, knowing what is about to happen. Others, when an example must be made, are found hacked to pieces by machetes or dismembered with chainsaws, in places where screams can't be heard or will not be reported. Others are not found at all, buried forever or dissolved in chemicals.

"It was very poorly done," says Macario carefully.

"Exactly. A butcher was sent to do the work of a surgeon. So much *combustible* wasted, and so much damage to the environment."

Gasoline, ready to pump or pour into an automobile tank, flows from the refineries on the coast through miles of pipeline in Puebla on its way to Mexico City. Not all of it arrives. Macario has seen *camionetas* loaded with square, plastic five-gallon containers of gasoline at the *tianguis* in Huejotzingo, has seen farmers selling it on the side of the road at a fraction of the government price.

"What would help us a great deal," continues the *huachicolero*, "is more accurate information about the system. When the *ductos* will be charged with fuel, when it will be flushed or shut down. You can imagine how anxious it makes someone with little experience cutting into a pipe when they don't know what lies within. When a single spark at the wrong moment– "

The man snaps his fingers.

The farmers usually do the digging on their own property, a shallow trench for the hose that leads to the *trailero* or reservoir, and down at least three feet to the pipeline itself. A narrow-diameter tap can milk the line slowly enough to escape detection by the pressure monitors but fill an eleven-thousand-gallon tanker in three days. One gang has learned to cut two holes, one to extract gasoline quickly and the other to pump in the same amount of creek water, fooling the monitors and ruining the quality of the fuel downstream.

"I'm not so high up as to be responsible for this kind of information," says Macario. "I only go where they send me."

"But you have access to it," smiles the *huachicolero*. "You can easily find out. The way that we can find out that you have a beautiful wife named Nilda and two little daughters, who have just traveled to visit relatives in DF."

Macario feels the fury rise up in him, tries to control his face. At first he was a supporter of Calderón's war. Put them in jail, execute them all if you have to, and do the nation a great service. But then it became clear that this was like trying to cut out your own cancerous lung— the operation would kill the patient.

"What do you want from me?"

"Information, as I've said. Then, perhaps, some technical advice so we can avoid these environmental hazards. And equipment," says the man. He taps the driver and they make a lazy U-turn to head back toward the abandoned Ram. Macario feels his stomach muscles loosen. "If you and your crew could leave certain items behind after your next few repair jobs, it would be very useful. You can help us prepare a list."

TOME SUS PRECAUCIONES! the safety sign on the Number 12 rig in Campeche advised, greeting them every shift when they stepped out onto the drilling platform. Macario has been thinking ahead for years, often the *encargado*, the foreman, always conscious of whatever could go wrong, wanting those first moments of crisis control to be based on planning and not panic.

"You haven't asked what your reward for this assistance will be," says the man behind the sunglasses.

"You've given me a lot to think about," says Macario. There is no bargaining with these people of course, any more than there is with Pemex or with the *petrolero* union. It is beyond your control. "I wouldn't want to disappoint you."

"No," says the *huachicolero*, still smiling. "You wouldn't."

They leave him by his pickup.

"People call me Flaco," says the man from his open window just before they pull away. "You can check with Colonel Estrada for my credentials."

It is no secret that they have allies in the government, in the military, in the police. The Zetas are supposed to have been founded by former elite troops, trained in weapons and combat. It does not pay to stir shit up.

Macario drives to work, arms shaky as he holds the wheel. There will likely be someone watching him at work, sure to report if he doesn't show up.

It is an unexceptional day. Much of the pipeline is cleaned and monitored by what the *yanquis* call 'pigs,' launched at a special entry and then driven the length of the system by the pressure of the flow, so he and the crew have only some routine valve inspection to do, out by San Matías. Jorge is a lover of *narcocorridos*, and sings them loudly as he drives the van–

> *I lift my bazooka*
> *To all who defy me*
> *A soldier of fortune*
> *A stranger to pity*

> *I toss away women*
> *And burn through my money*
> *The cops all respect me*
> *Or fall to my fury*

–Jorge who has certainly never lifted a bazooka to his shoulder or so much as cursed a police officer to his face, but comes from Sinaloa and grew up with the songs, with the culture–

> *A fast car, a gunfight*
> *Is all that I live for*
> *I take what I want and*
> *I pay you in bullets*

People think that the *politicos* are the biggest thieves of all, and nobody, especially its employees, loves Pemex. Milking gas isn't like helping to sell drugs.

"*Qué tal su casa?*" asks Hector, who put the windows into the first floor of Macario's *casa de sueño*, his dream house, and is always hungry for extra work. "When is that second story going up?"

"Maybe in a couple months," Macario tells him. "We may be coming into a bit of money." You never know who might be working for them, if only as a pair of ears, a passer-on of *chisme* from the job. "Nilda's aunt in DF can take her and the girls while the walls are going up."

All the dream houses have rebar poking through their flat roofs, an unfinished house taxed less than a finished one. If they were ever to add another floor, the plan since he was on the drill rig in the Gulf, there would be rebar sticking up from that as well.

"But only if prices go down," he lies. "When you fill your tank these days you drain your pockets."

Gas is up to eight pesos for a liter of Magna now, one of the reasons the roadside *vendedores* are doing so well.

Hector laughs. "Tell Don Pánfilo," he says. "Maybe he can put in a word with the Company."

Nobody follows him on the north road back to the highway. He makes the turn for the airport. It was just a matter of time, he thinks. The house will just sit there, like a thousand other *casas de sueño* whose owners are doing their dreaming up in the United States. He'll have to leave the old Ram, of course, and all the clothes he wasn't able to stash in the big toolbox in the pickup bed behind him. Nobody will report him missing for a few days.

TOME SUS PRECAUTIONES! They may have watched Nilda and the girls board the bus to DF, but he doubts if they had anyone at the huge terminal there to see her transfer to the one heading for Mérida, then Chixulub beyond it. When he turns onto the Cholula-Puebla road he calls her sister's number on his cellphone.

"*Quién es?*" Nilda's sister has only had a phone for a short while, and feels invaded when it rings.

"*Habla Macario*," he says. "*Está Nilda?*"

A pause, muffled voices, then his wife on the phone.

"*Hola, querido.*"

"It's happened," he says simply. "I'm on my way out."

A long silence as she absorbs the meaning of this.

"They threatened you?"

"With all courtesy."

"You can't work anything out?"

"Nilda," he says, realizing he may not see her or the girls for a very long time, "once you play along, they own you. Do you want that?"

218 YELLOW EARTH

In the movies, men leap from rooftop to rooftop, dodge between machine-gun bullets, vanquish their enemies in huge, flaming explosions that may knock them over from behind but never burn or kill them. But this is not the movies, only life in México.

"I miss you already," says Nilda.

"*Igualmente.* You know what to do."

They've never had that much in the bank, living from paycheck to paycheck, and Macario cashed the last couple with the *cambio* service in Tlaxcala, giving Nilda most of it and converting the rest into *yanqui* dollars. He's got those folded in one work boot and ten thousand Mexican pesos folded in the other, which should be enough for the flight and what comes after.

"They're giving away money up there," his cousin Félix, just back from the States, is telling anybody who will listen. "All you need is two legs and a strong back. But for an experienced *petrolero* like you, *híjole*, you could make a fortune."

He's found it on the map, way up near their border with Canada. He'll need some warmer clothes when he gets there.

Macario is not the only man in the Puebla airport carrying a canvas duffel bag, looking like he just got off work. They take cash at the Aerolitoral counter, and he shows the driver's license of his friend Rogelio, killed in a fall on the rig four years ago, as ID.

"To Nuevo Laredo," he says. "One way."

IT'S HALF PAST TWO in the afternoon and the Three-Mile is already packed. Leia's stomach does a flip in the parking lot, the usual convention of Rams, Tundras, Tacomas and Ford 150s, the sound of some hat act twanging about his little gal leaking out through the door and a set of longhorns– could be plastic, no, they're real– hung over the entrance. I will not crap out again. I will not go back to the apartment.

The ones that look at her, and most of them do as she makes her way to the empty stool at the end of the bar counter, shoot their eyes quickly from her butt (wearing ranger pants, who can tell?) to her chest (no tits to speak of) to her hair (what?). The reaction to her new white streaks ranges from wow, that's really different– different the local version of 'weird'– to look out, darlin, you got a skunk on your head.

"What'll it be, honey?"

The bartender looks like she sculpts tree stumps with a chainsaw for a hobby, incredibly defined delts with barbed wire loops inked around her biceps.

"Your draft– ?"

The bartender steps back to give Leia a look at the pump handles– all the mass-market stuff, and why would she expect otherwise.

"Blue Moon, I guess."

"Got it."

The jukebox switches to a woman with a nice voice and a tale of woe. Look out, darlin, you got a polecat for a husband. The first contestant approaches, early forties maybe, definitely balding under the oilfield services cap, STU sewn over the pocket of his tan work shirt.

"Hey there," he beams. "I'm Stu."

"I never would have guessed." If she's lucky he'll split before she has to get into her own name.

"What you drinking?"

"Uhm– beer? Blue Moon."

"That's just Coors you know. They say it's Belgian but it's made with all their other stuff."

"How can anything be considered 'just Coors'?"

A moment for this to register. "You're yanking my chain, right?"

There is a point, Jeff used to say, where irony ceases to be a form of humor and becomes a personality disorder. Just because she described him to her friends as 'serpentine.'

"You work in the oil business, Stu?"

"Twenty-two years and counting. If they're pumping, I'm jumping."

"Mud geologist?"

He looks offended. "Oh no. I *work* for a living. Rig mechanic– I mostly test and maintain BOPs."

"Big Old Pumps."

He grins. On a dentist's color chart his teeth would be Tobacco Road. "Blow-out preventers. Make sure the boys don't go sky-high."

The bartender leaves her beer in a glass with a slice of orange in it. Classy.

"You've got an important job, then. Shouldn't you be out somewhere, like, preventing a blowout?"

"In between calls." He nods to the crowd of men and the few women, who are mostly dressed for work and probably drivers of some sort. "Oil is a twenty-four-hour business, you grab your R and R when and where you can."

"Where's the best place you ever worked?"

"Texas. The best *place*, period. I can't imagine a better one. Where you from?"

"Minnesota. The Land of a Thousand Lakes."

"They don't drill there." He says it with heartfelt pity.

"Not that I know of, not for oil."

He is trying to lean on the bar close to her, but the guy at the next stool is an extra-wide load and isn't giving up any territory. Stu eyes the beer as she takes a sip.

"How's that?"

"Oh– kind of Belgian tasting. Maybe they import the bubbles."

He leans as close as he can. "You ever have a Jägerbomb?"

Even on Spring Break in South Padre Island this would get you eliminated from the competition.

"No, but I've cleaned up after people who drink them."

"I don't mean when you drop the shot in a *beer*, this is when you drop it in Red Bull."

"So you can keep throwing up all night long."

He gives out with a smiling wheeze. "Yanking my chain."

Leia swivels on her stool to look past Stu and He is there, alone at a table, watching the floor with a bottle of Budweiser Not-Lite in hand but obviously thinking about something else. Perhaps about this unusual young woman he's been dying to meet–

Stu says something she doesn't register.

"Pardon?"

"I said I can take you somewhere much better than this dump."

She feels for them, she really does. A lifetime of selling yourself door to door to women who are interested in *some*body or they wouldn't be there but not interested in *you*, stuck now in a town with a gender imbalance of epic proportions and when finally a nondiseased, nonprofessional, possibly receptive female wanders onto your territory she turns out to be a little snot of a varmint-chronicler from a nondrilling state.

"This bar happens to belong to my father," she says, standing, "and I can't imagine a better one. If you'll excuse me, I have to go speak with my parole officer."

She feels for them, but Nature is cruel.

He locks onto her halfway across the floor and watches her all the way to the table.

"The Wildlife Girl."

Standing over his table, glass of beer in hand, wishing there was a hard-wired bit of display behavior, a pheromone she could release, to substitute for whatever dialogue she can come up with.

Don't be a smartass, don't be a smartass, don't be a smartass–

"Is that what people are calling me?"

"You're legend." He half-stands, indicates the table. "Please– sit."

She obeys, sliding his hat to one side to make room for the beer. He cocks his head sideways to study her. Here it comes about the streaks–

"So– Swedish or Norwegian?"

"Guess."

"What's your name?"

"Leia Nilsson."

"So Swedish– "

"Actually, I'm a bit of both. Scandinavian half-breed."

"And Leia– "

"Yeah, my parents were *Star Wars* freaks. It could have been Padmé or Shmi."

"Leia's a real name."

"And you're Will."

Just a tiny stroke of surprise, which he struggles to keep off his face–

"Or should I call you Sheriff, or Sir, or Officer– ?"

"Will is fine."

Got that done. She nods toward the scrum of oilworkers. "Looking for a suspect?"

He smiles. Good smile. "They've had a few dustups in here, and Bud– that's the fella owns the place– asked me to come by."

"Push through the swinging doors, peacemaker on your hip."

He shrugs. "If I just sit back here quiet for a while they don't even have to look at me. There's a current or something, like with a herd of elk or buffalo when there's a wolf nearby– well, you'd know about that, wouldn't you?"

Her turn to smile. "I would. So you don't want to scatter the herd."

"And spoil Bud's business."

"–just keep them from locking horns with each other."

"Do your critters lock horns? Or whatever they got up there."

"Sure. It's a battleground."

"Prairie dogs."

"You used to shoot them, right?"

He considers, shrugs. "Couple, right after I got my first .22. Didn't much see the point of it."

"So you moved on to– what– ?"

"Targets. Mostly pop bottles off of fence posts."

"You grew up here?"

"Some, not too far away. Little town called Lignite."

"Low-grade coal."

"Way back. Mostly farming in my day, but my father was in the Air Force. My mother taught school. I been back in Yellow Earth about five years."

"What do you think of the invasion?"

He looks past her to the men, the volume of their talk and laughter nearly drowning out the jukebox.

"One on one they're mostly all right, but the numbers– "

"You get to hire more deputies?"

"One. And he's like to quit on me."

"You're overwhelmed."

He sighs. "Fights, stolen vehicles, nastier drugs and what folks do when they're whacked out on em, prostitution."

"I haven't seen any prostitutes."

"It's pretty much all phone hookups now."

"So you don't prosecute."

"It's against the *law*, sure, and they don't pay their taxes, which is a federal beef, but mostly it's what comes along with the trade. Like an atmosphere."

"Of lawlessness."

"You could say that." He sits back, considers her. "So you come in here to meet-and-greet or just to observe and take notes?"

Whoops. Attitude must be showing–

"Observe, I guess, and then I remembered– "

"They're the hawks and you're the field mouse."

"You could say that."

She finishes the beer and he doesn't jump to pour another one down her, instead looking all around the crowded room. "Roughnecks come in all colors," he says. "And the world won't function without them."

"A cornerstone species."

Will smiles. "They show up on time, do their job, the rest is mostly none of our business."

"Is that the royal we?"

"The Company we."

"Same thing."

Then he does that thing where they look in your eyes, like they've actually met somebody whose name they'll remember.

"So how's your– flock? Network?"

"Coterie. Smaller than a colony or a town."

"How they doing?"

"Oh, not too bad, thanks. You probably noticed I had to move them over."

"Off of reservation land onto A. J. Niles's ranch."

"He's complained?"

"No."

"But he's noticed."

"If he'd noticed," says Will, "he would have shot you already."

Leia gives him a tight smile. The first naturalists had it easy, blasting whatever bird or mammal they took a fancy to and having it stuffed to draw or sell to a museum later, dodging the occasional arrow, no institutions to bow to–

"So putting new prairie dogs on somebody's land is, like– "

"Like pissing in his well. If he doesn't see you do it, he probably won't notice."

"I'm there every day."

"If A. J. comes by and stops, just tell him they were already there and you're studying them for a statewide eradication program. But no more cages."

"You didn't stop me."

"Nobody complained and I wanted to see how it turned out."

No wedding ring. He hasn't once mentioned his ex–

"Thanks."

He turns away for a moment, pondering something, then looks back into her eyes.

"And making an arrest is a terrible introduction to someone you want to meet." He cocks his head again, evaluating. "Whatever that is with your hair looks really cool."

Contact.

STAGE THREE

EXTRACTION

By THE TIME THE second boom reached Yellow Earth, the slaughter of buffalo had become more harvest than hunt. The great northern herd flowed over the high plains like a huge, mobile lake– the shooters had only to find a suitable vantage on its shore and go to work, feeding long cartridges to their heavy old Sharps or state-of-the-art Remingtons, balancing them on support sticks, lining up the new tele-scopic sights and piercing the lungs of whichever shaggy beast seemed on the verge of upsetting the ruminant stasis of the group. Men killed fifty, eighty, more than a hundred bison from one stand, able to get off a shot a minute if their targets stayed close, careful to let the rifle barrel cool just enough before culling the next one. A fallen buffalo might be stepped around, sniffed, maybe even hooked momentarily with a young bull's horns, but the species was so physically powerful and had lived so long without an animal predator of any size that they were not so easily spooked as wild cattle or horses. The calm shooter, moving downwind, always downwind behind the edge of the herd, was far more wary of Indian competitors than of being gored or trampled. Loading, sighting, firing, then looking for the next hulk to be brought down before the last had finished its writhing and kicking in the grass.

In the shooter's wake came the skinners, at twenty-five cents a hide, hurrying to do their flensing before the blood cooled and the pelt began to stiffen. Drive a wagon rod through the nose of the just-killed beast to anchor it to the ground, cut a circle around the neck, slit down the underside from throat to tail, slit down the insides of the legs to the knees, then tie off the neck hide to your wagon horses hitched with a doubletree and crack the whip. Any wise team of skinners was already cutting while the shooter was still killing ahead of them, cold car-casses requiring painstaking tug-and-slice work with the curved skinning knife, and more opportunity to damage the hide. A troop of gleaners– wolves, coyotes, ravens, magpies– set up vigil just behind the skinners, waiting to feed on the yellow-white fat, the glistening red muscle, the innards suddenly spilt from their thick protection. Less experienced hands labored without a knife, rolling the liberated hides into bundles and lugging them back to wagons and then to the day's base camp, staking them out gory-side-up to dry in the cold prairie wind till stiff as planks for stacking.

Thick and lustrous winter hides brought the best price, with tongues and tallow taken as well if the Northern Pacific was nearby. Paired wagons, drawn by six yoked oxen, could haul three hundred bundled hides, the freighters often joining in long trains able to circle and provide shelter against Indian attack. There were hide thieves, of course, and occasionally an angry warrior would slash the staked pelts to diminish their value, while territorial disputes were settled at gunpoint. The outfitters, never more than a day's ride away, did handsomely without risk or gruesome toil. Rifles, primers, ball and bar lead, powder, knives, poisons to keep insects from ruining the hides, horses, mules, oxen, any grub but buffalo meat, tobacco and liquor for consumption or trade– only the most veteran hunters were grub-staked against their season's profit rather than paying cash.

A parallel industry grew up as the wolves grew fat and lazy gorging on carcasses they had no part in killing, their own winter pelts especially valuable, and laws were passed offering a bounty for their destruction. Wolfers, considered even a cut below the buffalo men, followed the slaughter, their prey gun-shy but vulnerable to poison, a gutted buffalo cow or tender prairie hen laced with just enough strychnine hard to pass up. Coyotes took the bait as well, and smaller predators, and there were stretches of ground left black and glistening with dead ravens as the stink of the rotting buffalo kill clouded the other senses.

Hide towns were thrown up hastily and then moved with the herd, enclosures of sod and stretched leather where anything a louse-infested, tangle-haired, blood-simple buffalo man could desire was for sale. The prices were jacked up as high as the lack of competition would allow, the women available only the most desperate and diseased. And even here, surrounded by bales of green hides stacked for shipment, the men weren't free of the buffalo gnats, the mosquitos, the greenhead flies, the odor of butchery on a massive scale.

But the real money was made by the furriers in St. Louis and the traders at the railheads, green hides likely to rot into worthlessness if you held out for too fair a price. The tanned winter robes became rugs and winter coats and wall hangings, while the patchier summer hides provided a durable, elastic leather useful for dozens of purposes and purchased in bulk by the British Army.

Meanwhile, the US Army kept patrols on the northern border, driving the herd south to keep it from Sitting Bull's renegade band in Canada, hoping to starve them back to the reservation, while the Cree, Assiniboine, Blackfoot, and Gros Ventre people had already been diminished in power and territory. By 1882 there were more than five thousand white shooters and skinners in the Montana and Dakota Territories, playing an endgame now, as the other three great herds to the south had already been obliterated. With robes selling at two to five dollars apiece at a time when cow punchers were making a dollar a day and keep, amateurs as well as seasoned buffalo men flocked to this last great slaughter once the railroad had penetrated deep enough to make the summer pelts pay. With the Sioux mostly forced onto reservations, the chief danger was from the temperamental high plains weather, dozens of skin men and thousands of buffalo killed every year in snap blizzards or floods of the unstable Missouri. But the market stayed hungry and the hunt was relentless, increasingly methodical by the end, when the herd was less a vast sea than a dozen isolated eddies, more than a million and a half animals killed in a three-year spree.

When the herd was reduced to a handful of stragglers most of the buffalo men left, off to find other work, none of it paying nearly as well. And once the maggots and flesh beetles were done with what the other scavengers left and wind and sun had bleached them white and dry, the bones were left for a final harvest, stacked into horse-high ricks and carted off by struggling farmers to sell for eight dollars a ton at railhead, to be ground for bone china, carbon for sugar production, phosphates for the soil, and finally all evidence of the great herd was gone, even the annual crop of dried shit that had lit a million campfires, gone from the land forever.

THE TRANSLOCATION, CONSIDERING THE short life span of the average prairie dog, has become another Trojan War, and she, Leia, is Helen. Aggressive staring, tooth chattering, tail flaring, bluff charging, defensive barking, reciprocal sniffing of scent glands– the outcasts of Poker Flats are not giving their territory up without resistance. But her invaders are healthier, more unified, desperate.

Odysseus has kept busy romancing some of the younger females, receptive perhaps because their coterie's adult males are too closely related– co-submerging with one, then the other, five or six times a day, symbolic nesting grass in his mouth. Ninety-eight percent of copulations occur underground, so she can only gauge his success by the females' behavior, each now preparing a nursery burrow, laying in dry grass and getting huffy with anyone who approaches. If this isolated bunch has been genetically drifting, new blood will pull them back into the heterogeneous current and perhaps avoid some inbred misfits. Mixed parentage of litters is possible, of course, and Leia imagines the steps to take to be sure, the drawing of blood samples from mother, pups, and potential fathers, sending them off to the lab for PCR amplification and DNA profiling. Nike and Niobe, impregnated back in the old colony, have each set themselves up in abandoned holes, and if not too damaged by hitting the padded extraction chamber at 300mph, should be nearing parturition.

Ajax, despite his advanced years, continues to be the enforcer, greeting each challenger with a display routine complete with anal sniffing, then choosing to fight rather than run. At least one rival has been chased, scarred and churring in submission, to the periphery of the town, and Ajax has come out of a few holes to meticulously lick his feet and rub his face in the grass, a sure sign that he's just killed and eaten the early litter of a resident female. Very Olympian of him. Lions kill their predecessor's cubs without cannibalizing them when they take over a pride, but even regular backyard fluffy-tail squirrel females will go for the protein while securing their genetic dominance. It is, in fact, a jungle out there.

The coterie will survive in a modified version. Leia has already recorded two instances of allogrooming between newcomer and resident juveniles, Romeo and Juliet action promising to unite the divided houses, and Hera, the oldest female, is working on a rim crater for her newly dug burrow, piling moist earth all around the opening and jackhammering it to rock-hardness with her nose. It's possible that the bunch over here started as a ward of the big colony, separated by the highway and the traffic, and that this is a reunion. Leia has checked every day since the move for fresh roadkill, and so far there's no evidence that any of her animals have tried to cross back to the old homestead. It could be nice for them here– a new start, room to grow. The only real advantage of dense colonization is mass warning and defense against predation, and the downsides– the stress, the constant territorial disputes, the tight-packed vulnerability to epidemic– all discourage big-city living. The grass is patchy here, and though it would derail any claim to a proper field study, she may have to consider provisioning the fledgling coterie, at least for the transition period.

A whining noise causes Leia to turn and look across the highway at the ever-developing fracking pad, a rat's nest of pipes and tanks and power hookups going in, at least twenty men and a half-dozen pickup trucks swarming over the area, working over and around each other day and night. Industrious little creatures, she thinks, but they're still varmints.

"WHAT HAPPENED TO MR. RUSHMORE?"

He made sure to check with Jonesy on the name. This one is younger, sharper suit, and comes bearing blueprints.

"He's really just a landman," says the young one, whose name might be Calkins or Dalkins. "He's the matchmaker and I'm the marriage counselor."

The young one smiles, what he thinks is pleasantly. Press steps around to his side so he has to turn in the chair, pretends to be pondering.

"So you're telling me the honeymoon is over?"

"All honeymoons end. By now your people have an idea of who's going to make a killing, who's going to do fine, and who's just waiting in traffic or staring at spoil pits." Dalkins holds up a roll of blueprint. "So it's a good moment to sweeten the pot."

"I thought this was about the housing ordinance."

"That's the tat," smiles the young one. "This is the tit. We have two workforce accommodation centers currently under construction– assembly would be a more accurate term– within your city limits, Mr. Mayor. The Company doesn't think it fair for you to change the rules on us without warning."

"There've been some fights, lots of drunken driving."

Will Crowder was in just before, explaining that he'd need at least two more qualified deputies to monitor the clubs all night, that he's got the whole county to worry about–

"We don't own or operate the strip clubs, Mayor."

"It's a tone that's been set."

"I understand. And we'd like to improve that tone. May I?"

Press nods and the Company rep stands to spread the blueprint out on his desk. It looks undecipherable, like they always do to him, but very big.

"Our men work long, hard hours, under a good deal of pressure to produce at speed. When they're off work, they need a place to unwind. Believe it or not, their first choice would often not be a titty bar."

The young one is from Texas, and the way he says 'titty bar' makes you think of a furry, big-breasted animal.

"What is it?"

"A three-story, multiuse recreational center. Gym, saunas, weight-lifting equipment, room for yoga or cardio classes, indoor track– we've taken the nature of the weather here into account– and an Olympic-sized swimming pool in the basement."

Press thinks of four places, three old warehouses and a failed big box store, that would make a good site.

"This is for your fellas."

"For the *public*. Company employees would have access twenty-four-seven, of course, but the people of Yellow Earth, especially if they're involved with a program sponsored by your city government, would be encouraged to use the facilities."

As the rep slides one blueprint on top of the other Press realizes that each is the plan for just one floor. He's not sure Bismarck has anything as grand.

"This is for reversing the man camp ordinance?"

"No, only for not applying it to projects already in progress."

"There's another outfit halfway through building one on the south side."

"We'd leave that up to your discretion, but I'd say any added clause would apply to them as well."

Press makes his move to the window. The state committee has already felt him out about lieutenant governor this next term, a shoo-in for election but considered a dead-end job. Unless–

"Totally funded by the Company?"

"Not only that," smiles the young one, rolling up his blueprints, "but we're willing to commit to a healthy percentage of local hire for the construction."

"Any chance of that going through us?"

"Absolutely. We could present it as a special concession you've badgered us into."

"I don't badger."

"Something you've won for the people. The staff, as well, once we're up and running, will have a lot of positions that could be filled from right here."

"And this is called what– the Case and Crosby Arena?"

"We were thinking of the Prescott Earle Recreational Center."

If he's already gone to Bismarck before the announcement, it will seem like an honor, a memorial. A legacy.

"So what happens if and when you people leave Yellow Earth?"

"That's the beauty of it. The way our contract is structured, we gradually cede ownership of the facility to the city. You end up owning it lock, stock, and barrel."

And taking on the cost of its operation, thinks Press. But if he's already gone, that's the next fella's lookout.

"It's a generous and attractive offer," he says to Hawkins. "I promise to take it up with my board right away."

It would be terrific for the people in town, especially while they're not paying for it. Even Jonesy might come around, get her girls in there for winter soccer.

The rep puts the plans under his arm, smiles like it's a done deal.

"As far as the specifications of the facility are concerned, I have only one important thing to ask you, Mr. Mayor. Do you people up here play hockey?"

SHE WAITS TILL THE hand is paid out, then taps Cheryl to take over the deal. Nice little posse around the table, the entire floor jumping though it is three o'clock in the morning. She claps her hands and shows them palm-up to the players, the old ritual, then burns a card and slides it into the discard tray.

"My name is Lady," she announces, "as in Lady Luck. Let's play some blackjack."

You try not to lose the momentum of the action when you tap in, in fact you hope to speed it up. The players push chips into their betting circles on the layout and Lady distributes cards from the dealer's shoe, sweeping them from left hand to right before flipping them face up as she checks the suspects across from her.

"How've we been doing tonight?"

"*We*'ve been up and down," answers the table-hopper at third base who the dealers call Just Ask Chuck. "*You*'ve been raking it in."

"Oh now, the last table I worked, the House was down a bit when I left."

She watches the hand signals, hit or stay, and feeds cards as she talks–

"What, five bucks down?"

"More than that."

"What's your play?"

Chuck taps his finger on the felt and she shoots him a jack that busts him.

"Ouch."

"Don't take it personally."

"Is your middle name 'Bad'?"

She's heard this one before–

"As in Lady Bad Luck?"

"I like all my people to walk away winners. Truly."

Cloyd, the pit boss, has explained that even with all her experience she'll still have to pool tips with the other dealers, but the more you throw in, the bigger the pot. And losers don't tip.

"Everybody set?" she asks, scanning the cards in front of the remaining players. Nobody signals for another hit.

"Let's see what we've got."

She flips a seven up next to her eight already showing, then hits herself again with a nine and goes bust.

"Everybody wins."

"Except me," says Chuck.

She gives him the dazzling smile. "Life is cruel, but blackjack has no memory."

It is a ten-dollar-minimum, five-hundred-max table, and Chuck is a ten-dollar-flat bettor, win or lose, rain or shine. He talks through so many hands without laying a wager and spends so much time kibitzing at other tables that he never has a really bad night.

"So I won with just sixteen?" asks a rig worker who is drunk but not as drunk as the buddy who leans over his shoulder, loudly advising his play.

"When the dealer busts, anybody still in play is a winner."

She matches the stacks of chips in their circles, running a finger over the even tops and proving her empty palm to the Eye in the Sky.

"I told you so," says Drunker.

"No you didn't," says Drunk. "You wanted me to hit again."

"Did I?"

"Yeah."

"Well, fuck me."

Drunk shoots Lady an apologetic look. "Boy was raised in the oil patch."

"Like you weren't," challenges Drunker.

"My mama taught me some manners," says Drunk. "Done it with a broom handle, but she *taught* em."

Bearpaw has just started the all-night shift, the place filled mostly with drillers and mud men and roughnecks, with a sprinkling of local insomniacs and degenerate gamblers. The Drunk brothers are new to her, as is the chain-smoking woman at first base to her left, a scrawny babe in her fifties who Lady files as Wheezy. Next is the Boss Man, a mid-level oil exec who apparently never sleeps and plays a different, complicated system every time he lands at her table, doubling his bet after losses, upping by a quarter after wins, dropping back to minimum every ten hands, whatever. He is a good, steady loser who makes tipping her a single every five hands part of his routine.

On his left are Drunk and Drunker, nice boys but clueless about the game, and then Sitting Bull, a member of one of the tribes that own the casino, who they say hit the jackpot with his oil leases, signing up early for a decent advance and already with four wells pumping on his land. He is a wide-faced, overweight, gloomy kind of guy who parks at whatever table he's chosen– blackjack, poker, roulette, keno– and doesn't budge for the session, hence the name. A real George, though, he slides a blue fifty to each dealer as they go on their break. We love Sitting Bull.

Beside him is an Einstein-looking character wearing X-ray specs and constantly looking around at the other tables, at the drinks waitresses coming and going, at nothing at all, often a tell for somebody trying to count cards and nervous about it.

Lady deals her up card, an ace, and asks if anybody wants to take insurance.

"I don't believe in insurance," announces Drunker. "Insurance is for weenies."

"She means in the *game*, dummy," says Drunk.

"What's that mean?"

"The dealer shows an ace up," Just Ask Chuck volunteers before Lady can speak, "and she has a good shot at a BJ– "

"Whoa, there's blow jobs in this thing?"

"A *black*jack, twenty-one. Insurance means you can make a side bet on her cards– half of what you've already laid out– that she *will* have a blackjack. Pays two-to-one so it hedges your bet on your own hand."

"Just ask Chuck," Lady smiles.

"It's a sucker bet," says Chuck. The Drunks look at him.

"Even with that ace up, the odds are really long against her nailing it. So for that return– "

Drunk looks to Lady. "What do you say?"

She is allowed, encouraged even, to explain basic rules and strategies with new players. The odds and human stupidity more than take care of the House.

"It *is* more of a hedge. Unless by insurance you mean a policy that covers lightning but nothing else."

"Insurance is for weenies," repeats Drunker.

"We'll pass on it," says Drunk.

"Pass on what?" injects a friend of theirs, a lost-looking guy a few years older who has been cruising the action at this table and that, one hand in his pocket probably gripping a roll of chips, waiting for Fortune to whisper his name.

"You wouldn't understand," says Drunk. "It involves higher mathematics."

"It's all a gamble, you know."

"Hell, that's quite an observation, Tuck, seeing as we're in a casino."

"I mean, since it's all up to the flip of the card or the roll of the dice, doesn't it make sense to just put your whole bundle on one play? Get it over, one way or the other?"

"You go test that bright idea out, buddy," says Drunker. "Come back and tell us how it works out."

The Lost Guy's face shuts down then, he turns and heads toward the roulette wheel, determined, but wishing he had an audience for his death-defying leap.

"That was Fuck– I mean Tuck. We let him pretend to work on the rig."

"Insurance?" says Lady, head never leaving the game. "Anybody else?"

The others have been sufficiently warned and Lady continues the deal. She hits a surprisingly long rocky streak, which includes busting on her third card three times in a row, the Drunks whooping and slapping five and upping their bets each time, a vibe you love to have at your table. After Lady dealt fifty-two hands in her first hour on the job, Cloyd has pretty much let her rock out, hovering near the few times there's been a beef but letting her work it out on her own. All the players but Chuck, too timid to jump on the streak, are up on the House when Sitting Bull starts to talk.

"The thing is, I got a bad ticker," he says. He is usually silent, a nice presence, quick with his play decisions, which seem to be based on mood and stamina. "Congestive heart failure. My father had the same thing."

"That's awful," says Lady. "What do the doctors say?"

"They say don't do this, don't eat that, get plenty of sleep. If I'm on borrowed time, what do I want to sleep for?"

"I'm with you, buddy," says Drunker, whose name is Ike. "Sleep is for weenies."

"Course my sons and daughter, they're already fighting over the money." He turns to the players on his right. "I got some wells coming in."

"Which ones?" asks Drunk, whose name is Mike.

"Hidatsa 13A, B, C and D."

"Hidatsa 13B!" cries Drunker. "We drilled that sucker!"

"Those are excellent sites." Boss Man constantly rearranges his chips as he plays, as if their arrangement is a mnemonic device for whatever system he's currently following. "They should produce for quite a while."

"They don't like me being here," says Sitting Bull, tapping his finger for another card. "Think I'm losing *their* money."

"Kids will break your heart." Wheezy lays her cigarette butts parallel to each other in the ashtray, which is in the shape of a bear paw, and then builds a pyramid with them like logs in a fireplace. She smokes Camel no-filters, Lady's least favorite. "I got a daughter in Phoenix, I never heard from her once that she didn't need some kind of bailout."

"In most states, you can disown your children once they're eighteen," Chuck observes. "There's a legal procedure."

"Worse than them bothering me is them fighting with each other," says Sitting Bull. "Brothers and sisters shouldn't do that, not over money."

"What else is there?"

"Maybe for white people, but for us– you're sposed to help each other, look out for your nieces and nephews."

"It takes a friggin village," says Wheezy. "And that's more than having the same zip code."

"Does it hurt?" Einstein asks Sitting Bull, the first time he's spoken.

"It feels heavy," says the big man. "It feels like my heart is made of lead and is gonna sink down into my belly."

"Blackjack," says Lady, softly. "Sorry folks, the House takes this one."

They tighten into a kind of crew then, which happens sometimes, Wheezy rasping about her daughter's hopeless boyfriends and surprising but equally abusive girlfriend, the Drunks, who really are nice boys even loaded to the gills, learning the game, Einstein making bolder and bolder wagers, his stacks of red becoming green as they get deeper into the shoe, as Lady effortlessly deals the hands, collects for the House and makes the payouts before sweeping the cards back up in the order they were dealt and parking them in the discard rack. She begins to think about Leonard, due sometime in the afternoon, the first she'll have seen him in almost a year.

He won't have any trouble catching on here, his record clean in Reno and Vegas and Louisiana, despite the longer and longer gaps between his periods of employment. He's never made a scene on the floor, Lenny, and is pretty much the default model for a stick man– thin, good-looking, speedy and glib. Lenny could talk Just Ask Chuck into a puddle.

As for giving him a second (third? fourth?) chance, it's tough to scope the odds. It was always streaky between them, from the first sawdust joint they worked together till the last awful meltdown in the parking lot at Foxwoods, blowing hot and cold, the high times so great, so much fun, that even knowing how it inevitably crashes has never kept her away from their game. Cards don't love you, dice do contortions to put you in the hole, man got a drug habit? Double down.

"Double down," says Einstein, hitting her with what might be a deep-and-meaningful with his eyes. He's been laying tens to ride for her every five or six hands, several of them winners, and though Just Ask Chuck always winks and says 'Gotta keep the dealer sweet' whenever he steers one of his own pink chips toward her toke box, she feels a message, an agenda, coming off this guy. It's not like she's in a party pit wearing Victoria's Secret and shaking her tits under his nose, and she's at least a decade older than he is. Is he asking her not to rat him out to the pit boss?

"You're killing me, handsome," she says and deals him a six that puts him at eighteen, where he'll stand.

"Breathe in my direction," says Chuck to Einstein. "I could use some of that stuff."

Streaks are intoxicating when they're not misery, but Lady knows they are only momentary ripples in a flow that is heading down the drain. She can quote you the numbers, and it matters not that half the table beats her seventeen, or that a few weary players will stagger out into the dawn with fattened wallets– she is only a factory hand servicing a machine that milks people for their money.

Drunk draws a second eight on the next hand.

"You might want to split that, honey."

"Right. And what's the point of that again?"

"Sixteen is tough to hit on, but eight is a good start, and if you play two hands– "

"I've got two chances to beat the House."

"And two chances to lose," adds Chuck.

"I'll do it."

"You have to make the signal," says Lady, holding up two fingers.

"The secret handshake."

She points to the ceiling. "The One Above records whatever it sees, but it might be too noisy in here to hear your voice."

"Right," says Drunk, forking two fingers to tap the table, "gotta go to the video-tape."

"And now you add your second bet."

He matches his green quarter on the second eight. Lady deals an eight and a deuce.

"All right, with what I'm showing, you probably want to stay on the first hand and hit the second."

Drunk makes exaggerated signs with his hand.

"Curveball on the inside corner," says Drunker, whose eyes have drooped to half-mast as he leans on his friend's back for support. Lady does Egoscue exercis-es for her hip every day, but by the end of the ten-hour shifts she's pulling here–

Another deuce.

"Again."

A king this time and he busts.

"The Lady giveth," says Chuck, "and the Lady taketh away."

She flips her hole card, a jack that beats everybody but Einstein.

"The Lady kicketh our asses," says Chuck.

The Lost Man calls out a loud goodnight to Drunk and Drunker as he passes, making a show of pulling his empty pockets out and letting them hang, a sad little smile on his face.

"When that industrial accident waiting to happen catches up with Schmuck," says Drunk to Drunker, "I hope I'm not anywhere near him."

Boss Man taps his watch face. "Four o'clock," he says, this quitting time obvi-ously in his night's strict protocol. "I'm done."

Lady helps him color out, trading his mess of reds, blues and greens for a trio of black hundreds. He does a quick mental calculation and leaves her fifteen for the toke, some percentage of some percentage he's predetermined. Probably a guy who stares at drilling logs all day, making decisions that can mean millions to the Company.

"It wasn't the Martingale and it wasn't the Paroli," Chuck observes after Boss Man has left the pit. "But the dude sure had *some* method cooking."

"Show me one that always works," Lady smiles, burning a card in the Boss Man's honor, "and I'll switch sides of the table."

"You ever gamble?" asks Wheezy, lighting up the first stick from a new pack. She is an inconsistent player, betting hunches from who knows what planet, and a lousy tipper, but Lady likes her.

"Only in love, darlin."

If there was only a breeze to carry the cancer cloud in the other direction.

They've got all blackjack dealers doing one-twenties before a break, so Lady continues to portion out the pasteboards. The tips are better at the poker table, but there are so many games and betting variations now and twice as many smokers. The drinks waitresses, the real lookers who know how to make it seem personal, probably do as well as she does, getting the same minimum base pay but allowed to take cash or chips and never in the position of beating their customers at a hand of cards. You make a living at this racket by making it fun, win or lose, and by keeping the action flowing steadily, mesmerizing them till there is nothing but your table in front of them, with slot noise, voices, the time of day or night all fading from consciousness.

Lady is a pro and can't think of a job she'd be better at, but she doesn't need it the way Leonard does. "I'm an adrenaline junkie," he told her on their first real date, and at that point it was all he was addicted to. This carpet joint will be hopping as long as the oil boom lasts, the colored lights and MIDI cacophony seeming natural when it's packed with fun-starved roughnecks. She's spent enough hours with lonely drunks at the one table left open to play in the wee hours to appreciate the energy here. You work the machine like crazy while there's still money to extract, then you move to the next spot. Lenny will love it, Lenny's eyes will shine when he steps into the lobby and the dice will tapdance with joy to know he's arrived. There is no shortage of meth floating around in Yellow Earth and on the reservation, of course, but availability is never the issue. If there was one crystal left in the Nevada desert, Lenny would know where to start sifting sand.

"Willpower is like luck with me, babe," he's told her more than once. "It comes and it goes."

A real player stays a little detached from the game. Keep your guts out of every roll, see the big picture, accept that success and failure are transient and not to be taken to heart. She'll smile and hug him close when he gets off the little plane, show him how she's set up the room the casino scored for her, listen to his excited chatter, his stories about the total losers he met in the Program this time, even make plans with him. But she'll be watching, looking for tells, four feet above it all, like the security cameras recording the conversation of cards and hand signals at the table. When there's a beef, a question of who's at fault and how things really went down, you can always roll back the video.

Sitting Bull makes his second two-hundred-dollar bet in a row, a sure sign that he's getting tired, his heart feeling heavy. He likes to go out firing ballsy wagers no matter what he's dealt. He's enough of a whale here to merit limitless RFB, but while he'll partake of the comped Food and Beverages, he's never taken them up on the free Room. 'Only ten minutes from my house,' he says.

Einstein is laying down black chips as well, not looking at anything but the cards as they come out of the shoe.

He wins again, his four cards adding up to twenty.

"My, you've had a lucky night," says Lady, as unloaded an observation as she can make it.

"You mean I should quit while I'm ahead?"

Again he has her in an eyelock. If he's counting he's new at it, and she doubts she'll say anything to Cloyd during her twenty off. The purse she left in the locker in the break room is made of transparent plastic to make things easier when she goes in and out through security. She started in the business dealing single decks by hand to retired beauticians from Bakersfield, back when half the players still called the game 'Twenty-One.' At the last seminar she went to it was conceded that some counters were indeed 'playing with advantage' and beating the House, but the interest the phenomenon had brought back to the game, the false hope, had triggered an increase in action that would offset that by millions.

"Your fate is in your own hands," she says gently. "I'm just the messenger girl."

Einstein colors out and slides her a hundred-dollar tip.

"When Lady Luck has smiled upon you," winks Just Ask Chuck, "you damn well better smile back."

There is yelling from over by the keno tables then, two men not playing anything standing nose to nose with each other, looking like they need a referee. Lady uses the distraction to pop the shoe open. Sometimes they work in teams, a departing player signaling the count to a newcomer.

"Time for a change," she says, pulling out the dozen and a half cards left and signaling the local girl, Nicolette, to take a drink order from her players. "This deck wants to go to *sleep*."

THE ROOFING LADDER IS a motherfucker to lug over the fields at night, bulky, noisy, heavy enough that Dickyboy has to keep switching shoulders and stopping to rest. The good thing is that the construction site he's stolen it from is only two miles from the ramp that Chairman Killdeer keeps calling 'the marina' in his newsletters, two miles from the propped-up hulk that hasn't moved an inch since the dedication ceremony. They had a security light on it the first couple months, which suddenly stopped working when the yacht started being pointed out as the symbol of everything wrong with the current tribal government. So when he finally sees the bulky silhouette against the sky over the lake, he can just sit for a few minutes and get his breath back.

There wasn't a scene at home, no big dramatic blowout, just more of the same old shit, and he's had it. There are uncles and aunts to stay with, sure, but they're all on your case about this and that, and who needs it? He's done vanishing acts– two weeks, three weeks– before, staying with friends or cousins on the edges of the rez, and nobody called the cops or anything. You show up at school most days of the week, don't knock out anybody's brains with a hammer, and you can stay under the radar.

The ladder at full extension is just long enough to reach the deck of the yacht with enough of a lean that he doesn't worry he'll fall backwards. Climbing high is a bitch though, would have been easier a year ago before he porked out so much, and he rests halfway up, listening to the coyotes on the other side of the water. It's getting cold, but once he's out of the wind–

He gives the ladder a little shake, feeling the ridge hook grab onto something above, resumes his climb up. At the top he's able to unloose enough boat cover to slide under and in, working the little flashlight out of his pocket to help him figure out what is where. Pulling the ladder up after is a nightmare, clattering and threatening to pull out of his hands when the wind takes it, but he finally gets it up, adjusted to its shortest height and stowed along the rail, hidden from outside view by the huge blue tarp.

On deck under the tarp frame is like being in a tent, the air smelling plasticky and stale, everything with a slight bluish tinge in his flashlight beam. Nothing is locked. Dickyboy enters the cabin, finds the house controls and flicks a map light on, then steps down into what will be the main casino area when it's all tricked out.

He'll need to keep selling to have operating funds, and school is still the best place to make connections, so developing a quick and secure boarding and exit system will be the first order of business. A place to stow the ladder out of sight near the marina, a good idea of who bothers to come down here during this season, some kind of peep hole or periscope to clock the outside before he shows himself. Dickyboy finds a room switch, turns the light on. He has to hope the tarp and the anti-sun windows are thick enough that nothing bleeds through. A bar counter, fixed benches, and some loose chairs pushed into one corner, three tables for gambling. He's disappointed that the slot machines aren't in yet.

The galley is a reasonable size, easy to get in and out of even with his bulk, and the stovetop comes on right away. He's learned to cook some things in self-defense, his grandmother's cooking marginal even when she's not fucked up on something. Dickyboy kneels on the floor, manages to plug the little refrigerator in, hear the hum that tells him it's operational. Cold beer if he has Dylan or any of the other few guys he trusts come in to hang. Or maybe this will just stay his own little secret as long as it lasts.

The head is fine for a pee, though he's clueless as to how the waste system works so he doesn't flush. Can't have a pile of your business piling up under the yacht. He feels like Goldilocks in the story, making himself at home in somebody else's space, a little too big for some of the furniture. Hey, it belongs to the tribe, he imagines himself saying if discovered. I just got here a little early.

Dickyboy finds a fold-out-bed setup in the crew compartment, lights a joint, lies down, and puts his headphones on. He sets his iPod on random, and the first thing it throws at him is Eminem, Dr. Dre and 50 Cent knocking out "Crack a Bottle." The wind outside on the prairie is gone, the rez and the rest of the world around it disappeared, just Dickyboy chilling with his herb and his sounds–

> *So crack a bottle, let your body waddle,*
> *Don't act like a snobby model, you just hit the lotto–*

–snug in the Drydock Hilton.

HE'S NEVER FOUGHT IN a pit before. In a container once, yeah, but with a pretty good floor laid down, and behind the Hooters in Ocala where the ring was just crime-scene tape stretched tight, and a couple times in a real octagon, though they weren't sanctioned fights, just smokers like this where the promoter had some money to lay out. But this has been dug for some kind of permanent tank to sit in, almost a perfect thirty-foot square sunk five feet into the ground. Nothing's been poured yet, so it's just dirt covered with black plastic on the sides, with big strips of hard matting on the ground, the seams gaffer-taped over. And somewhere, Brent, who put the whole thing together, has found metal bleachers to throw up on all four sides. Add the swords and sandals and we got gladiators.

Scorch sits on the tailgate of one of the ArrowFleet pickups while L. T. smears Vaseline on his face. He's got mineral oil rubbed everywhere else, slick as a weasel, which is against the rules in sanctioned fights, but Brent said this was "sort of kind of *vale tudo* rules," so what the hell. All he knows about the other guy is that he's big and he's never been in a pro fight.

"Kick his ass, man!" yells one of the spectators, passing through the jumble of pickups and rental cars on his way to the bleachers.

"Will do." Scorch waves a gloved hand. Half the crowd are likely to be assholes he's had to collar at Bazookas, so any support is welcome. In Tampa once, a half dozen buddies of the guy he'd just decked swarmed into the cage and he got a bad cut from somebody's ring before the rest of the crowd and the meatheads hired for security could drag them out. This deal, down in a hole in the ground, won't be easy to escape.

Shakes hurries back to them, looking nervously over his shoulder. Shakes is the guiltiest-looking fuck he's ever met, the kind the public defender takes one glance at and says we're copping a plea.

"He's *big,*" says Shakes.

"Fat big or big big?"

"He's got a belly, but his arms are like legs. Like a pro football lineman, you take the pads off."

"Terrific."

He's getting three grand just to step in the cage, triple what he's ever got before, and Brent is supposed to be laying another grand for him to win. He wonders if Brent has checked this other guy out, if he'll bet against him with his own money. Brent lives at the bottom line.

"I'd ask you to take a dive," he said this afternoon, not totally kidding, "only it's two-to-one you get creamed in there."

Fuck, fuck, fuck. Every other time he's fought he's either seen the guy in action, had a look at somebody's shaky iPhone video, or at least had an idea of who he'd beaten and lost to. This could be King-fucking-Kong.

"You sure you don't want the robe?"

L. T. has tricked this thing up, some kind of wall hanging of a grizzly bear glued onto the back of a bathrobe stolen from a fancy hotel.

"I wouldn't be caught dead in that shit."

"You'll stiffen up."

"Once I get down in the pit," says Scorch, "it'll cut the wind off."

The thing is it's *cold,* the wind never letting up, the spectators in down vests and jackets, restless now, stomping their feet on the bleachers and shouting "Fight, fight, fight, fight!"

Brent shows up then, smiling. Easy for him.

"*Show*time, Scorch. Take him apart."

Scorch is wearing work boots he bought at the Cenex today, unlaced, to get over the gravel to the pit. They've hooked four big work lights to a generator thrumming out in the field a couple hundred yards away, trained down into the hole and poled up high enough that they won't blind the fighters.

Shouting and cheers as he steps to the edge. There's an aluminum ladder leading down into the pit. The crowd is stoked, Brent selling beer out of a panel truck for at least an hour now, some guys with hard liquor bottles in hand, passing them around. They overpour at Bazookas, cheap stuff but potent, and figure the more wasted the guys are the more likely to go for extras, to go for a lap dance or stuff a twenty into a girl's g-string. Scorch can handle it, Vic always says. Vic, who gave him the night off and said if you break your fucking arm you're fired.

"Gentlemen!" calls Brent, already down in the cage with a cordless mic in hand. "I assume there's no ladies here."

A roar of what– approval, complaint?

"Welcome to the first annual Yellow Earth Invitational Mixed Martials Arts *Massacre!*"

Another roar. There are at least a thousand of the bloodthirsty pricks crowded around, amazing when you figure there was no advertising, just word of mouth, and the location only revealed this afternoon. Some guy who owns private land on the Indian rez gave Brent permission. Way off the main roads, they stopped at two other lit-up drill pads tonight before they finally found it. And the vibe, right from the minute they pulled up– probably how it felt like when they used to lynch people.

"The management respectfully requests," says Brent, deepening his voice like the character who does the Caesar's Palace fights, "that you refrain from throwing objects into the cage."

Laughter and some hoots. Brent said they'd do five-minute rounds, but he didn't say how many, which means it's till there's a clear winner.

"For our first contest," calls Brent, strutting around to face all four sides above him, "we have a pair of heavyweight warriors new to the oil patch. In this corner"– he turns toward Scorch– "wearing the– what is that– ?"

"Teal!" Shakes calls out, enjoying this too much.

"In the teal trunks, from Tampa, Florida, at two hundred and twenty pounds- Stanley– the *Scorch*er– Adamov!"

There is no way to spring into the cage. Scorch kicks the work boots off, turns around and backs down the ladder. A guy immediately yanks it up and trots around to the other side of the pit while Scorch throws his arms in the air and walks a circle around Brent, to cheers and jeers.

"In the opposite corner– from McAlester, Oklahoma– at two hundred and thirty-five pounds– Mike– The Mountain– Mul*laaaaaa*ney!"

The guy is two-fifty if he's an ounce, and the only thing in fucking McAlester is the state penitentiary. It takes a minute for him to climb down the ladder and turn, most of the gawkers above on their feet and hollering. Big bald-headed hunk of muscle, like if Kimbo Slice was a white guy, and yeah, he's got the shamrock with the 666 on one arm and A. B. over the SS lightning bolts on the other. No ink on his chest though, which is matted with hair.

Fuck, fuck, fuck.

Brent motions for them to step close, keeping his own body in between, and the eyeballing begins. The thing is to look right down through the pupils into the guy's brain tissue, and concentrate on how you're going to drive the fucker's nose bone into it.

"Fellas, let's have a good, clean fight," says Brent, then looks up to the crowd. "We are rockin in the Bakken! Let's get it *on*!" he shouts, and then flips up the hand mic end over end for the ladder guy to catch. Under the roar of anticipation he has a private word with the fighters.

"You boys are getting paid plenty," he says. "No tapping out. Now take three steps back."

So that's the deal. Snap but no tap. I'm going to have to kill this motherfucker or he'll kill me.

"Bong!" shouts the ladder guy over the mic, and there's only Scorch Adamov and Mike Mullaney facing each other in an overlit hole in the North Dakota prairie.

Scorch gets on his toes and begins to bounce and sidestep. Fucker this big, that kind of power, you don't want anything to do with grappling. He throws a few jabs and it's clear he's faster, the Aryan Brother barely moving his head to absorb the blows, then lunging to try to grab his arm. Boos as Scorch dances backwards out of the way. He's had the fundamentals shown to him in the gym a couple times by serious practitioners, but the sport pretty much boils down to kick the shit out of your opponent without getting disqualified. Scorch fakes a jab and hits him with a left overhand, right between the eyes, then throws in a muay thai kick to the side of the knee before backpedalling. Think Bruce Lee, think Jackie Chan. Whap! Whap! Stick and move, stick and move, but the last move backs him up against the wall, no give to it, and Mullaney crowds in, sending an uppercut into his jaw before trying to grab him around the neck, Scorch getting his forearm up just in time to protect his windpipe but crushed in the grip, digging his bare feet into the mat to keep from being thrown, the two of them staggering together this way and that, till the Mountain jerks him off his feet and falls backwards with a heavy smack, Scorch able to get a knee up and pry himself loose, immediately rolling away and scrambling to his feet. The Mountain takes his time, huge arms up for protection, pushing back against the wall to leg himself upright.

Neither of them is a marathon runner, both huffing for air as the crowd calls for mayhem. His best move in the clubs he works at is to step inside the other guy's defense while he's still cursing you out and then snap an elbow into his face. No talking down here in the pit.

Scorch exhausts his supply of striker moves, jabbing and running to boos and catcalls as Mullaney closes, closes, closes, taking most of the blows on his forearms, patient, flinging an occasional body shot to the ribs or hips, trying to rush him when the wall is at his back, not bothering with kicks or fancy footwork.

"Bong!" calls the ladder guy, and they separate into opposite corners, no stools there for them to sit on, just catching their breath and staring at each other. Brent comes over as if to check for damage.

"Better get busy, pal. Folks came to see a rumble."

Scorch hasn't ever been pinned in the cage like that, hasn't been held down that helpless since those shitbirds at the Okeechobee CI when he was waiting for trial, after all their bullshit about white cons got to stick together, dragged him behind the generator in the machine shop and took turns on some teenage ass. The smell of the shop floor, the weight of them.

It will not happen again.

Scorch bites down on his mouthguard, tasting blood, and runs the possibilities through his head. He beat a Cuban guy in Dade County with a double leg takedown and then some ground and pound, but the dude was a light-heavy at best. The couple straight rights he's landed haven't had much effect, so a knockout is unlikely. Got to get him off balance, which means taking some chances–

It is a very short minute.

The crowd yells "Bong!" this time and the Mountain lumbers toward him. Scorch takes a step, pivots and hard-kicks, hoping to hit groin but only smacking a hairy thigh and skipping away. A roar of approval– action is action. Mullaney rushes him and Scorch gets caught against the wall, the Mountain locking hands behind his head for a double collar tie, but Scorch thrusts up hard, butting him under the bloodied eye and trying to slip out, but he is hurled down and has only time to get one knee up before the man falls onto him, throwing short hooks to the head that Scorch mostly catches on his arms until Mullaney pins one of his wrists to the mat and continues to hammer with his left. He hurts but without full leverage or a clean shot at the face it won't kill him. The big man pounds away till his arm tires, then tries to press the point of his elbow into Scorch's Adam's apple, and now it's just wrestling, Scorch trying to hug close and the Mountain without the technique to even start a submission hold. Scorch has a sweaty, hairy shoulder grinding down on his mouth and nose, hard to catch a breath, and there is booing as it goes on too long, Brent slapping the Mountain on his back till he's got his attention and pulling them apart to start on their feet again.

Scorch feels dizzy for a moment, all the blood that was trapped up in his head draining out as he stands, but manages to move sideways leaning against the wall till he can get his balance.

Brent signals for them to engage again.

The Mountain's cheek on the bloody side is swollen, maybe broken by the butt, and when he sniffs it brings his lips up over his mouthguard, which has a shark-tooth pattern painted on it. Scorch lowers his hands a bit and steps forward.

If a bar fight lasts more than twenty seconds you're doing something wrong. The point is to put the asshole down quick and hard and then hope his friends don't have easy access to anything that shoots bullets. No feeling a man out, no playing with him, no referee, and if you're lucky, no security camera trained on the floor.

Scorch throws a couple jabs, leaving his left low, and the Mountain throws a tremendous haymaker hook to the side of his head, knocking him stumbling sideways, Scorch milking it a bit by bouncing hard off the wall before he skitters away. He brings the left up too high, jab, jab, and thwap! takes a sidearm hook in the ribs that almost knocks the wind out of him. He can hear the oil workers cheering, can vaguely see through the lights that they are on their feet. He goes flat-footed, bending his knees a bit as if he's in trouble, circles right, then moves forward again, dropping the left even more. He throws a pussy jab, leaning his head in too far, then ducks back quick as the Mountain throws a killer right hook at his head, the momentum as it misses twisting his whole body enough that Scorch can stomp his heel down on the side of the man's right knee, sending him to the mat, and the moment Mullaney's right arm goes stiff to catch his fall, dive on it knee first, rig drivers out on Route 12 able to hear the report as the big bone snaps, a collective *Ooooooooh!* from the crowd as their bodies wince at the thought of it. Scorch rolls away and hops to his feet, Brent just standing with his hands on his hips and a grin on his face, so he straddles the mound of Mullaney and pistons his elbow to the Mountain's thick neck, 12 to 6, just the way they say is forbidden in the instructional videos, just the way his Aryan Brother would have done to him if positions were reversed. Mullaney somehow rolls sideways and gets his good arm up to grab Scorch's face, fingers probing for the eyeballs, till Scorch clamps both hands on his wrist, rises up and drives his knee through that elbow socket as well. Brent has him in a choke hold from behind then, and he lets himself be pulled back as the derrick jockeys whoop and holler and stomp the metal bleachers and yes, throw bottles and cans into the pit.

L. T. and Shakes have to pull him from under the arms to get him the last two rungs up the ladder, the lamest corner men in history, while Brent squawks something over the mic and walks a little circle around the writhing Mountain, wondering, no doubt, how he's going to haul the big fuck out of the pit.

"And still unde-fucking-feated champion," yells Brent as well-wishers and backslapping drunks surround Scorch, a smile on Brent's mouth but his eyes reading that the prick did bet on Mullaney, "Scorcher– *Adamov*!!!" Serves him right.

L. T. and Shakes help Scorch stagger, still winded and feeling his cracked ribs like an ice pick in the side, through the bug-eyed, shouting throng. They can hear Brent announcing the next contest.

"That fucker owes me," growls Scorch, his legs starting to shake. "That fucker owes me something good."

RANDY WAKES AND DOESN'T know where he is.

It's a suite in a Best Western, he can tell that much right away. A plane outside, landing, so it's right by the airport. It takes him a minute to get to the little living room, turn the lamp on, find the stationery next to the phone.

Yellow Earth.

It was the blood fracking dream again.

He looks to the clock, does the math. It's too late to call Coral and the kids, even if they're in Seattle. She's very formal about the whole deal, likes a pre-call to repeat the ground rules and wipe her feet on him a little bit, remind him who ended up with full custody. He can't wait till they're old enough to have their own phones.

And Jewelle is out for the count by now, always saying how dead she is after a shift.

In the dream the blood is being driven by an enormous pumping heart, and he follows it out of the chamber in a tumbling flurry of platelets and red blood cells, the pressure straining the walls of the main arteries, making them bulge, then ripping through the smaller arterioles with a clattering sound and blasting out into the capillaries, and he is in one place and everywhere at once as the tiny vessels overload, circumference inadequate for the volume, endothelial cells suddenly rupturing and the fluid exploding outward into the muscle tissue, the skin flushing a purplish red, flesh torn from the bone, the blood-brain barrier giving way before a flood of leukocytes, and the cerebrum itself swelling, swelling, pushing outward against the thinnest wall of the skull at the temple–

The shale has been responding beautifully, the wells already tapped are in several cases out-producing his calculations. He's refined the technique a bit, adjusted it to the particular conditions of the play, but can't imagine why they still need him here. They've got plenty of people who can pound combustibles out of the ground with sludge.

In the dream, sometimes he is the heart, forcing the fluid through the vessels, sometimes he is only a tiny molecule swept along in the rush, and sometimes, at the end of the ones that wake him up, he becomes the organism, the man who is being blown apart from within.

Randy turns on the TV, finds a movie, mutes the sound. He sits, naked and sweating, on the couch. The movie looks familiar, something he's seen before, or maybe just a familiar genre, men in thin black leather jackets killing each other. They say the room service is twenty-four hours now, a sleepy cook downstairs probably watching the same show to keep himself awake, half the lights off till there's a call.

His father was in a Holiday Inn when the stroke hit him, a divorced mud man with so many wells to service that each assumed he was at another, and it was a full day, Do Not Disturb sign hung on the doorknob, before his body was found. He was a great admirer of room service, or at least pretended to be.

One of the men in leather jackets, who looks like an Eastern European of some sort, has another man's head stuck in the jaws of a vise, grilling him for information, steadily turning the handle. The pressure is unbearable–

MACARIO CATCHES THE TAXI at the corner of Paseo Colón and the Avenue of Beheaded Saints. When he says he wants to see the border fences the *taxista* does not hesitate, taking him east on Colón and then right on the ring road named after the assassinated presidential candidate.

There is not much to see. On the Mexican side, a massive cement ramp leading up to fenced-in *fábricas*, then the golf course, then a low, tree-covered flood plain leading to the Río Bravo and the United States beyond, on the other.

There are a lot of things to be climbed over.

"If there isn't much rain you can walk across," says the *taxista*. "You only get wet a little above the belt. But the current can be strong, so most people pay to be taken across on a raft, and for that the *Migra* is always watching. Those *yanquis* have cameras everywhere, even ones that see the heat of your body at night."

Macario has been trying not to look like an *indocumentado*, even carrying a second-hand toolbox, with no tools in it, when he goes into the bars where people know things.

"And worse than the *yanqui Migra* are the Zetas," adds the driver, singing the song Macario has heard a dozen times since he arrived in Nuevo Laredo. "You try to cross alone, or even in a group without paying their *cuota*, they kill you. A few come floating down that river every day."

They turn back in on Avenida Transformación, passing another cluster of the low, whitewashed factory buildings, all behind metal fencing with concertina wire strung across the top of it. But for the lack of gun towers, they look as much like a prison complex as the Centro de Ejecución de Sentencias #2.

The *taxista*'s warning is the same as he heard from Nacho, the skinny little *pollero* who made him an offer on the first day here, a teenage boy with nervous, shining eyes, wearing a Tecate cap.

"All my passengers pay me the *cuota*," he explained, "and then I pay the ones who own the river before we cross."

The ones who own the city of Nuevo Laredo, and most of the state of Tamaulipas. Macario had gone to an immigration lawyer on the second day, a man who sighed a lot and told him the United States government did not care if *huachicoleros* would kill him if he returned home, that the 'well-founded fear' they made exemption for was meant to save the victims, hopefully well-educated ones, of governments they were waging quiet wars against.

"You cross with me, I bring you past the first line of the *Migra*," said Nacho, disturbingly loud, grinning over the beer Macario had bought him. "Believe it, *güey*, I'm the best."

"I want to go further than that."

"*Yo soy solamente pollero del río.* You want to go all the way to Houston on one ride, you need to get on a truck. If there is something illegal moving on a truck, the *narcos* want it to be their product."

Macario has spent hours watching the World Trade Bridge, thousands of trucks passing over through Laredo and into the heart of America every day. They must be stopped and searched according to some kind of a system, sniffed by dogs for drugs, but if the *narcos* use them, most of what they send must get through.

"What do you say, *chango*, I lead you out of this *cagadero* and you go get rich in Paradise?"

Macario had smiled and said he wasn't looking to cross, legally or illegally, but thanked Nacho for the offer. The boy didn't seem like much more than a *ventana*, one hired to watch the river with binoculars and report on anything moving. It is a slippery world here so close to the border, some people claiming to be more than they are, others not revealing their claws until it is too late.

"You're not going to be *tan burro* to try it on your own, are you? *Un aviso, güey,* stay off the river unless you've got permission, and don't be hanging around with *chapinos* and *cotrachos*."

The people most obviously here to cross are, in fact, from Guatemala or Honduras, with others from El Salvador and even a few Cubans, who march up to the *Migra* officers on the bridges and get themselves put into the refugee process.

"You be sitting with those people, doesn't matter whether on the street, in a bus, even in the shelter where they let the ones who got caught and sent back stay– and before you know it there's six *tipos* wearing masks and carrying *cuernos de chivo* threatening to shoot and pushing you into their van. They take you where don't anybody care and they line you up and say hand over your money, hand over your cell phone if you got one, hand over that telephone number of your brother back in Huehuetenango or the *socio* you got waiting up in Tucson. They gonna call your family for some ransom."

"And if you don't have a number?"

"Then they going to *darle chicharón* right away instead of later. *Créame amigo,* when you get up the nerve to go, you look for Nacho."

They loop around north to the neighborhood of the shelter and Macario pays the driver and gets out. He had hoped to find work here while he was studying the situation, but with the flood of desperate people coming through there is nothing left. Nothing legal.

There is a television set playing at either end of the bar in El Rincón, turned to different channels. Macario sits on the Telemundo side and orders a beer. It is a familiar place, the same neon *cerveza* logos, the calendars with Aztec maidens showing off their huge *chichis*, the team photos of local *fútbol* teams on the wall, Los Tigres del Norte on the jukebox. But where at home the talk would be of work and sports and local politics, here it is assassinations and prison escapes, blood feuds, and the ever-changing tactics of *la Migra* on the other side of the water. It is a very *norteño*-looking crowd, all Mexicans as far as he can tell. He avoids the eyes of the ones with the most expensive boots. Too many predators locked in a single cage.

Twice he saw the baby turtles hatch on the beach in the Gulf. Thousands of them crawling out from their sandy nests on the same day, shells still soft and vulnerable, struggling with their little curved flippers across the broad beach to the surf, the sky filled with swooping *gaviotas* and *halcones*, the first half-kilometer of the surf boiling with silvery, razor-toothed fish, the beach itself patrolled by gorging dogs and half-wild pigs. Getting through to the open ocean is only a matter of numbers and blind luck.

Unless you are a more observant turtle.

Macario notices that the drinkers are all looking up at the TV screen and takes a glance, expecting to see Carmen Villalobos or Mónica Spear in something that barely covers their *nalgas*. Instead it is news footage from his home, San Martín Texmelucan, where a huge black cloud is blowing across the town. A huge black cloud caused by a pipeline explosion, says the newsreader, thought to be the result of *huachicoleros* attempting to install a hot tap.

"*Están buen jodidos*," mutters the man standing behind him, and yes, it looks like the people there are truly fucked– dozens dead, more burned or with ruined lungs.

There are many people in this city, in this Mexico, who have nothing to do with the *rateros* who have infested it, the ones who have made their deal with the devil and will soon, he hopes, die miserably at the hands of the government or their rivals in crime. These honest people must lock their doors and windows against the tempest roaring outside, praying for a change in the weather. Nuevo Laredo was always a border town, a haven for smugglers, but now it seems less a city than a way station to hell, the place where *gringos* come to manufacture what is too expensive or too poisonous to make in their own country, the place where the poor of Central America flock to be preyed upon by murderers.

The news camera, in a helicopter over the site of the explosion, is enveloped in black smoke.

"*Qué rollo con el hoyo, güey?*"

It is Nacho, slapping his back and sitting at the empty stool to his left. He immediately turns his back to the bar and scans the crowded room with nervous eyes.

"You're back."

"*Cómo no?* I deliver my *pollos* and I come back. *Estoy como un espírito, chango,* they don't see me."

"And if you can stop talking for a moment, they don't hear you."

"Listen, *amigo,*" says Nacho, leaning close, "I got to beg you a *favorzote.*"

The boy looks like he hasn't slept in days.

"*Dígame.*"

"Not here," says Nacho, getting up off the stool. "Take a walk with me."

They walk on Felipe Ángeles, passing the shelter that Macario looked into on his third day here, a roof and a meal for a few days, run by people with good hearts, but now seeming to him more like a corral meant to hold the sheep for the *narcos* until ready to be slaughtered. Nacho tries to seem carefree, but keeps turning completely around as he talks, making sure nobody is following.

"I cross with a group of ten *cotrachos pendejos*– you know how they are from down there. This one woman is pregnant, big as a whale, and I'm helping her off the raft on the other side when the *pinche Migra* step out of the reeds, two of them."

"You were caught."

"I was be*trayed, te juro,* somebody on this side who has a deal with those *ca-brones* and needs to throw them a couple fish now and then. So they take me to their processing and these idiot *hondureños*– I bet it was that pregnant bitch– tell them that I'm the *pollero.* Which means they charge me with transporting. And this fucking *pocho* behind the desk, this Garza, sounded like he was born there right in Laredo, he tells me *hijo,* I will let you go this time, but if you ever come back, transporting or not, you go to federal jail."

"They tell me those prisons are like hotels compared to ours."

"*Hombre,* they got gangs inside there I never even heard of."

"You could tell them you're with the Zetas."

"But I'm *not.*"

"I'm glad to hear that," says Macario. "Maybe you'll live to be twenty."

"But this is not over. They do all their typing into the computer, they take pictures of me, take my fingerprints with ink, and then this *hijo de puta* Garza holds me until it's dark again before he loads me into the van with a mess of *indios chapinos* who got caught that day and they back it up to the little crack you walk through on foot on the Juárez–Lincoln Bridge."

"So you're back home."

"No, I'm *completamente jodido, güey,* cause that's where the Zetas have their people waiting after midnight, looking for fresh meat."

"But if you paid your *cuota*– "

"I *was going* to, I just didn't have time before I left with the *pollos.*"

"And besides, you're invisible."

Nacho looks like he might cry. "This *rompehuevos* grabs ahold of me right there, the Border Patrol guys are behind their windows watching, probably laughing at me, and I try to explain to him."

"You said there was a favor I could do for you."

They have come to the corner of Independencia, the boy stopping, looking in all directions before he continues.

"They want five thousand *yanqui* dollars by tomorrow or I'm dead."

"I don't have that much."

"But you *do* have *some,* and you *do* want to cross over. I know a *truckero* who can drive you all the way to Houston."

"And how much do I pay you for bringing me to him?"

"Nothing. You pay him to take *me* along with you."

"It's called remediation," says Rick, like he's talking to a fucking third-grader. "We've got three sites you've contracted to clean up, two reserve pits full of cuttings and an oil spill, and your people haven't gone near them."

"Everybody is in a fucking hurry."

"One of the pits is right on the road into New Center. It looks bad."

"What"– says Brent, lounging in the Chairman's office while Harleigh is on his way back from some tribal event– "the real estate values are gonna suffer? This reservation was a fucking eyesore before the first drill spudded in, and that's what it's going back to."

"Harleigh's talking about a facelift."

"Harleigh's a politician, he's got to say shit like that, and you're supposed to be covering his ass. If you were doing your job people wouldn't be complaining about the reserve pit, they'd be looking at a big sign that says 'Site of Another Successful Energy Extraction– Keep America Strong.'"

"Are you planning to clean up those sites or not?"

If this kid got the job to shut his mother up, it hasn't worked. She's been mouthing off in the paper, specifically complaining about ArrowFleet.

"We'll do something."

"At least throw some dirt on top of it."

"If that's what it takes to shut people up, sure. You dig down miles underground, pump shit up from there under pressure, there's bound to be something to show for it."

"Something toxic."

"How bout a couple 'No Swimming Allowed' notices? Or don't enough of the people here read?"

Rick doesn't see the humor in this. "You push the Chairman too far," he says, "he'll cut you loose so fast."

"You think so?"

Brent can tell the kid doesn't like him sitting at Harleigh's desk. He leans back in the swivel chair, playing with a beautifully fashioned old spearhead.

"Big ship goes down, Ricky boy," he says, "the captain stays with it."

Rick crawls back into his hole.

Once they sense you're more than willing to take it all the way, they always blink first. It's what scares all the second-rate characters about Roark in *The Fountainhead*, it's what the Objectivist meant when she said that animals survive by adjusting themselves to their surroundings, but men, real men, succeed by adjusting their surroundings to themselves. Brent buzzes Doris, another one scared to look him in the eye.

"Doris," he says into the chief's squawk box, "can you get me that number in Idaho? And be sure to let him know the call is coming from Chairman Killdeer's office."

IT WAS A CAMARO in a custom-looking shade of gold, California plates, and the man with her could have been as old as thirty. By the time Clemson got himself turned back in their direction on the 2 they were long gone, though he hunted in ever-widening circles for an hour. Then he stopped in at the coffee shop that was the Dakota Diner and before that the Prairie Hen's Pantry that Don and Evelyn Nussbaum ran forever. Spartina is obviously very well liked there, a good worker, but nobody knew or would tell about the man in the Camaro.

It's not a fit place for women anymore, Yellow Earth, Clemson thinking of the shacks off base in Biloxi when he was stationed there, how the decent girls had to walk in squadrons and even that didn't spare them what the GIs had to say. He was young then, with the big war on, and never thought about what the folks in Biloxi thought of the invasion. Some made out pretty good, of course, the ones running the honkytonks and cathouses that weren't Off Limits for some reason. The army must have known everything that was going on, the army could do anything they wanted in that time, so they must have chosen not to shut it all down. Clemson remembers slot machines in the bus station, in the grocery stores, remembers half the fellas stationed at Keesler losing all their pay in one crooked game or another. And by some miracle he met Nora, survived the war, and took her back up here.

He remembers walking her home after a USO dance, through the worst of it, men calling out to her, women calling out to him, and how none of it seemed to touch her, chatting pleasantly to him in her musical voice. He thought at the time she was the most innocent girl he'd ever met, but later learned Nora had the Southern woman's skill of seeing without acknowledging. If I do not choose to recognize it, it does not exist.

He's never had that talent.

Jake Wiltorp had mentioned seeing her at the Havva Javva, and he figured she'd tell him sooner or later, and maybe good for her going out to make her own money instead of depending on him to come around on whatever new gadget she had her heart set on. Industrious. And it was a relief to see they don't make the girls wear some kind of short carhop uniform. If they took a day off his life for every little lie he told his Pa–

He can't bear the thought of a confrontation, of raising his voice to his Tina. He got the license number though, one of those vanity jobs– SRFZUP– which makes it easy to remember. And Busby Curtis's boy Tolliver is a deputy now, with access to all that law enforcement computer business–

His father shot a wolf once, back when there were wolves, that was raising hell with the stock. Left it out for the crows and the buzzards, and maybe as a warning for its friends, if it had any.

"You can scare em away," Pa said, "but they'll just come skulking back."

THE MEN ARE MAKING the drum talk. Six of them at the moment, big men sitting around in a circle and striking it in unison, a few with their traditional shirts and feathers on, some just with T-shirts and tractor caps, at least three of them wearing sunglasses, which seems to be accepted now as something like a traditional mask. They are the beating heart of the Powwow. Harleigh remembers as he passes, as he always does, the thrill of the first time Granpaw Pete brought him into the circle. The old man's leathery hand over his little boy hand over the stick, making the drum talk with the men, raising his thin voice with theirs to chant.

"This, at least," his grandfather would say each year, "remains unbroken."

The veterans have put up their flags, Harleigh at the microphone for the solemn moment before he handed it over to Nick Straighthorn, the rodeo announcer they brought over from Bozeman. His job now is to mingle in the stands and in the refreshment area, pressing the flesh, admiring how big the little ones have gotten, fielding compliments and complaints. There is no simple 'Hey, how's it going?' for the Chairman.

He stops in front of the grandstand to watch the Women's Traditional Dance for a moment, the ladies circled in their shawls and beads, bouncing lightly to the drumbeat, holding themselves like queens, raising their eagle feather fans when an honor beat comes. He knows all of the local women out there, some of them with enough personal tragedy to fill a TV miniseries, but they stand straight and serene, inhabiting the beautifully beaded cloths and buckskins rather than just wearing them, braids glistening and wrapped with ribbons or fur, all pride and elegance. He'd tried to get Fawn interested in taking part, but she was feuding with the daughter of Shirley Plenty Fox, who taught it on the reservation. Or that's what she said.

"We have to talk."

Rick McAllen has appeared beside him. Rick has been dogging him with this environmental business, even people with wells already paying off on their land getting into the act, as if you can bring the money up by magic.

"Not another spill, I hope."

A wastewater pipeline had bust over by Wabek, spewing brine over about twenty-three acres, and people were legitimately upset. 'Metal fatigue,' said the Company, though they didn't explain why they didn't use metal that wasn't so tired. They'd made good on some fencing to help people keep their stock off the poisoned ground, and were working up a remediation plan.

"Not that bad," says Rick, "but it's got to be dealt with. You know the PeteCo-Cloud Number Four?"

"White Shield?"

"It's paying out good, got the Christmas tree up, couple tanks, but they left the spoil-pit they dug behind."

"Sometimes it takes a while to– "

"Four months. There's some bad-looking sludge in the bottom of it, dead birds and animals by now, and the smell is– "

Harleigh starts to walk away. "I'll look into it."

Ricky follows after him. The job came with sixty grand a year, good pay for a reservation gig, but the kid looks like hell.

"You could use some sleep, buddy."

"People got my cell phone number. They call when the spirit moves them."

"Turn it off."

"Can *you* do that?"

"I got two. One where everybody's got the number, and that I shut down at nine o'clock every night. Then there's the emergency phone, only the law and a few other people got that number, and it better be an emergency."

"People aren't happy, Harleigh."

Harleigh puts his hand on Rick's shoulder. "The people who haven't struck it *rich* aren't happy," he says. "And they weren't happy before. Welcome to my world."

A final shout and drumbeat, the women in the arena stopping as one, holding their spot for a moment as there is applause and people crying out in the three languages and Nick back on the microphone telling folks to show their appreciation. Harleigh uses the moment to disengage from Rick and move on. Rick's job is to identify problems and deal with them, not to come to him with every sob story about a sick heifer.

But four months is not good.

He invited some of the Company men to the powwow, give them a taste of Indian culture, and sees a few high up in the stands. The way people are mixed these days they don't look so out of place, and the couple from Oklahoma might even be some bit Creek or Cherokee by blood. Harleigh climbs up, passing men who look like rig workers in between shifts. Good for them, they can say they've really been here.

He waves to Joe Dixon.

"Good to see you come out, Joe."

"It's so colorful."

"Yeah, they put on a good show." The Antelope Society are out in the middle now, fancy dancing, all swirling feathers and footwork.

"And it all *means* something, right?"

"Any big hunt, big move, big battle, we had a dance for it. Get everybody involved, put all our spirit behind it."

"Weddings and bar mitzvahs?"

Harleigh smiles. "We had our version of all of that. And like the beadwork you seen on the women– everybody understood the time and effort that went into that, that it wasn't something you could buy."

"There ought to be an oil-shale dance."

"Couldn't hurt."

Joe is something like a coordinator for the Company, seeing that the needed personnel and equipment move from well to well in the proper order, that nothing falls through the cracks.

"Listen, you know the PeteCo-Cloud Number Four."

"Still producing like a champion."

"You had a pit dug there."

"For the fluids, right."

"Shouldn't it be gone?"

Joe takes eyes away from the dance in the arena. "It hasn't been filled in?"

"Still there, still holding residue."

"But that's your outfit."

"My outfit?"

"Subbed to do the clean-up. Your outfit with Brent there, the body-builder character. What's it– ArrowFleet."

It's the third job he's heard of left undone. And then the Parker brothers saying they quit because they hadn't been paid for a couple hauls–

"You sure of that?"

"We subbed everything we could on the reservation to you. Keep it in the family."

They are pretty good old boys, the Company crowd, but are dead serious about their business.

"Well then, I got to get on somebody's tail, don't I? Thanks for clearing that up."

"Any news on that situation up north?"

The reservation is big enough to have regions, and Joe must mean the Looks for Water family, who hold mineral rights on a big area up at the top but can't stop fighting with each other long enough to settle on a lease agreement. Marjorie is the only intelligent one in the whole outfit but tends to have her head stuck in the latest conspiracy theory.

"Last I heard there was a brother they thought was dead, showed up from California wanting to claim his acreage. I'd say your best bet is to offer just what their closest neighbors got."

"The Mortensons."

"Right, and put the money in escrow for them to sort out later."

"You think they'll go for that?"

"I think enough would want to make a deal if you could get them all into the same room without a fatality."

"I don't want to be in that room. Don't you have some kind of mediation panel– "

"The old days, there'd be elders, there'd be the community and people would be shamed into getting right. Might not be a word spoken. But these days– " Harleigh shakes his head. "And the money bug has bit, which doesn't make it any easier."

"There's one fella outside of Yellow Earth, just flat turned us down."

"Clemson Dollarhide."

"Notorious crank, I take it."

"No, he's well thought-of. Son and daughter-in-law were hit by a truck on the highway."

"Not one of ours?"

There has been an increase in traffic fatalities, a few involving oil service vehicles.

"This is some years back. Stock-hauler, headed for Fort Peck."

"So he's what, bitter?"

Harleigh shrugs. "Philosophical. Like some of our traditionalists, don't like to see Mother Earth tore up. But here people are a lot hungrier."

Joe cocks his head, getting up his nerve to ask something. They're shy about the Indian stuff, so much bad feeling in the past.

"If you could turn back the clock," says Joe, nodding toward the Antelope Society men whirling in the arena, "go back to those buffalo days, would you do it?"

"Before the Company came?"

Joe grins. "Before Lewis and Clark, let's say."

It's something he's thought about. He loves to hunt and fish, but when he's
come home empty-handed there's still always something from the fridge to put
on the table. And you don't have to worry about the Sioux raiding anymore, or
starving if the snow is too deep for too long–

"Sure," says Harleigh. "From what I can tell, that was a good life." He indicates
the performers and the spectators around them. "All this week people been getting ready for the powwow, they feel good. But lots of days they get up, and
there's nothing they look forward to. No *purpose*. Buffalo days, everybody had
a purpose. Even the kids were expected to pull their weight, were eager to get
involved and earn people's respect."

"Hell," Joe nods, "*I'd* go back to that."

Harleigh claps Joe on the arm and moves away.

"Then we'll meet up there in the Happy Hunting Ground, buddy," he winks.
"Bring your own toilet paper."

Harleigh meets and greets with a half-dozen other little gatherings of spectators then, enrolled members mostly, some of them even thanking him for his
efforts in bringing the oil. A few have hit the jackpot, hundreds of thousands
in the bank and still pumping, while others are guessing at how the tribal-lease
money will shake down. He's hoping to come up with some projects that benefit
everybody– not the hospital, the Feds still owe them that– but improvements
the tribes can use. If you start to divide the money up into cash payments to the
enrollment it can get messy. Why are you giving cash to a person everybody
knows has a drug addiction, why should the members who've already struck it
big be included in the People's Pool profits, can you qualify for membership if
you haven't been living here for years, maybe for generations? At the big conferences he hears about membership purges in other tribes, people calling each
other out, some even surrendering to the cold percentages of DNA tests. The
Three Nations, like many others, have a long tradition of intermarriage and adop-
tion. Was Quanah Parker a Comanche? Was John Ross a Cherokee? Can his
cousin Nils, who looks like that Swedish guy Rocky had to fight in one of the
sequels, qualify just because he's one-sixteenth and has been the pipe-bearer of
the Kit Fox Society for twenty years? Things used to be so bad that the joke was

'Who would ever pretend to be an *Indian*?,' but first the Dawes Allotment and now this oil boom have attracted some pretty marginal types and pretenders.

Danny Two Strike is motioning to him from the edge of the arena, where groups are assembling for the Grass Dance. Danny is in his police uniform but with some of his military buttons and badges hung in front. He doesn't look like he's celebrating.

"We should step out of sight."

"It's powwow, Danny."

"You need to hear this."

Harleigh throws up his hands and lets Danny lead him under the bleachers. The drums have a strange echo here, the steady beat less certain, jumpier.

"I'm getting complaints from your former employees."

"I don't have employees."

"You own ArrowFleet Services."

"Co-own."

"Well, in the last week three different people, all of them enrolled members, have come to me complaining they were fired for asking your co-owner for their paycheck."

"You know I went out of my way to make as many TERO hires as possible, and some of those people– "

"These aren't deadbeats, Harleigh. They picked up other work right away."

"So, problem solved."

"They say they're owed for services rendered. Two, three weeks in a couple cases, one guy who filled his truck with diesel for a haul and was never reimbursed."

"They're bringing criminal charges?"

"They say your co-owner has surrounded himself with a bunch of hard cases and the workers are afraid to stand up for themselves."

"Trucking is a rough business to begin with, Danny, and you throw in the shifts these guys are working, the pharmaceuticals they may be taking to stay in the game– I'd want a few muscle men backing me up."

"Every one of the fellas who come to me said the same thing. 'Somebody's gonna get killed.'"

"All right, I'll have a word with Brent."

He hasn't seen Brent in that command mode ever, but can imagine his Cross-Fit training kicking in. Steroids? Those are supposed to affect your moods–

"How much do you actually know about the guy?"

Harleigh shrugs. "You've met him. Charming, a real go-getter. Like a Navy SEAL without the weapons system."

The last time he went by the shop it was hard to see who exactly was running the day-to-day– trucks coming in and out, lots of guys just hanging around, Brent on the phone yelling about what sounded like a lease-flipping deal he was trying to finance. Harleigh just gave him a wave and left a note about the oil socks piling up on his property.

Danny looks away as they hear the Grass Dance begin.

"My father and his family, even my older brothers when they were little," he says, "used to ride here for the powwow every year. The ladies would come later in a wagon. But the men, they'd have their ceremony at home in Makoti and mount up, ride all night. People be waking up in their tents– it was army surplus tents in those days– and our men would ride in, bare chested, sitting tall without a saddle. The women there already would all drop whatever they were doing and step out to raise up a cry."

They listen for a moment, standing among the candy wrappers and plastic soda bottles that have been dropped though the bleacher seats, imagining the dancers, imagining the swaying of the grass.

"No saddles."

"Just a blanket and a hawser. At night, whether there was a moon or no. When only the spirits are supposed to be out."

"That was a hell of a long ride."

"Just cause things get easier," says Danny, "doesn't mean they're better."

IT TAKES A LITTLE while to jockey around the drive-thru line, which hooks out to the shoulder of the main road, and get into the crowded parking lot. The Golden Arches have extended their hours, like all the other fast-food joints in town, and Wayne Lee is glad to see it is as mobbed inside as outside. Fargo is already standing in line to order.

"Throw a double cheeseburger onto whatever you're getting," says Wayne Lee, handing him a five, "and one of those chocolate sludgy shakes."

He takes the strap of the backpack from Fargo, swings it over his shoulder as he heads for the men's room. The more people crammed into a place the less they pay attention to anyone else. There's no line for the bathroom, three guys inside pissing, one stall open– perfect.

Wayne Lee locks the stall door, sits and starts opening compartments in the backpack. The bulk of it is weed, pressed together in a lump the size of a basketball. Mexican maybe, anything better than what they try to grow up here. He opens bottles and packets and takes inventory. Some coke powder for the old-school party hounds, meth in pills and crystal, anabolic steroids, Ecstasy, and a little taste of crack. He repacks, steps out and washes his hands, checking his hair in the mirror.

By the time he hits the floor again, backpack slung casually over one shoulder, their order is ready. He and Fargo take their trays out to the picnic tables out front, alone with the truck exhaust and the wind.

"Where you in from?"

"Last stop was Denver," says Fargo, a bearded, red-eyed character who smells like an ashtray.

"Get to see the sights?"

"Couple hours."

"Bookstores, brew pubs, six-story buildings, you can get a massage– "

"I slept in my cab while they got my load ready."

"Ah– the knights of the highway lead a glamorous life." Wayne Lee slips the envelope with the money under Fargo's tray, unwraps his double cheeseburger.

"You don't like it here?"

Wayne Lee indicates the crawl of pickups and water haulers on the street before them. "What's not to like?"

"How's the snatch?"

Wayne Lee hesitates. He's been thinking about Tina all day, the girl telling him she's ready to really get into it. Tina, who would never sleep if you gave her two hours in Denver.

"About what you'd expect," he says. "When's your next run?"

Fargo is opening ketchup packets, ready to deal with his mountain of fries. "Last trip."

"You're getting out of the business?"

"No, but Brent says no more deliveries, so why should I run all the way up here?"

"Why would he say that?"

"Shit if I know. He got that service company with the chief, I heard he's fronting for oil leases on the reservation, maybe he don't want to risk it for some side money."

First Brent taking him off the long runs, now this. Brent said nothing to him this morning, just that he'd be out of town till late and that Bunny was still in California.

"Could be," says Wayne Lee. "But what if I fronted the money, made it worth your while?"

"Step around Brent?"

"If he's not buying product anymore I'm not stepping around him, am I?"

Fargo leans forward, serious. "I would think twice before making a move like that, my friend. You know Brent."

BRENT HAS TO WALK away from the noise of the backhoes till he can hear Tillerman's voice on the cell phone, stepping through high grass. Dollarhide's property, he thinks with satisfaction. The old fart doesn't want to let them build an access road through his worthless cow pasture, fuck him, we'll run it along the edge, meticulously surveyed. Brent looks to the Dollarhide farmhouse, just a hundred yards up the rise.

"You still there?" shouts Tillerman on the other end.

"Just had to find another spot. These oil wells start paying off, they make a lot of noise."

Actually, the pumping is one of the quietest phases of the operation, but Tillerman is just a coupon-clipper in fucking Idaho and wouldn't know.

"So what's this about?"

Always better to do these things in person. He's read how Lyndon Johnson used to back senators against the walls of Congress, hang an arm around their necks, and steer them in the direction he wanted.

"What it is, Hal, we're closing one door and opening another. The Mandan 27 well– "

"My investment."

"–that you were one of the many investors in, has attracted somebody who wants to shout for the whole package. You can understand how when we bring a production company in they'd prefer to be doing business with only one entity, one set of paperwork to deal with when the royalties have to be paid."

"You have my money," says Hal Tillerman.

The Russians don't want anybody else on the lease, that's a dealbreaker, and without them he's only got eighty-five percent of a sure thing.

"Which is convenient," says Brent, stepping around a dried-up cow pie, "because it puts you in first position for an even better deal. Due to my privileged position here on the reservation, which I might add is the result of a substantial amount of diplomacy and cash outlay on my part, I am able to offer you– "

"You have my money in the bank," says Tillerman flatly. "Papers have been signed."

"Technically, until Mandan 27 is fully capitalized, no one investor– "

"You told me I was the last one in."

"Look, contracts are rewritten up here every day. It's a fluid situation."

"I own thirty percent of Mandan 27. You have guaranteed it will be drilled within six months. If you've got anything different to tell me, my lawyer should hear it first."

"I'm trying to help you here, Hal. These opportunities open and close so quickly– "

"The only deal I'm interested is outlined in our contract."

Fuck, fuck, fuck. The Russians need to hear by Friday, saying they might buy a hockey team instead, and it won't be long before the word escapes that not every inch of the reservation has oil under it.

"You don't want to get in the way of these people, Hal."

There is a pause on the other end. Brent turns and watches his machinery scrape out a new access road, waits to hear which way Hal will break.

"Is that a threat?"

"The first one who utters the word 'lawyer' is making the threat, Hal. I'm offering you the same deal, possibly a much better deal, or to wire your money back right now. Your alternative, to be honest, I wouldn't wish on an enemy, much less a business associate."

"His name is Andrew Wertheimer," says Hal. "Nicholson, Bridges, Bodine, and Wertheimer. I'll e-mail you his contact information."

The thing is, he's got everything tied up in this deal. If the Russians come in it's a massive score, but if it falls apart–

Clemson Dollarhide steps out of the farmhouse, looking down at the phalanx of backhoes reshaping the landscape at the very edge of his property. Another asshole who won't listen to reason. Brent makes a pistol with his thumb and forefinger, points it up at the old man.

Pow.

"I GOT YOUR WORK schedule from that coffee place."

So he knows about that.

Her grandfather is at his easel, head back the way he holds it for focus, able to see fine without glasses even at his age. So he knows about her job. Tough it out.

"Why would you need my schedule?"

He holds the brush halfway down on the handle, arm extended. "You shouldn't be relying on other people for rides. I'm going to teach you how to drive, get you something cheap but roadworthy, and I need to know when you're free."

He's gotten good at that, making me feel guilty–

"I know how to *drive*, Granpa."

For years he's let her take the wheel close to home, even showed her how to change a tire and watched while she went through the whole process.

"You got to get your license. When you go off to college– "

"Most of them you can't have a car your freshman year."

"It's a rite of passage," he says, "and an important proof of identification."

Fawn has had a fake ID since she was fourteen, but Fawn is the first to do everything. 'Indian princess by day,' she likes to say, 'international woman of mystery by night.'

And Fawn is pregnant, or at least thinks she is.

"I'll tell you what," she says, hanging up her jacket and coming around behind him. "You take me into town for some pointers, like that parallel parking thing? And then I'll sign up for the road test."

He knows something else, she can feel it, but doesn't want to fight it out in the open any more than she does. He was always been there for her, like daylight in the morning.

"That sounds fair," he says quietly. Schedules change, and there are the imaginary Science Club meetings she can skip if Wayne Lee wants to see her. He's been quieter lately, worried about something, and she hopes it's not her.

"How was work today?"

"Oh, you know. Caffeine for the troops."

There is something wrong on the canvas. The usual prairie-scape is there, this one featuring snowdrifts interspersed with open patches of stubble, Herefords clustered facing into the wind at the lower left. But there is a new element, dark and angular against the winter field and the light gray sky, *one, two, three, four, five*, painted in careful technical detail and perspective–

Oil rigs.

THE DAY MAN ON the desk at Killdeer City makes him wait in the lobby. He's picked up so many nicknames in the time he's been here that you forget who calls you what.

"If Wayne Lee doesn't ring a bell," he tells the day man, "try Surfer Dude."

Scorch comes into the lobby about ten minutes later, looking like he just woke up.

"This couldn't wait?"

They sit alone in the little visiting parlor, like it's a sorority house in the 1950s.

"My job is to distribute," says Wayne Lee. "Not to sit on it."

He gives Scorch four boxes, each about the size of a deck of cards, that hold the steroids in their punch-through sheets. Scorch looks like he's a user, though the muscle could just be from access to prison iron. Brent, on the other hand, brags about his reliance on gym candy when trying to bulk up, and has the sudden mood swings to prove it.

"You can't be nervous and deal," says Scorch, who only moves roids out here and is a vulture on drug use in the bathrooms at Bazookas. A time and a place for everything.

"Not nervous, just cautious. Listen, you heard anything from Brent about– you know– a change of plans, a change of product?"

"Why would he tell me that?"

"Well, he invited you up here."

"Same as you. What's your worry?"

"Oh, couple things I heard, maybe he's planning to phase out distribution."

"Or maybe he just got himself a new boy," says Scorch, giving him the deadeye and tucking the boxes of pills away.

"Dude owes me big time," smiles Wayne Lee, shaking his head. "Did you hear he's been speculating in leases?"

THERE IS ONLY A tiny bit of Rabbit peeking out from underneath the stickers. Along with various political candidates and their running mates are the simple classics– **Red Power, Proud to be Hidatsa,** a peeling **Free Leonard Peltier,** the new-agey **The Earth Does Not Belong to Us, We Belong to the Earth**– and a nice one he hasn't noticed before, **My Heroes Have Always Killed Cowboys.**

Marjorie Looks for Water is leaning against her old VW, parked just behind his patrol car, her eyes huge behind the thick lenses and that expectant smile on her face, when Danny steps out.

She nods back toward the Fetterjohns' trailer. "Any clues on who stole the Arctic Cat?"

Marjorie has jiggered some contraption that she keeps in the Rabbit, able to monitor the department's radio calls.

"Not until the first snowfall."

"Probably kids. What idiot steals a snowmobile in July?"

He looks at her car. What isn't stickered is pitted with rust. "You're back on the road?"

"It's been three months."

"I thought it was six."

"That's for full reinstatement. I've got restricted status back– no highway or night driving, already set my appointment at the clinic."

"You understand the responsibility? If it was only your own safety at stake– "

She has tonic-clonic seizures with no warning signs and has almost bitten through her tongue twice.

"I plan my routes," she smiles. "I take my meds."

"What have they got you on?"

"Carbatrol."

"Dizziness, drowsiness, nausea– "

Marjorie's smile widens. "Do I look drowsy to you?"

From all evidence, Marjorie doesn't sleep. When he pulls a graveyard shift there is always a light on at her little house, and he's stopped in for coffee and conspiracy theories more than once.

"The thing is, Chief, I've been noticing how thin you've been spread with all these new people coming in, and I thought you might want to reconsider."

She is one of the few who call him 'Chief,' though that is his department title.

"As a patrolman. Patrolperson."

"I passed the test three times."

"You passed the *written* test three times, and flunked pretty much every part of the physical."

"When the Sioux attacked us," she says, up there with Teresa Crow's Ghost for historical trivia, "did the People ask if you had 20/20 vision?"

"What's yours– 20/100?"

"With corrective lenses it's– "

"And do I remember something about limited peripheral acuity?"

When she ran Indian Country Tours, Marjorie had led people into the wrong chamber of a cave looking for pictographs, then had her flashlight batteries die–

"I *hear* things that other people don't."

"That's called an auditory hallucination, Marjorie. I wouldn't brag about it."

"But you need help."

"Your support and encouragement is an inspiration to the entire department."

Marjorie is addicted to *America's Most Wanted* and *Cops*. She is a constant blogger on Websleuths.com and chat partner of the people still wondering who killed the Black Dahlia. And if she could see past her nose and didn't fall down in eye-rolling, bone-wracking convulsions at inconvenient moments, Danny would love to have her on the force.

"How's the new business going?"

"*Schrecklich.*"

"And that's– ?"

"Terrific."

She runs an online catalogue, shipping Native handicrafts off to German people who are gaga about Indians.

"And your mother?"

"Hanging in there."

Marjorie lives with her mother, who carries a cell phone with the ambulance service on speed-dial in case the epilepsy strikes at home. So far Mrs. Looks For Water has only used it to report sightings of her son, gone missing in Vietnam forty years ago, on television.

"Good, that's good. And really, I'm sorry there's nothing to be done about the job."

"Just thought I'd try."

"You're taking it really well."

Marjorie has been known to persist, to plant herself in his office or block his path back into the patrol car.

"That's the Carbatrol. For me it might as well be Prozac."

"So your moods– "

"I don't have moods anymore, Chief. I am the eagle that never comes to earth. Floating above it all, observing."

"Through your corrective lenses."

"I see things," she says. "See things on the reservation."

Marjorie is not a snitch, exactly, but she does get around, does listen to the gossip, and has a forensic slant on life.

"Such as?"

"Oh– Dickyboy Burdette isn't missing, whatever his grandmother might have told you. He just doesn't come home very often."

"You've seen him?"

"All the time. He goes to *school*. You can't be missing if you attend class."

"Mystery solved. I'll tell his grandmother."

"She'll forget. And then I see things left on the land, piles of them, puddles of them, in places where they shouldn't be."

"The drilling stuff is not my beat. Take that up with Ricky McAllen. Or the Chairman."

"The Chairman's got his hands full. Business problems, family problems."

Danny opens the door of the patrol car to hear the radio. It's only Patty at the mic, singing. She leaves the Vox switched on sometimes.

"Terrific voice," says Marjorie. "She's in my church choir."

Danny sits into the patrol car. Marjorie is lonely and always ready to lay a recent unsolved murder on you, but tells such a good story you get caught up in it and time goes by–

"I really *do* hear things, Chief."

Another offering. Danny picks up the cue.

"What do you hear?"

"Noises. Loud voices, banging, slaps and weeping. From the Carter place."

J. C. Carter is a white guy, real piece of work, married to one of the Dozier girls who came up from Standing Rock. Put her in the hospital in Bismarck once.

"They're at least two miles down the road from you."

"*Very* loud noises. Somebody might need a talking to before he commits a capital crime."

She is looking at him intensely, Marjorie, those magnified eyes signaling that this is dead serious.

"He drinking again?"

"Amphetamines."

"That he gets from who?"

She might tell him if she knew, even if it was a relative, which considering some of Marjorie's relatives is entirely possible.

She shrugs. "Whole lot more of that floating around the rez these days. As you know."

Danny nods, shuts the door but rolls the window down. "I'll get over there and see what I can do," he says. "Thanks, Marjorie."

He drives toward the lake. J. C. spends a lot of time lifting cold ones at Lonnie's out in the county, but he might be home, and if not his ride is easy to spot. A jet-black Ram pickup with rocket-flame detailing on the sides and the single bumper sticker, red letters over the silhouette of an automatic pistol.

JUST KEEP HONKING– I'M RELOADING.

THEY SIT ON A blanket on the open tailgate of his pickup, Will off duty for once, looking out at the flare-offs dotting the black night, the white-and-ruby stream of highway traffic in the distance.

"Mostly old folks left around here," he says, "till the shale oil people come."

"But you stayed."

"I thought about leaving a bunch of times, but I never had– you know– like a definite *plan*."

Leia hears the high, electric *pyeeeeew* of a nighthawk. "So you turned to crime-fighting."

"To do the job right," says Will, "you got to read people. Which is the part that interests me."

"Hell of a lot more useful than what I do."

"You contribute to scientific knowledge."

"For a journal that five hundred people read. Or are supposed to read. And so far I've only recorded behavior that's already been documented."

"You get to work outdoors."

"And away from people." She smiles. "Which I suppose is good for society."

"Oh come on."

"My assistant, this girl Brandi? I thought she ran out because Yellow Earth was getting so weird, or she hated the fieldwork. Then I realized it was living with *me*."

"That couldn't be so awful."

She realizes she is leaning against him.

"You ever married?"

"Once, long time ago," he says. "It didn't take."

"Incompatible."

"She wanted to have kids and a house and all right away, and I– it didn't feel right in my gut. So she gave up on me."

"Got to listen to your gut."

The nighthawk buzzes again, cruising for moths. There were buffalo here, she thinks, and the people who followed them, and agriculture of some sort along the river. But now–

"You'll stick out this boom?"

"Seems like I ought to. I mean, people *voted* for me."

"Who lost?"

"The last time? Fella who's got a car lot. He'll clear a couple hundred grand this year."

"And I should have gone into geology. More money in rocks than in rodents."

"My parents' day," says Will, "especially when they were younger, there was more of a *cen*ter to things. Even out here where there's so much space between people. There was church, folks belonged to things that brought them together, they had to pitch in when there was weather."

"Community."

"Something like that."

"I think that's all gone to the internet. You're not on Facebook, are you?"

He laughs softly. "People are in my face all day and half the night, I don't need any more what do you call it– networking– "

"I'll be quiet then."

They sit there for a long spell, bugs and birds and the distant traffic providing a soft blanket of sound, and Leia begins to watch herself as she always does, semi-pathetic biology geek out in the middle of nowhere with a guy who's probably figuring the odds are good, but the goods are odd–

Then he turns her face to his, and irony surrenders to passion.

"THERE'S NOTHING WRONG WITH your work, it's just bullshit from Houston."

"They don't know I exist," says Tuck.

"And believe me, they don't want to know." He's in Hurry Upshaw's little shack on the deck, the tour already started outside, stands of pipe being craned into the slot for the day's drilling. "What it is, the insurance people are all over them about fatalities up here, so they say nobody without at least two years' experience."

"Fatalities?" He hasn't heard anything, not on the news, not from the guys, who are joyful purveyors of gossip.

"Fella they medevacced out just passed in the hospital," says Upshaw. "Fell off the damn platform while he was hosing it down."

"They really think they can find that many experienced hands?"

"I've had three different qualified hands approach me since you came on, Gatlin, but you were doing fine and they were gonna expect higher pay. You can't take it personal."

"But this is just the one company– "

"Company owns a good percentage of what's drilling here if you look through all the dummy operations. Tell you what, though– "

Upshaw scribbles on the back of yesterday's depth printout–

"You track this character down, tell him I'll vouch for you. He got one or two wells going in, what I hear, and he's not too particular about who he hires."

"Meaning?"

"Meaning he don't pay but half of what we do, so his outfit's likely to have some folks still trying to make the Big Show. I worked for him when I was coming up– you learn damn quick."

"Any idea where I could– "

"Try Buster's. Most likely spot he'll park himself when he's off work."

Tuck takes the name from the driller. Worth a try, though it sounds kind of fly-by-night.

"I want to thank you for the opportunity here," he says, and Upshaw waves it off.

"You got any damn brains you'll find something else to do," he grins. "Good luck to you."

Tuck hurries off the platform, Mike and Ike too busy wrestling pipe to see him go.

As he remembers, there isn't any vodka in the house, so he surrenders himself to the slow-moving procession into Yellow Earth. Like being in a wagon train, he thinks, but with diesel exhaust.

Econo Liquor is obviously having a hard time keeping the shelves stocked, but he scores a bottle of Stoli and some tonic. He's on 11th heading back to the 2 when he sees her.

She's in the Arby's parking lot, standing by a blue Chevy Malibu with the driver's-side door sporting rust-colored primer. He makes a left at the light and is the object of much horn blowing till he can scoot across lanes to turn into the empty drive-thru lane. He eases around to the lot, near empty but for a few early-bird employees and Jewelle. He parks in a far corner, adjusting his rearview mirror to get a better angle on her.

She's wearing a parka and what look like bowling shoes– Francine would know the name of them. Her hair blows around her face in the wind. A couple times at Bazookas she had sparkles in her hair, silver sparkles in golden hair, and he had to do a careful clothes check in the men's, lit as bright as a hospital operating room, after their dance.

It looks like she's waiting for somebody.

If he was to get out and accidentally bump into her, what a coincidence, gee, they're not open yet? He feels like their relationship is partly based on him being a rig worker, that and strapping on the healthy paycheck before he walks into the club. But there is definitely some chemistry, something beyond the dancer and client roles they've been playing–

He has his seatbelt off and the door half open when the gleaming black Hummer muscles into the lot. It has some mud-spatter around the hubs, looking like a search-and-destroy vehicle from another planet, dark-tinted windows obscuring whoever is at the wheel. She smiles, gets into the passenger side, and the machine rushes away.

It's only nine o'clock, thinks Tuck. What more can they hit me with today?

VIC TURNS THE NEON off so it won't be in the photographs. There have been national reporters wandering through town, grabbing a few quick quotes. 'Boomtown Blues,' all that. Bazookas is a good handle, catchy, and he may want to use it somewhere else.

From where he's standing with his back up against the club wall, the kid's head looks like it's part of the sidewalk, stuck there with drying blood. Scorch is next to him, while Oxana, who was behind the bar while the assailants were still on the floor, is talking to the sheriff, blue lights strobing on them from the patrol cars.

"Looks like he got it from behind," says Vic. "Could have been you."

Scorch has his yard face on, even though he's in the clear on this one. "When I bounced those assholes, I should have bounced them harder."

"Whatever you do, there's always that chance." Vic taps his hip. "Still got some lead in there, ricochet. We booted some character in Fairbanks, real pain in the ass, he drives home shitfaced, manages not to run into a moose or off the road, gets his automatic, drives back, head clearing up now but not enough to stop him from emptying a clip into the joint from the doorway. It's me and a couple of the staff, doling out the tip pool."

"Somebody left the door unlocked."

"He waited till a bargirl left, elbowed his way in. We were just sitting around, easy target."

"Could have been one to the heart, one to the head."

Vic gives Scorch a look, but that face gives nothing away.

"He was just a jack-off with a temper, not a hired assassin."

The night deputy, Clayton, throws some plastic over the kid on the sidewalk and clears a path through the crowd that has poured out of both clubs once the news spread. Teasers has had a half-dozen fights, but this had to happen with guys from his spot. The murder weapon is still on the ground between four orange traffic cones, a bloody three-foot length of metal pipe with a hexagonal nut the size of a grapefruit threaded onto the end of it. A couple EMTs step in with a stretcher, looking for a place that's not all bloody to lay it down, but there isn't one, and their feet are already sticky with it.

"Head injuries," says Vic. "Bleed like a motherfucker."

The sheriff comes over.

"Can I hear your version?"

"Guy comes in with friends, already loaded to the gills," says Vic, "and I give Oxana the eye, so she never quite gets to his drink order in the crowd. Makes himself obnoxious to everybody sitting there, louder than the music, which is saying something, and ends up pinning the kid on the ground there against the counter. Kid probably called him out for the douchebag that he was. Then Stanley here, my head of security, escorted him from the premises, followed by two of his posse." Vic looks to Scorch. "I don't believe any blows were exchanged."

"I had his arm behind his back, stayed with him till his friends had him calmed down, cut him loose."

"Description?"

"My height," says Scorch, "maybe two hundred, two fifteen on the scale– he's got a half keg where the six pack should be– two-day stubble, brown eyes, still got his lace-up work boots on and a T-shirt that says 'Pump Till it Squirts.'"

The sheriff looks impressed.

"I had him in my sights for a while before I give him the boot."

The sheriff nods. "Might need you two for ID sometime tomorrow."

"No problem."

The EMTs have gloves on, trying to get all of the kid's shattered head onto the stretcher now, the crowd oohing and aaahing. Vic has seen guys pretty messed up who survived somehow, but this one is a goner.

"And I'd advise you not to open tomorrow night."

Vic nods. Tomorrow is payday and he'll lose a fortune, but this kind of thing gets the church ladies riled up and the mayor might cave and pull their license altogether.

The sheriff steps away then, helping his deputy herd the rubberneckers out of the way. One of the regulars, a local who Jewelle has got a lock on, looking in pretty bad shape himself, crosses over to join them.

"I saw the whole thing," he says. "In case you need a witness."

"We'll be okay."

"The guy was out of line. Looking for trouble."

There are fight bars, of course, where a nose-buster or two every evening serves as the floor show, but the money is not worth the aggravation. He'd hoped the tone had been elevated a bit when he hired a DJ, plushed up the seating.

"Got plenty of trouble now," says Scorch. "Done screwed the pooch to *death*."

WHEN HE COMES IN late from his rounds with the boys he sleeps on the sofa. "Don't want to wake a fellow worker up," he says, but Francine figures it's so she can't gauge the liquor on his breath. She bowls with the other teachers on Wednesdays and they have a couple drinks, loosen up, but you have to imagine another level for oil workers. This won't last, this frenetic drilling, and she can't imagine Tuck wanting to follow the rigs to the next strike, or whatever it's called in that world.

And the money is great, good for Tuck to be contributing again, making a lot more than she does. Not that that should matter so much. He's never been the

macho type, considering himself more of a thinker, a spotter of trends and con-
noisseur of opportunities. Like the stock market, where he's got most of what's
left of his inherited money tied up, no rainmakers in the portfolio yet, but some
promising long shots. Francine has learned to think of it as a pastime of Tuck's,
like betting on the NFL games, rather than real money they'd be able to spend
if he cashed in.

He's left his shoes in the kitchen, considerate when she's such a light sleeper,
but they're big and in the way right now. And stuck to the floor with something.

In fact there are tracks, half a heel on one side and the whole shoeprint on
the other, leading backwards to the driveway. She peels a shoe up with a crackly
sound, something he stepped in last night–

THE TRUCK COMES DOWN Los Mayas in the Bellavista neighborhood an hour
after dark, stops halfway down the deserted street. The rear doors are unlocked.
Macario and Nacho haul themselves in, wriggle their way around what Macario
thinks are huge industrial heaters mounted on wooden pallets, till they can
crouch out of sight. It is very dark.

They hear the clunk of the rear doors being locked from the outside, then in
a moment the truck starts to move. It is not long, maybe twenty minutes, before
the truck stops again, the engine turned off. Macario quickly opens the jar he's
brought, dabs liquid on the metal around them. There is the biting smell of kerosene. The rear doors are thrown open, they hear voices and see flashlight beams
against the back wall of the trailer where they are squeezed behind the machinery. He has given Nacho six thousand pesos to pay to the *truckero*, but that is no
guarantee against betrayal.

A dog whines. The *yanqui* Customs people, Macario thinks with relief, the
dogs sniffing for *mota* or humans and smelling only kerosene.

The rear door is closed again, locked.

The engine comes to life. The truck rolls on.

"We're crossing the bridge, *chango*," Nacho says to him in the dark. "Right
under their noses."

It is very hard to judge time without light, with only the engine rumble and
the drone of the highway beneath you. The *yanqui* highway. I am a message in

a bottle, thinks Macario, adrift in the great ocean, at the mercy of currents and the pull of the moon. He called Nilda this morning, his voice floating into space, then caroming off a satellite back down to Xichulub, then the reply making the same journey. Nilda's sister, the computer voice informed him, was not available at the moment.

The girls will look different the next time he sees them, if he sees them, and little Azalea will have no memory of her father. Macario can tell from the rhythm of his breathing that Nacho is sleeping, exhausted.

"*Pan o plomo?*" the *narcos* are reported to have said to the chief of police of Nuevo Laredo. Bread or lead? Apparently he gave the wrong answer and was assassinated only hours after he was sworn into office. Bread or lead. Those should not be the only choices, to accept the *narcos'* world, their money, to do their bidding like a frightened dog or end up *encobijado*, rolled in a plastic tarp and sealed with tape. Macario hopes this oilfield in the far north of *el norte* will be better, even with the shadow of *la Migra* always looming above. He could make enough money to build them a house in Yucatán, or even bring his family up–

It is dangerous to think too far ahead. All that matters at the moment is to get himself out of the back of this truck and into the big sea of the United States.

Macario is not sure if he sleeps or not. It is never comfortable, his body bent around the metal heaters, the kerosene smell lingering. A coffin, he thinks, suddenly finding it hard to breathe. I've been buried before I'm dead.

At some point Nacho wakes and begins to talk. He is a boy afraid of silence.

"Do you know any English?"

"Some," Macario tells him. "There were *gringos* on the oil rig. And I watch their television shows."

"Me too. I know words."

"*Dígame unos.*"

"Ford. Chevy. Toyota."

"That's Japanese."

"Lexus. Jeep."

He says it *yip.*

"You can be a car salesman."

"It's no joke. I don't know anybody up here, I don't who the gangs are, who's in charge. I don't know how to *do* anything."

"You'll learn."

"They'll take one look," says Nacho in the dark, "and think *puro mojado*, this guy doesn't belong here, and throw me into their federal prison."

"There are thousands of people who look just like you in their cities. Believe me."

"If you pay what the Zetas demand," says Nacho wistfully, "you never really make enough. You eat, but you're still nothing compared to them."

"Don't compare yourself to them."

"*Güey*, I was not born in a mansion. I'm not some *fresa* who takes tennis lessons and goes to *una academia privada*. Anything I get, I have to rip it from the world."

"Take your time when we get out," counsels Macario. "Look around, see what's here, don't start ripping things right away."

When the truck finally stops and the rear doors are opened there is a tentative dawn in the *yanqui* sky outside.

"*Fuera!*" calls the *truckero*. Macario does not like the tone in his voice.

They wriggle out past the heaters and let themselves down, legs cramped and unsteady, onto the ground. There is nothing but flat, scrubby plain around them and the *truckero*, holding a shotgun.

"There's a checkpoint just south of the next town," he says. "You'll have to walk around it."

"We got through at the bridge," says Nacho.

"This is as far as you go with me," says the man. "Dump out what you're carrying and turn your pockets inside out."

They've turned off the highway onto a dirt road. The man with the shotgun is nervous, his face frozen in a scowl. Unless he is truly stupid, thinks Macario, he won't kill them here, his tire tracks like fingerprints in the sand.

"I already paid you!" cries Nacho as he empties his plastic sack onto the ground. The *truckero* kicks at what falls out, eyes Macario's few clothes and bottles of water. He takes the roll of pesos from Macario's hand.

"Pick up your things and start walking," he says, indicating the direction with the barrel of the shotgun.

An amateur, thinks Macario as he gathers his belongings, hearing the truck grind gears as it turns around. He still has the *yanqui* bills in his shoe.

"*Hijo de la chingada!*" Nacho spits as the truck rolls past them on its way back to the highway, Macario memorizing the license number to tell to the Border Patrol if he is caught by them today.

"We can't walk along the *pinche* highway," says Nacho, turning to look at the nothingness that surrounds them.

"We don't have to. *Mira*."

Macario points to the faint strip of clearing, only a few feet wide, that runs for miles in a straight line in either direction. "There's an oil pipeline buried under there. It will go parallel to the big road all the way to a refinery, or maybe right to a city."

They walk, Nacho cursing the *truckero* and all his ancestors, the sun still mercifully low in the sky. In less than an hour they see what must be buildings off to the left.

"Where do you think we are?" asks Nacho.

"*Tejas*."

Nacho glares at the little bumps of civilization in the distance, shakes his head. "Let's get it over with. I don't want to die in this *pinche desierto*."

It is very early, not much moving in the little town when they arrive, looking like refugees. From the sign next to the huge statue of a rattlesnake, it seems the place is called Freer.

"What does this mean?"

"*Más libre*," Macario guesses. "More free."

They sit to drink the last plastic bottle of Macario's water on the concrete steps of the statue's base. The *cascabél* is poised to strike, head erect, rattles in the air.

"What kind of people," asks Nacho, "honor a fucking snake?"

"What kind of people," Macario responds, "wear a tattoo of Jesús Malverde on their skin?"

"Assholes from Sinaloa."

"Or San Judas Tadeo, or *la Santa Muerte*, or any of the other narco-saints?"

"Those spirits can protect you. But a snake."

Macario points to the metal cut-out in the shape of the state of Texas on a pole beside them. "That sign says there is a *rodeo de cascabéles* here. A rattlesnake round-up."

Nacho shakes his head, looking around miserably. "I want to go home."

"You fucked yourself there. If I want to go back I just turn myself in. But they've got you in their computers for transporting– you'll have to sneak back in to your own country, and when you do the Zetas will be waiting."

They continue down the highway, passing a tire store and a pair of motels. They are between two low stores with empty parking lots, one called Dollar Value and the other called Family Dollar, when a pair of old cars pull up beside them. The driver of the second one, a *güero* about the same age as Nacho, calls to them in English through his open window.

"Need a ride?"

Macario steps closer to talk to him.

"Yes. We are needing to go to Houston."

"San Antonio," grins the blond boy, pointing ahead. "Straight north from here."

"*Igual,*" says Macario, making the thumbs-up gesture the *gringos* on the rig always used when it was too loud to hear.

"The way it works," says the blond boy, "is my buddy up there rides ahead, and if the Border Patrol has thrown up a spot check he calls me." The blond boy has a cell phone resting on his thigh. "That means you get out, wherever we are, no refund. *Comprendo?*"

"I understand."

"Two-fifty each, Americano," says the boy, his eyes moving to Nacho, who has backed into the Family Dollar parking lot to watch. "And that's only because we were going there anyway."

Macario hesitates. He has only a few more dollars than that in his shoe.

"Or you can keep walking."

"Is okay," says Macario, and waves for Nacho to come over. He starts to get in next to the *güero,* but the boy pushes a button and there is the click of the door lock.

"Sorry, *amigo.* Gotta see the cash first."

Macario is not sure he understands. The boy makes a gesture with his fingers, rubbing them together, and speaks very slowly.

"Show– me– the– *money.*"

"Ah, *por supuesto,*" says Macario. These are just boys in cars, the ones you see in their television shows, lovers of speed and girls and Coca Cola. He and Nacho will not be left murdered in the desert by these two. He steps back from the car, smiling at the *güero.*

"Excuse me, please. For this I must take off the shoe."

BULLETINS FROM THE BLACK STUFF

Comeback of the Century – North Dakota.

Since the Pashas of Petroleum have encamped in the Bakken oil field, the former Gateway to Manitoba can now boast a paltry 3% jobless rate, the lowest in the country (in Williams County it is under 1%), enormous growth in population and personal income, strong housing and construction markets, and an enviable state budget surplus. Thousands of residents have become millionaires from oil and gas revenues, and there's more to come!

This month we count nearly eighty new rigs in the mix, many of the wells nearing completion.

With crude holding at $95.70 a barrel and gasoline back up to a respectable $3.67 ($3.90 for diesel) we're bullish on the Bakken!

O when I die
Please bury me low
So I can hear
The petroleum flow–

EVERYTHING IS NEW. EVERYTHING in the kitchen– pots and pans, set of plates and glasses, microwave, even the stove and dishwasher look like they're right out of the box. Only the blender has a film on it, Wayne Lee saying that his man Brent makes himself protein shakes. Tina feels a little weird to be here, knowing what she does from Fawn, but Wayne Lee said it was chill, his man Brent gone for the day and always running an open house. The wife is gone too– whether it's about-to-divorce gone or just out-of-town gone is not clear– and Tina wonders if she was the one who chose the colors, who picked out the appliances online or in catalogues. There is only beer and energy bars in the fridge, so it's probably been a while since she was here.

Nothing at home is new. Her grandfather eats shredded wheat from a chipped bowl every morning, and the furniture was old when her parents were still alive. He plays music, old croony love songs with lots of orchestra behind the singers, on a record player where you have to place the needle by hand.

Wayne Lee said he wanted her first time to be somewhere nicer than a Days Inn. It was nice, better than she expected, though he smelled a little like Mc-Donalds and she smelled like Colombian Roast. She insisted they change the sheets after, and they finally found some, still in plastic, from a place called Pottery Barn.

"Look what's happening to me," Wayne Lee had said, "just looking at you." And it was pretty amazing, like his thing had a life of its own.

It went slow and then fast and then slow again for a bit and then really fast till it was over. He was nice and lay around playing with her braid for a long time after.

"Never sleep with somebody you don't want to wake up with," he said, meant as a compliment, she thinks, but kind of like he was giving her advice on how to go out and deal with other guys. And then he saw the fancy digital clock and said he needed to make some business calls.

None of the rooms look like anybody has been in them, a house waiting for its people. Fawn said there are colored lights, but it's still daytime. Tina supposes that if she had a lot of money she wouldn't build a house but would travel, see different places and find out what the people who lived in them are like. She knows this Brent and his wife went to Hawaii, which is part of the United States but like another world. And if you really had a lot of money you'd fly first class, where stewardesses bring you drinks and bake you cookies.

Or so they say.

It's like a big deal at school, girls kind of bragging, but she's not going to tell anybody. Keep it hers. Hers and Wayne Lee's. He doesn't seem like he'll talk about it either, even to his man Brent, though you can't be sure. He used the rubber at the end, which if Fawn wasn't such a nitwit she would have insisted on. Tina has seen the guy, Brent, around town more than a few times, driving his Corvette. Not her type, with all that muscle, but Fawn says he's 'dynamic.' She thought only cars and planes and speedy boats could be that, like 'hydrodynamic,' but everybody's got their own taste.

When she saw the backpack she had the sudden thought that they were going to camp out and do it in a tent, but that was just her being a little panicky when she got into his car. She'd been a mess pouring coffee all afternoon, knowing this was The Day and she signed herself up for it. She tries to think now about what comes next, but draws a blank. A lot of people, not her grandfather but a lot of people, seem to be living that way since the boom started, making crazy money, buying things, partying, trying not to think about tomorrow.

'If you never hope for anything, you're rarely disappointed,' her grandfather says. 'But then you're a pretty dull character.'

Mrs. Gatlin says she should go out of state for college, and Mr. Reidy, her guidance counselor, says her grades and SATs could get her a scholarship somewhere. She already feels more confident about going. Wayne Lee, who has been all over the place, wants to be with her, she's not a virgin anymore, and she's had a real job.

She turns into a room with lots of big leather-covered chairs, with an entertainment center that has more units than she can guess the functions of, with posters of almost-naked women looking at you with puffy lips from the walls. A room with the smell of marijuana she recognizes from parties at Dylan's house and a glass-faced display case full of guns.

There are pistols, the sleek kind you see in James Bond movies, and rifles of different kinds, some with beautiful wood and metal and others looking like high-tech plastic. There are a couple of things that must be machine guns, or whatever the ones the Navy SEALs or school shooters use are called, that can kill a whole classroom in the blink of an eye.

She hears Wayne Lee moving toward her, finishing up a conversation on the phone. This is a 'man cave,' like what they joke about on TV, and suddenly she feels like Goldilocks in the three bears' house. Not supposed to be there.

Wayne Lee steps in, pocketing his phone, his mind a million miles away. He looks at her, then at the guns in the display case.

"Yeah," he says, shrugging his shoulders. "My man Brent is way into this stuff."

THE ONLY THING HE and Fawn really don't agree about is the radio. He's a Nirvana and Chili Peppers guy, and she likes rap of all things, black guys rhyming about their dicks and their hos and their money and how they'd like to fuck the police up. Maybe it's an Indian thing. So no radio, which makes it a long drive with her in a mood.

A legitimate clinic, you'd need the parent's permission, and that ditzy mother of hers would already be picking out baby clothes. If this guy that the buddy of his buddy recommended is as good as advertised, there won't be any medical issues. And Fawn is such a slick little operator, a natural talent, that they'll never know. Best for everybody, give a young girl her childhood back, all that shit. He's at least not taking her across state lines or into Canada.

With Bunny the first time she went to this Asian woman, vouched for by Planned Parenthood, diploma on the wall, the whole deal. A few questions and then, "Well, if that's what you've decided," and bingo, case closed. The second one she lost on her own, just one of those things, and started to get mopey about it. Children were never a clause in their agreement, not portable enough, not resilient. He's read where with some nomadic people, the women fuck all they want but only get pregnant when they stay put for a while.

Or maybe it was wildebeest.

But Bunny is moping back in California and Fawn is sitting next to him, hair blowing in the wind as they eat up highway heading to Dr. Fixit.

"Brent," she says, looking moonily out at the prairie flying by, "if we like– if we *were* going to keep it, what names do you like?"

"You want to name something, get a turtle."

"Just pretending."

"Okay. For a boy, Rocket. It's already cool, and for nicknames you get Rock, Rocky, Rockabilly."

"And for a girl?"

"Fallujah."

"I'm serious."

"So am I. It's a beautiful name."

"It's a *place*."

"So's Dakota. So's Georgia. There are girls named– "

"It's a place where there was a *bat*tle."

"Even better. Kind of sexy, kind of mysterious, but like, don't fuck with me. Another good boy name would be Armageddon."

"You're mean."

"I'm bad to the bone. That's why you love me."

The girl gives him an appraising look, as if deciding whether this is true or not.

"You know, if something bad happens to me, my stepfather will kill you."

"Bow and arrow?"

"With his bare hands."

Brent flexes a bicep, keeping the other hand on the wheel. "Like to see him try."

She's quiet for a long time then, which gives him time to think about the Hal Tillerman problem. Gotta get that piano off my back.

"It makes me feel old," she says finally. "Having the procedure."

"Mature old or decrepit old?"

"Like something that's been used. Not new anymore."

"Darlin," he says, patting her on the knee, "you weren't new on the day you were born."

When they get to the place she won't get out of the car.

"I changed my mind."

The place could be more impressive. Stuck alone out where the suburbs become the country, decent-looking woodpile under the carport, a mailbox that looks like a cardinal, an old satellite dish with dead leaves in the bowl, a snowmobile up on cinderblocks.

"You gotta be fucking kidding me."

"I'm not going in."

"So what, you're gonna blow up like a blimp, go through a day or two of agony and then play mommy to little Fallujah?"

She glares at him. "I don't know yet. But I'm not going in *here*."

They say you're supposed to count to ten, but it's never worked, just giving him a moment to decide which to fuck up first, the teeth or the eyes. He looks to the sky. It's getting late.

"I'm going to take a very short walk, and when I come back I hope you'll have made the right decision."

He heads down the steep driveway and hooks around onto the country road. He can see Fawn sitting in his Vette. She isn't moving.

He pulls out his phone and the number Scorch gave him, punches it in. The guy answers on the third ring.

"Yeah?"

"This is the man in North Dakota," says Brent, turning his back on Fawn and the doctor's house. "I believe our mutual friend told you I might be calling."

"Right. You understand I don't perform the service itself. I'm a middleman."

Fucking subcontractors. Next he'll want an indemnity clause–

"I understand that."

"And you know it's half on engagement of services, half on completion."

"It's a lot of money."

"It's a serious undertaking."

Could be a nice little scam, he thinks. Anybody contracting a murder probably lacks the stones to get physical themselves, so if you take the half up front and don't deliver, what are they gonna do? Call a cop? Out you on Craigslist?

"Knock that down to a third up front and we keep talking," he says.

A pause. Brent wonders how much he'll have to pay Dr. Fixit up there for services not rendered.

"All right," says the guy on the other end. "Tell me the play."

"I got a problem in Pocatello."

"Not a word," he says as he slams back into the car. "One fucking syllable out of you and you walk back to the reservation." He jams his *Uplift Mofo Party Plan* disc into the slot, cranks it up loud, and peels out for Yellow Earth.

THERE AREN'T ANY MANDANS on the Mandan Braves this year. Lots of German names from the people who built Bismarck up, one black kid at forward who can jam. The Three Nations Warriors have their hands full, playing on the road against a bigger school, less height and no point-machine since Ziggy White Elk graduated. Good ball-movement, though, with the coach, Ed Munger, sixth man on the team Harleigh captained back when they went to the state semis. Ed always puts together a killer defense, zone or man-to-man, the kids flying back and calling out the switches. It won't be embarrassing.

They're only down four, halfway through the second quarter, when he comes in, looking for an open seat on the visitors' side. The only one left is next to Claude LaMere, whose grandson is on the JVs.

"How we doing?" he asks as he squeezes in.

"We better shoot damn good," says Claude, eyes not leaving the gym floor, "cause we won't get an offensive rebound off this bunch."

The black kid goes under and makes a reverse layup.

"I got stuck behind a convoy of tank trucks, coming and going so there's no chance to pass," says Harleigh, wondering why he's explaining himself. The job description doesn't include attendance at every minute of every tribal sporting event. "JVs win?"

"Got massacred. Couldn't buy a bucket, then they started with the turnovers."

Harleigh settles in, watches the back and forth. No mental mistakes from the Warriors, just the lack of size and superstar. The game has changed a hell of a lot since his day, no more calling out a play and making three good passes before you think about scoring, no more weave, and now you got high-schoolers jamming the ball, which had been outlawed while Kareem was in college, all the white dinosaur coaches afraid they were losing their game. They lost it, and saw it replaced by something much more fluid, more improvised, more acrobatic.

The Fox kid, related to all the Foxes over at Mandaree, has a classic jump shot, beautiful backspin as he sinks one with his toe on the three-point line. Too bad he's short and slow.

"You know where I live," says Claude.

Claude is a good mechanic, fix anything on your car that's not a computerized unit, lives by the lake at Sanish.

"I do."

"Been out there lately?"

"Can't say I have." The Chairman is never off the clock, which he supposes is the biggest negative of the job. But Claude is not a squawker, so if there's something wrong–

"Looks like a second Dust Bowl out there."

"The trucks."

"They run em fast as they can, down a dirt road."

"It's been dry."

"I thought there was somebody sposed to wet it down now and then."

"We hired a company." Actually, the job went to ArrowFleet when Brent said it could be done by his people on the cheap.

"I look out at the road from my shop every day. Never seen any water truck."

It was a no-bid contract, over a half-million dollars, that he ran through the council without a vote.

"Then I'll have to talk to the fella we contracted."

Claude nods across the court. "He's right there."

And yes, Brent is sitting over behind the Braves' bench, glad-handing with a white fella in a turquoise cowboy shirt. Claude must have looked up the contract, learned what the numbers were. People see six digits, they get excited, not figuring in just how many hundreds of miles of dirt road there are on the reservation.

But you never want them to think you been caught off guard. "Well, that's convenient, idn't it?"

He's been chasing after Brent for a week, trying to cut him loose, and was hoping to do it quick and professional and private. A 'just business' kind of thing.

"Wind blows west, the dust settles on Old Man Good Iron's pasture," says Claude, "and his milkers turn their noses up. He wanted me to fix up some concrete speed bumps, slow them oil trucks down."

"And start a war."

"That's what I told him. Oil folks have paid off the right people, they can do anything they want on the rez."

"It's called a lease."

"Any time an Indin signs a piece of paper, I call it a *robbery*."

The half ends with the Fox kid just missing a buzzer-beater from midcourt, the Warriors down eight. Harleigh is careful to walk around the court and not on it with his new boots, waving to Coach Munger, who is limbering up for his halftime chalk-throwing.

Harleigh catches Brent by the table where they sell the pizza squares.

"You're a hard man to track down."

Brent does a good job making light of the ambush.

"Heyyyyy– there you are! You see what I got on my line?"

"Looks like a wax figure from the Cowboy Hall of Fame?"

Brent lowers his voice and takes Harleigh's arm, steering him further from the refreshment counter, moving down the hallway by the vice principal's office.

"Texas beef money, wants to get into oil without making a fuss about it. I'm brokering a lease on Shorty Winstead's acres."

"That's not reservation land."

"But it's surrounded by reservation land, and my man's been burned by the PC police a couple times– built a strip mall on sacred land or something– so I've promised him I can get you to smooth things over with the neighbors."

"There's nothing to smooth."

"*He* doesn't know that." Brent looks like he just ate the whole pie. "I figure to throw maybe ten percent of my end your way. I'll just bring you over for a quick intro before the second half, shake your head about what wildasses the folks parked around the lease can be, but how you know how to talk to them."

"Brent, it's over."

Brent looks at him like he didn't hear.

"If you think fifteen is right, I can go for that. This is basically a no-show job."

"I'm dissolving the partnership."

Brent's face doesn't change but something in the air between them does, Harleigh feeling an icy ripple up the back of his neck.

"You can't do that."

"I already talked to Ruby, she got the paperwork with your wife in progress."

"Bunny doesn't run *shit*!"

Harleigh lowers his voice, hoping Brent will take the cue, people looking down the hall at them. "Everything is in her *name*. It'll be a fair split, profits and liabilities, don't worry. I just can't have my position with the tribes hooked up to your service company any more, can't having you using me like a tire iron to jack open the door to Indian Country."

"You can't."

"I can and I have."

Brent's color is different now, like something terrible is rising up to bust out of him.

"You'll regret it."

It is more of a threat than a prediction.

"I already do, buddy. I already do."

Harleigh heads back down the hall to the crowd buying sodas and candy and Cheetos, stuff he didn't allow when he ran the rez high school. He'd had to cut bait a couple times back then, firing relatives, passing a friend up for a janitor job, and it was never easy dropping the bomb and walking away. But this is the first time he's been scared to look behind.

Fawn steps out from the gaggle of her old rez girlfriends clustered by the stairs.

"Were you talking about me?"

Fawn doesn't come to Warriors events anymore, and this is an away game. He wonders how she got here.

"Why would I be talking about you with Brent?"

"You were arguing."

"Business dispute, darling. You need a ride home?"

She looks upset about something, something more than him suddenly appearing on what used to be her turf.

"I'm covered," she says, and flicks her reddened eyes to Brent as he walks by, the buzzer from the gym blatting to call the crowd back in. "I'm going to a party after."

"Don't get back too late. Your mom will blame me."

"She's *your* girlfriend," says Fawn, rebounding with that little wicked smile that always makes him hope she's listened to Connie's birth control lectures. "Deal with it."

HITCH AND DENNY HAVE thrown plastic dropcloths, the cheap ones you get at Walmart, over any of the furniture that can stain. They pulled this off once before when their parents went to an Herbalife conference in Fargo, and this is a weekend trip up to Regina to visit some of their mother's Lakota relatives. The house is pretty isolated to start with, and they've told everyone to park around back where they won't attract attention from the road.

"The wide and the narrow!" Hitch calls out when Dickyboy lands with Dylan. "Come to party or just making a delivery?"

It's not like they put out invitations, word just travels and whoever shows up shows up. Dickyboy made the last party, chugging a ceremonial Red Bull at dawn and pitching in with the frenetic cleanup drive the boys insisted on, a half-dozen survivors still there and just sober enough to put the house back in order.

"Little of both," says Dickyboy, "if that's cool with you."

"You know the password?"

"Fuck no," mutters Dylan, who smoked a J behind the wheel on the way over.

"That's it! Step inside, step inside."

The music is cranked way up and kids are shouting over it and there's a good chunk of the junior and senior class there, heads, drinkers, straight arrows, almost as many girls as boys, which is an improvement over the last time. Dickyboy has on the hunting vest he just bought, the pockets have pockets, while Dylan, on probation, serves as the bank.

"Yo, Dickyboy, where you been hanging?" the guys shout when they see him, or "Here comes trouble!" or just "Yo, you got anything?"

The bathrooms are all taken, girls mostly, going in two and three at a time, so he sets up in the kitchen, using the little island counter to deal out product and getting bumped every time someone passes to grab a beer from the fridge.

"It's the walking drugstore," says Armand Fox, yanking a pair of cans off the plastic rings. "Looks like you've expanded."

They never liked each other, him and Armand, even if they were on teams together back when Dickyboy was into sports. Everybody's buzzing about the big comeback, Armand hitting three three-pointers in a row, so he's strutting even when he's standing still.

"If you break your own scoring record this year," says Dickyboy, "will they have to put an asterisk on it?"

Armand is a senior and should have graduated in '09, but was notably absent from the ceremony.

"Says the guy who comes to school for the free lunch."

Dylan doesn't look so good. He's one of the few white guys here and was nervous about coming, and has the asthma thing on top of it. He says smoking dope helps him breathe, but it's really hot in here with all the bodies, and his forehead is all sweaty.

"Any scholarship offers?"

Armand just glares at him and pushes out to the front room.

"Football player?" asks Dylan.

"Basketball. No jump, no D, but he hits nothing but net. If we lived in Pygmyland he'd be a superstar."

The kids around him seem pretty psyched to see each other without adults present, the ones least comfortable with a simple conversation getting the most wrecked. Katy Perry is singing "Teenage Dream," Dylan bouncing up and down in time with the beat, a couple making out in the pantry with the door not totally closed–

Fawn steps in, looking bored and miserable.

Somehow Fawn manages to go to Yellow Earth and still keep her Three Nations friends. She's wearing something that really shows her legs off and is looking different somehow–

"Dickyboy in the kitchen," she shouts over the song, "what a surprise."

"You on a field trip? Visit the natives in their habitat?"

"Somebody told me you went missing, and I said, 'What could Dickyboy possibly *hide* behind?'"

"You're looking pretty chunky yourself." That's it, she has a belly. Fawn who used to look like a runway girl on a TV fashion show.

"You're such a flatterer."

This always happens to them, like chemicals that shouldn't be mixed together. And what's this– the beginning of actual *tears*?

Something neutral, maybe call a truce, derail the usual fight.

"How you been?"

"Busy."

"Doing what?"

He's heard rumors, but people make up crazy shit, especially about people who leave them to go to Yellow Earth or anywhere else off the reservation. A kind of jealousy maybe, or just imaginations in overdrive.

"Oh, driving around," says Fawn, looking away from him. "Trying to stay cool. I got my own car now."

Of course she does. Word is her stepfather has got people throwing money at him to let them do business on tribal property.

"What kind?"

"You wouldn't fit in it," she says, and moves back to the main party.

"Bee-*yitch*," says Dylan.

"Yeah, she needs a stepladder to climb on her own ego, Fawn."

If he'd known she was going to be here he wouldn't have come. Their worlds are totally separate now, no reason to give a shit, but there isn't anybody else on the planet who can make him feel worse.

"Yo– you got anything?"

They do a little business, nothing hard core, and then Dickyboy tells Dylan to chill for a minute, maybe go out back and light up another stick, while he cruises the party. Mostly he doesn't want to seem like some leper who gets stuck in the kitchen and never circulates, the guy who DJs the songs but never gets out to dance.

There's more thrashing than dancing going on now, Alice in Chains wailing

"Man in the Box," and there's most of the guys chummed together on one side of the room and Fawn at the center of a bunch of the girls in another and then some pairs going at it in various stages. Jolene tugs his arm.

Jolene?

"That really upset Fawn," she shouts into his ear.

"Yeah," he says, "kicking somebody in the nuts and then running off must be traumatic."

Jolene's another one going to school in Yellow Earth, a real Braniac, but even in the summer this is *way* past her bedtime.

"What are you doing here?" he asks, Jolene nowhere near as prickly as Fawn.

"What?"

"I said what are you *doing* here?"

"They're my cousins."

She means Hitch and Denny.

"They're not *my* cousins."

"So?"

"But you're my like– what– second cousin? So how can– ?"

"Different sides of the family."

She looks a little scared, Jolene, and hasn't let go of his arm.

"Do you remember the word?" he asks.

"What word?"

In the sixth grade they were the last ones standing at the school spelling bee. He was really into school then, got good grades, but there was always Jolene Otis, and nobody did better than her.

"The word I blew you away with."

A hint of memory comes into her eyes. "Oh– you mean the spelling."

He digs into one of the hunting vest pockets and comes out with a small yellow pill, holds it in his palm in front of her face.

"What's that?"

"That's the word. Ecstasy. You spelled it with two c's instead of two s's."

Jolene frowns, looks at the pill.

"That's Ecstasy?"

"Yup."

"What does it do?"

"Oh– chills you out. Makes you feel good."

"And then you're like an addict."

"Never been an Ecstasy addict in the history of the world. Not even rats and monkeys."

"And you want to sell it to me?"

"Free sample."

"I don't need anything."

"You may not *want* anything, Jolene, but you definitely *need* something. You're here because Fawn snapped the whip and you were too afraid of her to say no, so now you're hanging onto me because it keeps you from looking alone and constipated."

She lets go of his arm.

"It's good for constipation too?"

He has to smile. He has never, ever heard Jolene make a wisecrack before.

"Have you had a beer?"

"I don't like beer."

"The point is to change your consciousness. Our people been doing that for centuries– "

"That's peyote."

"Got some in my other pocket if you want to try it. Can be tough on the stomach, though. Whereas this"– he presses the yellow pill into her hand– "has virtually no side effects, unless you're wearing braces or need to get to sleep right away."

She doesn't give him the pill back, looking into his eyes. Really cute girl if she'd smile once in a while.

"What's gonna happen to you, Dickyboy?"

It's something he doesn't like to think about a lot. The best thing about smoke, at least the stuff he and Dylan have been getting from the bouncer, is the way it puts you in a hazy, no worries place, where even breakfast is too much future to deal with.

She's still looking at him, and it prompts another memory, a poem they had to stand up and trade verses on in class, Jolene barely able to muster the volume to be heard.

"Nothing's going to *happen* to me. 'I am the master of my fate, I am the captain of my soul.'"

Dylan is waving from the doorway to the kitchen, maybe another customer or some problem. Dickyboy starts away, turning back to call to Jolene.

"But thank you for asking."

IT'S BAD ENOUGH TO have to wear a rubber. But these assholes, the ones who come in here and next door at Teasers, don't even get to take their pants off. Otto has the door and Scorch is floating in the big room for a couple hours, just letting his presence, his existence, be known to the mob. It's as much for the girls as for the customers, and if they try to pull any of their bullshit likely to lose Vic his license Scorch will be on them like white on rice. Zeena, executing a chopper on the pole as "American Woman" thumps out, has been coming in all jacked up, maybe even getting high in the dressing room toilet, and he has already had to lay a hot word in her ear. And Tuesday night she had her fingers inside her performance panties on stage, a big hit with the drillers but a definite no-no if anybody from the state is checking up. Zeena slithers down the pole head first and crawls on hands and knees to the edge of the stage so the front row boys can slip fives and singles in between her knockers– the hundred-and-first of a hundred-and-one uses for silicone.

I mean if you want to get off, just bring up Backpage.com on your phone and book a party. *Horton Hires a Ho.* But all this other business, suckers getting milked for more cash every step of the way– Teasers is the perfect name for it.

Oxana and Chelsea are working the bar, all smiles and no bullshit, pouring the liquids and harvesting the green, watering the drinks of the ones who've already had enough, and always aware of where the floor man is if somebody needs to be shown the door. There are three or four of the girls out doing table dances, taxi meters running in their heads as they grind for gold, and Brent is at a table in the corner, getting into something with Wayne Lee Hickey.

"My man Scorch!" Wayne Lee calls out when he spots him, like they're friends or something. "Sheriff of the Pussy Posse."

Scorch nods to Brent, whose jaw is out the way it gets when he's pissed.

Brent nods back. "Whassup?"

"We had a guy who claimed to be a health inspector in the other day," Scorch says, leaning down so they can hear him over Lenny Kravitz. "Five o'clock but we already got girls working, the guy spent twenty seconds checking out the toilets and two hours gaping at the T and A. Mostly the A– cat was definitely a back-door man."

"Like I was just saying to Wayne Lee here," says Brent, deadpan, "eatin beaver is a tough job, but somebody's got to do it."

"Surfer Dude whining again?" Wayne Lee has maybe never been to a beach in his life but looks like he belongs there, wearing those fruity shorts and with a smear of white sunblock on his nose. Type of guy who wouldn't last a day in the joint, like throwing a bleeding baby into a shark tank. Whereas Brent, the cons would have to take their time making book on Brent, and by then he'd be running the tier.

"You're not gonna share the wealth with your people," says Wayne Lee, gazing off across the smoky floor to the red-lit stage, where Zeena is picking up twenties with her snatch, "don't go rubbing it in their noses."

Scorch's deal with Vic is he gets paid with cash straight from the bank, virgin stuff with the wrappers still on that hasn't ever been wedged in anybody's crevices.

"What this overpaid brainfuck doesn't get is that flashing the bling is part of my *job*. Like hanging shiners on a fishhook. Christ, renting that fucking Vette by the week nearly busted me. But I landed the Chairman."

"And now you *own* that ride. And that house with all the toys in it– "

Brent has put up what by local standards is a mansion, just outside of Yellow Earth, paying, or maybe just promising, a fortune in overtime to get it finished before the fucking Dakota winter kicks in again.

"You think the landmen who do leases for the Company come on with please, baby, please? No fucking way. They lay those full-color brochures on them, the Company is in Texas, the Company is in Alaska, the Company is in Kuwait, the Company is in outer fucking *space*, and if you want to join our exclusive club and get filthy rich just sign on the dotted line. How do I pull investors in without I look like a high roller myself?"

"I thought we were running an oil service company."

Brent trades a look with Scorch and shakes his head. "And Vic Barboni here is running a dance academy."

Scorch sees Fontayne, plastered to a beefy pipe-pusher's lap, giving him the eye.

"I'll have to leave you gentlemen," he says. "Enjoy the show."

The thing is, Fontayne thinks she's done and Burger Boy wants more mileage for his money.

"Better let her loose," he says with a smile, the friendly one, not the don't-fuck-with-me one. "You get to play with them but you don't get to keep them."

"Hey, for forty bucks– "

Scorch claps his hands over his ears. Zeena is done now, taking prisoners on the floor, while Nurse Betty wipes down the pole, wearing the latex disposable gloves that are the first to come off in her routine.

"I'm not here to mediate financial transactions," he says. "Please unhand the young lady."

You try to keep it on a joking level, boys together being naughty, unless somebody really pushes your buttons and you need to fuck their face up.

"Besides, I gotta weewee," says Fontayne, which might even be true.

Burger Boy frowns, still with the death grip on her thighs.

"Unless it's your thing, I seen her unload on a guy's lap once. Not the wet spot he was hoping for."

The guy lets go and Fontayne is gone like a shot. Time is money to these girls, they got a number in their head for every hour they spend on the floor, and while the guy might have been only thirty seconds short of his Promised Land, something like a smoke detector was shrieking in her head.

Scorch gives the sap a light pat on the shoulder. "Women," he says, "you can't live *with* em and you can't drown em in a bathtub."

He sees L. T. and Shakes at the bar then, L. T. arranging empty shot glasses into a double row formation, ready for review. My entourage, thinks Scorch, heading over, with three quarters of a brain between the two of them.

"*There is no sex in the Champagne Room!*" quotes Shakes loudly as Scorch slaloms through the crowd to the pair.

"We don't have a Champagne Room. It's called the VIP Lounge."

"Next door," says L. T.

"You went in Teasers?"

"What, your feelings are hurt?"

"You could get a disease just breathing the air in that joint."

"Shakes got booted for propositioning a stripper."

"That's what they're there for."

"Perhaps his language was overly explicit."

"This bouncer with, like, metal teeth– Russian guy, I think– come over to lean on me, so's I told him how you and me were tight, Scorch." Shakes is really lit up, face flushed, eyes bright. "He wasn't impressed."

"I understand. Anybody with you for a friend must be a real sack of shit."

There is a shout as Betty puts her stethoscope chest piece on some guy's crotch to listen for a heartbeat.

L. T. gets off his barstool, teetering a bit, breath that could strip paint off a battleship hull. "And we have decided that the skanks in this establishment, despite its employment of our good buddy Scorch, are cold-hearted and mercenary."

"Plus none of them will take a check," says Shakes, standing and almost falling into Scorch. They are always broke, no matter how much work he and Brent throw them, and usually unable to remember what they spent it on.

"Therefore we have decided to embark on a squaw hunt out on the rez."

"You watch what you say out there."

"What, they gonna lift our scalps?"

"No, they'll cut off your dicks and nail em to a telephone pole. Neither of you is in any shape to drive."

"He'll brake," says Shakes, leaning on L. T. for balance as they start away, "I'll steer."

If they're lucky they'll skid into a ditch before they get into real trouble.

"Yo, Scorch!"

It is Bo, signaling that it's time to change the guard in the Lounge. Betty is down to her white hospital hose and nurse's hat as he passes the stage. You only see that gear in porno movies now, the real ones at the clinic where he goes for his Hep C cleanout wearing those pajamas with patterns off of Kleenex boxes on them.

A drunk leaning on the wall by the door to the VIP Lounge is singing along, somehow getting the simple lyrics to "Pour Some Sugar on Me" wrong.

The music inside is always mellower, lower volume, Donna Summer having vocal orgasms, and even some stuff in French. The light, what there is of it, is a kind of rosy pink, and Nora Jones is on the system, soft-edged even with the thump of Def Leppard's bass line hammering through from the big room.

Scorch sits on the upholstered chair in the little niche the guys call the Throne, visible but not intrusive, just meant as a reminder to everybody that Willy better stay under wraps. Sasha has her big Ukrainian butt parked on a guy who has his eyes closed, her back to him, hands on knees for leverage as she gives his crotch rocket a generous grind. Scorch hopes he won't start moaning– he hates it when they moan. And Jewelle is straddling one of her regulars, local guy who works mud on the rigs, moving her ass in circles, rubbing her breasts against his face and whispering what she'd love to do if things were different into his ear.

In other words, a relationship.

Jewelle, looking over the guy's shoulder, catches Scorch's eye and then crosses hers, still crooning in the man's ear. Jewelle is a real pro– no bullshit, good earner, and since she came up to No Man's Land here right away when he called, Vic doesn't charge her to work in the club. He gets cover charge for the guys who come to see her, of course, and a bump whenever she steers one into the Lounge, of which she is the undisputed queen, but for the rest she's on her own. Class the joint up a bit. And Vic knows she'll never tell the other girls, just like she won't rat out the ones who are making dates for later or providing happy endings when Otto, who is also working days on one of Brent's trucks, is on duty in the Lounge. Once Otto's on the throne, chin down on his chest copping Zs, a girl could give *him* a BJ and he wouldn't wake up.

The pink *My Little Pony* lunchbox that Jewelle keeps her dance tips and lap revenue in sits on the floor by the chair she cohabits with her regular, though it is her only little-girl touch, unlike Araceli, who claims to be from Panama and does the full plaid skirt and knee socks routine. Araceli has a regular, a headquarters honcho from the look of him, who monopolizes her twice a week and only pays with plastic. Either the guy is not married or he's laying it on the Company. Maybe that's what Wayne Lee is pouting about, thinks Scorch, Brent won't give him an expense account for transporting product and moving it among the drillers and Yellow Earthlings.

The guy Sasha is sitting on starts to moan, eyes still shut tight.

"Oooh, baby," Sasha gasps, working her buns and checking the paint job on her nails. Vic has a thing about nails, even inspecting them a couple times a week. Rules about how long the glue-ons can be, advice about what colors glow best under the black light. "Ooooh *baby!*"

Thing is, up here a real pro like Jewelle can knock down as much in a year as one of these oil platform monkeys, even the best of them, and she doesn't have to wrestle drill pipe twelve hours as day. Scorch pointed the fact out to her one night and she nodded toward one of her regulars, who they called Pizza Face because of the permanent rash on his mug.

"You're right, Stanley," she said, somehow knowing his birth name. "Why don't *you* go sit on his dick for a while?"

The door opens and "La Tortura" pounds in, Araceli's favorite number, and Bo is waving for help. There is a camera in the ceiling, Vic glancing at the monitor once in a blue moon but there for inspection and insurance, and Scorch never worries about leaving when Jewelle is working the room. The moaner has his head thrown back like he's had a heart attack, and now the local sap is whispering into Jewelle's ear.

"I could of handled it myself," says Bo as they step out into the big room, "only the guy ast for you personal."

Brent has Wayne Lee face down on the table, both arms pinned behind his back, leaning down to shout over the music.

"You never learn! You never *fuck*in learn!"

Only a few of the customers have interrupted their schoolgirl-banging fantasies to look over at the disturbance, Araceli with her plaid dress hiked over her hips and slowly peeling her lace panties down, various assholes shouting "*Olé!*" and "*Más, más!* The whole enchilada!"

"I'm done with you, fucker," shouts Wayne Lee, breath bubbling the puddled beer his face is pressed into. "You are fuckin *history*, man, and you come after me I'll fuck you where you live!"

Brent gives one of Wayne Lee's wrists a quick twist and he cries out, legs buckling a bit. Scorch taps Brent on the shoulder, moving to where he can be seen.

"Nice and gentle," Brent says, jaw out but voice steady. "But I don't want him bouncing back in here tonight."

A huge cheer. Araceli does a thing where she pulls the panties off, then drapes them over the face of one of the front row boys, a souvenir. Must buy the things in job lots.

Scorch takes one of Wayne Lee's wrists and gets a tight grip at the back of his neck, Brent easing away.

"Come on, buddy," he says. "We're going for a walk."

He lets Wayne Lee straighten up as he steers him through the crowd, keeping the arm twisted behind, ready to put him to the floor if he balks. But Wayne Lee seems resigned, even eager to leave.

"Believe that shit?" he mutters. "Going off like that in front of the whole world."

Otto gives him a look when they come out the side door, and Scorch shakes his head no. Under control.

"Where's your ride, hoss?"

"I can find it."

"Gonna have to walk you there. Boss's orders."

He lets go of the wrist but keeps his hand on Wayne Lee's neck as they walk.

"How can you work for that fuck?"

Brent said he wrestled, hundred ninety-five pounds, and used to wipe the mat with guys.

"I know, he can be a pain in the butt."

"You can't *trust* the dude. I'd watch your ass, Scorch."

Like they're friends.

"What you got to do, my man, is settle up and get outa Dodge. I mean *way* out. Shouldn't be hard to put this shithole in the rearview mirror."

"He *owes* me. Promises were made."

They are out on the main drag, the usual late night parade of big rigs and pickups rolling in each direction, some kind of techno music and strobe-light effect leaking out from the front of Teasers. Give you an epileptic fit working in that place.

"How many people you think Brent is in the process of ripping off as we speak? It's what he *does*, man, you heard him brag about it."

"You're not supposed to con the people who work with you."

"Hey, you lie down with dogs, you get rabies."

He sees Wayne Lee's tricked-up Camaro ahead, parked in the light spill of an all-night drugstore that wasn't there last week.

"You're going home now, right?"

"Fucking *bar*racks."

"Tell me about it. I been in county lockups that were way more fun. But you're not gonna be stupid and antagonize the guy anymore, right? Cause Brent don't play that."

Wayne Lee pulls his keys from his pocket and stands looking out at the ugly mile-long strip, neon and sodium vapor lights and vehicle headlights streaming east and west, as if it might be something to fight and die for. Money is being made flushing oil out of the ground and money is being made getting guys' dicks hard and shit, money is being made, good money, selling razor blades and toothpaste at boomtown prices, but there's not a thing or a person that Scorch would care to spend it on as far as the eye can see.

"Brent don't own Yellow Earth," says Wayne Lee Hickey, "and he ain't the king of *me*."

THE APARTMENT, WITHOUT BRANDI to fill it up, is the biggest space she's ever had to herself. She doesn't have to throw anything on to go to the bathroom. She doesn't have to do her dishes right away. She can play whatever music she likes, keep the lights on late at night if she's working, floss while she's watching TV without grossing anybody out. It's an ideal situation to go mental in.

Leia runs her paper through spell-check, though the program is unfamiliar with some of the scientific terms and leaves them highlighted. It is a bit more of a plea bargain than a thesis and proofs, the computer thesaurus not much help in alternative ways to say 'invites more study.' The gist of it is that so many species are under pressure from modern industry and human habitation that there is no objectively 'natural state' to investigate, that the norm from which group behavior deviates is not the community but the refugee camp.

In other words, bullshit elegantly stated. She was much sought-after in grad school for her ability to synthesize, to flesh out a malnourished thesis with layers of verbiage, to express somewhat wobbly ideas in academese and transform them into insights.

Depending on how much time the professor had to read.

It's the community part of the p-dogs that interests her, and if their habitat hadn't been blitzed she might have found some things out. Is it only a multitude of individuals obeying their selfish genes, hard-wired with a limited repertory of interactive gambits, or do they consider the group before they act? Is Odysseus really cunning or just testosterone-imbalanced? What is the trigger that makes them feel there's too many of us or too few of us and then do something about it? Are they afraid even when they're underground?

There wasn't any moping when they were translocated, she's got that much in the paper, something like the old coterie up and running within days. Ants are pretty much ruled by what they can smell, to the point where they are easily fooled by parasites. With thousands to choose from, how does a dog tell one hole from another? With a bad head cold are they more likely to get lost? What would a single individual, male or female, dropped out somewhere there wasn't another prairie dog for hundreds of miles, do?

It invites further study.

Leia looks at the last two days' dishes and decides she will definitely wash them tomorrow morning. Not that she's inviting him over, her visible conduct is unusual enough in this place without inviting him into her lair, but she doesn't want to walk the windy streets of Yellow Earth feeling like a secret slattern. A creature with an untidy nest. Just as there are actions and behaviors to attract a mate, there must be prairie dog turn-offs. Fleas, which would definitely put her off, don't happen to be among them, but there must be something a gal in heat can do that will drive away the horniest p-male. And with humans, who knows? One look at the playlist on her iPod and he might run screaming–

She thinks of the solo mammals– some predators, some large ungulates, house cats– maybe meeting up with somebody cospecific for a few minutes a year, fulfilling their genetic imperative, and then back on their own. Do they *feel* alone? Is any one of her study subjects out in the fledgling colony, surrounded by hundreds of near-clones, even the slightest bit alienated? Not with the program? Or do the others sense that kind of thing right away and terminate the imposter?

She can't read the paper one more time, it is what it is. Her finger hovers over SEND, then takes the plunge.

It doesn't require physical proximity anymore, she knows. There are coteries of people who play Scrabble online, of people who root for the Golden Gophers, of people who love to watch specially built cars scream around a track again and again and again. And for a while she believed her coterie was the savants who studied animal behavior, who discussed cadre dynamics and pair bonding and published incisive dissertations that increased the store of human knowledge. As soon as her e-mailed offering, her plea for leniency, is read, she'll be cast out from that secular sodality, and then what? Dwell in the Land of Nod, to the East of Eden?

Leia gets up, finds her shoes. The circulation in the apartment has never been any good. Stale thoughts hang in the air, depression clings to the walls like mold. What she needs, thinks Leia, what will recharge her failing batteries, is to get out and watch some methane pollute the atmosphere.

IT'S NOT LIKE YOU can dance to that stuff. Some of the guys thrash around if they're wasted enough, but you might as well be playing football in a closet. And what does rap have to do with anything out here? Ludacris? Or for that matter, Megadeth? Really?

There is enough moon that Jolene doesn't wish she had a flashlight. At least the road home hasn't been taken over by oil traffic yet, though there's a story that a pipeline will come through here. She can see their lights moving way over on the 12, a steady stream in both directions, night and day, and four different wellheads in between where they're flaring the gas off. She's done this walk in the dark plenty of times, not much more than two miles, but tonight there's the feeling hanging over it, the bad vibe thing, which started even before she swallowed the pill.

Boys will take over a party if there's too much to drink or somebody's got leapers to pass around, and then it's time to leave. She wanted to pull Fawn out with her but Fawn and Dickyboy were going at it, what's she been up to, why is she so distant, and it was a temptation to just step in and say forget about her, don't you know she's doing it with a married guy who works with her stepfather? I mean, Dickyboy is Jolene's friend too, sort of, his grandmother used to leave him at her house when they were little so she could go to her job in Yellow Earth, but Fawn and her are like supposed to be friends forever and you don't betray a confidence. Loyalty comes first, even if sticking with Fawn is a lot of work sometimes. Not just because Fawn has money to spend and she doesn't– Fawn is really generous when she *thinks* of it and doesn't rank people on how they dress or what they can drive. I mean Dickyboy was always in like the world's oldest pair of sneakers till he went into business and could afford to pimp up a bit. And in junior high Fawn stayed true to Dickyboy even when Armand Fox was after her, and he gets his picture in the newspaper three times a week and might be going places if he can ever graduate. Or Lyle Cunningham, whose family has two wells on their property and owns everything the Apple Corporation ever invented– Fawn wouldn't even let him give her a ride on his ATV.

Jolene has a shivery feeling but it's not that cold and there's no wind tonight. Something terrible is going to happen, she just knows it, knew it even before the pill and before they played "Check My Brain" at full volume for the third time. The whatever that Dickyboy gave her, said it was Ecstasy, hasn't helped any. He's a walking pharmacy these days, and she swallowed the mildest-sounding thing he offered, just to get him off her back. Made her feel kind of rubbery and took the edge off the thrash music, but it sure didn't make her feel *good*.

What Dickyboy should be looking for is a drug that will help him lose some weight. Not that Fawn was ever into jocks that much, but her stepfather looks like he could still play ball and this Brent guy pumps iron and Dickyboy just keeps getting wider. Hard to get your arms around him to dance, if anybody danced anymore, and there wasn't a boy at the party you could really get excited about unless you had like a death wish.

She goes over the story in her head, the one she'll tell her parents about Fawn's new car breaking down and nobody stopping to help them for an hour. She hopes the whatever doesn't show, make her eyes look funny or something. They always threaten to pull her out of Yellow Earth, and facing a senior year back at Three Nations is not appealing.

When she was eight there was a tornado, and she remembers her mother talking outside to a friend with the sky changing behind her, clouds like cow's udders bulging down toward the ground, and she started to cry. She didn't even know what a tornado was yet or the word for it, but the feeling in the air before it hit made her sick and scared inside. Something terrible going to happen. And if it's going to happen at the party I don't want to be there to see it.

Jolene hears something– senses it more than hears it– moving parallel to her at the side of the road. Something walking? Maybe it's just the pill she swallowed, gives you hallucinations. These are definitely not running shoes she's got on, so it would be better if it's not real.

And then she sees the eye-shine.

Yellow eyes. Stopped to stare at her. Jolene stops to stare back. Maybe twenty feet away, yellow eyes, unblinking. And then, maybe it's the pill putting weird ideas in her head, she hops into one of the routines, shouting as loud as she can–

> *Vinegar is sour*
> *Sugar is sweet*
> *Yellow Earth High School*
> *Can't! Be! Beat!*

The yellow eyes disappear. She tried out for the cheerleaders, made the squad, then her parents found out and she had to tell Miss Rumbauer she'd wasted everybody's time. It was a coyote, probably, which are never a problem unless you're run over by a truck and left alone at the side of the road and there's more than one of them. Or that's what people say.

It's supposed to be 'beaten,' according to Miss Rumbauer, but that's a tough rhyme to make and you want the last syllable to be a plosive. Cheerleading is basically really dumb but it would have been fun to go on road trips with the girls and you jump around and yell and work up a sweat without all the competitive thing that's on the playing field. I win, you lose. Armand Fox is a nice enough guy, but when the Warriors lose he kicks chairs and punches metal lockers and sits alone in the cafeteria the next day, and when they win it's like he's bouncing off the walls, more amped than the meth heads at the party tonight, and who wants to deal with all that up and down? "It evens you out," Dickyboy said about the pill she finally swallowed, as if she needs a drug to do that. This Brent guy, the one time she met him, looked like a Ken doll with lifter muscles and starting to lose his hair on top, definitely not her type, and she's sure a lot of Fawn's interest is the drama of the whole deal. Married man, sneaking around, like something you'd see on *Glee* or one of those reality shows that seem so fakey. Fawn would seriously love to have a camera crew follow her around, the way she screams at her mother even when Jolene is in the room and then five minutes later they're sitting on the bed looking at catalogs together. Coming from a family where people speak in tongues and believe the Final Judgment is just around the corner, Jolene figures why would you want more drama. An old married guy? *Really?*

The headlights from behind throw her shadow across the road, then the car passes and pulls over a little bit ahead. She doesn't recognize the car, but if it's somebody from the party she'll turn down a ride. Never know what somebody might be high on.

"Excuse me– you know where Sonny Hardin's place is?"

Two white guys, oil workers probably, looking lost.

"I don't know who that is."

The guy in the passenger seat unfolds a piece of paper. "Can you tell if this address makes any sense?"

Addresses are tricky on the reservation. Unless it's in one of the towns, people mostly end up telling you the biggest nearest road and then start talking about landmarks. She steps up to read and the guy over in the driver's seat gets out, maybe to go urinate. She can smell beer in the air, really strong– maybe the Ecstasy gives you super-sensitive smelling abilities. Maybe she'll be a mutant from now on, like the kids in the *X-Men* movies.

The guy in the passenger seat turns the dome light on to help see, holds the paper up to it. She has to lean into the open window a bit to get a good look and hears the crunch of gravel behind her. There's only one word written on the piece of paper and at first it doesn't make sense.

Gotcha

THE GIRL APPEARS IN her headlights, not totally off the road, and is gone. There was blood. Leia slows and turns– she was going seventy, crazy at night though the roads are so straight– but when she gets back to where she thinks the spot was there is nobody. She stops, gets out, calls.

"Hello?"

Nothing.

"Are you okay?"

Again no response, but then a sound to the side. It is black night, only the cones of her headlights and the half-dozen distant intense pockets of light where gas flares are lit or all-night crews lay out drilling pads.

The girl steps up to the shoulder, more a presence than something Leia can see yet.

"I don't know where I am," she says.

Under the dome light as she sits into the car, Leia can see that the girl has a smudge of dirt on her face, that there's blood from her nose dried on her lip and staining her blouse.

"You're hurt."

"No. I'm all right." The Native American girl stares out at the nearly featureless prairie. It's the warmest night they've had all month, barely a breeze.

"Where is this?"

"I think it's called Route 10 here. We're just west of Hawkeye." Leia has a good sense of the reservation roads from her initial colony scouting, knows which side of the Missouri she's on and can skirt around the oilfield traffic most of the way to Yellow Earth.

"I need to go back the other way, then," says the girl, and even in the dark Leia can tell she's crying. She slows, turns the car again.

"How did you get out here?"

No response for a long moment. There is a feeling you get from wild-caught animals when you transport them, even when they're not moving in the cage, not a smell or a sound but a tightness in the air, something ready to snap.

"It's where they left me."

What she was afraid of, the first thing that clicked in her head when the girl was caught in her lights.

"I should take you to your hospital."

"We don't have one."

"Then into Yellow Earth."

"No."

"–and then to the police."

"No."

"You can't just– "

"My parents– we're Christians," says the girl, shaking now. "I wasn't supposed to be there."

"There– ?"

"At the party. It got kind of out of control and nobody was in any shape to drive me so I walked. It's not much more than a mile."

"You've got bigger problems than trouble with your parents."

Leia slows down but the girl is silent. Yellow Earth is in the other direction.

"Was it somebody you knew?"

"No. Two men– it was too dark to see."

Leia turns the car for the third time.

"I'll take you to the emergency room. I'll stay with you– we can call your parents from there."

The girl says nothing, which she takes as acquiescence. Leia feels like if she saw one of them on the road she'd run him over.

"What's your name?"

"Jolene."

What the hell, maybe try to change the subject–

"Like the Dolly Parton song."

"I get to hear it a lot."

"At least it's a great song. You could be something else– Clementine."

"Yeah."

Driving out here is a little less lonely since the platform crews have come with their powerful work lights and the highways are streaming with trucks all through the night. Leia knows where all the gas stations are, most never closing these days, but there is still all this *space* to get lost in. And they are still out there, the predators, maybe somewhere near. They are always out there, somewhere, but you can't live your life thinking about that. Prairie dogs, described in one of the journals as 'the Chicken McNuggets of the high plains,' spend a third of their waking day scanning for danger. But even with all the hardtails crowding the town, with all the stares and comments she now gets, Leia has never felt endangered.

Which is just magical thinking.

Leia drives to Mercy. They sit in the car under the parking lot lights and the girl, Jolene, is still shaking, and Leia takes her hand and squeezes it.

"This is a *thing*," she says. "A thing that happened to you– like a car accident or a bad flu. The men, they're gone now and they won't come back, and the important thing to remember is they don't own you, they don't own any little bit of you. You're the same Jolene who woke up in bed this morning. Really."

It may be bullshit but that's the way she would want to feel about it and that's the best she can do.

"If you have to call the police," says Jolene, pleading with her eyes, "would you call Mr. Two Strike at the reservation? Cause that's where it happened, and I, like, used to go to school with his kids."

Leia walks the girl into the hospital, the reception lights assaulting them and two young men with their faces scraped and bleeding half asleep, still drunk, in two of the plastic chairs waiting for stitches.

The woman behind the glass panel gets Jolene in to be seen right away, and Leia sits as far as she can from the two fighters, air heavy with booze breath for yards around them. She is getting out her phone to call Will's office when the other one, the one who's name she should remember but who she always calls Deputy Dipshit, comes into the lobby.

"Another brawl in front of Bazookas," he says when she tells him what she knows. "I got to talk to those two."

"But then you'll deal with her?"

"Sure," he says, clearly annoyed at the extra work on his shift. "When she comes out from the Doc. Then I spose I could drive her home."

"I can do that. I don't think she wants to be alone with a man in a car. Even in the back seat."

"Suit yourself," says the deputy, whose name she now remembers is Clayton. "But if she was to a party out there, I'm not sure that story of hers gonna hold water."

Hitting the deputy is not an option, and Will has explained that with what the county is able to pay you're not going to get the brightest lights to join the sheriff's department.

"Is Sheriff Crowder on duty?" She hopes he takes it as a vote of no confidence in his abilities.

"Off the clock. What were you doing out on the rez?"

"Just driving, thinking." And if you had a decent fucking radio station, I'd have been listening to that.

"Lucky you come along, then."

He moves away to rouse the fighters and write down the answers to his questions on a small notepad, then goes in to the emergency room to find

Jolene. She hopes the doctor is thorough and at least kind. She gets the number for the reservation police, and the dispatcher says the chief will meet them at Jolene's house. The fighters nod off again, and the receptionist behind the glass calls her over.

"Her mom and dad are pretty religious." The receptionist is in her fifties, dyed blonde with a smoker's rasp. "They believe in that thing where all the good people suddenly disappear?"

"The Rapture."

"Yeah. Her mom told me at sewing how the airlines have to have either the pilot or the co-pilot who's a sinner, or at least a nonbeliever, or the insurance won't cover them."

"Because– ?"

"Just cause it's the Rapture it don't mean the ones that's left won't sue. And if both your pilots disappear– "

"I never thought of that."

"Anyhow, if she comes home and has to tell them that story– well, they're probly the type that think wickedness comes from with*in*."

"She's their daughter."

"I wouldn't want to have to tell them what she's got to. Not alone."

Since Brandi bugged out there is the other bed in the apartment. Hell, I could just adopt her–

"Maybe I could go in with her, if she wants. Help her through the story. Be like a– like a buffer."

The receptionist winks at her. People still wink here, like in Frank Capra movies.

"You're an angel."

WILL RECOGNIZES THE GUARD at the gate of the man camp.

"Evenin, Sheriff," says Cory Stufflebean, who Will has never seen under anything but a Stetson. "Your red brother's already inside."

He hits the buzzer and the gate slides open. "I'll join you in the lobby."

Back in Yellow Earth the main camp is three stories of stacked ISO containers with doors and windows cut into them, what the long-time town folks are calling 'the Pile.' This one, called Killdeer City after the council chairman of the rez, is six rows of long, trailer-like structures behind some security fencing, dumped on a flat spot in some patchy grazing land. He parks next to Danny Two Strike's patrol car among the collection of mud-spattered pickups and gleaming muscle cars in the front lot, and heads for the admin building entrance, with Cory hurrying herky-jerky to catch up with him.

"How's that leg doing?"

Cory stops and bends to rap his shin hard with his knuckles. "Terrific, now that I swapped it out. Plastic and titanium, like a jet fighter."

"They took it off?"

"Just under the knee. The sumbitch was hurting me so bad I decided the hell with it."

Cory was a bronc-riding champion in the '50s before he got trapped under a ride at the Wildhorse Stampede, the animal twisting and kicking even after it slammed sideways into the arena dirt. Will has brought Cory in for D&D a dozen times over the years but thought he'd left the area.

"You look good in the uniform."

"Bull turds I do." The old man taps a code on a keypad to open the front door for them. "I look like that bank guard in the movies, the one that always gets kilt reaching for his pistol."

"They pay pretty good?"

"Better than anything else I could handle. My sponsor hooked me up here."

"AA?"

"Yeah, the old-time religion. Doctor said how there wasn't any space-age replacement for a liver, so I hung up my drinking spurs."

"Good for you."

They step into the lobby area, just an unmanned reception desk and a couple long brown-leather couches, a lame instrumental of "Raindrops Keep Fallin' on My Head" oozing out from somewhere.

"Tell you the truth, Will, I feel like hammered shit. But I spose it's better than being dead."

Danny stands up from one of the couches, his hat in his hand. "Morning, Will."

"*Early* morning."

"Thanks for coming out."

"No problem. We got an assault?"

Danny nods his head. "One of our girls and two fellas sound like they're probably white. She was walking home from a house party at her cousins', the two stopped by her in their car to ask directions, then one pulled her inside and they took off. Left her out in the boonies about four hours ago, banged up pretty bad. She wandered around till that Wildlife Girl come along, doing who knows what out here, and– "

"Clayton filled me in on it when I came on."

"You got Clayton on nights?"

Will shrugs. "He'd make more hauling gravel, but he likes to carry a gun." He looks around the lobby. It feels more like a display room than anything real, with Harleigh's arrow logo on the wall behind the reception desk. "What are we doing here?"

"Show him the card."

Cory pulls a plastic card out of his shirt pocket, hands it to Will.

"You swipe this little bugger to get in through the gate, use it like a credit card at the convenience store on site, gets you into the gym, the rec room, the Wifi café."

"The girl saw one of these on the dashboard of the car," says Danny.

Will nods, hands the card back to Cory. "Description of the car?"

Danny shrugs. "A four-door something. I sat with her and flipped through our auto look-book, but she couldn't even give me a color. Not a pickup, not a van."

"She saw their faces?"

Danny sighs, pulls out his notepad, flips to the page he wants.

"White male, slender and strong, dark hair, one- or two-day stubble, noticeable gold crown on what is probably his upper left bicuspid, probably chews tobacco– no visible tattoos. Wearing a monocolor hooded sweatshirt, khaki pants. Second perp is older, heavy-set, brown-to-black hair which is thinning, wearing jeans and a maroon windbreaker, belt with a heavy belt buckle, black grit under his fingernails."

"That's it?"

"It was dark and they pushed a bag that'd probably had some kind of fast food in it over her face. She smelled fries and onions."

They both look to Cory, who shakes his head.

"We got four-fifty, five hundred hardtails in here at any one time, coming and going. You coulda just described a third of em."

"You got a camera on the parking lot entrance?"

"Live feed so's we can get a look, but it don't record."

"Damn." Will looks to Danny.

"I figure we take a little walk-through," says Danny, "see if two badges makes anybody flinch. If we flush anything out and they're white, I got you to make the arrest. If nothing pops, then I'll sit with Cory and go through ID photos on their database."

Will nods to Cory. "You're the Man."

The old cowboy leads, access card in his hand. "I can take you into all the public spaces," he says. "The residences, you're gonna need a warrant."

"Is that what they call them, residences?"

"Jack-and-Jill rooms– you got a bed unit with a storage drawer under it, half-fridge, microwave, sink, flat-screen TV, share a toilet with the fella next door. Couple feet bigger all around than your county lockup, Will. Plus they got cable."

They leave the lobby and walk down a narrow chute to the next structure.

"Temperature drops and the wind gets howlin, you can access pert near all the amenities without stepping outside. Mostly fellas come here to *sleep*."

They step into the dining hall, a low-ceilinged quadruple-wide with a cafeteria-style food line and a few dozen plastic tables scattered around. Fifteen or twenty men, all white, eat at or lounge around the tables, a few with their music hooked up to their heads.

"Our tenants are all pretty much of the Caucasian persuasion," says Cory. "There's a few Mexicans working the mud jobs and low end on construction crews, but they can't afford it out here. And then your folks, Danny, they got their own homes or relatives to stay with nearby."

Cory waits by the tray of lemon squares at the end of the chow line while the two lawmen stroll around the room, one on either side of every occupied table, looking into eyes. Mostly the men don't respond, too exhausted or disinterested to do more than look up, though a few nod. Lots of tats, some notable beer bellies, guys with sunburned necks and forearms, and you could run a small engine on what they got jammed under their fingernails. They rejoin Cory, passing the insistently humming bank of food vending machines and heading through the security door to walk down the next connective chute.

"You're right. It is a bit nicer than the county lockup," says Will to Cory.

"Yeah, them bars tend to fuck up your *ambience*." Cory says it with the French pronunciation. "This is more like that assisted living I was in over to Spring-brook, probly use the same kit to put it together. 'Panelized Flat Pack Structures.'"

"Listen to you."

"Working the graveyard out here," says Cory, "you got plenty time to peruse the brochures. This here's a 'portable modular housing facility custom-built to the locale, workforce size, and other needs unique to your project.'"

"Nicer than the government housing on the rez," says Danny. "Nicer than what half the people out here living in."

"Harleigh get out here much?" asks Will.

"I only seen the chief once," Cory grins. "Come out for some photographs, shake a few hands. Manager is a fella who does these all over the country. Runs it like one of them corporate feed lots, but he knows his bidness."

They step into the Wifi café then, a white-walled little box with three men sitting at the row of six computers, their faces washed by the bluish glow of the screens. One of the men is Skyping, talking to his kids in a thick Texas accent.

"I don't see no oil bein pumped," he says. "Just drill the holes and leave em for the frack boys. But without your Daddy and his friends there wouldn't be no gas for Momma's Explorer– well, darlin, then you shouldn't *spill*. Momma got to keep her eye on the road."

Danny cruises along the backs of the computers, getting a good look, then nods and they enter the next chute.

"I lived in one of these deals once," says Cory. "Back when they built the dam."

"You're that old?"

"Son, I'm two years older than *dirt*. Broke my hip the first time, so I'se off the circuit for a spell, and I chewed down enough aspirins to get through the interview without whimpering too bad, and they put me on a bulldozer. Rode it for two years and it never throwed me once."

"This is when?"

The light is harder in the chutes, and all from above, the broken vessels in Cory's nose looking purple.

"I started pushing dirt in '49, but went back to the rodeo before they finished it. There was a couple towns sprung up– Pick City's still there, but I was out in what they called Silver City. Wunt no silver there ever, far as I know, just put up a couple rows of these little boxy things converted from grain bins– called em 'cabins'– shaped like the plastic houses in that board game."

"Monopoly."

"Played a lot of Monopoly in the hospital, when I was doing my sheet time between stompings. Learnt I wasn't cut out for the real estate bidness. Not like the fellas who put up these little boomtowns– four or five of em dumped alongside the road we cut between the dam site and 83. They'd have three, four of us fellas in each unit, somebody opened a little store, there was a bar they threw up from lumber off the barns about to go under, dance hall."

"My grandparents lost their place," says Danny.

"Hell, it was what, nine outta ten people on the rez had to pick up and move, we seen em leaving with what they could carry."

"Any Indians on the crew?"

"Couple fellas, maybe– drivers, pick-and-shovel men." Cory shakes his head. "The cabins was just bare inside– you got a frame and a mattress, little stove to make coffee on if you had your own pot, no housekeeping or any of the services that come with this here deal. Pay was good, though, and Jesus, we had fun on our off time. Wasn't but one of those cabins with the TV antennae and nothing to watch back then, so it was card games and races."

"Races."

"Anything that had wheels and we got keys to or could hotwire, we'd race it. You fellas are too young to remember what a steam shovel is."

"I had a children's book," says Danny. "My mother read that to me most every night so's I'd shut up and nod off."

"Well the trick to racing one is not to tip it over on the turns. We're racing in muck, see, so you get a nice sideslip on the turns."

"Don't suppose the law was ever called out there," says Will.

"Wasn't nobody to bother but each other, and we kind of policed ourselves. When there was fights, you'd just let the loser lie there, rest up a bit, and some-body'd throw a bucket of water on him if he had his shift coming up."

"You must of worked on ranches before, lived in a bunkhouse."

"More than a few. And I'll tell you one thing– this here," says Cory as they step into the gym, "you can live here for months and never come up on the radar. Don't need to talk to nobody, you can stick your headphones on, lay back in your room and look at two thousand channels' worth of nonsense, sleep till you go out for another twelve. Try that on a ranch and the boys are like to take a brand-ing iron to your tender parts."

The gym is the same white box as the lobby and Wifi café, all the machines and benches taken, even at six in the morning. Will lingers beside a stocky, over-muscled guy bench pressing what looks like four hundred pounds of free weight several times.

"Who's the girl?" he asks Danny, as if it's just conversation.

"Jolene Otis. Religious family, goes to school in Yellow Earth now, I never heard nothing bad about her."

"How she doing?"

"Bout like what you'd imagine. Word leaked out awful fast, and her boy cousins– she got a truckload of cousins, couple of em hosted the party she was at– they're out looking nasty and talking about gelding somebody. I had to have a talk."

The lifter makes a final *Whoo!*, thrusting the loaded bar up and racking it, staring past Will to the ceiling, then sits up, grabs his towel, and steps quickly out the door that leads behind the structure.

Will looks to Danny. Danny taps his lip and the side of his neck– the man had a Fu Manchu moustache and a three-color tat of a screaming skull on fire on the left side of his neck.

"Don't think she'd have missed that," he says.

"Call him Scorch," says Cory. "Works for the chief's outfit."

"ArrowFleet?"

Cory nods.

"He works at Bazookas too," says Will. "Bouncer."

"Know his real name? Scorch?"

"It'll be in the data up at the desk," Cory volunteers.

"He's not one of our perps from tonight," says Danny.

"Probably not." Will stares at the bench the man was laying back on, black vinyl still slick with his sweat. "But I'll guarantee you he's doing *something* we should run him in for."

THEY'RE EACH TUGGING AT one side of a suitcase, the pink carry-on with a butterfly pattern he bought Fawn for the Hawaii trip.

"You're not going anywhere."

"You're not stopping me!"

"I can have him arrested."

"For what? It was consensual."

"Where did you learn *that* word?"

"I'm not as stupid as you think I am."

"Says the high school girl who's got herself knocked up."

Fawn lets go and Connie almost falls to the floor with the suitcase. Fawn looks to Harleigh.

"Can you get her off my back?"

"She's your mother."

This observation has never worked before and it doesn't work again.

"Call 911," Connie orders him.

"Connie."

"Call Danny Two Strike, call whoever is in charge of statutary rape."

"It's statu*tory*, Mom."

The look of exasperation from Connie, on cue. "Where does she get this stuff?"

"Television, most likely. We're not having anybody arrested."

"Just because he's your partner– "

"My *ex*-partner."

"You brought those people into our lives."

"And you thought it was a pretty good deal. You and Bunny out on your shopping binges, thick as thieves."

"While her husband is fucking my daughter!"

Now Fawn pretends to be shocked. "Are you gonna let her talk to me that way?"

"You two just simmer down." He is standing in the doorway to Fawn's bedroom, the avenue of retreat unimpeded behind him. "Where, exactly, do you plan on going?"

Fawn thrusts her jaw out the way she does when she's out of ammunition. "Texas or California. Or Florida. He hasn't made up his mind."

"Brent has responsibilities here. Contracts to honor."

"Bunny owns the companies."

"Bunny," says Harleigh softly, "is the girl in the car ad who sits on the hood in a short dress and smiles. She doesn't know diddly about the oil service business."

It was never more than a tease with Bunny, he thinks, or he never pushed it any further between them, and is now mightily relieved that he didn't.

"And Brent is the guy in the beer ads hanging out with his meathead buddies," says Connie. "What's he know about helping a young girl pregnant with her first baby?"

Fawn mutters, having wondered the same thing. "He doesn't even *like* beer. He drinks Bacardi cocktails."

"Well excuse me," says Connie, tossing the suitcase back on the bed. "I had him mixed up with a lowlife who can't keep his hands off of underaged girls."

"He bought me a car!"

"You don't have a drivers' license!"

"I'll *get* one!"

Harleigh takes a half step forward. Boxing refs must face this all the time, how to separate the opponents without getting pasted.

"That belly gets any bigger," says Connie, pointing, "you won't be able to reach the pedals."

Fawn is just starting to show, Harleigh thinking it was all pizza and Coke till she hit them with the news.

"You *knew*, didn't you," Fawn accuses, narrowing her eyes at him. "That's why you fired Brent."

"Brent was never my employee, we were partners. I dissolved the partnership."

"Because of him and me."

"Because he's not an honest man."

She only hesitates for a beat. "And you *are?*"

And that's when Connie slaps her.

They both start to cry then and Harleigh slips in between.

"Okay, you two– time *out*. Connie, this isn't a thing about you as a mother, it's just how life is these days. Fawn– I love you and I will consider this baby my grandchild."

Connie runs out then. They both listen for a crash, but she is too upset to assault the ceramics, not even slamming the door to their bedroom.

"You'd better go to her."

"In a minute. You sit."

Fawn sits, her biggest worry with Harleigh settled now, her defenses coming down. He sits beside her, considering his options. Picking a fight with Brent and then shooting him is his favorite at the moment, but he's sure Ruby, back in his corner now that he's left ArrowFleet, would advise against it. Connie pulled this same routine when she was Fawn's age and ended up stranded in a motel room in Kalispell, going into labor.

"You're gonna do what you're gonna do," he says as gently as he can, "but I don't trust him."

"You don't know him."

"The more I know about him, the more I worry for you. You know you can call me, any time of the day or night, no explanations necessary."

"Your emergency number."

"And I will come and get you. Texas, California, Florida."

"We're gonna be fine. We're in love."

Harleigh sighs, looks at the walls– Britney Spears, Katy Perry, Miley Cyrus, some skinny boy singer from the *Idol* show with his shirt pulled open. He'd been sorry to see the Little Mermaid go.

"What kind of ride did he buy you?"

"It's an M-thing."

"Miata?"

"Mazda Miata. Baby blue."

Baby blue has always been Fawn's color.

"It's really cute."

Harleigh nods. "Son of a bitch knows his automobiles."

MAKE YOUR OWN BOX, be your own trainer. There must be an AA meeting here in Yellow Earth, and various other Loser Lobbies, but forget about CrossFit. The people who hadn't left here before the oil came were the ones with no initiative, the ones too clueless to move.

Brent is on the treadmill to start, already pushing his lactate threshold, and thinking about what to do about Wayne Lee. "Never think of your enemies a moment longer than is necessary to fight them," said the Objectivist, and it's true, worrying about the people in your way can be a suckhole. He adjusts the slant on the mill to max, digs in. The Workout of the Day he's chosen is all attack, with ninety-second recovery periods in between. There's the slacker thing with Wayne Lee, of course, always willing to go with the flow, but that is just border-line laziness. And there's a new element, a petulance, like Brent owes him something. He tries to bring his knees all the way up to his chest, quads screaming, and imagines the Crusader armies. Basically a Christian biker gang, in it for the rape and pillage and the bragging rights back home if you make it there in one piece. None of this 'team member' shit, though they were all aware of a certain power in sheer numbers. Overrun the sons of bitches before they get the second arrow out of the quiver. The machine beeps and he steps off the tread before it stops rolling.

Ninety seconds. Shake out the quads, couple deep breaths.

The hero in your soul. She talks about that a lot. Listen to what he really wants, don't accept compromises, don't let himself down. Bunny, right now, is a compromise. Have to deal with that situation, unless she's willing to read the writing on the wall and do the right thing. All the legal tangle, ownership, paper signing, all that weight they tie on to try to handicap you, will be fine. She knows what's at stake, knows the consequences if she doesn't hold up her end.

Not a dumb Bunny.

Power cleans now. The architect, just a contractor with an attitude really, wondered why the basement room had to be so high. So I don't smash these weights through the ceiling, numbnuts. You don't push, you don't *lift*, you give gravity a good hard shot in the ass.

Right into the Bulgarian split squats, no breather in between. He's started designing his own WODs instead of finding them online, each meant to punish a different muscle group. If you're not infuriated at least two or three times during your workout, you might as well hang it up.

Break now. The chief has turned chickenshit, listening to the whiners in his tribe. She had a few bombshells for the red man, too, "They fought to live like animals, and had no rights to the land," something like that. Which, if you don't get all romantic about it, is pretty much true. Let them try to live on beef jerky some winter, they think it was so wonderful.

Buffalo jerky.

He only got the book because he'd been outbid on the Victoria's Secret catalog that had been smuggled in. "It's like science fiction," said Hummer from the second tier, who rented it to him. "Only more complicated."

At first it was slow going, some babe who owned a railroad, and he kept waiting for this Atlas character to show up. Then the ideas kicked in. Things started to make sense, and not just in the book. It was a new way of seeing the world. He was already hitting the iron at Walkaround, just out of boredom, but once he was into the book he started being disciplined about it, setting goals. Looking around on the yard you could see it in the eyes, in the attitude– the ones who ran the joint, who would run the world if they'd take the shackles off, and the extra baggage. From now on I carry nobody.

Wall ball shots, getting into a rhythm with the medicine ball, nobody in the house to freak out with the impact. Throw it like you mean it, like the point is to put a *hole* in the wall. He practiced sending the vibes out– do not fuck with me– and they must have gotten the message. He did his own time and read the big book three times, cover to cover. The picture of her on the back wasn't impressive, little dumpy Russian woman, but she was into some righteous theories. No complaints, no excuses– the next go-round he was going to rock the joint. I'm tougher than the smart ones and smarter than the tough ones, and I know how simple it all should be.

See it, want it, *get* it.

Walk up the wall for handstand pushups, that great rush. Hard to lose your focus, all that blood in your brain, and focus is the whole story from this point on. All the rest of it, the trucking scam, the product, is just for operating cash, just what you need to show to sit at the Big Table. But you get a piece of an oil lease or two–

He steps out and lets the blood redistribute.

"The smallest minority on earth is the individual," she said somewhere. So people who fuck with the rights of the individual can't pretend they aren't racists. Or something like that. You get to the Big Table the stakes are higher, the risk greater, but when you win, you get to leave all the others behind, the ones who cling, the ones who can't hack it. Scorch is a bad man in his own little world, takes care of business, but he doesn't have the imagination to play on that level, doesn't have the *vi*sion. But when you need shit done and no questions about it–

Box jumps. Get your plyometrics in gear, engage the abs. The floor is a sizzling hot griddle, don't let your feet burn. Once you're there, an accepted player, they can't touch you. How much money do these Wall Street characters, these greenmailers and corporate raiders steal in a year, and if they're caught, do they ever do time? No fucking way. Because the little lawmakers and their enforcement goons know the secret– you take those people down, it *all* comes down. The whole system. Because they *need* you, need whoever is willing to stick their neck out and make a move, dig a hole, build a skyscraper, give them something to tie down with regulations and taxes so it doesn't lift off the ground and *fly.*

Brent sits in the rowing machine, imagines himself a half boat-length ahead of a competitor, begins to pull. Faster. Harder. Think of other men's envy as rocket fuel, let it charge you up. He thinks about making it with Fawn down here. She's still pliable, even if she's a little spoiled, and he can make her into whatever he wants. A matter of focus, a matter of will. He begins to pull away from the other boat. If he'd been into tats, there was one of the Objectivist's quotes he'd have on his chest, maybe backwards so he could read it in the mirror every morning.

"The question isn't who's going to let me– it's who's going to *stop* me."

IT'S SUPPOSED TO BE a tradition.

"Rookies always light the first flare stack," Nicky the derrickman told him, rummaging around for a length of PVC pipe the right length and diameter. "It's like an initiation."

Tuck has only been with the new outfit a week, nice enough guys but a little slapdash compared to Upshaw's crew. Nothing he can put his finger on, just that they seem like they're racing to catch *up*, not to get ahead. They've been making hole like crazy, though, at least till the gas started coming up, surprising since they're only into the first shale layer and nothing's been fracked yet. Just some natural pockets, says Kelsey, the driller, something that has to be vented and burned off before they can go deeper. So Tuck is squatting with his back to the wind, running through safety matches, trying to get the damn rags to catch fire.

He'd feel more confident if Nub, who's supposed to be supervising all this, wasn't at his other well, or if the other guys weren't all up on the platform, hugging close to something big to duck behind. Grunt told him to stay on the edge of the pad, fine, and to approach from the far side, away from the ground pipes that send the gas to the stack, in case of leaks. In case of leaks, he thinks, I am *toast*. He's maybe three hundred feet back from it, just a big steel pipe sticking straight up, fifteen feet or so from the ground. The idea is to throw the pole up like a baton, end over end, so the lit end passes over the gas blowing out of the stack–

There will be a much bigger one eventually, says Kelsey, thirty, forty feet high, with an electrical sparking device built onto it. But that's for the production boys, weeks after this crew has finished drilling and moved on to a new well. Just part of the macho routine, thinks Tuck, proving yourself under fire.

The ball of gas-soaked rags catches. He stands and waves to the platform, holding the payload as far from his body as he can, flames whipping in the wind.

Then there is the noise they told him about, a loud rushing as the gas is released, a bit like an airplane engine revving up if you've got a seat right over the wing. He thought it would hiss. "If there's too much nitrogen and not enough methane," Nicky told him, "she might not even light."

Tuck starts toward the stack. If he'd known about this he might have practiced throwing poles in the air. Circus people do stuff like that all the time, with precision, but they rehearse like crazy when there's no audience.

He's halfway to the stack when there is a *Pop*! and he sees a streak of smoke in the air and then *WHOOOOOM*! an explosion from the top of the stack, a column of flame roaring up twenty, thirty feet, slanting slightly in the wind.

He's on his knees on the pad, the torch he was carrying having set some weeds on fire, the assholes on the platform hooting with laughter. Tom Hicks holds what looks like a small shotgun, which must have fired the flare that flew over the stack. Tuck stands carefully– nothing bleeding, nothing burnt or even singed, the flare-off lowering but continuing to roar. There goes my entire winter heating supply in twenty seconds, he thinks, up into the atmosphere.

They come down then to slap his back and ask if he shat himself and relive his reaction and help him throw gravel on the torch and the smoldering weeds. Nicky stands facing the flame-throwing stack, hand over his heart.

"I officially declare," he yells over the roar, "these Olympic Games to be *open*."

STAGE FOUR

ABSQUATULATION

"*THE WEST! THE MIGHTY West!*" rhapsodized the oft-wounded Civil War general James Sank Brisbin in 1881, in his *The Beef Bonanza: or How to Get Rich on the Plains,* explaining how in the former Great American Desert, "The poor professional young man, flying from the over-crowded East and the tyranny of a moneyed aristocracy, finds honor and wealth."

That book and the earlier Homestead Act helped precipitate a rush that filled the high plains with strivers, the majority of them either foreign-born or first-generation Americans. With pasture land further south and east played out or swarming with nesters, experienced cattlemen as well as ambitious greenhorns like young Theodore Roosevelt came to the Dakotas to build up great herds, which the Northern Pacific Railway, at one point owner of a quarter of the upper state's land, shipped to market once filled out on free grass. Vast 'bonanza farms' were cleared and planted along the Missouri River, some with hundreds of migrant laborers hired for the wheat harvest, while the smaller family operations of Norwegians and ethnic Germans from Russia filled the lands that lay further from easy water.

Dusty processions of cattle, mostly Hereford by blood now, ambled down Broadway in Bismarck. Advances in refrigeration and the highest price-per-pound in decades excited a whirlwind of British investment. Millions of cattle and billions of cow chips festooned the grasslands, and wheat farmers, flush from their own bumper crops, invested in the relatively new technology of barbed wire to keep the beeves out of their fields. Yellow Earth, located near the confluence of the Missouri and the Yellowstone, grew from a side-track tent colony beside the just arrived Great Northern Railway to a passenger and freight division point, replete with roundhouse, car repair shop, icehouse, and stockyards capable of holding over a hundred carloads' worth of livestock, eventually becoming the county seat and trade center. People who walked to the Territory with a bindle over their shoulder or pawned the family heirlooms for a train ticket suddenly owned horses and wagons, ate regularly, and built schools for their children.

The cattle went first, in the Great Blizzard of '87. After a brutally hot summer, prairie dogs had gone underground early, elk had banded to migrate southward, birds vanished. In early January snow fell, then fell again, then fell again, covering the tallest of the wild forage, and in parts of the state the temperature plummeted to 50 below, the cold locking up water holes and streams that were then buried in more snow. The wind rattled the boards of farmhouses, blew head-high drifts over roads. Unprovisioned by their owners, steers found buildings in the blasting wind and pressed their starving bodies against them for shelter, or wandered into riverbeds and coulees, where they bogged shoulder-deep and were buried. When the weather finally broke for spring, flocks of turkey buzzards circled the sky and blanketed the carcasses of dead animals that covered the land like tiny hillocks, rotting carcasses that choked the streams and rivers, that polluted the water and befouled the air. Some outfits were completely wiped out in the Great Die-Up, most losing nine out of every ten of their stock, and cattlemen left the state in herds.

With the wheat it was a longer, more tantalizing process. Good years and poor, prices sliding up and down, shipping costs eating into whatever bounty advances in agriculture produced, mortgages taken to tide farmers over through seasons of too little water or too many grasshoppers. The death blow came in the Dirty Thirties, when in the western half of the state soil depletion from overuse and severe drought was followed by black blizzards up from Texas that dumped layers of sterile dust on the stubbled fields, blinding horses, short-circuiting tractor engines, and driving people inside for days on end, cloth stuffed in the cracks around doors and windows in a doomed effort to keep the disaster at bay. A perfect storm of misery. Most of July of '36 was over one hundred degrees, and more than half the people in the state had to grudgingly seek some form of public assistance to survive. Mortgages were foreclosed, farmers were found hanging dead in dust-drifted barns. Yellow Earth bled citizens, some stopping in Fargo, others continuing out of state. And the trains of the Northern Pacific and the Great Northern rolled further westward, carrying young men away to their uncertain futures.

THE GIRL SEEMS SURPRISED.

"Now that I look at it," she says, frowning at her computer screen, "we do have you booked." She shrugs. "New system, it's driving everybody crazy."

From the reception desk Dudley can hear the MIDI noise of the slots. The girl looks kind of Indian, pretty in a plump, youthful way. He tries to avoid looking down at the ubiquitous carpet, a swirly, petit-mal epilepsy trigger of purple and orange.

"Just the one week?"

"That's right." If he needs to stay longer he can hack into their system again.

"May I see a credit card for incidentals?"

He gives her the Amex, which charges through the Company. At least for now.

"Dudley Nickles," she reads off the plastic. "There's a girl I know in town named Dollarhide."

"And you probably listen to Johnny Cash."

"My grandfather does."

He's supposed to be here incognito, none of the rig managers or field staff aware of his visit till he's ensconced in their trailers, but there's no need for disguise. He's always been like the people caught on Google Earth, faces a feature-less smear no matter what activity they're engaged in. Muddy Duddy, the wags at HQ back in Houston call him, when it's not Studly Dudley or Nickles and Dimes or just plain The Dud. In five minutes she'll forget he existed. In a week–

"You have a vehicle?"

There are so many pickups parked in the lot, she's learned to use the generic nomenclature. Dudley slides the keys for the rental to her, the license number written on the tab. The girl keyboards it in. Somebody shouts from the casino floor, a winner. He's been into their slot machine database, tracked the last two weeks of payoffs. No advantage there, somebody who knows their job constantly adjusting the machines. When he was in college he was in a posse that hit casinos, counting blackjack cards– five tech students ambling from table to table to allay suspicion, one or the other retiring to the bathroom for a few minutes at a time, with a set of signals to pass on to the counter taking your place. Two-up, one-up, even, one-down, two-down. That simple, just a statistical hiccup and you had the slightest edge on the house, which meant if you all played without tactical error you'd aggregate between five and ten grand an evening. Twice, the others were asked to leave and Dudley ignored. Like he wasn't there.

He almost never comes to the scene of the grime. But they're remodeling in Houston, new computer system, lighting, layout, the whole nine yards, and Boomer said, "Dud, get you a pair of shitkicker boots and pack your GPS, you're heading to the Bakken." Then a thump on the back. Boomer thumps him, in passing, once or twice a week. "Like to check an see you're still *there*, buddy."

The girl gives him back his car keys and encodes the entry card for the room, number 108 around the back, as he requested in the hack. The door-lock memory will be battery operated and not connected to the front desk, but it keeps a printable log of time, date, and key code for every entry. Next they'll monitor when and how often you flush the toilet.

"It's just through the casino floor on the left," she says, handing him his Amex and the entry card and pasting on a smile she's obviously received a memo about. "I hope you have time to enjoy our gymnasium and spa facilities during your stay."

And be sure to drop a bundle in the betting parlor.

The room is fine, buffalo roaming on the wall and a view of the parking lot. Dudley opens his suitcase on the stand, pulls out his computer and sets it up on the little desk, uses his smartphone to connect to the internet, bypassing the hotel's link. He opens the diet cola and Cheetos he bought in the gift shop, hangs his jacket in the closet, brings up the records of all the Company's drilling operations in the Bakken play.

Locked and loaded.

THE PARTS WHERE YOU'RE strapped to the chair and interrogated make his stomach hurt. Or maybe it's just the double cheeseburger with bacon settling in. The idea is that you, inside of Alex Mason, are going to be jolted back into memories of Black Ops missions, complete with firefights and hand-to-hand combat. Since I'm here in the chair, thinks Dickyboy, I must not have gotten whacked in any of the flashbacks, though it seems I was probably brainwashed to do some killing for the enemy–

Georgie Price, who graduated last year and manages this shift, lets him play in one of the corner booths as long as he buys something. It's mostly drive-thru action anyway, the oil workers wanting to grab and go, and he's finished the burger and fries and is working on his second vanilla shake. With the headset on you only hear the soundtrack from the game, running his xBox 360 onto a little stand-up

monitor. Nothing like the flat-screen on the den wall at Dylan's, but Dylan's parents have him on lockdown for the week.

Which kind of puts a dent in the old financial outlook.

Now I'm in what– Cuba? Trying to assassinate this guy with a beard, all the
politics flying at you fast and furious if you don't word up on the game before
you start playing it.

The shit hits the fan again and his fingers fly on the controller. He's playing
single-shooter today but has beat every local player he knows and kicked some
ass online. The graphics are so much better in this new version, he thinks, blasting away, only he should be smelling cordite and not French fries.

Things get confusing again– did he actually assassinate Fidel Castro or only
a look-alike and should he take advantage of his kill-streak reward to call in a
chopper gunner to get all these Spetznatz commandos off his back– and for
some reason he looks up from the screen and sees Fawn pull into the lot in a
baby-blue Miata.

She's with her posse, Tina Dollarhide and poor Jolene, pushing in through
the door with that little strut of hers, look at me, I got the goods, blowing right
by him to the counter without a glance. The other two stop so he puts the game
on hold.

Tina says something and he realizes he's still got the headset on.

"*Grand Theft Auto?*" she repeats when he's snatched them off.

"*Call of Duty.*"

"That's like, really violent, right?"

"Uhm, yeah, there's a lot of fighting and assassinations." He looks to Jolene.
"But you can set it for less blood and cut out all the cursing if you want."

As if Jolene might be a gamer. Jolene who is standing here but not really
meeting his eye, knowing that everybody knows what happened.

"You get points for how many people you kill?"

"It's a *story* you're in, and it's– it's kind of educational, this one, all this stuff
about the Cold War."

"Which was?"

"Like in the '60s, I think? So far it's the US and Russia and Cuba, but there's
like this old Nazi who invented Nova 6 nerve gas and has sleeper agents waiting
to release it."

"This really happened?"

"No, not exactly. It's like alternative history."

"Uh-huh."

He missed school today, overslept in the boat. He's told his grandmother he's staying with his uncle, his uncle that he's staying with his cousin, and his cousin that he's staying with Dylan and so far nobody's thought to call the school and see if he's showing up.

Not that anybody's likely to care one way or the other.

"That car is the bomb," he says, looking out to the Miata. "The Chairman must be doing okay for himself."

Tina makes a face. "It wasn't him. It was that guy."

Dickyboy knows who 'that guy' is. Very hot topic in the cafeteria.

"Well, wheels are wheels."

They say nice to see you, then get in line to order. Tina is nice for a Yellow Earth girl, no attitude about you being from the rez, and Jolene is the one of her old friends Fawn kept when she transferred out after junior high. *Friends* might be pushing it some, Jolene probably flattered just to tag along with the Savage Princess and after what happened really glad to stand by somebody who draws all the attention away from her. Fawn will have them sit on the other side of the room, so she can talk loud about how fat he's gotten.

Fawn who is looking really puffy now.

But he's got more pressing issues to deal with– chopper down and in flames, the van turned over with machine-gun fire tearing it to shreds, Alex Mason neck-deep in the shit again, got to think fast, how to respond, how to survive– Dickyboy falls back on his old reliable.

Dragon's Breath rounds.

PEOPLE ARE A SEPARATE skill. He's been painting for a long time, feels like he's got a pretty good handle on it, but whenever he's done people they've been way off on the horizon. Couple little strokes with the tip of the brush, indicate the way they bend to the wind, carry a pail. For a full-face job, a portrait, you've got to get the flesh tones right.

Which he's never tried before.

Clemson mixes from the dabs of primaries, making little splotches on the palette, storehouses of the shades he thinks he'll need, referring constantly to the photograph. The snap is from three years ago, with a real camera, not one of these telephone deals, Tina with her feeder calf before the county fair, smiling at the lens with an aerosol can of show foam in her hand. It was the last year she did the 4-H, a three-month-old they'd bought from Wiley Cobb. She'd named it Jonas, after some boy singing group she liked then, and worked with the animal every day.

He mixes the yellow ochre and cadmium red, dulls it down a bit with ultramarine blue. Splotch of orange, splotch of pink, a bunch in between, a blue that looks good with them. Tina was out in the sun a lot in those days, had a bit of a farmer's tan. Her eyes will be easy, at least the colored part of them, and he's already thinking about how to do denim up close. It won't be just like the photograph, it should be more how the picture makes him *feel* when he looks at it. There are much more recent shots of her, of course, but he doesn't know that girl nearly as much as he did this one.

He tried to paint his wife once, from memory, and never got too far.

She won't be staying around, he can tell that much. Whether it's college, which would be good, which would be what her parents wanted, or something else, she'll be gone next year. His mission is to make sure she doesn't feel too bad about it, encourage her to leave the nest. He helped with the calf when she asked, but it was supposed to be her project and she took that seriously. Before, when he was doing more with the land, she couldn't bear to be left out, always full of questions, wanting to hold the other end of things. 'My shadow,' he used to call her.

He's done the fence rails, the barn in the background, putting it in cloud shadow so the red doesn't overwhelm the frame. With the calf he did the castrating, and after that Tina took over, hauling sacks of feed and buckets of water, getting up early before school, spray washing the animal once a month. The problem when you've only got one is that it gets lonely and forgets it's a cow, and you start treating it like a pet. She'd seen sheep slaughtered at Prairie Packing, but there's something different when there's so many, the mind flips a switch and it's like you're in a factory. So even with winning best in class at the fair and selling Jonas for a profit if you didn't count all the hours of work she'd put in, Tina told him it was her last. They'd both looked so good in the arena, Spartina straight and strong, the young beef shaved, scotch-combed, and oiled, thrifty and long-bodied.

Clemson dots a little titanium white into one of the blotches, mixes it in. Oils are great for surface, but it takes a lot of skill to suggest what lies just beneath. The way Tina's cheeks would glow when she was happy or excited, the special light in her eyes. The shape of her smile in a face yet devoid of creases. Tears drop on the palette and Clemson has to wick them away with a Kleenex. Oil and water don't mix.

He sits back to look at the empty part of the canvas, the big hole where Tina should be. This is going to be really difficult, he thinks, and decides to start on Jonas.

Cattle are easy.

"Guy just asked for you," says Shakes, smeared with black from changing tires.

Scorch looks out through the dirty window. Skinny character, leaning against a white Ford Focus and looking around as if there's anything to see.

"I'll check him out."

Brent bought the garage when he set up the service company, a spot to do whatever repair work was needed on the old dinosaurs he brought up from Texas and overbilled the company for. Plus the long-haulers carrying product always stop here first. He's okayed Scorch, not officially on the payroll, using it for a pickup spot, which keeps all his commerce away from the club.

The skinny guy looks appropriately intimidated when he gets an eyeful of the tats.

"I help you?"

"You're Scorch?"

"That's right. What seems to be the problem?"

This, nodding toward the car.

"I was told that you could– like– hook me up."

Scorch lays a look on the guy. Shiny black shoes, silky blue shirt, bow tie. Who the fuck wears a bow tie?

"How exactly did you get my name?"

"You know, people say things."

"I need a name."

The Indian casino maybe. There's like a uniform they wear–

"Doyle."

Doyle is at the casino, tends bar in the lounge. Bingo.

"Let's see what we've got here," says Scorch, popping the hood and raising it up. "See if I can do anything for you."

Narcs have stamina but not much imagination. The plates tell him the car is a rental, the sweat on the character's forehead as he leans in to stare at the engine says he's nervous or strung out or both.

"You know, if you just call Enterprise," says Scorch, playing it out a bit further, "they'll bring you a new ride and take this one back to their shop."

"There's something coming out of the crankcase," says the skinny guy. "Sort of like black tar."

Very cute.

Scorch is a bike guy, ride em but don't fix em, and a car engine to him is just a bunch of metal shit and hoses.

"Smoking?"

"Yeah, smoking," says the skinny guy. He looks more like a meth head, but whatever floats your boat–

"Chasing the dragon, are we?"

"Can you hook me up or not?"

Tough on all the pilgrims who come in here, have to find a new connection. One of the ArrowFleet haulers rolls in, sounding like shit. A job for the real mechanics.

"How much are we talking about?"

Shiny shoes, silky shirt, bow tie– must be a dealer. One dealer to another.

"Uhm– it depends on how much it goes for."

"Hundred-twenty a gram."

A quick calculation. Casino dealers can sling numbers with anybody.

"How do I know it's worth that? The quality?"

"What's your name?"

He could give a phony one, of course, but it doesn't matter. You just need something to hang on a guy if he's going to be a regular, going to bring you other customers.

"Lenny."

"It's like this, Lenny. Buy what you think you can afford, and if you don't like it, don't come back to me. *Caveat emptor.*" Brent taught him that phrase and he loves the sound of it. "You want a half a gram?"

"I don't want to keep coming down here."

As if they'll start selling it at the Albertsons.

"So?"

"I'll take two."

Scorch gives him a quick pat down. Nothing under the silky shirt.

"Jesus."

"For your protection and mine, Lenny. Lay the cash on the engine block, then go back into our restroom– it's just past the service desk, go in and play with yourself or whatever for a couple minutes. When you come back out it'll be in your glove compartment."

The skinny guy leaves a pile of bank-fresh twenties and goes inside. Scorch slips the money into his shirt pocket, lets the hood down, heads back to his tool-box. He couldn't name half the shit in it, but from under a ring of washers he pulls out a little envelope with the shit in it, the stuff that's been coming up baked hard, like a little chip of coal. He's on his way back to the Focus when Wayne Lee rolls up in his Camaro, shit-eating grin on his face like always.

"Yo, Mr. Badwrench!" he calls. "Good to see you minding the store."

"You making a run?"

"Just looking for your boss."

If he has a boss it's Vic at the club. With Brent he's just an independent con-tractor.

"Haven't seen him all day. Don't know if he'll be in."

"Well tell him I stopped by. We need to parley."

"Is that a good idea?"

"Maybe you'd like to referee."

Scorch holds up his hands. "Leave me out of it."

Wayne Lee laughs and drives off and Scorch puts the shit in the glove com-partment, goes back inside. He watches the skinny guy come out and sit into the car, check to see that the deal has been completed, then zoom away to wherever he's going to fire up.

The beauty of simple commerce, thinks Scorch. Buy low, sell high.

THE CALL CAME IN just after he left the office, Julie on the radio, saying to call his sister for an emergency. He waited in traffic to pull into the Walmart lot, but then the radio again and a wreck out on 1804.

It's a kid he recognizes from before, the Mustang totaled, the guy driving the water hauler pissed that he's losing time.

"My brake lights were working fine!" he yells before Will is completely out of the patrol car. "He must have been fucking asleep back there."

His father, the Colonel, is retired, wings folded, kicking back in Colorado Springs. Plays some golf, hikes twice a week, grumbles about politicians giving away the store. He brags that he's only five pounds over his weight when he went to the Academy and still operates on military time, rising precisely at 0700 hours.

The kid is sitting on a hummock just off the road, an I-don't-care look on his face. On another day Will might bother to walk around, kick the weeds for whatever pharmaceuticals he's dumped.

"You hurt?" he asks the boy, who just shakes his head.

"Want to tell me what happened?"

"I rear-ended the dude."

"I didn't even hear brakes," says the glowering trucker. "It was stop-and-go for like fifteen minutes, only this dipshit forgets to *stop*." The trucker has already written down his company information, insurance, phone number on a slip of paper. Will looks back to the boy.

"I must have just spaced out."

He still looks pretty spacey. The Mustang is halfway off the road, hood like an accordion bellows, and the water hauler parked up ahead without much damage visible on the rear.

"Can I get out of here?" asks the trucker.

"You don't feel any twinges in your back or your neck?"

"I've got four thousand gallons of shock absorber in that tank. Didn't feel a jolt."

He's called Julie to send the wrecker. Traffic is slowed but moving around the Mustang, and Tolliver will be here in a minute to wave people through, cut down on the gawk time. He hands the trucker his license back.

"You can go ahead."

There was a heart thing a couple years back, the Colonel ordering them not to call it an attack, that hastened his retirement. He didn't love teaching, even if it was for the next generation of birdmen. He liked to say there was *flying* and then there was garbage time.

Being home with the wife and kids was not flying.

"Stand up."

The boy stands, not too shaky.

"You're sure you aren't hurt?"

There's no airbag in a car that old, but he doesn't see any dents in the kid. The boy takes a couple steps, shrugs his shoulders.

"Not even sore."

"Let me smell your breath."

The kid opens his mouth wide to send out a blast.

"Arby's?"

"About an hour ago."

"Okay, Jason."

"Dylan."

"Right, Dylan. I'll take you back to the department office."

With alcohol you want to do the test on site, but the other possibilities hang in the blood longer. He hears the siren approaching. Tolliver loves the siren. Will guides Dylan into the back seat, throws the flasher on, gives a *bwoop* for the civilian drivers to make room and turns between them to head back toward town, stopping to roll his window down and call to the deputy.

"Give the car a shakedown when you get a chance."

Will puts his own siren on then, driving mostly on the shoulder to pass the inbound stuff.

"He won't find anything," says Dylan.

"You never know. People sample their own product, they get sloppy."

The kid shrugs again but Will sees him check out the mile marker as they pass it. Stuff in a ziplock bag somewhere in the field probably and he'll get a ride back out when he can to try to find it.

"DWI while on probation, you're going to lose your license, Dylan. Might be some criminal charges, depending. You could do yourself a favor."

"Not interested."

"Whoever is selling to you is in deep shit, and if we find out *you*'ve been selling–"

The boy closes his eyes and puts his head back against the seat.

Will can't remember much about the first couple bases they lived on, all stateside. Then the Colonel, only a captain then, was transferred to Minot to fly B-52s for the Strategic Air Command. 'Part of the triad of national defense,' he used to say. The marriage blew apart pretty soon after that, and his mother moved them to Lignite and got back into teaching in Yellow Earth, Will and his sister ensconced in their first completely civilian housing. Every weekend he was shuttled over to the base, the Colonel grilling him in math and science, encouraging him to develop a good technical understanding despite his low opinion of the 'rocket geeks' who shared the real estate. And there was the assumption, always, that like father like son, and talk of the senator who would vouch for Will when it came time to apply for the Academy.

"You got your cell phone?"

"Yup." Without opening his eyes.

"You want to call your parents?"

"Not especially."

"Our holding cell is pretty basic," he tells the boy. "A bench, a sink, common toilet. No TV."

Dylan squirms to pull his phone from his pocket, flips it open. "I got no bars out here."

"You can call them when we get to the office."

Will remembers from the first time that the father was a lawyer and drove up in a black Lexus.

Julie is on the radio again.

"We have a complaint from ArrowFleet," she says. "Trying to service a well over in– "

"A. J. Niles?"

"Obstructing access."

"I'll drop this one off and swing out there."

With Julie he doesn't bother with all the '10-4' stuff unless the deputies are involved. Don't want them to get too relaxed.

His mother sparred with the Colonel for a while, then surrendered Will to military school in Virginia for two years. But the asthma and the discipline problems gave him an out. He hated wearing a uniform, hated taking orders all the time, and unlike his father had never stayed up nights staring at the heavens and dreaming of flight. His sister at least leaves the ground a few times a week now, though stewardess is more of a waitressing job than being master of the skies. The asthma, which involved prescriptions of bronchodilators and corticosteroids and one scary trip to the emergency room, was the equivalent of losing an eye for anyone who wanted to be a pilot.

Which he didn't.

"Any idea what you'd like to do with your life?"

The boy opens his eyes again, thinks.

"I know things I *don't* want to do."

"That's all I knew at your age, but it's a start. I'm not a career counselor, but I'd advise against the drug-dealer option. The people who make it in that field are real go-getters. Entrepreneurial skills. And you"– he glances into the rearview mirror– "don't strike me as the self-starter type."

Dylan has nothing to say.

So back to Yellow Earth High, were he stayed out of trouble, played sports just for fun, and had no problems with his breathing. Thinking about it, he began to suspect it was the uniform itself, a fabric he was allergic to, but kept this idea to himself.

"How's school?" the Colonel would say on his visits, Sundays only now because there were games on Saturdays. It clearly pained him to see Will in civilian clothes. The Colonel would take Will around to introduce him to support personnel on the base, vital to the defense effort but clearly lesser creatures than the men who slipped the surly bonds of Earth. He remembers watching the Colonel endure a barrage of insults from a pair of fighter pilots, all implying that being a jockey on what they called a Big Ugly Fat Fucker was something akin to driving a bus, until he shut them down with a reminder of the superior destructive potential of his payload, quoting Oppenheimer.

"I am become Death, destroyer of worlds."

If it wasn't the Academy, the Colonel really didn't care where or if Will went to college, so he tried UND for a couple years, majoring in Psych, till even the in-state tuition seemed like a waste.

Payton is in the office and takes Dylan for the urine test. Will calls his sister.

"The Colonel's gone," she says.

He is not surprised.

"Heart?"

"A stroke, this morning on the golf course."

"At least he wasn't behind the controls."

The Colonel had a little Cessna Skycatcher, flew it up to Sloulin Field once and took Will for a steak at the El Rancho Hotel restaurant. 'Your basic transportation,' he called it, but went up a couple times a week just to look around.

"Can you get down? I'm hitching a flight to Denver."

"Yeah. I'll see you at his house."

She isn't crying. As a girl she was both off the Colonel's hook and beneath his radar.

"Some finish, huh?" she says. "The guys he was with say he'd just sunk a putt, bent over to pick up the ball, said 'Oh no,' and that was it."

Will sees Payton on the way out.

"That boy sure had to pee. Two days for the verdict. I called the mother to come take him to Mercy– he could be all fucked up internally and not feel it."

"You book him?"

"He's in the system, reckless driving and probation violation for the moment. Took his license away for safekeeping."

There was dope in the high school back in the '90s, and Will smoked his share of it, though he never reached full pothead status. Locally grown stuff as far as he knew, not very potent, and none of the heavier drugs they saw on the news or in cop shows. There were amphetamines and even coke in Yellow Earth and on the reservation before the shale oil hit, but nothing like now, the Stupid Behavior Index shooting up within a week of the invasion.

He counts three pump jacks on Wiley Cobb's property, visible from the 2, one of them with a stack spewing flame next to it. He turns up the bumpy access road, still just Caterpillar tracks, onto the Niles place. A quarter mile in he comes to a huge rust farm of a tractor, an old Massey Ferguson that A. J. has parked across the road and pulled the front wheels off of. Hell of a lot of work just to make a point.

There are two ArrowFleet fuel tankers waiting to get in and one waiting to get out.

"The first time he left the wheels on and we rolled it," says one of the truckers. "We go in that field after this rain, tank empty or full, we'll get bogged down for sure."

Even in the patrol car it's pretty hairy, one hummock after another and sinkholes in between. Picked the perfect spot for a blockade.

The Colonel was still just young enough to be allowed to fly missions in Desert Storm, nothing he would go into detail about, and remained tight-lipped about the fact that Will did not enlist. But he was married to Sheila then, a bad idea, and trying to start a construction business, a worse one. Liking to work with tools and knowing how to make a reasonable bid and control a half-dozen employees were clearly distinct aspects of the trade, and at the time Yellow Earth was in something of a building slump. The marriage ended without children or any terrible fireworks, and three years of nail-gunning for Gunnar Bjornson's roofing outfit got him square with the vendors in town. His mother had remarried and moved to California and he was thinking of following to check it out, when old Sam Kearny, who'd had the job for as long as anyone could remember, announced he was packing it in.

The guys on his crew used to call Will 'the sheriff' when he'd walk on site, because he wouldn't let them fudge on the building codes and made them clean up the work space every night.

"Watch it, here comes the sheriff!"

So it was kind of a joke when Lou Josephson from the Democrats asked him to throw his name in, embarrassing to leave a slot empty on the ballot even if Sam's long-time deputy was a shoo-in. Though Sam was mysteriously noncommittal on the subject.

"Let the boys run," he said.

Will didn't campaign much, standing up at rallies to say a few words, the newcomer at the bottom of the ticket. But he read up on the job, even went to talk to Sam about what he thought the position should be.

And then the long-time deputy's wife sued for divorce, citing years of physical abuse, with one post-beating photograph that garnered a slew of hits on the Web.

"You look good," said the Colonel the first time he saw Will in the uniform, a cotton/synthetic blend that didn't even make him sniffle. "You look like you mean business."

And once Will got used to the idea he found that he actually liked it, liked having a window into people's lives, even if two times out of three they weren't exactly thrilled to see him drive up.

A. J. Niles, in fact, looks markedly unenthusiastic about his presence. A. J. has pulled a chair out onto his porch and is looking beyond Will to a pair of jacks bobbing up and down on his front forty, pumping crude oil that will add nothing to his personal worth.

"It's my land," he says. "I can leave my equipment wherever I want to."

"We've been over this before, A. J."

"I own the *sur*face. The tractor is on the surface."

"Mineral rights include access. You want the Company guy out here with a court order?"

"It shouldn't be legal."

"If you've got some modifications to the law, some restrictions to unbridled commerce to suggest, I'm sure your elected representatives would love to hear them."

The last time he talked with Press Earle the mayor told him it was mostly complaints now, how could the city, how could the *state* let these oil people ride roughshod over everything?

Not that we want them to leave.

"They got machinery," says A. J. "Let em come and move their road around it."

"That will cost them money, and you cost them money they will sue you and they will *win*. Believe me."

The last time he talked to the Colonel, only two weeks ago, he got to say it. Just under the wire, as it turns out.

"You know, Dad, I always thought it was really cool what you did. Important. It was just never what I wanted to do with my own life."

A long silence over the phone. "I thought about getting that asthma business expunged," his father said finally. "Wipe your record clean. But then I'd picture you up at forty thousand feet, trying to suck air out of your oxygen mask with your lungs shut tight."

At least A. J. doesn't have the shotgun lying across his knees, the one he keeps in the kitchen utility closet in case of Third World invasion. He's in the wrong and he knows it, a dangerous combination.

"I'll tell you what we're going to do," Will says, turning to look out at the pump jacks, bobbing, bobbing, out of sync with each other. "We'll throw those tractor tires and whatever else you need in the back of your pickup and head down that access road. I'm sure those truckers will lend us a hand when we get there."

THEY SPEND A HALF hour recording trucks rolling over rumble strips. Press watches them from his office window, the soundman with a machine hung over his shoulder, holding the boom microphone almost to the pavement as they parade by. He calls Jonesy in.

"What are they doing?"

"What does it look like?"

"They came all this way for traffic noise?"

"It's *our* traffic noise. That's what they do, they put authentic sound effects in with the interview, to give you a feeling for the place."

Phyllis listens to it while she makes dinner, which means he tries to be in a different part of the house. The theme songs alone drive him up a wall, and all the male announcers are named Scott and sound like they went to the same Ivy League universities their fathers went to. Now and then, if that Terry Gross has

somebody interesting enough on he'll listen to a bit, but when the request came
in he took a long time before saying yes.

He pulls the city map down, arranges his desk. He knows there's no visuals,
but it makes him feel more confident, like a sea captain flying his colors. Jonesy
brings the young woman, the interviewer, in. She's African American but doesn't
sound like it, probably how she got the radio job, and must be turning some
heads here in Yellow Earth.

"How long have you been in office here?"

They're good at hiding attitude if they have one, about being strangers up
here in the high plains. It's the sixth or maybe seventh interview he's done, the
third with a national outlet, and what's never said is that if they didn't think
there was something *wrong* going on they wouldn't be here. It's one thing to
be the man in the spotlight, trapeze bar in hand, and another to be the geek in
the sideshow.

"Halfway through my second term," he tells her. "So I was here well before
the boom."

The soundman comes up then and clips one of the little body mics on him
and another onto the interviewer, whose name is Reese, Reese as a first name,
like Prescott. The soundman also has the boom microphone on a pole, and has
Press count off a few times to get a level. Jonesy turns the ringer off the phone in
the next room.

"We're talking with mayor Prescott Earle in Yellow Earth, North Dakota," says
Reese in her non-radio voice, then looks up at him, raising her eyebrows. He
wonders if she knows she does that, or does it on purpose.

"Let's get straight into it," she says. "Talk about the biggest changes, positive
and negative, which have come to your city with the fracking."

The F Word.

"Well, first of all, hydraulic fracturing is only one part of the resource recovery process. There are so many different phases, each with its own procedures
and specialists involved, and we have wells in all of these stages, from drilling
to stimulation to actual production, in play simultaneously. Our population has
increased threefold, with the attendant pressure on infrastructure and social
services."

A mouthful, but when Jonesy wrote it for him she assured him it could be
delivered in one breath.

"So is this good or bad?"

"Everything," he says, "has its price. Development means change, in some cases dislocation. But I can tell you that in purely economic terms, wages here have gone up far more than the cost of living."

"That's across the board?"

"Oh, our teachers and other public officials aren't making any more than they used to, but our service employees and small businessmen are doing very well."

"And some people have gotten wealthy from selling oil leases."

Phyllis's brother, for instance, who has never had a clue how to support a family, has three wells pumping on his formerly worthless thirty-five acres–

"I'm not one of them," says Press, smiling the smile, "but yes, we've had some folks experience quite a windfall."

"Will those people stay?"

"Too early to tell, but I imagine many of them will be spending our winters in a warmer climate."

"If you could kind of repeat the question in your answers," say Reese, "it would be really helpful."

He always forgets that part. This isn't a conversation, he reminds himself, but an opportunity to position Yellow Earth, to position himself, in people's minds. A branding exercise.

"I'll try to do that."

"Have you seen an increase in crime?"

"We've seen an increase in every statistic related to the population tripling in size overnight."

"And most of those people are men."

If you know the answer, he thinks, why ask the question?

"The sort of rapid growth we've experienced here presents unique challenges. Housing has been particularly difficult, despite the efforts of the energy companies to put up their own facilities. So many people other than rig workers come along for the carnival."

"Robberies, drunken driving, rapes?"

We're a modern-day Sodom and Gomorrah, he thinks. You have to step over dead bodies on the sidewalks–

"You'd have to speak with our chief of police and county sheriff for those details. I personally notice the change most dramatically at the gas station. There didn't use to be lines at the pumps."

It has slacked off quite a bit lately, and Phyllis says it's the same at the Albertsons. But you don't want to spread the rumor that it's about to bust–

"Do you think the average– Yellow Earther? Yellow Earthling?– "

"Resident of Yellow Earth."

"Do you think they view all this as a positive or a negative experience?"

"It's so personal– there is no *average* resident of our city. The complaints are mostly about traffic and noise, but then there are some shared benefits. We have a new sports facility, built hand in hand with the energy companies, about to open. Everybody's water bill has gone down."

Gone down because the county has been selling water at inflated rates to the oil companies. And about to shoot up again now that the companies say they're done fracking for the moment and won't be needing so much–

"Do you think– can I call this an invasion?"

"We've had a rapid *in*flux of activity."

"How do you think it's affected the women in your community?"

They have their story written no matter what you say, just fishing for sound bites that fit the plot line.

"You should talk to my assistant," he says, indicating the door that separates their offices. "She'll have a better perspective on that issue. She works with girls."

And is capable of tearing you a new one if you get out of line. Jonesy has been keeping him up on the environmental impact, on the downtown crime wave, on the companies overstepping their mandate here and there, on the mood of the people who will still be here to vote when most of it goes away.

Because it *will* go away.

"If you had to work the scoreboard," says Reese, smiling for the first time, "Big Oil versus Yellow Earth, how do you think the match is going so far?"

"I don't accept the idea that we're in adversarial positions," Press answers. Now the Democrats, of all people, have also gotten in touch to see if he wants to drop the Independent act and run for lieutenant governor in 2012. No thank you, and I wouldn't care to throw myself off the top of the State Capitol Building, highest structure in North Dakota, either. "But if you see it as a contest between our city and a potentially disastrous natural phenomenon, like a tornado or a tidal wave– "

This feels like the punch line, the bit they're likely to actually use in their piece–

"–I'd say we've fought it to a *draw*."

They're setting up in the next room, taking his advice to interview Jonesy, when he approaches with a slip of city hall stationery.

"My wife is such a huge fan," he says to the black girl. "Could I trouble you for an autograph?"

DUD IS CERTAIN HE'S seen the same girl do her routine in one of the strip mall clubs in Houston. That hard hat, the tool belt that comes off first and has all the naughty battery-operated necessities in it. Who would have thought Makita made one of those? He lays a twenty on the bar counter, leans in very close to the girl sitting beside him– she's a woman, actually, still a babe but no kid– to be heard over the throbbing music.

"Here's the deal– was it Janelle?"

"Jewelle."

"I don't need more liquor, I don't want a lap dance, but one of these is yours anytime to want to come over and rest your feet for a few minutes without the floor supervisor busting your chops. Tell the other girls there's more where that came from."

"You're a generous man."

"Just redistributing a little wealth. Good night at the casino."

He had played poker with live bodies, a couple of the players with some game, one poor old Indian guy who was too drunk, or maybe too rich, to keep track of how much he was bleeding. There were computer poker machines behind them with intent acolytes pushing the buttons, an abomination even if you can hack them. "I own your *soul*," said Boomer to a commodities guy he fleeced the one night Dudley was invited to the big boys' game. Dudley pretended to be intimidated by the stakes and walked away with a wad of Other People's Money. He is known as a quiet, conservative player, just a fill-in at the table between the titans who've come to do battle. 'Dud does awright for himself,' say the good old boys, 'but he don't ever clean *up*.'

True if you don't make a *per annum* tally, which none of the good steady losers bother to do. Last year he took over eight thousand dollars off Dippy Beauregard and nearly seventeen grand from Hump Phillips. Not their souls exactly, but there is real satisfaction watching their faces, discreetly, while you rake in their green stuff. It helps to pile your winnings neatly, blushing a little at the anal accountant jokes, and palm some of it off the table during the night.

"Did she use to work in Houston?" he asks, nodding at the now upside-down pole dancer in the mirror.

"Don't see why not," says Jewelle. "It's a popular stop on the circuit. Wherever she's from, the bitch stole my routine."

There are men at headquarters and elsewhere throughout the Company's far-flung empire who are afraid of him, at least the ones who know he's an actual person and not just a concept. The Determinator, some call him, the guy who figures out if your job is necessary, or if one employee can handle the work presently done by three, or if you're too high on the pay scale and should be replaced by somebody younger, hungrier, cheaper. 'Don't fuck with the Determinator,' they joke, and leave him pretty much alone. Boomer and the others above him are good business heads but not facile with the numbers technology, and at times he feels like an overpaid IT scrub. Well, not *that* overpaid.

"I liked your routine."

"Thank you."

"Some of the girls just spin around on it and wiggle their stuff, but you– it was like a real *dance*."

"Thanks. I used to love to dance."

"And you don't any more?"

"If there was a disco in Yellow Earth," she says, "you could take me to it."

"Sorry. I've got a black belt in dancing. People get hurt."

She bumps against him playfully. "I bet you're not that bad. You just have to let *go*."

"You have no idea. People call 911."

"Anyway," says Jewelle, "you ride that pole a couple hours a night, it takes some of the hop out of you. Like you figure those Indians that used to do their rain dances, for like a ritual? Then they start doing them for tour buses, three, four times a day, and it's not the same thing."

"Going through the motions."

"And you never get the love back."

"But you're doing good here?"

"Business-wise? Sure." She shrugs. "Though the rent's high and it's– you know– kind of an Alaska Pipeline vibe."

"Hairy mountain men lacking the social graces."

She grins a nonprofessional grin. "They're just men away from home, the ones that claim a home. You from Houston?"

"Used to be. Right now I'm in transit."

"From where to where?"

Enigmatic is always better than the real you. All of these girls have club names, have to for security and mental health purposes, and have a doctored story to tell if you want to pay to hear it.

"Oh," says Dudley, "from this barstool to the rest of my life."

Jewelle smiles again and gets up from her stool, putting her hand on his shoulder for support. A little touch is nice, even if you've bought it. He had a female barber once, did the little palm-vibrator thing on his neck at the end of the cut, always made him hum in appreciation.

"If you're still around, Mr. In Transit, I might come park myself here some a bit later."

Then Jewelle is gone and so is the twenty.

AMERICANS MELT CHEESE ON everything. Gaspar has told him that the plates with cheese on them won't come clean just going through the *lavavajillas*, hot and powerful as it is, and have to be scrubbed first. But it seems like two out of every three plates that come back have some sort of cheese stuck on them, baked on in the case of the onion soup, and have to sit for a moment in the soapy water sink with the pot pie bowls before Macario can even get busy with the scrubbing sponges. The cooks are shouting for sauté pans so he tackles those first, then blasts a rack Orestes the Guatemalan has filled with plates with the spray hose before pushing it into the machine to get hammered with scalding water for a half a minute, time to scrub one soup pot, then hustling around to pull the rack out and roll it to the Haitian, whose name is Dauphin, who will dry the glasses and stack everything back at the bussing stations. Macario is sweating already, a half hour into the shift, wearing a black trash bag like a poncho the way the others do, relying on his years of *fútbol* to dodge around bodies and equipment and stay in the rhythm of the cleanup galley.

There is nothing in Mexico, he muses, that stains a plate as thoroughly as blueberry pie.

"*Adelante, muchachos!*" shouts Gaspar over the attack of the dishwasher and the sharp banging of metal and ceramic. "*A toda velocidad!*"

Gaspar is the senior man on the crew, the one who ran into Macario in City Park and told him there was an opening at the restaurant.

"Gringo comfor' food," he said in English. "Lotsa burger, *macaroni y queso.*"

Reuben, the fry cook, brings in real corn tortillas and makes them tacos for the staff meal, which half the time they eat standing up. The job pays seven-fifty an hour, twenty-five cents more than the minimum wage, and so far Macario has not been able to wire anything home. When he ran out of money in San Antonio he got on a patio-laying crew that paid a little bit better, but had to put in for the house they were all sharing and his share of gas for the van that got them to jobs and to eat and to buy new work shoes after the old ones got ruined fording the river when he saw the *Migra* set up checking identification on the bridge, and to share a couple beers with the *muchachos* every week–

A busboy, one of the new hires, thumps a plastic tub loaded with dinner dishes onto the counter and Macario is on it, scraping uneaten food into the trash with a chunk of garlic bread. They don't wear gloves, which tire your fingers and make you drop things, and he's gotten used to his hands being burned and being as wrinkled as raisins by the end of a shift. Orestes is grabbing the plates from Macario as soon as he can clear them, the three *lavaplatos* immediately dealing with whatever is in front of them rather than breaking the job into stations, all without words except for Gaspar's shouts of encouragement.

"*Rápido, rápido!*" he cries. "*El Yaxon* getting hungry!"

The huge, rumbling and hissing dishwasher that everything in the galley revolves around is made by a company called Jackson, and Gaspar treats it like a monster that must be fed to keep it tame. All the restaurant ceramics are white, and it has begun to please Macario more than he can account for to see them coming out of *Yaxon* only slightly wet and gleaming, like the milk bottles used to illustrate a pure soul in the *catecismo* he was given to study in church as a boy. When he worked on the oil platforms you could spray till you ran out of water and the deck would never really come clean.

It is a Saturday night, voices of the diners surging through whenever a busboy butts through the swinging door, and there is no letup in the flood of dirty dishes and utensils, nothing but the immediate task that needs to be done or everything will back up and there will be a meltdown. Sometimes he imagines they are the firemen on an old locomotive, shoveling coal to fuel the boiler to make the steam to keep the engine speeding ahead, and sometimes it's a war and they are feeding artillery shells as fast as they can to ward off a charging enemy, and sometimes it's just Macario sweating his *culo* off supplying clean plates to overfed *gringos* and making just enough to keep his own head above the water.

Gaspar has a phone, and twice now he's been able to borrow it to call Nilda in Yucatán, telling her he's doing all he can, that he hasn't forgotten them, the little one almost too shy to say hello. Nilda has heard that the *huachicoleros* came by their old house a couple times, and then somebody just moved in, *usurpadores*, probably given permission by the gangsters in return for some service they provided, some little risk they took. You can't fight these things face-to-face and hope to survive.

Gaspar bangs a heavy ladle against the rim of the trashcan to get his attention. About to overflow. Macario pushes a sprayed rack into the washer, hurries to deal with the garbage.

Howie, the blond kid who works in the cold room prepping chops and ribs, is listening to the radio as usual, one of those news-and-talk shows that Macario will listen to to see how his English is coming along. He thinks he hears the name of the place he is supposed to be going.

It is cool outside behind the restaurant, a nice change even with the smell of the day's refuse from the dumpster. Denver is a spread-out city, lots of different neighborhoods, and once he found Federal Boulevard it seemed a lot like San Antonio, only harder to breathe. He's spent the rest of his life at sea level.

You have to be careful with the trash bags, which might have broken glass in them, and be sure to get your legs underneath when you heave them over the side of the dumpster. On really slow nights they'll come out here to smoke and talk, leaving only one man on duty inside. Orestes had a hard time of it, robbed and beaten by *pandilleros* on his way up through Mexico, but Dauphin's stories are worse. He is Haitian but born in the Dominican Republic, and seems never to have known a moment of peace.

"This is the best," he tells them. "Until I am captured."

Macario has only had to run once, in San Antonio, from a parking lot where dozens of the *indocumentados* would gather every morning to wait for men driving pickups or vans with a day's work to offer. A pair of cruisers sped into the lot with lights flashing and sirens whooping and everybody tore away in their own direction, Macario able to get a look back and see that the officers weren't even getting out of their cars, just making a display to watch everybody panic.

The same show is on Howie's radio and he hears the name again. Yellow Earth. *Tierra Amarilla*, he thinks, and makes a picture of it in his head, kind of a desert with yellow sand and a forest of oil derricks in every direction. It is the mayor of the city speaking, and if he understands what the man is saying there is so much drilling going on there the workers can't find a place to sleep.

The cleanup galley slaps him in the face like a wave. Orestes has put a new trash liner in the garbage and is scraping plates into it, Gaspar is spraying a rack, and Orestes is elbow-deep in the sink, scrubbing cheese.

"*Yaxon está asfixiando!*" shouts Gaspar over the racket and the dishwasher is indeed choking, Macario scooping a slimy handful of blasted scraps from the food drain in the machine, squishing over the rubber mat below to toss it in the bin. He gets paid on Friday. It's time to go north, he thinks. *A la Tierra Amarilla.*

AT LEAST NOBODY SHE has ever known is likely to come to the Yellow Earth Walmart and see her behind a cash register. When she tried to explain the relocation of the coterie and the intent of her paper on the phone there was a long silence, then Dr. Paulsen said, "So that's finished." The stipend withdrawn, no invitation to come back and launch something related in a less environmentally challenged area. Then coming in here, a PC sin but everywhere else was out of milk again and black coffee makes her stomach raw, and she saw the sign advertising seventeen-fifty an hour and did the math. Put in forty, fifty hours a week, which they're begging for with the hiring crisis, and it comes out much better than she was making as a prairie dog peeper.

Only a temporary position, she told Will. Two months left on the apartment lease, it would be wasteful to just pack up and go.

She sees the Native American girl, Jolene, two checkout aisles away, paying for supersized containers of cleaning products and trying not to meet eyes. Fine, thinks Leia, I'm just a reminder of something she should try to forget. But as the girl wheels her purchases out she gives a little nod, blushing.

"Is it okay if I get one for my husband?"

An older woman stands before her with two identical sets of headphones in her hands.

"Pardon?"

"They're on sale, but it says 'One per customer' and my husband's not here."

Leia is sure there's a store policy, but doesn't see a supervisor near.

"We listen to books on tape," the woman continues, "but he's Ross McDonald and I'm Philippa Gregory."

"Does your husband ever come in here?"

"Oh, all the time."

"Then he's a customer," says Leia, and discounts the headphones.

THE TRAILERS ARE ALL the same, dirty floor, cheap laptop on a metal desk next to the mud engineer's blender, paperwork covering the desktop and walls, which are rattling, buffeted by the wind that hasn't let up all day. And the hydraulics noise, the thumping, groaning, grinding of the big animal above and below them, as constant as the boops and beeps at the casino hotel but with weightier consequences, tons of force being thrown into a narrow fissure in the earth. The fracker– Hardaway? Hardacre? Hardass?– runs through the usual litany.

"There's service companies and there's service companies," he explains, his attention still half focused on the sounds outside, monitoring the rhythm of the pumping like a cardiologist with a heart patient in crisis. "A few we've got to use because Houston set them up, just as a firewall in case something goes wrong."

Dudley did the heavy lifting on the actuarial numbers back in the early 2000s, setting levels of restitution– first offer, second offer, final offer, sue us and stand in line– and establishing the prevention versus compensation variances. Deciding what you've really got to get right the first time, when it's a lot cheaper to pay the fine, and when to stonewall and go to court. Just patterns of numbers, nickels and dimes.

"Then there's outfits you're expected to deal with for political reasons, like they're connected to the honchos at the reservation here, which is a case of don't expect to get what you pay for."

"To the point of physical danger?"

"No, I get my wells drilled and fracked out and my people off the platform in one piece. But what's left behind– that's somebody else's lookout."

Dudley glances at the daily logs from Hardwhatever's three wells currently in process. Nothing out of line with what he's seen from the other site managers he surprised this morning with his Company card– Boomer said it ought to say '007, License to Drill.' Fracking is a complex process, constantly becoming more refined but rarely any cheaper. When gas was over four dollars a gallon at the pump it was like printing money, but now–

"Anything you can send back to the Company, ideas for operational improvements from what you're learned here?"

The trailer gives a booming, violent shake, the long wall warping in then popping out, Dudley worried for a bad instant that the well has blown up till he sees from the manager's face that it is just the wind.

"Tell them to find a deposit under someplace that grows palm trees," says Hardwater. "With a quiet hotel with decent room service and no damn hurricanes."

SHE FEELS IT VIBRATING in her shirt pocket, hurries through the men calling out Excuse me, Miss, and Hey Honey, to the back room. She's started to associate his voice with the coffee fumes, or maybe she's just been thinking about him a lot. It's been two days since he called.

"Hello."

"You're at work, right?"

"Yes."

"I'm sorry, I know they keep you hopping, but I had to hear your voice."

"Where've you been?"

"Oh, couple moves I've had to make, should play out good in the next couple days."

"*Where* are you?"

"On my way out to the rez, settle a little business. When you get off?"

"Five."

"I swing by?"

"Okay– you know– "

"Yeah, wait on the parallel block so the snitches don't see us."

"I'll be there."

"You know– just cause you don't hear from me a couple days doesn't mean I'm not thinking about you."

"I know."

"I can smell the java through the phone. You'd better go."

"I love you."

A pause then. He's driving, maybe has to pay attention to the road.

"We'll talk about that at five."

Spartina grabs two bags of roast, hustles back to the floor. She knows you're not supposed to, like, lose yourself to a man and all that, but it's hard to think about anything else. She finds herself drifting off in class or here at work, replaying moments between them, the way he looks at her and touches her, or worrying that it's going to end. Or that he's got other girls. He could have, he's so good-looking, and there's no way she could know unless it was like another girl in her high school, which is pretty unlikely. She can't imagine any one of them he would go for. Some days she can't imagine why he's at all interested in *her*, it can't just be sex cause she's not so good at it yet and he could get that somewhere else. Well, maybe not in Yellow Earth, where there's so few women compared to men right now, but like in Bismarck or Minot. Sometimes she just starts thinking about his *car*–

"Hey Honey."

A guy in a quilted vest and a Mack truck hat with a bulldog on it, looking up at her from his table.

"You gonna *pour* that coffee, or just stand there lookin good with it in your hand?"

VERY FEW CAN CLOSE the deal.

Scorch sees them every night at Bazookas, chins up, eyes hard, looking for a fight. But if you fight in a bar or strip club you're asking for it to be stopped, to be pulled away by a half-dozen volunteer referees. You want to beat the guy down without a court date at the end of it, show off for your friends. Even the guys who did that kid out in front of the club, all of them drunk as skunks, seemed surprised when six hard shots with a hunk of plumbing sent him to the morgue and them to the joint. Amateurs.

The minute he sees Wayne Lee's pimped Camaro rolling up he tosses the keys to the wrecker to Shakes and tells him to go on a beer run, even though the cooler is still half full. Shakes has too much imagination for this.

"Wait out here," he says to L. T., not the brightest bulb, but able to follow a simple instruction.

Wayne Lee still has that idiot grin plastered on his face, even with all the bad blood between him and Brent.

"Hey, it's the pit bull himself," he cracks, leaving his keys in the Camaro. "Bust any good skulls lately?"

It's the dead hour between shifts, just getting dark, and Brent has given most of his gravel haulers the evening off.

"Brent's running late– he called to say it'll be ten, fifteen minutes," says Scorch, not taking the bait. "But he's got the paperwork ready for you to sign in the back."

Wayne Lee has been whining louder than usual lately, appointing himself spokesman for all the other bellyachers on the payroll, like he's the fucking shop steward or something, and too stupid to sniff out that Scorch is taking over the trade. And now this idea that he's going to jump over to work for Phil Enterlodge and take half the drivers with him.

"I always wonder," kids Wayne Lee as they walk between trucks to the back, "why they call it a 'bouncer.' That guy you threw out last night sure didn't *bounce*."

Wayne Lee is one of those characters who wants everybody to like him, even if they don't. There's three guys Scorch knows of who are stepping the powdered goods down and reselling them, fucking with the quality of the brand, and some asshole from Bakersfield who's set up shop out at one of the man camps, and Wayne Lee is all like, 'Free market, dude, there's room for everybody.'

Well there's not room for Wayne Lee Hickey.

"I consider my job sort of an escort service," says Scorch. "Only I escort people *out* of clubs instead of into them."

Wayne Lee laughs and then steps a couple feet into the back office, looking down at the oily tarp spread out on the floor.

"What's this for?" he says and then Scorch hits him, using both hands to swing the thirty-six-inch cast-iron pipe wrench, a good twenty pounds of heft to it, and there is a sound like a pumpkin landing on the sidewalk from a third floor window and Wayne Lee falls straight, *tiiiiimberrrrr*! onto his face in the center of the plastic tarp. If it was an Olympic event Scorch would get a ten on every card.

"L. T.!" he calls, wiping the wrench handle down with an oily rag and tossing it on top of the body.

By the time L. T. joins him Scorch has it all rolled up like a burrito, ends tucked in.

"Help me put this in the back of that Camaro. We're going for a drive."

And L. T., God love him, doesn't blink an eye.

"Bend your knees when you lift," he says to Scorch, hunkering down to get a grip. "Watch that lower back."

SHE'S WAITING BY LEIA'S car in the parking lot, mostly empty as the store lights go off.

"Could you give me a ride?" she asks in a little voice.

Or should I just swallow water and swim for the bottom?

"Okay– uhm– where to?"

"Home?"

There is a shuttle bus that goes around town and even out into the boonies a ways, but the girl could have caught that an hour ago.

"I think I remember the way– "

"Just a couple miles past where your critters are."

"You know that?" Leia hits the button on the keys to unlock the doors. She's kept the same rental even though they've jacked the rates up again.

"My ride to school used to pass you on the way in," she says. "You were usually busy looking through your binoculars."

Jolene slides in next to her, pulling the bag of cleaning stuff onto her lap. Leia eases the car out of the lot. It isn't that far away–

"Did you get fired?"

I've been outed, thinks Leia. The internet must be buzzing with it– "Wildlife Girl Surrenders Career, Dignity to Chain Retailer."

"Not exactly," she says. "The study was ended. Sometimes when your data are compromised– " She shrugs. "The world of science was not holding its breath."

"But you like it."

Leia squeezes her way into the eastbound flow between two rumbling trucks, considering the question. "I do. I like figuring out how the animals interact, how they deal with challenges. But that kind of knowledge doesn't turn into money if it's not like a domesticated food animal, so getting grants is pretty iffy."

"And prairie dogs– "

"Happened to have nobody major hogging the field when I started in on them. I've observed other species– when I wasn't too much older than you I spent a summer in Madagascar, following lemurs around."

"Prosimians," says Jolene.

Leia gives her a look.

"That have great big eyes? I remember some pictures from a biology book."

Leia turns off on the county road, still busy but not bumper to bumper.

"The rarer species are up in the Madagascar rainforest," she tells the girl, "what's left of it. We wrote our sightings in grease pencil on these laminated pads because it was so damp that paper would just dissolve."

"Is that in Africa?"

"Just off the coast of Mozambique, in the Indian Ocean."

They drive in silence for what seems a long time then, oncoming headlights washing over the girl's face.

"Everybody knows," she says finally. "About me."

Leia understands what she means, but you can't just agree. "I work with twenty, twenty-five people at the store. Say four, five hundred shoppers wandered through on my shift. I'd be surprised if one percent even know you exist."

"But everybody who *does* know who I am, who live here, knows about it. People at the police and the hospital talk, one person tells another."

"Do you know any other kids who've had bad things happen to them?"

Jolene considers. "A boy named Quentin died of cancer. And Dickyboy Burdette's father committed suicide."

"But is that who Dickyboy *is*? Just 'the kid whose dad killed himself'?"

"No. It was a long time ago, but he's still kind of a mess."

"In not too long your story will be a long time ago. We think everybody's paying attention, but we're barely on most people's radar."

"I guess." She doesn't sound convinced.

"How's it been with your parents?"

"They had me pray with them."

"Did that help?"

"No."

Leia nods. Her own short-of-penetration incident during undergrad never made it into her phone calls home. Her parents were paranoid enough without giving them something real to chew on.

Another silence. Leia's freshman roommate did a lot of whatever was available on campus and would come back wrecked and too freaked to be alone. Long, arrhythmic conversations about God, boys, bands, whether she looked fat or just voluptuous. Silence is fine, silence should be respected.

"So how do you do it?" Jolene asks her when they are beyond the traffic and cutting into the night alone. "How do you just pick up and go somewhere you've never been before, where you don't know anybody?"

What now– three, four major moves? Active dislike of where she's *from* has played a part, general cluelessness–

"I can't say I've done it very *well*," she tells the girl, "but I've done it. There's good things and bad things. At first, or maybe even for a long time, you feel shy and lonely. But on the other hand, if nobody knows you, knows your history, you can totally reinvent yourself."

"Like pre*tend*?"

"No, but– let's say you can emphasize an aspect of your personality you really like, and just jettison anything that embarrasses you."

"You like who you are here?"

This kid doesn't take any prisoners.

"Uhm– I have had my moments. Kind of made a *stand*– this is who I am, deal with it– and that I feel good about."

"Here's where your colony is."

Leia would have passed it without noticing.

"It's called a coterie– the little subsection I was observing."

"Are they nocturnal?"

"Let's see."

Leia pulls to the side of the road, jockeys the car around so her low beams spread over the field.

Not a furry soul.

"Too many predators out at night," she says softly. They aren't too far from where the girl was attacked, which makes sense if she was walking home. "So they're diurnal under normal conditions. But of course conditions haven't been exactly normal up here for quite a while."

Jolene studies her face for a moment.

"Are you going to stay? Now that your project is finished?"

"For a while."

"Why?"

It is flattering in a way, a kid, a thoughtful kid like this one, asking you questions about stuff that counts.

"Okay, don't laugh at me, but I met a guy."

"In Yellow *Earth*?"

"There's possibly-cool guys everywhere. Few and far between, sure, but if you get lucky– "

"So you're in."

"I am testing a hyp*o*thesis," she says. "And most of those don't work out. But you always learn something by seeing it through."

Jolene nods, looks at the empty field. Behind them, on the other side of the road, sits an oil derrick with a few lights here and there but no workers on it, towering over the section where the whole town used to be. No activity, no pumping, no noise– Leia wonders what the deal is.

"So it's called a coterie."

"That's right."

"And they live right on top of each other."

"Shoulder to shoulder, if they actually had shoulders."

"They must feel really safe together."

"Maybe," says Leia. "But they're *not*, honey. That's the sad thing. Not even from each other."

HE TAKES HER OUT of town and onto the Indian reservation, parking in a spot where they can look out on a lake. Like always he doesn't like to talk till they get there, which is fine with Jewelle, who needs the time for her face to wake up. She must look like hell.

"Weird-looking lake," she says. The Hummer has a huge windshield to see through.

"It's man-made."

"Oh. Is that what it is. I could tell there's something wrong with it– like a guy who colors his hair."

"You color your hair."

She looks at him. "You know that?"

"Sure. Women your age don't still have that shade of blonde."

"My age."

Randy Hardacre, or 'Heartacher,' as the girls at work tease her now that they know, smiles. "Digging myself in pretty deep here."

"That's what you do. Dig."

"I *drill*, actually. It's a little bit more to the point."

She looks back over the water. Here it comes–

"So," she says, "you wanted to see me."

"I always want to see you."

"–really early in the morning. So this must be where you tell me you're married."

"No, I am extremely divorced. As a matter of fact, I think my ex-wife used the same product. L'Oréal."

"You like blondes."

"If you turned brunette overnight, my feelings wouldn't change a whit."

His feelings, whatever they might be–

"So."

"So I'm supposed to go back to Houston for a while."

"A while."

"They only booked me one way, so they haven't decided how long yet."

"Something the matter?"

"Naw, just– this whole circus, the leases, the drilling, the fracking, depends on international price per barrel."

"How much is in a barrel?"

"Forty-two gallons, and we're over a hundred ten dollars a barrel right now. But there was some thought that OPEC would jack their prices up."

"OPEC?"

"Oil Arabs."

"So they need you in Houston to figure this out? I'm impressed."

"The Company likes to get everybody from different stages of the process together in a room, give our opinions, tell our stories, then one or two guys who weren't even there will make a gut-guess on what to do next. But their asses have officially been covered if it comes up at a stockholder meeting. 'After exploring all options– '"

"When?"

"I fly out tomorrow."

There are no ducks on the lake. Maybe it is too windy or too cold for them, maybe there're all in Florida, but the lake would look a lot better with ducks on it. What there is is a very big, very white boat, like a yacht on steroids, sitting propped up on dry land just across the water.

"Who do you think owns that boat?" she asks.

"Well, we're on the reservation."

"Indians have yachts?"

"Why not?"

"I don't know. I picture them in, like, ca*noes.*"

"It's the twenty-first century. I got my job in the oil business cause I'm good at computers."

"You're like a big deal, huh?"

"Not so big."

"Bigger than the guys who come into the club."

"How would I know? You still haven't invited me to."

"I told you, it'd make me self-conscious, having a real person there."

"The customers aren't real?"

"Not as *people.* They're like– I don't know– like a herd of cattle sometimes, and sometimes like lions and tigers, in the cage with the guy with the whip and the chair."

"Wow."

"I'll tell you, it doesn't make you crazy about men as a species."

"We're just a sex," says Randy. "Same species as you."

"Not in Bazookas you're not."

She can't imagine Randy in the club any more than she can imagine herself on a real oil platform in her tool belt and hardhat outfit.

"So there's some chance you're coming back."

"No telling, but if I do I hope you're still here."

"If you're still drilling, I'm still dancing."

She's socked away a bundle since she's come up here, and unlike these idiot roughnecks she's not going to spend it on pretend sex with strangers.

"We were just getting started, I think," he says.

He doesn't say I'll call you every day, or would you like to come to Houston with me and forget about the dancing, or any of the other things that might change her life. He's the best man she's met up here, the best one she's met in a long while, but when the music stops the ride is over.

"At least you didn't buy a house," she says.

Across the wind-whipped water, a figure pops out from under the tarp on the boat and clumsily maneuvers a ladder to the ground.

THE ACTION FACTION LOVES Leonard.

"Nina, Nina, the in-betweenah!"

He is fast, good-looking, and wired in to the job. There's never much hedging at his table and he's a wizard with the proposition bets, so the action flies along, lots of chips down on the come out roll, an easy fifteen to twenty more rolls an hour than any other stickman on the floor.

"Fiver, fever, don't believe her."

Lady is on her break, watching him wield the stick. She's never worked the craps table, too many bets to keep track of, too many hyper bettors at your elbows, not her rhythm. But Lenny was born for it, eyes everywhere at once, stick changing hands on the roll, the patter inexhaustible–

"Jimmy Hicks from the sticks, rolls the dice and wins on six. That's six, six, six, wasn't sleazy, it came easy."

The casino hired him on sight, had him in harness the minute his background check cleared. He looks good in the uniform, has already made friends with all the dealers and the boxmen, and the high-octane players are drawn to his table like moths to a flame.

"Mr. Natural, pass line wins." He offers the bowl to the next shooter. "Pick your bones, Jones," he says, and then when the dice are being shaken, "Hands high, let 'em fly!"

They try to work the same shift in order to see more of each other, but it's not always possible. And at least here there's only the one casino– in Reno and Vegas she'd never hear the door creak till the dawn's early light. Lenny is breaking in a new dealer tonight, gently, working instructions and reminders into his spiel without embarrassing the kid, controlling the vibe of the table.

"Boxcars, pass line loses, push on the don't pass."

He never bends to mop the dice around, moving only from the elbows out, but the rocks never sit still for long–

"Aces, double the field."

He was a little distant the first couple days, distracted, just getting the feel of the town, of the vast, underpopulated reservation, the silent lake and the raucous casino. And then she came back from work one night and he was the old Lenny, the old *good* Lenny, smiling and relaxed and full of plans.

"Eighter, eighter, see ya later, eight is the point."

He's in the same groove now, acknowledging each player with eye contact, urging them along, goosing the volume on a hot roll, coaxing the tough bets from the vets who know the odds–

"Three craps out, don't comes win."

He is high as a Georgia pine.

"Little Joe from Kokomo, tell your daddy what you know! That's four the hard way, folks, shooter rolls again."

The thing is, he's never been good to live with when he's straight. Even totally cleaned out, not sick, he stays anxious, not really with you. Something is missing and they both know it. They've talked it to death, with and without the drug counselors, but a junkie is always a junkie. 'I wish I was addicted to brake fluid,' he always jokes, 'so I could stop whenever I wanted.'

"Pay the don'ts, double the field."

With both of them working, the expense won't be overwhelming. This new habit is so much better than the crystal, the highs and lows less extreme, no temper tantrums, and he's willing to eat at least one full meal a day. He claims to just be a dip-and-dab man instead of carrying a King Kong habit, and she has only found him unconscious once, getting the lecture when she drove him to the ER at Mercy. "If I still got a pulse, baby," he told her, "just let me dream."

"Hard ten, the ladies' friend, no one wins unless they spend. Dice are in the middle, folks."

Lady looks into the too-bright eyes of the players glued to the rail. Adrenaline freaks, all of them, hooked on the tumbling cubes, the colored chips, the noise, Leonard's play-by-play chatter–

"That's yo-leven, feels like Heaven, somebody paid the light bill."

When he is in the Zone like this he can skip sleep, food, trips to the bathroom. Now and then, at a certain stage of the downslide, they'll make love. 'Want to make sure I can feel it, Lady,' he tells her. 'Even if I'm starting to get ragged.' She hopes whatever connection he's made here is a safe one, but has learned not to ask. There should be enough shit floating around that it's not too expensive, decent quality. She's learned to tell when he's gotten something laced with another drug, too speedy or talking in slo-mo. He's always been shy of needles, sensible about the health issues and the wear and tear on his veins. So the apartment is full of beeswax candles and aluminum foil, she keeps the cardboard tubes when the toilet paper is gone–

"Came easy, bet it hard!"

Lady turns to head for the break room. Lenny and his posse at the craps table will always want more. Need more. And you can have more, you can, but you have to pay the price. Not right away, maybe, but it will catch up to you. This whole crazy oil field, this drilling, pumping, this rush of money and people, cannot stay in the air forever. Gravity exists. The House always wins.

"Up pops the devil!" calls Leonard, raking snake eyes off the rail. "Shooter goes down."

THE MOUNTAIN LION IS looking a little scruffy. Not that they aren't scruffy out in Nature– dirty, scarred-up, hide full of ticks– but most stuffed animals get a makeover before they're put out in public. Ruby wonders if this one was actually killed on the reservation and when that might have been. If it was in the last two years the thing would have tire marks from an oil truck on it.

Harleigh, on the other hand, has his look totally together as he stands at the lectern behind the big cat. Hat pushed back on his head so you can see his eyes, fringed buckskin jacket over a red cowboy shirt, silver and turquoise flashing from his fingers.

"The Three Nations," he says, "is the leader in tribal oil produced in the continental United States."

There's always a little wonder at the Alaskan tribes holding out for their own nomenclature, just because they came late to the party and are sitting on an ocean of the black stuff. Alaska Natives. Hard to imagine a place with more brutal winters than here.

"And we've only just gotten started!" Harleigh crows, and there is clapping and whistling and stomping of the feet. The Events Center is filled mostly with oil people and wannabe oil people, and then the enrolled members who've signed leases and want to get rich, or in a few cases, richer.

"There's a family," Harleigh tells them, voice dropping into the tale-swapping frequency, "in the Middle East called the Sauds. A family that's got their own *coun*try, which with all the troubles over there, never seems to get invaded by anybody. Their sovereignty remains un*vi*olated. Now why is that?"

In three corners of the Events Center there are mock-ups of the traditional dwellings of the three tribes, little kids allowed to go in and play inside them during the Christmas shows and winter powwows. Newly added, to the far left and far right, are facsimiles of early twentieth- and early twenty-first-century oil derricks, each with Do Not Lean or Climb signs on them.

"Is it because they have a large and expensively maintained military? Oh, they do– they bought over sixty *billion* dollars' worth of weaponry from our government and solved their unemployment troubles by keeping a hell of a lot of men in the field. They *bought* that army, they *bought* that sovereignty with *oil*. Their freedom and self-determination comes by the barrel!"

More applause and a few shouts. Ruby has never heard the Saudis get this much love.

"It doesn't matter what you think of their culture, it doesn't matter what you think of their politics, when folks think of Saudi Arabia a big sign starts flashing that says 'Hands Off'!"

She sees Rodney Pierce, who had one of the first frack jobs come in on his acreage, jump to his feet and throw a fist in the air. Rodney saw combat somewhere, Panama maybe, and has a collection of sexist T-shirts, though today he's opted for a simple 'Drill Her Deep and Pump Her Hard' over an American flag.

"Oil and gas extraction on the reservation," says Harleigh, looking around as if he could actually see individuals with the hall darkened and the spotlight trained at him, "is not only supplying America with its energy needs, but it is forging a new and more respected status for our tribes– not a poor cousin, not a ward of the state, but a strong and self-governing nation within a nation!"

The oilmen, the Texans and Okies and pipeline people from Alaska, are applauding harder than anybody. Harleigh is hosting this expo for them, with the same lure of fewer rules and tax-free operations that bring the casino people here, or the firecracker peddlers in states where they're restricted, or the outlaws and cattle rustlers who used Indian Territory for their personal free-trade zone, thumbing their noses at Hanging Judge Parker. Ruby can hear the digital cacophony of the slot machines from the back of the hall, the Events Center connected to the casino by a short walkway, not only for comfort in the hard, wind-whipping winter months but so people never have the fun parlor out of their minds. To the oilmen it must sound like money falling into the coffers– Harleigh should have taped some oil-pump thumping and played it here to get their blood up even more.

"We live in a corporate climate," Harleigh tells them. "There are businesses with more financial resources than most of the countries in the world, with more employees than most armed forces, with more *power*"– he does a nice dramatic pause here, looking around the hall, letting this sink in to the enrolled members present– "than most of the outfits making trouble on the nightly news. What I have tried to do in my capacity as Chairman is let the world know that the Three Nations are in the game, that we are *open for business!*"

More people stand to applaud now, believers in the gospel he is preaching. Ruby's Aunt Earline got caught up with the evangelicals for a while and took her to a couple mass revivals in Santa Fe. There was the same near-ecstatic vibe in the room, the same sense of belonging to something big together, Aunt Earline shaking and testifying even though most of it was in Spanish, which she didn't speak. Like a Burning Man concert with bad music. And Harleigh eats it up, loves to hear the *amens* hollered out. He had only nodded to Ruby when they passed backstage before, caution in his eyes now. She has sent him a half-dozen self-serving letters, detailing her concerns about his oil service activities, his executive measures taken without council deliberation, his drift into what might be considered influence peddling. Her concerns and cautions are on record, held in duplicate, in a volume thick enough to legally cover her ass. She has put feelers out, mostly to southern and southwestern tribes, discreetly letting it be known that she is open to a move. You want to leave before the ship is obviously sinking, when the feces might be already launched in the air but have yet to contact the whirring blades.

"What I have tried to insure," Harleigh adds, "is that the resources go out to where they're needed, but the *money stays here!*"

The thing is, he's the best she's lawyered for. The most dynamic, the hardest working, the best sense of the world away from the reservation. But whenever she's tried to put the brakes on, to counsel a little restraint, a little caution, he looks at her like the enemy. She wonders if mob lawyers ever suggest to their clients that abstaining from future murders might be a wise legal strategy–

"We got some videos, we got some numbers for you all to chew on now," Harleigh smiles, "and after the reception you're welcome to cross over to the casino and try to win some of that lease bonus money back."

Laughter at this.

"But I just wanted to welcome you to our third annual exposition here, and to remind you all that a rising tide lifts all boats. We're *partners* in this adventure, folks, and here's hoping for good long run."

The applause is genuine. Fall out of a plane without a parachute and you can tell yourself that skydiving is a blast, right up until you hit the ground.

Florida, maybe. See what the Muskogees and Miccosukees are up to. Give all those parkas and thermal underwear to the women's shelter.

Harleigh is shaking hands by the side of the stage while the documentary he commissioned, made by a kid who grew up on the rez and got into advertising in Minneapolis, plays on the big screen. He sees Danny Two Strike waiting, and it isn't to congratulate him.

"Tell me what."

"You know Brent's boy Wayne?"

"Wayne Lee Hickey."

"Right."

"Tall, skinny surfer-looking dude, drives that pimped-up Camaro."

"You seen him?

"You know that me and Brent are not– "

"The partnership is dissolved, yeah. Have you seen Wayne?"

"Can't remember the last time."

"He's missing."

"You mean he left."

"His mother hasn't heard from him in three months."

Harleigh smiles. "If I see him I'll tell him to phone his mama."

"She's working up a search party, coming here."

On the screen there is a montage of all the things that depend on oil and gas energy.

"I don't get it. You send his plate number to the state police?"

"We found his car in Yellow Earth. Fella across the street says it's been sitting there since late September."

The shot where they caught a dozen antelope grazing right up by a pumping wellhead is playing now. Nature can take a punch and roll with it.

"These kind of fellas come and go. Out at my man camp you find their rooms cleaned out– not a trace, no notice they were moving on."

"The last anybody saw of him," says Danny Two Strike, standing in front of the stuffed grizzly that, legend has it, was the last killed in the state, "he told Phil Enterlodge he was coming to work for him, that he just had to stop by your garage to get his back pay and hand in his company gas card."

"Only met the guy twice. Nice enough kid, maybe a little wild. Heard he raced motorcycles in California."

"And you don't know of any bad blood between him and Brent?"

"Asshole buddies, the last I knew of it."

Danny does not look happy. "Well, these people are coming to poke around. They've contacted a few enrolled members, got their own website."

"Might as well look into that little Jon Benet killing while they're at it. And the Kennedy assassination."

"Meaning Marjorie Looks for Water."

"As I said."

"So there's gonna be some press."

"You send them all to me, Danny. Anything I can do to help, get it over with. How bout you, everything running smooth in the enforcement sector?"

"Oh– nothing wrong ten more paid officers wouldn't help."

"I thought we approved– "

"The pay's not enough if they don't already live here, Harleigh."

"Yeah, housing's a bear right now. I might be able to swing a discount out at Killdeer City."

"Cops come with families. Coming here shouldn't be like a tour of duty in Afghanistan."

"So you're suggesting– "

"We shop around, find the best deal on some decent apartments, and offer free housing with the job."

It's the hidden expenses that kill you, thinks Harleigh. Mr. and Mrs. America, sticking the nozzle into their vehicles, got no idea what you got to go through to fill that pump.

"Next council meeting," he tells Danny. "We'll take it up."

Danny nods and goes out through the back.

He and Brent and Wayne Lee went hunting a few times, Wayne Lee telling racing stories and talking motors with him. Up for fun, but not a total flake. Spent a lot of time at the casino, maybe got in over his head, but if it's money trouble you'd think he could have just sold that ritzy muscle car to one of these roughnecks. A mystery.

Harleigh steps back out so he can see the video better, him up there talking about the boom with two dozen of his best Herefords grazing in the background.

It's his favorite part.

Buzzy has no idea who or if anybody is waiting to unload at the next site, just directions how to get there, east on 20 toward the Indian reservation. He signs the invoice, climbs into the cab, touches the glow-in-the-dark Jesus he picked up with a supply of beef jerky at the Cenex, and swings the rig away from the well and over the Caterpillar bumps of the outfit's access road. He's asked to have a tailboard put on too, but the guys in the shop just laugh and make jokes about wearing a rubber on top of your rubber. Of course none of them ever crushed a family to death with a breakaway tumble of pipe.

There is an art, when taking a beating, of directing the blows where they'll do the least damage. Tuck had a few lessons in this when he was young and stupid and prone to revealing that fact in badass bars, and has never forgotten the basics.

"You don't sit and have a few with the boys, you're not *one* of the boys," he explains to Francine, who is circling him at the breakfast table with his toast still in her hand. "You're not one of the boys, you don't get work. It's that simple."

"Bullshit."

"How do you think I got on this new rig? I was in the club, and I met the guy who runs the day-to-day, the toolpusher."

"Who also had some pole dancer rubbing her fanny in his face."

Elbows over the kidneys if you think it's coming there next, otherwise protect your head and keep your balls tucked in–

"Oh come on, Francine."

It is true about meeting Nub Hammond there, and it was at the bar, not in the back room–

"According to Butch Bjornson– "

"Butch Bjornson is an idiot."

"Absolutely. Only an idiot would charge his lap dances on a credit card when he's got a joint account with his wife. I'm sure you're a cash customer."

She'd been asleep, or pretending to be, when he came in last night, so the first warning of the onslaught was her blasting her protein shake in the blender before he was awake, a willful breach of protocol. Then the sullen stare, the kidnapping of his toast before he could get his hands on it, the one-word opening volley, uttered with heartfelt contempt–

"Bazookas."

"The things we go through together on the job," says Tuck, adding a strain of weariness to his voice, "you don't want to carry them straight home."

"You're not in fucking Fallujah fighting the rebels!"

She frisbees the toast across the room. This is bad– Francine is not a thrower or a smasher– and all you can hope for in the situation is that they get tired or distracted–

"Yesterday the hole starts *talking*"– Tuck continues– "that's gas building up in the borehole, too much pressure coming from underneath, and it can– well, you don't want to think about the worst-case scenario, you just keep *drilling*, cause the real pressure is coming from the Company, which has got millions of dollars invested in that hole and not a bit of profit pumped out of it yet."

"You're saying it's dangerous."

"We take the necessary precautions, sure, but the *pressure*– it's the same principle that makes volcanoes go off."

"If it's that dangerous I want you to *quit*. I've still got my job, which I'm going to be late for."

"I'm late too," he says but doesn't stand. You show signs of life, the slightest movement, they'll kick you harder–

"I thought you said they shut it down."

"That was just temporary– Nub threw some saltwater down the pipe, got it stable. We'll probably be back at it when my tour starts."

Francine stops pacing, fixing him in her headlights across the table. "How much does that kind of thing cost, anyway? Do you pay by the minute, by the results– "

"Francine– "

"Oh fuck it!" She turns away from him and is halfway out the door. "I don't want to know!"

The door is slammed, hard, and Tuck sits for a moment, listening. He hears the Camry engine fire up, tires crunching gravel. He finds the toast on the floor, throws it in the bin under the sink, grabs a microwave burrito from the fridge, which will have to do for lunch. No matter what they've been up to the night before, the hands are never late for work.

There are no signs of fury having been vented on his pickup, a controversial purchase his second week on the rigs, but no way he was pulling up in Francine's sister's Honda Civic. It is a battered Tacoma with some good miles left in it.

"You start slapping bumper stickers on that thing," joked Francine, scowling at it that first evening in the driveway, "I'm filing for a divorce."

The 20 is a fucking nightmare, even worse than usual. You can't call it *rush* hour cause nothing's moving that fast, but a lot of shifts, not just on the rigs, are beginning now, adding to the usual stream of water and equipment haulers. Nothing to do but hold your place in line and wait it out, hope the other hands, or even Nub, are stuck in the same mess. It is a thrown-together crew, guys spun off, like him, from outfits broken up or able to replace them with more experienced hands. Nicky, the derrickman, is just twenty, a high-school dropout from Odessa, and Grunt, whose real name he hasn't been able to learn yet, is a vet from the various Gulf wars, a fact conjectured from his tats and not from his occasional monosyllables. Nub, who grew up in the Alaska fields and has done every other job on a rig, is managing two wells a mile apart from each other and seems a little over his head, arriving on the platform every day with a worried-sounding "How we doin, fellas?" before hovering over the shoulder of the driller, Kelsey, for an hour or so. Kelsey wears a sushi-chef headband and a biker moustache, Tuck feeling some days like he's on the deck of a pirate ship. But before yesterday's gas farts they were making hole like crazy, well ahead of the curve and cruising for a bonus. And Tom Hicks, the motorman, has promised to show him how to throw chain–

Your Hole is Our Goal says the sticker on the tailgate of the Dodge Ram inching forward ahead of him. Fucking Butch Bjornson, who he hardly knows, has got to see him in Bazookas and have a wife who teaches with Francine. He can say, when it comes to the showdown tonight, that no, he's not having an affair, because that's not the nature of his relationship with Jewelle, not exactly. Explaining to her exactly what it *is*– that's not going to happen.

Buzzy turns off on the parallel road to the north– 40th, 43rd, they've got it numbered like Tulsa or Okie City, even though there's nothing but prairie. Lucky for him the next drill site is up this way because the 20 is a nightmare right now, crawling along, and he's feeling like he should stop and check the straps on the load. It's only been what, fifteen, twenty minutes, but it was awful bumpy coming out from that last site and pipe likes to shift–

The truck shudders as if hit by a wave, Buzzy's eyes immediately darting to the side mirror but the load is all there, the pyramid holding its shape, and then a spiral of black smoke expands upward just ahead, a fireball spilling out from the middle of it. Not the rig he's headed for, but close, only a quarter mile ahead. A slap of sudden heat through his open window, the smell of burning oil. He eases off the road, leaves the engine running, hops down and begins to sprint toward the blowout.

The first man is naked but for his underpants and his work boots, which are smoking, and is running along the shoulder of the road. Buzzy thinks it is the man's gloves hanging from his fingers in strings, then realizes it's his skin.

"They're over there, they're over there!" screams the man, whose bare skin is livid red, waving an arm back toward the burning rig and then continuing to run.

Buzzy hits the superheated wall of air and is driven back, circling the blazing deck, only a few twisted struts of derrick left, till he first smells then comes upon the second man, lying on his back in the hayfield. This man is naked as well, skin bubbled like overfried chicken, all hair singed away, but somehow still alive.

"The derrickman is dead!" the second man shouts. "The derrickman is dead! Find Kelsey!"

Buzzy doesn't know who this is, but keeps working his way around the tower of fire till he sees a pickup bumping over the field from the road. Two guys in oil-drenched coveralls jump out.

"You call it in?"

Buzzy feels like an idiot. "I left my phone in the cab."

"Well get it and call 911! We'll do what we can."

"The derrickman is dead," he tells them, "and there's a guy named Kelsey you got to find."

"Go!"

Buzzy runs back to his truck, calls in the explosion, able to pinpoint the exact location for them. He realizes he is shaking, rolls up the window against the smoke, which is starting to blow parallel to the ground as the wind picks up. He can see the two deckhands, probably just coming home from their shift, carrying the man in the hayfield toward their pickup. He looks in the mirror, sees that his load is still there, realizes he'll be in the way. He pulls back onto the road and moves ahead in second gear, scanning the shoulders for the running man.

Tuck hears the boom, sees the smoke, and has to pull over like everybody else to let the fire trucks and ambulance by, but it's another half hour before he passes the flashing patrol cars at the turnoff and can see that it's Gorbus 327, his rig. He tilts the rearview mirror to keep it in sight as he drives away with the rest of the eastbound flow, all feeling gone from his hands and feet. "It's all computers and gauges now," Nub told him that first night in Bazookas, shouting over the throb of Jewelle's set. "The day of the old-fashioned gusher is *gone*, my friend, and the world is a poorer place."

Will is first on the scene, sealing the access except for responders, till Tolliver shows up to take over traffic and he can move to the site. He's cleaned up after a couple of head-ons back when you could actually speed on the highway around Yellow Earth, stepped in on a suicide six days dead in a locked apartment, but never seen anything like the two fellas the EMTs slide off the pickup bed and into the ambulance. The one who is burnt black is holding the cell phone of one of the deckhands who brought them out to the road, talking to his wife in another state.

"It ain't nothing, darling," he says. "Just a little sheet time and a lot of insurance forms. I love you."

From the look of him he'll be gone before sundown.

"This is the manager," says Danny Two Strike, leading over a wiry, sweating man in his forties by the arm. "Name is Hammond."

"The well was *static*," says the toolpusher, before Will can ask him anything. "I went through every reading before we started up again."

"You were here for the blast?"

"Not at the moment, no. I'm kind of doing double duty, supervising this site and another one Fossilco owns down the road."

"That's the company? Fossilco?"

"They're indemnified," says Hammond quickly. "I work for EnDak Oil Services, which is a subcontractor."

"And what do you figure happened?"

"Just a *kick*, you know, gas pressure below gets too strong and it comes up the well bore."

"This happens a lot?"

"It happens now and again, but we always have a blowout preventer."

"Which didn't work today."

The toolpusher shakes his head. "I never seen nothing like this, in all my years."

"Can you give me the names of your crew members?"

"Oh, Jeez, I got em written down somewhere in the doghouse, but that's gone. Uhm– Barry Kelsey is my driller, then Grunt, whose real name is Jerome something– I seen both of them go into the ambulance– they found Tom Hicks wandering around up the road. Then Nicky Metaxes, he's the derrickman." Hammond shakes his head. "If he was up top you won't find much of him left. Oh, shit, and the new guy, general helper, who knows where he was when it blew. Tucker something, local guy."

"Not Tuck Gatlin?"

"That's him. They should look in the mud tanks, there's shit blown all over creation here."

"Nub!" calls a young guy in a jacket and tie, running up with a cell phone in hand. "I got Houston!"

Hammond looks confused. "What?"

"Corporate needs to talk to you, *now*. The shock of this thing, you got to get in the right frame of mind."

Hammond takes the phone and steps away, mostly listening, saying, "I understand, I understand," every now and then. The young guy in the suit stands between him and Will.

"He'll finish his statement, whatever it is you were doing, when Legal gets here."

Will sees one of the firemen holding up a blackened safety helmet. The fire is out now, but the smell of burnt oil sours the air and there are brush fires still smoldering in the field on the periphery of the drilling pad. "It isn't a criminal investigation yet," he says to the company flack, stepping past to go to his car. "I'm just getting a body count."

Tolliver hasn't managed to screw anything up too badly when Will gets back to the main road and shuts himself into the car. Bearer of bad tidings is his least favorite aspect of the job.

"Francine Gatlin please– you'd better call her out of her classroom. Yes it is, but try not to alarm her."

The Colonel told him that in combat a wing commander had to write to the family of every flyer who got killed, and how in a hot war like Vietnam there were some who suffered nervous breakdowns.

"Francine? Will Crowder here. I'm over at the well Tuck's been working on? I'm so sorry, but I got some awful bad news for you."

Jewelle is walking back from the Albertsons with a sack of groceries when she sees him sitting outside her apartment on the hood of his car. She has her street gear on, exercise pants and a hooded sweatshirt, no makeup, what she thinks of as the pole-dancer protection program. He looks at her with moony eyes.

"Oh no," she says, stopping short. "You can't do this. You'll get me fired."

It isn't true, of course, she'd have to strangle a customer or three before Vic would even consider letting her go, but it's a line the sane ones usually respond to. He looks shaken up, like there's been a death in the family or he's about to propose marriage to her.

"We had a blowout at the rig," he says. "Guys have been killed."

The groceries weigh a ton but she keeps them out in front of her. This one, Tuck, has been a steady payer and pretty much of a gentleman, but when they snap you got to walk careful.

"You were there?"

"I should have been. I got caught in traffic and was late. They were all burned."

"That's awful, honey," she says, sidestepping very casually toward the door, keys already in her hand like always, "but it sounds to me like you just dodged a *bullet*. Somebody up there is looking out for you."

Most of the drillers' stories are either bad boss or near-death-and-dismemberment tales, drawled through a curtain of Jack Daniels as the club is ready to close. They've never made her want to trade jobs with a roughneck.

"It makes you think, something like this," says Tuck. "About your life. About the decisions you make."

Oh Lord, he *is* gonna propose, she thinks, and backs up the three steps and tries to get the key started in the slot behind her back. "What you want to do," she says, as kindly older-sister as she can muster, "is go home and take a long shower and then just lie down. You're in shock, honey, and you need to just *chill* till your head clears."

Nobody at the club would ever give out her address, so he must have followed her here at some point, spent who knows how many nights parked outside, running the heater in his pickup and fantasies through his head. No matter how you play it, the job sticks to you.

"I just drove on past the fire and ended up here," he says.

Comes a time when you've got to cut bait and paddle on, no matter how much income you leave behind. "Well that's just a wrong turn, darlin," says Jewelle, feeling the lock click open behind her. "You ain't thinking straight."

Tuck is halfway home when he hears the sirens again and he realizes where they'll take them, dead or alive, and that he should be there. That whatever this is, the part he's been playing in it isn't over yet. They aren't friends, really, despite the long tours on the rig and some serious bar time together, they're more like– what– brothers in arms? He turns for the hospital, brake linings complaining like they do whenever he hangs a left. Kirk at the dealership was bragging how he couldn't get pickups in fast enough, wrecks or not. Better to sell it now, he thinks, than put any money into maintenance.

Francine is in the lobby out front arguing with the implacable emergency room gorgon when Cindy Liu comes down and says to buzz her in. Cindy has something blue and official on, not like the nurses at the clinic, whose uniforms make you think they tend to pre-school children.

"There's three in intensive care, none of them is Tuck," Cindy tells her in the elevator. "But we have a body."

"Oh God."

"I don't think it's him either, but there's no telling."

"He was wearing– "

"No clothes left. We'll need dental records."

"Oh God."

"Tuck goes to– ?"

"Goldschmidt."

"We'll send over to his office." Cindy walks her into the cafeteria, sits her down and brings her some hot tea. "What I heard, they're still out at the site, searching the area."

"I don't even know how many men were at that well."

"You just sit here, and when I get any more information I'll tell you right away. I'll call Goldschmidt for the X-rays."

Francine sits and watches herself from a place a little above and behind, watches herself watching the other family members and staff scattered around the cafeteria. She was here earlier in the year, one of her former students dying of leukemia, and she had been struck by how nothing else– race, gender, class, age– separated people more than the Land of the Well and the Land of the Sick. As sad as she felt seeing Quentin that day, the whole while she kept thinking, 'This is not my tragedy.'

And now it is.

"Tucker Gatlin. I work with these guys."

"You're welcome to wait here, Mr. Gatlin," drones the woman in the booth, looking at something on her PalmPilot or whatever they're called now, Francine has one, "but the doctors are obviously engaged at the moment. When any information becomes public, you will have access to it."

"They're my *friends*."

"I understand. Would you take a seat, please?"

When he turns there is a young guy in a suit who he doesn't recognize blocking his way.

"Tucker Gatlin?"

"That's right."

"You were at 327."

"I was late. Traffic."

"So you didn't witness the incident."

The man is steering him away from the admission desk by the arm.

"I saw the– you know, I was close, so I heard the explosion, saw the fire, but they blocked off the access road before I got there."

The young guy nods like this is the last piece of a puzzle. "Okay, Gatlin," he says, "you're going to be debriefed about the condition of the well, asked your opinion of things. People from OSHA will be here within the hour. I need you to seriously consider one thing– do you desire to have a future in oil and gas recovery?"

He is thinking no, no I don't, when the elevator behind the glass door opens and Francine comes out into the lobby. He pulls away from the young guy in the suit. When Francine sees him she begins to weep, her body shaking, and he crosses to hold onto her. This may be it, he thinks. This may be the day his real life begins.

BULLETINS FROM THE BLACK STUFF

Though the going gets tough, the stuff keeps flowing.

This month saw a record of 36,100,722 barrels of oil produced from the Bakken and Three Rivers formations, though an atmosphere of caution has taken hold as several of the new rigs, over a hundred started just in April, have ceased drilling or been stacked till the numbers improve. What's going on out there?

We're back on the rollercoaster with crude, the benchmarks dropping from June's $105 per barrel to a shaky $59, lowest in years.

Meanwhile, US average gas prices have declined $1.44 per gallon (39%) since reaching a respectable $3.70 in August. The current $2.51 at the pump is the lowest since way back in '09.

The hardest thing to explain is the glaringly evident which everybody has decided _not_ to see. – Ayn Rand

THE SHERIFF IS PUTTING the notice up on the door when Vic arrives.

"What's this?"

"You're shut down."

"I cleared up that liquor thing."

"This is zoning. They don't want you here anymore."

Vic points over toward Teasers–

"Already posted."

Vic reads the notice, short and sweet. It was a terrific run, the most he's ever cleared, even if he never fell in love with the town. Or it with him.

"If I find a place outside city limits?"

Crowder considers for a moment, shakes his head. "With the present county supervisors, forget it. One's Church of God, two are up for election this cycle."

"And you're not going to bat for me, are you?"

The sheriff smiles. "Honestly, it might be better to have a bullshit-magnet or two downtown instead of the trouble being spread all around, but this isn't Las Vegas."

"So we're done Saturday night."

"You're done *now*. Closed is closed."

Vic goes inside and harvests his couple of cash stashes. A few of the items might be salable on eBay, the lighting is all rental, and he'll pack his lucky disco ball for the road. In the Old West the first saloons at any bonanza site were in tents, only growing wooden walls if the ore held out. He's got the books spread out on the bar counter when Scorch pokes his head in from the side, letting himself in.

"That on the door for real?"

"Afraid so."

Scorch nods, steps in to stare at Vic's pile of greenbacks.

"Gittin out while the gittin's good."

"Yeah. What I owe you?"

"Four hundred."

Vic separates the bills from the stack, hands them to Scorch. "Know where you're heading?"

"Away," says the bouncer, and leaves. Vic hears his motorcycle, a new acquisition, roar to life and trail off past the train station.

He's never actually been run out of town before. When the Katrina clean-up slowed down in New Orleans it was time to move on, and sometimes it's been competition, too many clubs, too many girls offering it to the same pool of pussy hounds. In Michigan there was an offer of partnership from some wise guys he didn't want anything to do with, but they were happy to take the club off his hands for a reasonable bump, and tossed one of their clueless nephews the keys to the kingdom. The laws changed on him in a couple other spots, less contact, more enforcement, and he chose to move on. It is a gypsy trade. Shirleen, when they were still married and partners, would put on Connie Francis belting "Where the Boys Are" once a night and peel while she lip-synched to it. 'Our theme song,' she called it.

There is a rattle at the rear door, which he's neglected to unlock. He'll have to start calling the girls, the bar staff, everybody.

It's Jewelle, not due back on stage till Friday, in her schlubby street outfit.

"Hey, stranger. How's Lake Tahoe?"

"The usual suspects. What's with the traffic? There's like *space* between the sixteen-wheelers."

"Bunch of the rigs are shutting down half-drilled."

"They make a mistake about what's down there?"

Vic shrugs. "Orders from headquarters. Had a bunch of guys coming in before their two weeks off, been told to go home and not to come back."

Jewelle looks worried. "But you've still got customers?"

"Nope. Shut us down as of an hour ago. Yellow Earth just developed moral compunctions."

"Shut *down*?"

"Next door too."

She looks around the club, always sobering under the ugly lights. "Where does that leave me?"

Vic slips the rest of the cash into the zipper compartment under his jacket, closes the ledger. Plenty of time for that now.

"Up Shit Mountain," he says, "without a backpack."

THE MOTHER ACTS LIKE they're all in a conspiracy together. Blonde and scrawny, with a tattoo that says *ELVIS* in script on the back of her right hand.

"He texts me," she says. "Even when he'd be down in Mexico, I'd hear from him once, maybe twice a week."

"I can understand why you're concerned." Harleigh has moved his chair out from behind his desk, the mother sitting across from him with their knees almost touching, the daughter and Marjorie Looks for Water, who is hosting them on the reservation, standing behind. "You been in contact with our chief of– "

"We just came from there. He showed me all the reports– who's been killed or arrested in the state."

"We have excellent relations with the surrounding counties."

"But none of that tells me where Wayne Lee *is*."

I'm not hiding him under my desk, lady. If your kid doesn't want to communicate with you, it's none of my–

"I met your son a couple times," says Harleigh. "A very– *per*sonable young man."

"Your partner."

"Brent? Former partner."

"They said at the garage he's away. They didn't know how long."

"I don't really keep track of Mr.– "

"They said there was a fight."

"Blows were struck?"

He's heard this from Danny Two Strike, heard it from a couple of the drivers, but it didn't sound so different from any of the other times Brent lit into an employee.

"They had a yelling argument. *Scream*ing argument."

"The oil business, Ma'am, has a bit of the Wild West to it. Lots of men without women, competing with each other for economic survival. Tempers flare up."

"I want to search his house."

And take a look at his books for me while you're at it.

"You'll have to get a court order for that, be accompanied by law enforcement."

"You can't just okay it?"

"Mr. Stiles's house is not on reservation property. Even if it was– "

"But the *gara*ge is."

"Absolutely." Though the partnership is dissolved, Brent still has a lease on Harleigh's garage, good through the end of the year.

"That was the last place he was seen alive."

He thinks of Alice Looks for Water, Marjorie's mom, whose boy Jimmy went to Vietnam and didn't come back, flying that black MIA-POW flag for the next thirty years and still convinced he's Out There, alive somewhere.

"What you might try," and here he locks eyes with Marjorie for a moment, who is a responsible person even if she spends too much time making friends on the internet and wants to play girl detective, "is to speak with Brent's wife. Her name is Bunny, and she knew– knows– your son too, and might be able to clear a few things up."

The mother, not expecting this, just stares at him.

"My secretary can give you the phone number. And take some of these."

He hands her a half-dozen of the printouts.

"That's a letter of introduction from me, requesting that folks cooperate with you, answer questions, whatever, and the other is a rough map of the reservation with both the man camps– those are residences for visiting workers– and the well sites marked on it. I have to warn you," he says, indicating the world outside his window, "that we're talking about four thousand square miles."

The mother nods, mollified if not satisfied, and stands up. From what little time he spent with Wayne Lee he could tell he was the daredevil type, always up for an adventure. Odds are he's shacked up in a motel room over in Montana, telling lies to some pretty lady he met.

"What do *you* think happened?" asks the mother. There is something so past-tense about it, like she knows the answer and is just testing him, that it gives Harleigh a bit of a chill.

"What I think, what I *hope*," says Harleigh, "is that your boy has just got distracted by something, forgot about calling his momma."

The mother leaves without thank you or goodbye, Marjorie giving him a little wave as she steps out last. He pops his cell phone out, speed-dials Rick McAllen as Doris appears in the doorway.

"Hey buddy, what's shakin? Listen, I been fielding some complaints, and this is embarrassing, but it's about something on *my* land."

"Is that right," says Rick flatly on the other end. In fact most of the complaints he's been fielding have to do with Rick handing people his emergency phone number. Like he's not being paid a bundle to catch a little flak.

"Yeah, kind of slipped past me. Somebody's been dumping those oil socks– you know, the filters– "

"The ones that pick up all the radium."

"Right, right, it can build up in there. Well there's a bunch of them been dumped out behind my grazing property, and I just got word we might be having another camera outfit– "

"I just had the Bismarck people put me on the grill for a half hour. KNDX."

"Well this is a national outfit, *Attack of the Frack Monster* kind of stuff."

"So I guess you'd like me to send a crew to pick them up." Ricky is a sulker. And always the voice of doom– this thing spilled, that thing's in violation, another doesn't have its permits yet, they're burning methane off in the air, like anybody but the eco-freaks and the soreheads think you can make an omelet without busting a few eggs.

"Yes, Ricky, since you're Mr. EPA around here, I would *like* that, and to*day* would be a good time. *Yesterday* would have been better, but I just got the word on this."

"I'll send some fellas over." Grudgingly though, like it's a big favor and not his job. And fucking Brent, who contracted to haul the fucking things to the hazardous waste site, had better fucking *stay* missing.

"Good, good, you do that– countin on you, buddy."

Doris, hearing all this, is wearing her bearer-of-bad-tidings look. Harleigh terminates the call.

"Tell me."

"A gentleman from the FBI?" she says. "For you?"

THE VOLUNTEERS HAVE COME through. Everywhere they drive there are flyers tacked up, in the man camp lobbies, on the corkboards in the drill site trailers, in every bar in Yellow Earth and its environs, at the Pool-N-Pong and the lobby of the new recreation center, at the diners and fast food places.

HAVE YOU SEEN THIS MAN?

–above the photo Mrs. Hickey sent, Wayne Lee smiling at the camera in a motorcycle racing outfit, his helmet under his arm, and then the phone numbers and e-mail addresses to contact. Nice-looking boy, like an actor on a TV show if his hair was shorter, and Marjorie is sorry she never got to meet him.

And probably never will.

"So much room to get lost in." Mrs. Hickey is staring out the window at the prairie again, brooding. This time of year, no wildflowers out, the cattle mostly in at their winter feed lots, it is pretty bleak. And then with the wind, rocking the car sideways now and then as they travel west on 23.

"E-mails, telephones, all that stuff," says Marjorie, resigned to tuck in between water trucks and go their speed, "make you forget how big the world is."

"He'd be passing everybody right now, Wayne Lee."

She hopes it's only an observation and not a criticism of her driving. There's just as many trucks in the opposite lane, coming into the rez, and weaving in and out to pass won't get you anywhere.

"Couldn't bear to *wait* for anything, even when he's little."

"They had him on Ritalin," says the sister from the back seat. "Or else he'd be bouncing off the walls in school."

The sister still has her arms folded across her chest like she has since she got here. Either she thinks this is a waste of time or is jealous of Wayne Lee getting all the attention. "She likes girls," Mrs. Hickey muttered the first minute they had alone, as if this explained everything.

The trailer is just off the highway and Marjorie pulls over. There's an ATV parked out front, same model as what the Cunningham kid has got, only with nice-looking **Indian Power** and **Fueled by Frybread** stickers on it. Marjorie hasn't heard about anybody in Dickyboy's family getting an oil lease.

She probably bangs on the door too hard, but the TV is on real loud inside, a game show playing, probably cranked up to compete with the constant rumble of trucks going by. Olivia Burdette answers, wearing a sweatshirt for some sports team, a big wolf head on the front of it. She looks puzzled to see them.

"Yeah?"

Marjorie's mom used to go to the bingo with Olivia, said she could handle five cards at once and smoked a pack of Luckies before the night was over.

"Good afternoon, Mrs. Burdette– is Dickyboy home?"

"He in trouble?"

"No, Ma'am, but we're trying to find somebody that he knows."

Olivia scowls at Mrs. Hickey, trying to place her and coming up with nothing. Dickyboy is her grandson, living with her on and off since his father checked out and his mother Ella had the breakdown.

"Yeah, he come by today. Out back," she says, and closes the door.

There's a shed out back that's been patched with different materials over the years, and a metal DO NOT DISTURB sign hung on the door knob. Marjorie gets one of her twinges and signals for Mrs. Hickey and the sister to hang back.

"Let me go first."

With the oil money and whatnot floating around, there's more guns than ever on the rez, and as her heartthrob Steve Earle sings, a pistol is the devil's right hand. She doesn't knock, but calls out loud.

"Dickyboy? It's Marjorie Looks for Water."

Some quick shuffling of items inside, then the reply. "What do you want?"

"I need to talk to you."

"About what?"

"Wayne Lee Hickey."

Nothing for a moment, just the truck noise from the road.

"Never heard of him."

"Come on, Dickyboy, it's just me and his family here. No cops, no problem."

Another long moment and then he opens the door. He looks too wide to fit through it, the whites of his eyes tinted red, not a happy boy.

"What about him?"

"You knew him. Know him."

"I seen him around."

"When's the last time?"

"Can't say."

He looks past her to Mrs. and the sister.

"This is Wayne Lee's mother and his sister"– what was her name again?– "Patty. He's gone missing."

Dickyboy shrugs. "I ain't in charge of him."

He was a nice boy, smart, and she babysat him regular on bingo nights. Glued together plastic battleships.

"I'm not interested in whatever you're up to," she says, holding his eyes with hers. "It's just everybody says that you and that Dylan Foster who was in the accident were hanging around with him. Riding in that Camaro."

"So?"

He's just a little younger than Jimmy was when he left, Marjorie only nine then and riding in to Yellow Earth to see him get the pictures taken in his dress uniform. So handsome. He said Parris Island wasn't so bad, just a lot of screaming and pushups, and you only did one tour, 365 days, where the fighting was. And then he got on the bus and they never saw him again.

"What was he up to?"

"He was a driver for Chairman Killdeer's company."

"I mean hanging around with high school kids?"

Dickyboy shrugs again. Drop sixty, seventy pounds and lose that sullen look and he'd be good-looking.

"Liked to party," he says. "Sold a little pot."

"A little."

"When he had something," says Dickyboy, practicing his hard-eyes for the day the police come to see him, "he'd share it or sell it."

"He liked young girls?"

"What do you think?"

"Anyone in particular?"

He looks away then. He used to go with the Chairman's stepdaughter, Fawn, back in junior high, and there's rumors about her, but none involving Wayne Lee Hickey.

"Tina," he says.

"I don't know a Tina."

"She lives out south of Yellow Earth, on a farm. Tina Dollarhide."

With True Crime you never know what little bit of evidence will be the key. You build the picture, try to get into people's heads, follow your hunches. It was embarrassing the one time she contacted *America's Most Wanted* and it turned out to be somebody else when they caught him, but Mr. Glaser at the finance company really *did* look like the guy from New Jersey who killed his whole family, or at least what the face-artist had guessed he'd look like twenty years later. And he did give her a creepy feeling, like they say certain people get when they're in the room with a genuine psychopath.

"Anybody you can think of," she asks, Mrs. Hickey standing just behind her now to hear better, "who might have wanted to do Wayne Lee harm?"

"Naw," says Dickyboy, flicking a glance of what might be sympathy to the mother. "He was a cool dude."

SPARTINA, WHICH IS HER whole name, is not in, so they are sitting with Clemson Dollarhide. Her uncle Brewster has grazing scenes by the same painter up on his rec room wall– you can't miss the style. Each one in this room has got a different breed in the distance– Angus against dry yellow grass over here, Charolais white on a green hill over there, a huge herd of Herefords spread out over the fireplace mantel. He's asked them to come in and sit, old-school polite and formal, and takes his time getting into his chair.

"I never had the pleasure of meeting your son," he says to Mrs. Hickey. "But

I've heard some about him."

"Your daughter knows him?" The sister now, Pat, getting bolder as the long day wears her mother down.

"That's what I understand. She's still at school. Fashion Club, I believe."

Something tense here, Marjorie thinks. The way he's sitting, and it isn't just arthritis.

"Has she ever talked to you about him?" she asks.

"We had"– and here the old man looks up as if searching for a word– "we had a discussion. Some might call it a heated discussion."

"Because– ?"

"Because it isn't appropriate for a young lady of her age to be spending time with somebody his age."

His gaze comes down to Mrs. Hickey, not hostile, just straight talking.

"As a matter of fact," says Mr. Dollarhide, "I've been looking for your son myself."

"To have a word with him– " Marjorie says, trying to head it off.

"To kick his young ass and tell him to stay away from my granddaughter."

Mrs. Hickey is just staring holes into the man. It's clear that in her mind her son has never been guilty of a single thing, not even the felonies he did time for back home.

"But you didn't track him down?"

"No. And I already told Crowder I had my rifle in the back seat, but that was just a precaution."

Marjorie turns to Mrs. Hickey and Pat. "Sheriff Crowder is in charge over to Yellow Earth," she says. "We talk to him tomorrow."

"If he is missing," says Mr. Dollarhide, "it's because he has chosen to absquatulate."

"Abs– what?"

"To retreat without honor."

In the True Crime books sometimes the perpetrators are very bold, almost daring the detectives to come after them. But Marjorie isn't feeling a killer vibe in here.

"I want to talk to this granddaughter," says Mrs. Hickey, eyes hard and fixed on Clemson.

"I'll tell her you come by. Leave one of those flyers."

He's still a suspect, for sure, but not likely to give anything up that he doesn't want to. The paper has done a couple articles about his fight with the state over right of way for the oil people, got drilling operations on properties all around him that have to loop way around his land to get to the highway. Acting as his own lawyer and not doing a bad job of it, from what she can tell. Good for old people to have a hobby.

Mrs. Hickey stands and Marjorie and Pat do the same. Time to leave.

"I do hope you find what you're looking for, M'am."

THEY MEET IN GINGER'S Café across the street from the Yellow Earth Cinema, which is featuring *The Expendables*. That's me, thinks Danny Two Strike, pulling up to the curb. A tired action hero trudging toward one more payday.

"You fellas planning a bust?" asks the waitress who pours their coffee, a local woman in her forties.

"If you don't have real milk instead of that damn whitener," says Will, "it might be this place."

"I'll get you some."

"So," says Danny, sitting back, "I say it's fifty-fifty he's in Mexico, drinking margaritas and waiting for the whole thing to blow over."

"Could be. With some of the characters Skiles has got hanging around him, if he was mad at me I'd want to blow town."

"But then *you* got more than half a brain and aren't a drug dealer."

"Good point. I brought Clem Dollarhide in for a talk, but there was nothing there."

"What's he got to do with Wayne Lee Hickey?"

"Hickey's been seeing his granddaughter Tina."

"Seeing."

"Assume the worst."

"She's not eighteen yet."

Tina Dollarhide works at the Havva Javva. Very nice girl, seems sensible–

"If we ever find the guy," says Will, "I can try to bust him for it. But she's all worried and weepy about him disappearing, so I don't expect any cooperation."

"The one I'd love to nail is that Skiles."

"Stand in line. But through the wonders of subcontracting, I can't get much of anything on him. Jim Wilson from the Bureau is looking into his financial dealings, but those boys take forever."

"He and Harleigh have called it quits."

"Good for Harleigh."

"And they were tight. Vacation together, went out hunting."

"Bows and arrows?"

"I doubt it. Think he got an elk last year, Brent."

"Which suggests a rifle. Which he can't have, not with a felony record."

"You've checked? He's got a record?"

"It isn't a record, it's a double album," says Will. "Fraud, robbery, assault, jumping bail a couple times, credit card theft."

"Assault?"

"Two convictions. Did county time in Texas. The officer I talked to there says they were readying a drug indictment when he left. The thing is, most of his business here is in his wife's name. Some tax deal."

"You could get a writ, search his house."

"*He* doesn't have a house. The one he built is in his wife's name."

"And she is– ?"

"His wife."

"Right. And she might be terrified of disappearing like Wayne Lee Hickey."

Both of them have had bad guys waltz out of their jurisdictions due to insufficient evidence, both have guys just as bad still infecting their turf. It would be nice to take one off the board.

Will digs into his turkey burger, checking out the street through the window. Danny knows the reflex, in or out of uniform– whatever is going on is my business. He tries to remember back before he put his antennae out, before he noticed every out-of-state license plate or trailer with a funny smell coming out of it. He's only been shot once, by the wife in a domestic he was breaking up, who claimed she was trying to hit her boyfriend but they both knew that was bullshit. The guy put her in the hospital again just last week, jaw wired shut, the wife just shaking her head with oxycontin eyes when Danny asked her to testify.

"So tell me," says Will, still gazing out the window, "you ever been in a relationship with somebody from a totally different world?"

A personal question from Sheriff Crowder.

"Well– I married Winona, who was like Dakota Sioux with a vengeance. "

"But you were both Indians."

"And Swedes and Italians are both white people."

"I get it."

"It took me a couple years to figure out I was never going to be invited to join her club."

"Which you wanted?"

"Honorary member, sure, I was willing to go that far. But her club was her personality, not her, like, tribal affiliation."

"And you and that Ruby?"

Danny is stunned for a moment, recovers.

"You know about that?"

"I'm not supposed to?"

Try to keep a secret on the fucking reservation. Danny has only had one call from Ruby since she left to work for the Lummis, lots of complaining about the weather, saying how him coming there would improve her mood a hundred percent. Totem poles in the drizzling rain– it depresses him just thinking about it.

"Her people and mine never even met in the old days, much less warred against each other," says Danny, "but mostly she's a lot more educated than me."

"That's what I mean, different worlds."

"You thinking of marrying an extraterrestrial or something?"

Will frowns, shakes his head slightly. "I figure you should be willing to meet someone halfway. But halfway between Yellow Earth and New Center is different than halfway between here and China."

"She's Chinese?"

Will shakes his head again. "She's a field biologist."

"Nature Girl!"

"That's what you call her?"

"If she had an Indian name it would be Dances With Rodents."

Will laughs. "She's not totally dorky or anything."

"I'm sure she's great. Looks good in those khaki shorts."

"The thing is, she's *young*er."

"How's your lateral movement these days?"

Will had been a basketball, football, and baseball standout in high school, not quite Division 1 material but a force to deal with.

"My knees pop when I roll over in bed."

"Right. The older you get, the less *flex*ible you are. So if something feels good right now, I wouldn't overthink it."

"You're saying this could be my last shot?"

Danny can see that the man is serious, seriously asking his opinion. "Have you ever thought about who you'd be," he asks, "if you moved away from here?"

SPARTINA WAITS TILL THE car is out of sight, till her grandfather stops walking around, obviously upset by the visit. She came in through the back, quiet as usual, and heard the last part of it. Something has happened. Something bad. And she's sure it has to do with the guy he worked for, that Brent who got Fawn pregnant and then wanted her to have it fixed.

Tina takes her shoes off and pads past her grandfather, who doesn't hear so well anymore, and into the kitchen. She knows if she uses her cell phone there will immediately be a record of who it is, but maybe from a landline–

She uses the old rotary in the kitchen, the dial loudly clicking as it rolls back into position. Once Fawn came over and made fun of it, saying with a phone like that the whole house should be in black and white. The dispatcher answers.

"Sheriff Crowder, please?" she says, pressing her mouth close to the receiver. "It's personal."

The woman says he's not in but can connect him if this is his sister again. Tina says it is and there is a little wait.

Sheriff Crowder comes on the phone.

"Brent Skiles who owns the truck company?" she says. "He's got *guns* in his house. Like army guns that can't be legal, lots of them."

And hangs up.

THEY DON'T TALK ON the way back, Mrs. Hickey staring out at the empty plain again. Marjorie remembers when the Google Earth thing became available and she found Khe Sanh in Vietnam on it and went to the satellite view, zooming down in to check out the area where Jimmy disappeared. He was on a patrol 'outside the wire,' the Marines said. And they took fire and some were killed and wounded and when it was all over Jimmy wasn't accounted for. And sure, maybe like her mother always says, he could have been hit on the head and got amnesia and be a prisoner there with no idea who he is, but all Marjorie thought staring at the different splotches of green, like a whole country of camouflage cloth, was how are you going to find a set of dogtags in all that?

There's still not an affordable room to be had in Yellow Earth or Watford City, so the Hickeys are staying with her, Mrs. Hickey on the foldout and Pat on an air mattress on the floor. If she'd let Chairman Killdeer know this he probably would have found something better, but he's got an agenda of his own and it was clear Mrs. Hickey didn't trust him.

Marjorie keeps to Dollarhide's dirt road as long as it goes, not an oilfield truck in sight, then has to join the parade, squeezing in behind a crude-oil-hauling armada heading east. The buffalo grass on the road shoulders, usually impossible to kill, is looking bad, suffocating under a layer of dust. And up on a rise to the left are three coyotes, sitting, looking at something down on the other side. You don't often see that many together in the daytime.

IT ISN'T EXACTLY A vision quest. For starters, it was never really a woman's tradition, and Teresa is not planning to cut off a joint of her little finger, or any other part of her body, to offer the Spirits. But she needs guidance, some indication of what to do, which way to turn.

It takes her an hour to find a place where there are no drill rigs visible, a little bowl made by some rock outcroppings. The old places, the holy places her father told her about, are mostly under the lake now.

Teresa sits on a flat spot on one of the rocks. She's been fasting for two days but has brought a thermos of water. It's a bit warmer in here, out of the wind, and the sky above is clear in patches. She doesn't try to conjure anything, just kick back and free associate, see what comes.

A certain amount of it was metaphor of course, recognizing traits in the animals– swiftness, strength, stealth, persistence– that you admired and then tried to emulate. Probably why so many sports teams are named after predators. If your life was ruled by the availability of game, the cycles of weather, your observation of those things went beyond practicality. Science and religion were one.

But another part had to be that you did it in isolation, you as an individual were touched by a greater power, a power that found you worthy of visitation.

The Christians are always praying for Jesus to come into their lives, to talk to them, to sign on as their Personal Savior. As much as the People depended on each other to survive and lived on top of each other in earthen huts, as much as it takes a village and all that, there was always a hunger for individuality, to sing your own unique song. You had it both ways. When you came back from your quest there was a shaman of some sort to help you interpret the vision, and your family and your tribe were eager to take you back in and to learn how you had changed, what they should call you now.

The Spirits have lost interest in us, thinks Teresa Crow's Ghost, and we belong to nothing.

She can hear machine noise on the wind now. It isn't traffic– she's too far in from the highway– so it must be one of the oil rigs, or the pipes with gas burning up from them day and night, or even the pump jacks, bobbing up and down, up and down. The Earth has been stabbed and is bleeding, she thinks, there's a metaphor for you. But stabbing and bleeding was no rarity in the old life, and the problem can't be just a matter of scale. There is no ceremony to this taking, no more than there is at a slaughterhouse when the cattle are run through it. Cattlemen talk about the worth of the 'carcass' that will be left, while the animals are still growing. With the buffalo each bull, cow, or calf was a manifestation, a gift from the greater spirit of Buffalo, and the hunt was celebrated with dances before and after. Now there are only commodities.

When buffalo cross her mind the image is of the patchy old bull in the petting zoo in Fargo, the first live one she ever saw, an animal that seemed embarrassed to have its picture taken with small children perched behind its hump. She closes her eyes and other images come, more recent ones, trucks and other heavy equipment rumbling and growling, afraid of nothing on earth or in the sky. Consuming. Consuming. Teresa begins to sing one of the river songs, softly, the words simple but the melody always making her want to cry.

You can't go backwards in time. Even if you could, there are negative things, role expectations, the whole Crips-versus-Bloods aspect of tribal warfare, that she is glad are over. Young men don't have to kill an enemy to gain status, to impress the young women anymore. Not that they don't enlist in the military, but that's something that happens far away. There was a sense of being part of a whole then, of your destiny being attached, being an important part of that, of the People–

Somebody is singing along with her.

Teresa opens her eyes to see Danny Two Strike, in his badge and uniform, standing a few feet away from her.

"Sorry," he says. "Search party."

"Searching for what?"

Danny is one of the success stories, a pretty wild kid who straightened out, has stayed to give something back.

"White guy who went missing a while back, used to work for ArrowFleet. Marjorie is all over it, she's hosting the guy's family."

"You're being pretty thorough."

Danny shrugs, looks around. "I was trying to think of a place not in sight of any of the drilling operations."

"You've been here before?"

He sits by her on the rock. "Yeah. We used to come up here to get out of the wind, smoke weed."

Teresa shows him her hands.

"I'm not holding."

He smiles. "Anyhow, we're finding all kinds of stuff lying around that shouldn't be there, but so far no bodies."

"Would you share that information? So I can bring it up at the next council meeting?"

Danny is too polite to ask her what she's doing here. A good boy, such a shame his marriage didn't work out–

"Sure. You know more about the environmental stuff than me, but it just doesn't look right, what they leave behind."

"Sovereignty by the barrel."

"Not the worst idea."

"Turn the Three Nations into Saudi Arabia."

Danny laughs. "I wonder what it's like for those people– I mean the real people, not just the oil sheiks driving Rolls-Royces around the desert. I hear nobody has to work, they bring in people from Egypt and the Philippines."

"I haven't noticed any great uplifting going on."

"Me neither. How's Ricky hanging in?"

"You lie down with dogs," says Teresa, "you get up with fleas."

Danny stands, brushes off the seat of his pants. "Well– I'll leave you to it."

"Take care, Danny. I hope you find– you know. I hope he's alive somewhere."

A turkey buzzard floats overhead. If she stays here a while, doesn't move, there will be a half-dozen in no time, circling lower and lower to see if she's ready to be picked at.

Teresa begins to sing again, a song about the grass, and the animals that will come to eat it.

THE OLD EKSTROM PLACE has been empty for thirty years, but the probate is tangled enough that it hasn't been torn down. What had been a mowed yard around it is overrun now with spurge, Canada thistle, yellow foxtail. The composition board tacked over the missing widows has begun to curl apart, tall weeds have grown up through the cracks in the porch planks and several hundred bats fly out of the top story every night until mid-November. You can't see the house from the highway, which was only a wagon trail when the first Ekstrom in the county built it. The structure has begun to lean heavily to the west, as if it wants to lie down.

The coyotes come down the hill cautiously, the lead one, patchy and yellow-brown, whining a little. The dead smell is stronger every day, cutting through the other, the reek of oil. The coyotes come to within a few yards of the big gap that has rotted under the porch, and sit again, heads low, the tips of their tails wiggling like fishing lures.

There are toadstools growing in the dark of the crawlspace beneath the old house, and critters, the rodents growing curious about the smell from what is wrapped in the oil-splotched plastic tarp. A tiny bar of light reaches it once a day through holes in the roof, second floor, and ground floor, all lining up for a few minutes every afternoon, the tarp shining blue where it isn't stained, and then the Earth keeps rolling and it returns to darkness.

DICKYBOY IS REHEATING THE pizza in the galley oven when he hears the car door slam. He'd had a vision of Timmy Coates who delivers for the Hut bringing it all the way out to the yacht, climbing up the roofing ladder with the box balanced in one hand. He'd be a legend for at least a week, the balls of it, and then probably in jail. As it was, having Timmy meet him at the casino with the hot pie after work will be good for a day or two of gossip at school. He's been mostly using the oven to thaw and heat frozen dinners, as cooking on the stovetop presents a venting problem sooner or later with the boat cover laying over everything. He finds his flashlight and steps out on the deck, bending under the rain-puddled tarp, sagging with the weight between frame supports, moving to the side of the boat facing land rather than water. He wiggles into his observation post, taking up the binoculars he stole from the Sportsman's Warehouse and scanning around. He's studied the yacht from the ground enough to know that you'd have to be accidentally looking directly at the spot where he's loosened the boat cover to notice the slight bump the binoculars make, and has watched plenty of people drive up to check out the *Savage Princess* without them knowing it.

It's Brent Skiles, standing next to his red Corvette, looking pissed about something. From this height you can see he's really starting to lose his hair on top.

With Dylan off the road, Wayne Lee missing, and the Bazookas bouncer gone with the wind, an alteration of income flow was inevitable. They're hiring pretty much anybody in the enrollment who can breathe over at Bearpaw, and as long as he can call himself Spa Attendant instead of Towel Boy he's resigned to work for only three bucks an hour over minimum.

It's only a minute or so when Fawn's stepfather pulls up in his Denali and gets out, standing to talk to Skiles over the hood of the Vette.

"Chief. How's it going?"

Mr. Killdeer does not look pleased.

"You're using my name."

"Negative on that. There's people who might as*sume* that we're still– "

"ArrowFleet is dissolved."

"Yeah, I saw the paperwork you sent over, the notice in that excuse for a newspaper you got here. If we weren't so busy I'd have the boys change the logo on the trucks."

"I want you off the reservation."

"No can do, Chief. You know how it works– somebody signs an oil lease, the driller gets access, hires service companies at their discretion. We got contracts to fulfill."

"You're still hooking in investors."

"The free market. It's what makes capitalism great."

And Fawn is letting this guy do her.

The council chairman just stares at Skiles for a long moment.

"Wayne Lee Hickey. Your boy."

"Hey, dude worked for me for a while, then he didn't. Happens a hundred times a day up here."

"I've got his relatives stumbling around out in the fields, plastering the reservation with his photo."

"People watch too much television. They imagine things."

"He's *missing*."

The binoculars make the two men look like they're right on top of each other, like one could reach out and strangle the other, even with the car between them. Puffs of frozen breath come out of their mouths as they speak.

"Wayne Lee was missing when he was *here*, missing a shitload load of brain cells. The dude lacked *focus*. Look, he probably just got bored, or got some local chick pregnant, and he bugged out."

"I heard you had a screaming fight with him."

"More than one, but nobody threw a punch. He could piss people off."

"Was he dealing drugs for you?"

It's Brent Skiles's turn to stare at Chairman Killdeer.

"You should keep in mind," he says evenly, "that loose talk is kind of like an oil spill. Sticks to whoever and whatever is close to it."

"I don't make people disappear."

"You see," says Skiles, "it's a matter of *loyalty*. What Wayne Lee and people like him don't understand is that once you're in, you're *in*, balls and all. Or else you got to face the consequences."

"Are you *threat*ening me?"

It is all Dickyboy can do to keep from grabbing the flare gun he found in the cabin and taking a shot at the fucker. Not that Chairman Killdeer is like a daddy to him, or like he was anything but Fawn's practice partner for making out in the eight grade, but you fuck with the Nations–

"Relatives are out looking for him, huh? That's unfortunate. So much space out here to get lost in."

Skiles slides into his Vette then, and drives away.

Harleigh Killdeer stands thinking for a minute, then seems to look straight up at Dickyboy. Dickyboy holds the binoculars steady, doesn't budge. The council chairman walks to the yacht, reaches up to lay a hand on the hull.

"Soon," he says, softly, then gets in his car and leaves.

Dickyboy can smell the pizza now, crisping in the hold below.

EVERY ONCE IN A while they need an attitude correction. Remind them how things stand. Bunny has been on the ride long enough, you'd think she'd know the rules by now. The idea of waltzing back from a shopping binge in Jackson Hole, barely laying her credit card trophies on the floor before she's on his case, screaming at him. *Screaming*. Brent flexes his hand on the steering wheel, knuckles starting to swell. He should have brought the arnica along, but she'd already made him late to leave.

He'll zip across the top of the rez, get his head together, then turn north through Minot and across the border. And please give me no shit about getting into your second-string country, as if I want to go to fucking Winnipeg. The Russian insisted, maybe got some border issues of his own that keep him out of the States, and a face-to-face means he's close to taking the plunge. Big chunk of change, looking for somewhere legitimate to park it.

He did remember the copy of his birth certificate, folded in the glove compartment, in case they actually patrol that crossing. It will be his second foreign country, if you count Tijuana as part of Mexico and not just Duty Free for sleazebags.

Brent eases off, coasting down under eighty, sees that he'll need gas. Chuck's, where he ambushed the Chairman that first time, is up ahead.

He made her try to wiggle all her teeth, make sure nothing was loosened, and got her one of the ice packs he uses for his knees, wrapped in a towel. And she apologized, even if she didn't exactly have her heart in it. Good to have a business trip though– go to your separate corners, let her start to miss you, wonder if you'll ever come back–

He pulls into the pumps. Premium, he always puts Premium in the Vette, is down to three-forty a gallon, which even here on the rez seems low. A guy with a limp steps out.

"Fill her up?"

"Premium."

The man flips open the compartment, twists the gas cap off. "Nothing but the best for this baby, huh?"

"How's Chuck doing?"

"I would imagine he's doing just fine. Sitting on a beach somewhere in Florida. Retired."

"He sold this place?"

"To me."

"You'll make out like a bandit."

"That's what I thought," says the man, watching the numbers on the pump roll. It's the old-fashioned kind, no digital readouts. "Volume is way off from when I checked it out last year."

Brent has set up a dummy corporation, bought Chuck's main competitor on the south side of the rez. The ArrowFleet trucks all fuel up there, you dicker with the numbers a little and it's good on both sides of the equation. Only an idiot can't make a killing during an oil boom.

"Want me to get that windshield?"

"Thanks, but I got to roll," says Brent, handing the man cash. He's been paying cash whenever possible these days, leaving as few tracks as possible. Like spraying yourself with scent elimination before you go hunting.

"Good luck, here," he says to the man as he fires the Vette up. "Bound to pick up again, any day now."

The Vette is running smooth. Decent mechanic, way over in Fargo, has a nice touch with engines. Since he bought it from the lease company it's behaved pretty well, but high-performance machines need even more attention than moody women. Can't solve a carburetor imbalance with a love tap.

Shadows, which means mostly telephone pole shadows out here, are getting long. He'll miss dinner, which is fine, feeling a little thick lately, get up to the hotel there and take a shower, go over his plan of attack. Get up early, do an hour in their gym, clean up, and meet the Russian for breakfast. This is the game-changer. This is Showtime.

He's thinking about the case he'll present to the Russian when he passes the patrol car, different markings than the Yellow Earth units he sees all the time. Going what– ninety at least. Shit.

He could take the chance that the cop, whatever they're called out here, didn't get his plate number, but the Vette stands out like red meat on white carpet and with the chief on the warpath– better to take it and roll with the punch. He slows to sixty-five. If he can't catch up to that he's not trying.

Brent pulls over the minute he sees the flasher in his rearview mirror, steps out of the car and waits, pulling his license out. Make it quick and simple.

The patrol car stops a car length behind and the prick at the wheel leaves him standing there for at least five minutes. Psychological warfare, like he's calling your plate number in to higher authorities. When he gets out it's an Indian about the Chief's age, in good shape, wears his hair cut short.

"I know, I know," says Brent, holding his license out. "I'm sorry. When there's nobody on the road you start to space out."

"Nobody but a couple hundred trucks," says the rez cop, who from the plastic shield on his uniform is their chief of police. Brent has heard his name, maybe even had Harleigh point him out–

"You know I've driven across here a bunch of times with your Chairman, and he always goes– "

"I know who you are," says the cop. "And Harleigh holds it to five over the limit."

Danny something. Been on the job for quite a while.

"So I'm not totally straight on how this jurisdiction thing works," says Brent. You have to push back a little bit or they'll steamroller you. "You can give me a speeding ticket?"

"Doing it right now."

Danny what's his name is writing on a pad of forms.

"And I have to pay it?"

The chief of reservation police glances up at him. "You plan to set foot on this reservation again? Drive on it?"

He has to smile. "You got me there."

"You want to be careful out here," says the officer, tearing off forms and handing him the carbon copy. "We got a lot of drunken white men on the road these days."

He keeps it under seventy-five till he's off the rez. That kind of petty shit, harassment when you can't strike back, always knocks his *chi* down some, leaves him feeling deflated. There is a moment where he wants to just keep driving east, fuck Winnipeg, fuck the Russian, it's all too fucking complicated. Cherkov is the guy's name, sounds like jerk-off. Which is what the whole meeting might turn out to be, the Soviets are famous for that.

It's the flame-off stacks that bring him back up, now that it's dark enough to really see the gas burning against the sky. There are so *many* of them now, more light than this prairie has ever seen at night. How the Objectivist would have loved this, the way she loved all of man's great transformative endeavors, his industry, his skyscrapers. It's like driving over the top of a birthday cake with all the candles lit, he thinks, and gooses the Vette up to eighty.

A cake for somebody very, very old.

DUDLEY HAD ONE MORE scotch than usual at the club, but his head is clear enough to make the report. His machine comes on without a noise. He's got a spot bandage over the video eye and retaliatory malware to protect his keystrokes from being monitored. You sneak into other people's systems, you have to assume some of them might try to do the same.

The mission is straightforward, the health and future of the Company at stake. Dudley has studied complexity theory, he's written code for predictive models used throughout the industry, but this one is simple mathematics. Oh, he'll throw in the usual graphs and color charts, coat it in fiduciary obfuscation, but in the wrap-up paragraph the guillotine will have to drop. Crude had been hanging at ninety-five dollars a barrel for a good while but now has started to drop and will keep dropping as long as there's so much oil and gas flooding the market, so at eight cents lower than the present rate it makes no sense to keep hydraulically fracturing wells in the Bakken. Nickels and dimes. Keep pumping whatever is producing already, fine, but pull your equipment out of anything you're still drilling or stimulating and walk away. *Frackus interruptus.*

Dudley breaks his report into three sections and sends them delayed release, the first section to land in Houston the day after tomorrow, more to come. By the time they're reading the inevitable conclusion he'll be lost in the ether.

He developed the Ultimate Determinator over the last two years, the screen output enough to send even the nosiest office mates retreating from his carrel, and he's been able to test it out on a couple of Mexican roustabouts who died on the job in the Permian. It quickly became clear that their names and social security numbers were fake, and in the interest of avoiding insurance payouts to family, Dudley was given the case. Once he teased out their real identities, he set the Program to erasing them. One had a credit card in Mexico, and the first run-through obliterated over twenty-four thousand pesos' worth of debt, then computer records of his marriage, his two parking violations in Odessa, his fatal last hours in the emergency room. There is lots of paper still in Mexico, of course, so he still exists on the yellowing books and in the hearts and minds of his loved ones. The other worker, who he remembers was named Jesús, had managed to live most of his life untouched by the web, a nonperson to government agencies, to law enforcement, Nigerian pyramid schemers and online retailers. Jesús did not rise again three days after he was buried– in fact the little bit of encoded data he'd accumulated in his brief span (he was, by the coroner's estimate, in his early twenties) was expunged forever.

But those were entities with friends and relatives unlikely to mount sophisti-cated cybersearches. Dudley, virtually friendless, distant to all his relatives, still has the Company, the federal government and the leechlike coterie of creditors and their client preference databanks to deal with. He pictures Ahab, pinioned to the submerging albino leviathan by his own lines and harpoons, dragged to a watery death.

If you can devise a program to discover every appearance of an individual in the great e-Book of Life, you can design one to wipe *out* that individual's million coded footprints. Locked systems must be breached, of course, most with elab-orate systems of protection and the ability to detect– Who? What? A program that will scour the universe for any sign of its creator for a few more months, then delete itself, a virus with a genetically coded end date.

The rental car's continued absence will trip no warning at Enterprise, their paperwork revealing a credit card that no longer exists, that, when searched for, *nev*er existed. If found, without a license plate and with the VIN number re-moved, the gray Kia Rio will be only a mystery with an interior unsullied by blood or fingerprints, should anyone bother to check. The hotel will have no record of his visit, maids and desk personnel unable to describe his face if asked, only Caucasian, average this, average that. There will be a bit of a tail to the story of course, the computer record of the Company's attempts to find him, to know how much he stole– no, that's not the proper word. The breadth of the gold-en parachute he incrementally awarded himself during his years of service, web transactions overseen by only one privileged employee.

A guy known as The Dud.

Records of Dudley's past interactions with the recorded world flash on the screen, then dissolve. He feels lighter already. Nobody can live in this modern world, they say, on a cash basis, no matter how much of it they've got stashed away. It will be intriguing to try.

Farewell to Virtual America. Dudley, we never knew ye.

MAKEUP CAN ONLY DO so much. The woman is young, not yet thirty, and looks like she's been using this much base since she was in high school, but the evidence tends to ripen after a day. Right there along the left side of her jaw, and the way she holds her arm so close to her body. There they are on the bench together, less than six feet between them, the only people in the station at this hour.

"*Empire Builder*?" asks Jewelle.

"I'm sorry, what?" the woman replies, breaking out of a reverie.

"Are you waiting for the *Empire Builder*? The train."

"Is that what they call it?" The woman glances at her ticket. "Yes, I am."

"Spokane?"

"That far, then switching trains to Los Angeles."

"Wow. Long haul."

The woman, a natural blonde, at least from this distance, indicates the pile of magazines in her lap. "I'm prepared."

What she doesn't have is a suitcase.

"I get off in Spokane," says Jewelle.

"Home?"

"Just a job."

Jewelle doesn't recognize her, but Teasers had gone to open booking in the last year, girls from all over the map swarming the place to try their luck on the floor. Like the Gold Rush, thinks Jewelle, when everyone and his sister showed up with a shovel and a tin pan.

She doesn't look like she'll be insulted to be asked, but you never know.

"Dancer?"

"I'm sorry– ?"

"Are you a dancer? We might have worked together."

"Oh no– but I was a cheerleader in college."

"Kilgore Rangerettes?"

"Apache Belles."

"Close."

"That's a matter of opinion. You dance in like, what– shows?"

"Clubs. Like the one right next door."

It takes a moment to register.

"*Oh.* Like swinging from the pole."

"That's part of it."

"That must take so much core strength. I've seen it in movies, where the men talk and there's girls snaking around on it in the background."

"I can snake with the best of them."

"But to make it seem so effortless. It should be an Olympic event."

Jewelle smiles. "Don't hold your breath."

The woman doesn't move, but it feels like they're closer.

"And you'll be doing that in Spokane?"

"Stateline Showgirls, just across the border in Idaho."

"Do they have oil too?"

"Not yet. It's a different scene."

The woman thinks for a moment, decides.

"Are you ever afraid?"

"In a club? There's security, these big gorillas."

"But when you walk around all those men, like, not wearing much."

"It's kind of like acting in a movie. Julia Roberts or whoever knows the monster isn't really going to step on her."

The woman nods. Jewelle gives it a beat, then, softly–

"Are *you* afraid?"

"Yes," says the woman, in a very small voice.

"Of what?"

"Roid rage."

Not a familiar term. "*Hemorrhoids?*"

She laughs. "God no."

"Cause I was gonna say, I wouldn't advise a marathon train ride if– "

"*Steroids.*"

"Ah. Too much gym candy– "

"They can alter your personality," she says. "Or maybe he's just a mean son of a bitch."

Jewelle wonders if she's danced for the guy. Sat in his lap.

"Well don't be afraid here."

"Oh no, I'm not. Trains are like– like under his radar? He'd never think of me leaving this way."

"You live in Los Angeles?"

"No, but there's a lawyer there I've got to see." She holds up the magazine on the top of her pile, last month's *People*. "He shows up in these all the time, doing big celebrity divorces."

"You go, girl."

She smiles. "My name's Roberta, but I get called Bunny."

"I was born Donna, but nobody calls me that anymore, unless it's for a motel booking or a credit card thing."

Jewelle glances past the woman. Just a handbag, and not a very big one.

"I've got Tylenol if you need any," she says.

"Maybe later," says Roberta. "It hurts some to open and close my mouth."

"And I'm making you talk."

"Oh no, it's fine, it's good. I didn't get a chance to meet too many women here."

"I think if you're not local it's hard."

"Yeah. And how were you able to function here without a car?"

"It gave up the ghost yesterday. And the prices are still so jacked up here it makes no sense to buy another one."

Roberta nods, thinking.

"You think you'll ever come back here?"

Towns shut down and open up again, officials get greedy, lose office, the new ones make a clean sweep and then come up short on cash–

"Do you know what purgatory is?"

"Like in religion?"

"If you're Catholic, it's where they keep you till your sins are worn away enough by time or by people praying for you that you're allowed into Heaven. I've done my time in Yellow Earth."

"You think anybody will miss you?"

Jewelle has to smile. "No," she says. "They've seen my act."

THEY DON'T GET TO use the Blackhawk Dynamic Entry Ram. Or the Flashbang grenade or the tear gas, or any of the other cop gear Tolliver is so impressed by. Will feels like an idiot standing in the brand-new house in a Kevlar vest, he and Jim Wilson from the Bureau facing the pregnant girl with her bare feet tucked under her on the huge brown leather couch. She was watching a video on the giant flat-screen TV when they charged in, Tolliver no doubt bummed that the front door was unlocked, and she held her arms up like it was a stagecoach robbery in an old Western. The video is still playing with the sound muted, something about teen vampires warring with teen werewolves.

"I'm not sure you can arrest me," says the girl, who is wearing short shorts and a T-shirt with the logo of a band Will has never heard of printed on it. "I'm an enrolled member of the– "

"The federal government has jurisdiction here, young lady," says Jim Wilson, carefully placing his helmet with the bulletproof visor on an end table, "and nobody is being arrested yet."

"You're Fawn," says Will, finally placing her. "Harleigh Killdeer is your stepfather."

"That's right." Behind her the teen werewolves, in their human form, are running through dense forest with incredible speed.

Jim Wilson does not look happy. "Would you state your relationship with Brent Skiles?"

The girl, Fawn, thinks for a moment.

"Friend of the family? He– they– him and Bunny– said I could come by and hang out."

At the other end of the room, Tolliver, who always has his nose stuck in *Guns and Ammo* back at the office, is identifying the weapons in the arsenal as the ATF officer removes them from the cabinet.

"A Glock 34," he says, "an AMT AutoMag III, an old Desert Eagle, Beretta 92– that's a classic– Walther PK380, Smith & Wesson 1911– "

"You have any idea where they are now, Fawn?" asks Will.

"No. I mean Bunny is sposed to be in Jackson Hole, and Brent, Mr. Skiles, he's always real busy."

"Semiautomatic Mossberg 930 Watchdog Shotgun, chamber holds eight rounds," Will hears Tolliver say. "Pump-Action Winchester Defender– "

"Have you ever fired any of these weapons?" asks Jim Wilson, nodding back toward the case.

"I never even *held* one. People shouldn't own guns, unless they're like– you know– to shoot snakes or whatever. If you have to be where there's a lot of snakes."

"Have you ever seen Mr. Skiles firing them?"

"No."

"Fawn," says Will, "how did you get here? There isn't a car outside."

"Uhmm– Mr. Skiles gave me a ride."

"So he's nearby?"

"I guess. He dropped me here about an hour ago, but he didn't say where he was going."

"And he drives a Corvette."

"Yeah. He put the top down today cause it wasn't so cold."

"Stag Model 3 Highlander AR 15– see the camo?" the deputy is saying. "That retro-looking thing is a Henry Big Boy, then a Remington 700, that's just a hunting rifle– "

Will sits down on the far end of the couch, new leather squeaking under him. The girl is a little scared and a little excited.

"You weren't going to spend the night here, were you?" he asks.

"No."

"So I'm assuming that Brent– Mr. Skiles– is going to give you a ride home."

He's heard the rumors. He watches the girl weigh her options.

"He said he'd be back about five."

Will looks to Jim Wilson, who nods. Will stands, takes off the Kevlar vest.

"I'm going to give you a ride home instead," he says. "Let's get your stuff together."

"Mossberg 715T" says Tolliver, eyes gleaming, as they pass him and the ATF officer, "Steyr M1– "

Will lifts the mirror to see Fawn brooding in the rear of the patrol car.

"It'll come out, you know," he says. "About you and Brent."

"He never gave me drugs or anything. It was totally consensual."

They watch cop shows, forensics shows. Half the kids he hauls in are playing roles they've seen on TV.

"The trouble he's in doesn't have anything to do with you. But you'll have to testify, and if you tell the absolute truth you'll come out fine."

"They'll be under Bunny's name, you know," she says. "The guns. That's how they work their business."

"I believe the law will see through that."

They'd found a stash of Dianabol in the little exercise room, might be an old prescription, might not, but nothing else indictable. The gun charge will keep him in the state till the killing in Idaho can be investigated, and maybe the Hickey boy's body will turn up.

"Is my stepfather in trouble too?" asks Fawn. She sounds genuinely worried.

"I hope not," says Will.

HE COULD HAVE SWORN there was a workover rig there just yesterday. Harleigh pulls the Denali off the road, crosses the mucky field to the edge of the drill pad. One of the workmen throwing equipment into the rear of a box truck acknowledges him with a nod.

"What happened to the well?"

"Never got to be one," says the man, who has *SARGE* stitched on the front of his coveralls.

"But they were drilling."

"They stopped."

"Why?"

Sarge heaves something metal and bulky onto the pile already in the truck, shrugs. "Got a bad reading, decided it wouldn't produce, who knows? We just move shit from one place to the next."

"Where's this stuff going?"

"Out of state."

Only the collar of the annulus is still poking up above the surface, the gravel around it strewn with beams and struts, with equipment Harleigh couldn't name if you paid him.

"They can't just *leave* it."

Another guy, whose empty hands indicate he is probably the foreman, steps over. "It's been capped."

"I don't see any."

"Probably bridge plugs and cement, and if we're here the top plug has been tapped to be sure it'll hold. Plugged and abandoned. We're part of 'abandoned.'"

There is a cuttings pit, most of the liquid gone so you can see the liner.

"So who does the reclamation?"

The foreman looks around, raising his eyebrows. "What's to reclaim?"

"They're supposed to put it back the way it was– pull out the gravel and any drilling fluid left behind, regrade to the original contour, reseed."

"As far as I know they got a year for all that, unless the surface owner takes a pass on it."

This is tribal land. Stepping closer, Harleigh sees that the liquid is gone because the liner is ripped in a couple places.

"*Some*body's got to be responsible for this."

The foreman sighs like Harleigh has ruined his day, and moves off to look at a clipboard left on the front seat of his pickup. When they started on the rez they gave notice before every move, they sent him websites to visit and understand the process better. The access road he's driven down is almost a half-mile long, and that should be removed as well–

"Got it!" calls the foreman, reading off one of the forms stuck on his clipboard. "Reclamation contractor– Skilldeer Incorporated. It's an outfit called ArrowFleet."

Connie finds him out on the new deck that Arne built, drinking a Scotch.

"What's the occasion?"

"Nothing. Just thinking about places we could go."

"You know how I feel about flying."

"I mean places we could drive. See the country."

"Like for your conferences."

She sits on his lap. When Fawn isn't around she loosens up, gets more affectionate. And who knows if Fawn will really get it together to leave–

"Not conferences– that's just hotels and cities, other reservations with casinos. I mean the country in between."

She gives him a concerned look. "And just when is this likely to happen?"

"After the next election," Harleigh tells her. "I think me and the Three Nations are gonna need a vacation from each other."

BUZZY HAS SEEN MORE hitchhikers in the last two weeks. There were plenty in the first months of the Bakken boom, you'd see them in town later sitting on their duffel bags with hand-lettered cardboard signs, NEED A JOB, and in those days they probably didn't have to wait more than a few hours before getting an offer. And then, starting a couple months ago, the retreat, the ones who must have spent too much time at the Indian casino and can't even pop for a bus ticket. But this one is going the wrong direction–

From the way he wears his jeans and his belt, Buzzy has him figured for a Mexican, probably a wet, but way up here who gives a shit?

"You got family up here? *Familia*?"

"No," says the man, who is strong-looking, in his thirties. "I am looking for work."

Buzzy shakes his head, "Getting here a little late for that."

"I am trying," says the man, "but it takes me very long to come here. In *Tejas* there are too many Mexicans."

Buzzy laughs. "Got that right."

"So there is not good work. Other places, where they have the oil rig, I am not in the union or I am not somebody's brother."

"I know that routine."

"But I am hearing all the time there is so much work here, so I continue to the north."

Buzzy nods his head toward a pair of pump jacks, ducking up and down at the side of the highway.

"That's what's doing all the work right now, *amigo*. They pumping like crazy but they left off drilling and fracking some while ago. Hell, this might be my last run, they get serious about that pipeline."

"But there is still oil."

"Sure, it's still down there. What was it– Mac something– "

"Macario."

"The thing is, Macario, we done too good a job here. Put so much oil and gas on the market the pump price fell to half of what it was when we started. I'm sorry, buddy, but that heifer's left the *barn*."

The man stares out his window silently as they pass an abandoned well head. He seems like he's barely able to stay awake. Buzzy muscles the wheel, fighting a crosswind, the wind that's been trying to flip him wheels-up since he came to this prairie.

"There's a Taco John's in town that ain't bad," he says to the brooding traveller. "Maybe they got something in the kitchen."

Spartina tapes the boxes shut, identifying the contents on the outside in black Magic Marker. Shipping labels will come later, when the owner sells the lot of it or sets up somewhere else. One whole wall is stacked with boxes, and some-body is supposed to come in the afternoon with tools to disassemble the metal work counters.

When Tina goes out onto the floor she sees that the man is still standing there, just staring at the main street. There is still traffic, oil tankers and a service truck now and then, but nothing like during the fracking. The man has been there at least two hours, Latino-looking, and must be cold now that the wind has really picked up. She steps out to talk to him.

"Hello."

The man holds his hands up as if surrendering. "I am sorry. I stand in another place."

"Oh, don't worry. We're closing."

The man looks in through the window, seems to notice for the first time that Havva Javva is empty.

"So early in the day?"

"We're closing for good. Not enough customers."

"Ah," says the lost man. "*Entiendo.*"

"But I've still got one machine hooked up. Would you like some coffee?"

IN THE EARLY MORNING, before the slots have begun to chirp, the man from room 108, the one with the face you can't quite remember even if you saw it only a moment ago, steps into the little sauna cabinet with only a hotel towel around his waist and new-bought flip-flops on his feet, just beating the well-cement salesman who's finished his interval training on the recumbent bike, who sits on the bench outside, hand over his heart, feeling it settle down to normal. He starts to get cold after ten minutes, pissed after fifteen.

"Yo, buddy," he calls, rapping his knuckles lightly on the fiberglass, "you don't want to fall asleep in there. Won't be nothing left of you."

There is no response, and the salesman considers just barging in and crowding the guy out, or pretending there's a posted time limit and that he's got a watch on.

"Hey in there?"

Nothing. He waits another few minutes, thinking about heart attacks and his last physical with the specter of Lipitor to add to his arsenal of daily pills, then sees the towel boy, or whatever you call the kid who mopes around the gym and spa.

"You better get the manager," he says. "I think there's somebody in trouble in there."

The boy, an overweight Indian kid who probably can't even fit on the recumbent bike, doesn't want to peek inside either and goes to find somebody above his pay grade. The salesman walks in place. Not good to stiffen up and get cold after the intervals, but he has to see this out. Finally a manager type, white guy with worries, appears and calls at the door several times. No answer.

"You saw him go in?"

"Yes."

"And you've been right here?"

"Yes."

The manager considers for a moment, then pushes the door open.

No nondescript man. No towel, no flip-flops. A puddle of water on the floor.

THEY'RE ON RESERVATION LAND, the patrol car left at the side of the road ten minutes ago. There is some slope to the land here as they get close to the lake, what might be called dells back in Minnesota. The lupines and coneflowers are up by now and there are bright yellow meadowlarks flapping up from the ground as they walk, red-legged grasshoppers clicking like castanets and flicking away to clear a path for them a couple footfalls ahead.

"Hell, it would be great if people didn't need me, didn't need somebody to do my job. But as long as people are the way they are, there's got to be somebody serve as– you know."

"A referee."

"Sure. You could call it that."

"To uphold the law."

Will frowns, points up a slope to the left. "The law is just a tool you use to get it done. The job, to me, the *point* of it all, is that people respect each other."

"You think you can enforce that?"

Will has promised her something, some surprise, but he says she has to be patient. She can wait hours, maybe days for rodents to emerge from their holes, but with people she expects service or entertainment and pretty damn quick. It is not her favorite trait, and Will does not cut to the chase.

"When somebody's really out of line, when somebody's really getting screwed, sure, we can usually step in and at least stop it from going further. But the things I see now"– he shakes his head, truly upset– "like there's no center anymore. No moral code."

He's not a church guy, that has been established, and he doesn't seem to be afraid of gays or blacks or Indians taking over the country, but there is this Boy Scout part of him that is endearing and makes Leia worry at the same time.

"My prairie dogs," she says, "are pretty hard-wired for behavior, and that includes some really awful stuff."

"We're *people*, not critters," says Will. "We ought to be able to do better than that."

Leia has a slightly sick feeling, worried that this spot they're headed for is where he takes women for the Big Kiss-Off, someplace where if they scream or cry the scene won't have an audience–

"Here we go."

She sees the lake spread out below them now, looking beautiful and somewhat man-made at the same time. They start to descend toward it.

"Beaver Creek Bay," says Will. "Good fishing spot."

She has told him about applying for the Animal Control job, how she was informed they were looking for a long-term resident to fill it, told him she has given her notice at Walmart. He nodded and didn't ask why she was still in Yellow Earth, then, and they haven't discussed it since. He has another two years on his term as sheriff. She has been to his apartment, relieved to find he owns and reads books, mostly history and not exclusively about war. They've had a rendezvous in Bismarck, where he did business at the state penitentiary and joined her at an old downtown place that served enormous slabs of meat. He does not harbor snakes or reptiles of any species.

They come to a rock outcropping just above the steep earthen bank and sit, watching the water.

"Place I used to come to think," he says.

"It's pretty." The bay curves enough that they can't see across to the yacht that is still sitting on shore, the one that people have been making jokes about. A little breeze kicks up, no moan to it. When they make her Queen of the Universe her first act will be to turn that fucking wind off for a while, give people's heads a rest. There are no boats on the water, no motor sounds, no drilling.

"I suppose you've been wondering– " she starts, and he puts a finger to his lips.

He points.

There are three of them, though it is hard to distinguish at first from the liquid, graceful weaving of their long bodies in the water. They make a complicated wake, go under, come back up, one with its belly to the sky.

"Oh my."

"There's a bunch come down from Canada to live along the Red River," says Will, almost whispering, "on the border with Minnesota. But this far west, in this lake– not since the beaver were trapped out."

"Plenty for them to eat."

"Oh yeah– suckers, carp, a lot of nice slow fish. And look at the size of them."

The otters are all roughly the same size, maybe three feet long including the powerful tail, which is thicker than their hind legs, swirling and twisting and looping backwards under the water, then sliding along with their flat heads barely above the waterline.

"They can stay under for eight minutes," says Leia.

"You've studied them?"

"No, but they're– they're pretty fascinating. The social groupings are relatively anarchic, their territories overlap, they commandeer other mammals' burrows– "

"I never seen more than these three, and only started seeing them last spring."

They are long and lithe, pelts glistening as they roll and intertwine, one occasionally racing away only to yo-yo back and snake playfully around the other two.

"I'd love to know how they got here, hopping rivers and streams– did they do it in one big odyssey or did it take a couple generations, drifting west?"

"Somebody ought to do a study."

That might, she thinks, in his Andy of Mayberry roundabout manner, be Will's version of an invitation.

"So what do you think?"

He is looking at her rather than the otters, which in their aquatic nearsightedness must have heard rather then seen them and are now flowing three abreast toward the bank, little noses tilted, testing the air.

"I think I'm in love."

ABOUT HAYMARKET BOOKS

Haymarket Books is a radical, independent, nonprofit book publisher based in Chicago.

Our mission is to publish books that contribute to struggles for social and economic justice. We strive to make our books a vibrant and organic part of social movements and the education and development of a critical, engaged, international left.

We take inspiration and courage from our namesakes, the Haymarket martyrs, who gave their lives fighting for a better world. Their 1886 struggle for the eight-hour day—which gave us May Day, the international workers' holiday—reminds workers around the world that ordinary people can organize and struggle for their own liberation. These struggles continue today across the globe—struggles against oppression, exploitation, poverty, and war.

Since our founding in 2001, Haymarket Books has published more than five hundred titles. Radically independent, we seek to drive a wedge into the risk-averse world of corporate book publishing. Our authors include Noam Chomsky, Arundhati Roy, Rebecca Solnit, Angela Y. Davis, Howard Zinn, Amy Goodman, Wallace Shawn, Mike Davis, Winona LaDuke, Ilan Pappé, Richard Wolff, Dave Zirin, Keeanga-Yamahtta Taylor, Nick Turse, Dahr Jamail, David Barsamian, Elizabeth Laird, Amira Hass, Mark Steel, Avi Lewis, Naomi Klein, and Neil Davidson. We are also the trade publishers of the acclaimed Historical Materialism Book Series and of Dispatch Books.

ALSO AVAILABLE FROM HAYMARKET BOOKS

The Battle For Paradise: Puerto Rico Takes on the Disaster Capitalists, Naomi Klein

Freedom Is a Constant Struggle: Ferguson, Palestine, and the Foundations of a Movement, Angela Y. Davis, edited by Frank Barat, preface by Cornel West

Is Just a Movie, Earl Lovelace

Whose Story Is This? Old Conflicts, New Chapters, Rebecca Solnit